SIGNS OF LIFE

A NOVEL BY RANDY KRAFT

Randy Kraft
www.Maple57Press.com
Dana Point, California

randykraftwriter.blogspot.com
@ocbookblogger

Cover Photograph by Byron Cann
Cover Design by David Smith
Text set in Minion

Also by Randy Kraft
COLORS OF THE WHEEL
First published 2014 by Infinity Publishing
Available in print and for Kindle.

Who but the Gods go woundless all the way?

Sophocles

"Where would you go back to?" Anna asked.

"Where?" I answered.

"Where as in when. What time in your life?"

"Isn't that obvious?"

"Yes, but the day before, a month, a year?"

"The day before."

"Why not farther? Start again. All those precious moments, relived, in this lifetime."

"What's the point?"

"The point is to experience everything anew, recreate memories."

"An oxymoron. Memory is past tense."

Anna smiled. A Mona Lisa smile, befitting her enigmatic persona, although at moments like these, Anna the inquisitor, no nuance at all, and I was well aware the conversation would not conclude until it had played out to her satisfaction, so I played along, as I always do.

"Where would you go back to?" I asked.

"Not too young, certainly not high school. No one in their right mind would go through that again."

"For sure. College?"

"Too little sleep. Too much past tense."

I nodded in accord. "Although…"

"Although?"

"We met my senior year, Jason and I."

"Oh, I'd forgotten."

"Second semester. April."

So long ago. More than twenty years. I shifted in my seat and sat up a bit taller, hoping to quaff the snake that at such moments slithers down the throat to revel in gloom.

"Springtime. Renewal." Anna was speaking, but not to me.

"I would need to be sure, you know…"

"Yes, you would have to be sure Jeremy arrived."

"Five years. A long time to wait."

"Ah, but the anticipation would be sweet."

The snake had stretched deep into my gut. Hateful feeling, and Anna knew what I was feeling, she knew everything there was to know about me, and I of her, so I believed, so why was she putting me through this?

"This conversation is absurd," I muttered, squirming a little in my perch on the bench, impatience flagrant, also genuine discomfort. We were seated on wood slatted benches, which are notoriously uncomfortable. Not meant to encourage lingering, as one would imagine, thus the last refuge even for homeless sleepers. Horrible thought. I had to banish the image from my mind, easy to do on that nearly spring afternoon, the air warming even as the wind retained the scent of winter.

There we were, my dear friend Anna and I, engaged in nonsensical banter. A bird watching from above might have imagined us strays from a flock of pigeons, cooing and shivering despite wool scarves around our necks, hands tucked into fleece jacket pockets. I knew at any moment Anna's hands would spring forth to punctuate the dialogue in that way she has of dangling her limbs between us, like a magician waving a wand, or a witch weaving a spell, her fingers sloping like the barren tree branches surrounding us.

She would be the good witch, whereas these days I might be mistaken for a wicked witch. Nearly black rims circle my dark eyes from lack of sleep. Lips perpetually pursed into a solemn expression. Skin terribly pale and torso nearly skeletal from too much wine, too few nutritious meals, too often sedentary. A dreadful doppelganger. I would never have imagined being who I am now. I suppose none of us do.

"What?" Anna asked, aware that my mind had drifted.

I shivered. "I'm cold."

"Just a contemplation, Nell," she said, determined to hold me captive to the dialogue.

Not the first conversation between us that toyed with hypotheticals. Nor the last, I assumed. Two middle-aged, modestly dressed women nestled onto a dark green bench in the great park of Manhattan, in the throes of an ontological inquiry without resolution.

"Hardly a practical contemplation," I remarked, zipping my jacket all the way to the chin.

"You know better than that. Conjecture can be useful, if only to assess our reality. Imagine, going back in time, knowing what we know, we consider who we truly are."

"Only if we can alter the outcome."

"We can alter very little."

"So what does that mean? Could I even protect my husband and son?"

"Maybe. Maybe not. Maybe them, no one else."

"I don't know if I could live with the knowing."

"If that were the only option, would you go back?"

"Yes. But only to the day before."

Anna gaped at me in wonder. "Do you not have a greedy bone in your body? You would not seize every possible moment?"

"Knowing even for one day would be hard enough."

ONE

Fear not the pain.
Let its weight fall back into the earth;
for heavy are the mountains, heavy are the seas.

Rainer Maria Rilke

We had that conversation last Wednesday, Anna and I. We spend this mid-week day together, almost every week, always in Manhattan, because I rarely wander beyond its borders. She had phoned as she emerged from Grand Central Station and asked me to meet her at the Plaza Hotel.

"A startling day, Nell. Not even Monet could capture the color of this sky."

I couldn't help but smile, Anna's voice always uplifting.

"There's a bit of wind. The clouds like floating strips of filament." She paused for a moment, in thrall to the very thing she hoped to describe. "The clouds are racing the wind."

"Might be a storm brewing."

"These are not storm clouds. Not yet. I'd like to capture these clouds."

She paused again. I knew she was studying the sky. "Are you dressed? Hop on the bus, help me photograph the clouds."

Anna knows I prefer the bus to the subway. Sluggishness suits me. Horns blare, taxis weave in and out; the bustle buffers melancholy. As I have few time constraints, I can sit endlessly watching the city go by. Sometimes I do just that, board the bus and ride to its end-point, then reboard, watch the opposite view, and yes, everything, well, most things, look different in reverse.

"Leaving now."

"I'll wait near the fountain."

Of course Anna would want to meet at the Plaza fountain. The fountain is the gateway to Central Park, a grand sculpture mid-town that demarcates the shift from the gallant buildings of the central business district to the bucolic landscape of our magnificent green. She was fond of such meeting places, admiring of the monuments and artifacts that serve as markers of time and place, as if markers of her personal timeline.

My husband Jason, from the first, was charmed by Anna's eccentric ruminations. He dubbed her the duck, as in odd duck. He appreciated her wit and lack of airs, which made her appealing to a simple man like him. He always listened attentively to what she had to say, and while not one to judge, I occasionally heard his internal chuckle through the expression in his hazel-brown eyes, eyes with the eyelashes of a woman, for which he was forever teased. Now and then, Jason and Anna's husband, David, shared a nod, a subtle glance of bewilderment, as men will do with a woman like Anna, not so much dismissive as amused.

Jason was especially fond of Anna's annual photography hunt, an outing modeled on a scavenger hunt requiring the detection and photography of select subjects tied to a theme. "On the trail of the duck," he would exclaim when we received our instructions.

In truth, I enjoyed his delight in the pursuit more than the hunt itself, although we always had a great time, days I remember as equally silly and sublime, and from place to place, we never looked back, always on to the next image, which was Anna's message, we knew that.

My favorite was the flower hunt, an early spring happening that began at dawn at the flower market near the tip of Manhattan, followed by a quick breakfast on the way uptown to Central Park. There we photographed the first signs of the season: voluptuous pink blooms on the Yoshino Cherry trees lining the east side of the reservoir, the first purple hyacinth at Shakespeare's Garden or tiny white snowdrops clustered along tree roots and rock gardens, before wandering the winding lilac and azalea paths, shooting close-ups of pale blossoms on crabapple trees and the smattering of crocuses and daffodils near the pond. We landed further west at Riverside Park, along the Hudson River, where we might be in time for elegant tulips as their red and orange heads pressed up through the ground. Flowers inspired us to greatness, so we thought, although, in the end, our cameras captured mostly masses of generic color against waves of grass or jumbled branches, the beauty of the blooms obfuscated by our enthusiasm.

Jason's favorite was the fish hunt, a search for strangely formed creatures with markings that seemed sketched in crayon. That trek started at the aquarium in Brooklyn where only Anna was good at photographing fish swimming behind glass, then progressed to the search for bass and bluefish at the tip of the East River, and a hidden koi pond near the UN, before heading to the western embankment, where seahorses, northern pike and naked goby might be discovered in the Hudson River because the lower waters are so salty. There we jostled each other out of the way, clamoring for the best angle, laughing and ogling fish with flat faces and eyes in odd places.

Always exhausted at the end of the day, we celebrated our escapades at one or another neighborhood bar where we devoured aromatic fried food and buckets of beer, toasting our success with each sip as if conquerors.

In those days, Jason and I insisted on using point and click cameras, while Anna had a collection of Leicas, each better suited to a particular view, which she condescended now and then to permit David to use. A good camera was her imperative and even when our children were quite young, she made sure each had a Canon with a zoom lens. To launch them into the fundamentals of good photography, she taught group lessons on cold winter days using a camera obscura into which they pressed their tiny eyes, delighting in capturing the vision of what to the naked eye seemed ordinary, but through the pinhole, extraordinary.

Jason, an arts book editor, repeatedly tried to convince Anna to publish the photography hunt as a coffee table book, but she was never interested in sharing that pastime. He eventually gave up the quest, Anna not one to be convinced of anything.

Jason called us Frick and Frack, and David refers to us as the long and the short of it: Anna graceful and luminescent, me diminutive and dark. Compatriot souls nonetheless. And as Anna became more and more important to me over the years, I was pleased that she and Jason were friends, whereas David and I never cemented more than cordial relations. Men like him, an architect, imagine they can read people by the way they're built. By our exterior shape and elevations, the texture of our facades. So he, like most people, I imagine, assumed, because I am small in stature, that I might be fragile. Unstable. I prefer to picture myself as a hand-hewn stone farmhouse, while Jason would have been the

Brooklyn Bridge, perhaps the Golden Gate. David might be compared to skyscrapers in Dubai, impressive and unyielding.

Anna? Anna might be the Guggenheim Museum, asymmetrical and graceful, no sharp edges, although that may be too modern a comparison. More likely a Buddhist monastery perched on a remote hillside in Tibet, where she would await the wanderer seeking enlightenment.

Yes, Anna would always be an extension of a journey and we the scavengers. Just as we followed her all over the city to photograph flowers or fish, we tracked along with her metaphysical philosophy, in her thrall all these years in large part because she trusts that everything exists for a reason, everything happens for a reason, and believes that the reason will be revealed when the time is right. Don't we all secretly hope for the same?

We met at New York Hospital the day my son Jeremy was born. 1995. A bright spring day, and now that I think of it, a Wednesday. Anna was visiting her father, who succumbed to a severe heart attack while on a visit to the city, lingering in semi-consciousness for three days. Moments after he passed, she wandered downstairs to the maternity ward. She needed to connect herself to the perfect symmetry of life and death, she told me some time later.

I noticed her standing before the protective glass around the newborns, rows of squiggling masses bundled in pinks and blues, names printed in bold capital letters on labels clipped to the edges of clear plastic bins, without which they might have been interchangeable. She seemed more like a sketch than a human being, as if a concept, whereas most of us are the sum of more concrete disparate parts. Slender and elegant, with high cheekbones that slope to a tapered chin, her shapely legs peeked beneath a mid-calf length skirt and her mahogany hair was longer then, pulled into a ponytail that hung down her back and landed dead center between her shoulder blades, nearly touching her hands clasped behind her.

I looked up at her from a wheelchair, having had a Caesarian the day before. The birth nearly killed me, my hips too narrow, the passage squashed, so in the end they had to rip the baby from me just in time, even though he too was small. They cautioned us about risking another pregnancy. I didn't mind, not then, because my son was perfect, and we relished lavishing all our affection on him. I never worried about that only-child thing, only later, for me, although in truth, I don't know how I could have loved another child the way I loved that boy.

They delivered Jeremy to me frequently for feedings throughout that first day; however they refused to allow him to stay in a bassinet in my room, as if that might hinder my recovery. A kindly nurse understood that I needed to stare at my beautiful son. "Just a few moments, now and then," she acquiesced, and I agreed, gratefully, too tired for more, as sore as if someone had torn me open and removed a large object before stitching me closed, which they had.

As I stared at my newborn, stunned by his presence, despite the many months of anticipation, I looked up to see Anna's eyes glistening with unshed tears. At the same time, she had a hint of a smile on her lips as she stared at the babies, stepping back to take in the panorama. Even as the joy of Jeremy's arrival was uppermost on my mind, I could not help but be conscious of Anna's magisterial presence. Impossible, even without knowing her, not to be aware of her, not to feel drawn to her, as one might be moved to light a candle in a dark church.

"Which one is yours?" she asked.

I smiled, gazing proudly as I pointed to the tiny wriggling mass, wrapped so tightly that every single joint and limb pushed out, a movement he repeated throughout his brief life whenever bound by winter clothing or tucked too tightly in his bed, determined to spread out.

She smiled. "My son was born here last year," she said. "They grow quickly."

"I imagine."

"Your first?"

"Yes."

"You are at the threshold of a great journey," Anna proclaimed, turning now to focus her piercing eyes on me.

"You have more than the one?" I asked.

She nodded. "A girl, nearly three. Bethany Sara Miller, named for Beth in *Little Women*. Sara was my great-great-grandmother, descendent of Puritans, although I prefer to imagine she was a witch."

She chuckled and I smiled. "And your son?" I asked.

"Will. No middle name. Aptly so, as he is a determined soul, since the day he was born. Strong and earthy, like a sturdy tree, and he seems to be growing that tall."

I pictured my own son as a tree, his branches reaching out for sunlight, taking nourishment from the well-balanced eco-system I intended to provide.

"My father died today," Anna said.

I thought I had misunderstood her words. "Sorry?"

"Less than an hour ago he stopped breathing, although I felt his spirit depart some time yesterday, yes, yesterday afternoon, around three. The air stirred around me, a gentle flurry, as if a hummingbird had fluttered close to my face. I was holding his hand. I felt his body relax, every muscle seemed to release at once. At last at peace. In his time, without interference. A good death."

I was speechless. What can you possibly say to a stranger who speaks poetically about the ending of a life, surrounded as we were by beginnings? I recognized at once that she was a person of a higher intellect, or, at the very least, had greater comprehension of those things that most of us take for granted. Or choose to ignore.

"His name was James, my father. Perhaps more than a coincidence, I think, that your son Jeremy was born at roughly the same time yesterday."

"I'm not sure I understand."

"Well, in the more ancient cultures, it is believed the soul permeates the host body mid-way through the pregnancy, like twenty weeks. However, in other cultures, the soul arrives at the moment of birth. So your son may be my father's next host. James passes on to Jeremy. Quite possible, although it is awfully soon. No time for transition." Anna chuckled. "On the other hand, my father was an impatient man, wouldn't surprise me if he leapfrogged the usual path. The very fact that we are here together at this moment suggests the probability. Spirits travel in packs, you know. Again and again, through multiple lives. That's why we so often meet people we are certain we recognize, when we have not yet met them in this life. My own father might have been my lover in a past life. He might also have been a mortal enemy, although I think I would have sensed that. I'm sure you understand. Your Jeremy might have been in my father's orbit at another time. You and I have likely traveled together as well, meant to meet again."

Anna's pastel blue eyes, nearly gray, stared into mine so intently I might have turned away under the intensity of her gaze, were I not transfixed. If I had been a disciple of the concept of endless lives, I might have believed I had been summoned from another place in time.

"Yes, I think we have met before," she mused. "But we'll never know, will we? The secret remains buried with the past life and only a hint of memory remains. Newborns are closer to their pasts, they intuit so much more, but that sadly fades with age. Each of us born with mysteries that will never be solved, but which inform our existence. Spiritual DNA. Fascinating, isn't it?"

I nodded, although without conviction.

"Ah, you are not a believer of such things," Anna pronounced.

"I believe in, well, the possibilities. I'm afraid I cannot do more than that."

"Only believe in what you can see?"

"I also believe in what we cannot see, but know is there."

"For example?"

"The speed of light, or the color spectrum. The existence of distant solar systems. But when it comes to souls migrating between lives, I'm not sure I can accept that. I believe, I guess I prefer to believe, that loved ones inhabit a heaven, or some sort of netherworld that allows them to hold on, or lets us hold on to them. At least, that's the way I was raised."

"You know, otherworldliness is not religion and the soul is not the spirit. What I'm talking about is the very essence of spirituality. Cerebral as much as divine. The movement of the spirit from one time and place to another is a concept embraced by the earliest spiritualists and mystics, and the elders of most religions. The connections between us, in this life and beyond, form the fundamental spiritual network."

She peered into my eyes again. "You are more a believer than you know."

I smiled. Not convinced, rather captivated. Anna spoke with surprising nonchalance about surreal and mystical possibilities, and while I found the commentary, which would ultimately come to be familiar and precious to me, a bit daunting at that moment, I was willing from the first to accept our differences in favor of common ground.

Years later she would confess that when she saw me that day she had the overwhelming impression we had been separated for centuries. "There you are, I wanted to cry out," she told me, but restrained herself, aware, even then, I might take umbrage.

She could not have known that while I would come to honor her way of thinking, I would find such optimism impossible to sustain.

Anna surprised me the next day with a visit to the hospital, providing much-needed counsel from breastfeeding to bathing. We were strangers, yet before long we seemed to move in tandem and finish each other's sentences. Despite our often-quirky conversations, I grew accustomed to her ramblings about spirits and past lives, the fates, the master plan and the journey to enlightenment. She, in return, was accepting of my pragmatic nature, and, ultimately, more acutely attuned to my sorrow.

We lived across town from each other then and met regularly on sunny afternoons at a playground midway, near Gramercy Park, or, when the weather turned cold, at one of our apartments. Our husbands quickly became friends, if only to avoid becoming mere appendages. David, the young idealistic draftsman, and my beloved bookish Jason, shared a visual approach to life as well as the bonds forged by their wives. Anna's children treated Jeremy like a junior sibling, although with greater reverence than they might have treated a baby brother, and he adopted them as his own. All united by virtue of our friendship.

While I'm not certain I ever truly accepted her philosophy of the never-ending trek of the human spirit, I conceded there was a real possibility in what she believed, and that seemed to satisfy her.

In the last decade, we've shared nearly five hundred Wednesdays and I await Wednesdays as a schoolgirl awaits weekends. Few have friends they can count on in this way, and each time she cancels, which she has more often in the last year, I fear she has at last grown weary of me, but she assures me that work has been more intense, not to mention the challenges of adolescent children, community life. The day gets away from all of us. I understand. It is not my place to make demands.

I have survived largely because of Anna's friendship. She is my lifeline. I cannot imagine what I would do without her and I might have done anything in my power to prevent that possibility.

Anna and David, Beth and Will, moved some years ago to a picturesque suburban town barely an hour's train ride to Grand Central Station, a community established in the mid-nineteenth century and co-opted frequently by filmmakers for exterior shots meant to be colonial New England. David convinced her to leave the city and her engine still engages more fully when she returns, so perhaps I am doing her a favor by enticing her regularly into the urban milieu. She claims she cherishes the hour-long train ride during which she watches the landscape steadily shift from towering trees and graceful lawns to the swarm of steel and concrete. She rarely reads, she keeps her camera stored in its case, and she often meditates, her mantra the galloping sway and clack of the train on its tracks. She arrives no later than mid-morning, as a rule, anxious to scope out the day, to vitalize one day a week with an otherwise passive inhabitant.

We originally chose Wednesday because it is the mid-week matinee day at Manhattan theaters and we wanted to be among the ladies-who-matinee crowd, those chic women dressed in designer silks and shoes, a faint odor of garlic and wine lingering on their breaths after a leisurely lunch. Anna donned skirts that rustle against the calf, topped with swishy sweaters, or, in warmer months, long fitted T-shirts, a style of dress fashionable enough for the theater but sufficiently casual to suit her persona. I shifted from jeans into slacks, with a blouse or fitted sweater rather than a floppy T-shirt, my version of dressing up and the same clothes I wore on dinner dates with my husband. I rarely accessorize, never wear the sort of colorful silk scarves that frequently adorn Anna's stately neck, and most often wear dark colors. Basic black and its variants, charcoal gray or navy blue, these shades always suit my mood.

The theater was only one of our Wednesday rituals. More often we walked, either from the station, where we met below the large legendary clock, or from my apartment on 22nd Street and Eighth Avenue, the northern edge of a lower west side neighborhood known as Chelsea. Over the years, we have wandered the length and breadth of Manhattan, more than once, one Wednesday at a time.

We frequently strolled the Highline as it evolved, an open-air penthouse to the former meatpacking district. Crafted on elevated train tracks once dedicated to commercial transport, and left for years to rust and wither, the tracks were repurposed into an oasis of gardens and fountains, pathways and vistas. Urban restoration is a favorite subject for Anna's camera, so I patiently wait as she shoots, and at times, although I never say so, I imagine loved ones lurking there, hidden in a photograph the way one occasionally notices strange shapes or light not seen by the naked eye, but captured by the lens.

Recently we meandered south along the Hudson River to the tip of the island, where we stared at the Statue of Liberty as if she'd just landed, before strolling to Battery Park and along Wall Street to watch perfectly appointed money-makers scramble around during lunch hour.

When we find ourselves in lower Manhattan we avoid Ground Zero, although, on occasion, we have stood starkly still among the giant cranes and construction equipment hell-bent on restoration, like those mimes draped in white that appear to be statues until they suddenly blink. Like those mimes, we never speak a word, in commiseration with fellow New Yorkers. Almost ten years later, I still feel a great kinship to all those who suffered.

On rainy or snowy days, we spend hours in bookstores or museums, dawdling over lunches at museum café's or at the food court at the train station where we have tasted every ordinary culinary concoction, rating them as if critics. When conversation is too difficult for me or the weather too bitterly cold, we take shelter at a movie theater where we skitter like rats from screen to screen, one after another, enjoying two, sometimes three movies in one day, popcorn and M&M's our only sustenance.

Five years ago, we picked up a guide listing the fifty best places in the city to find peace and we have visited every one of them – yoga institutes, Zen meditation retreats, a Kabbalah center, aged church sanctuaries, secreted gardens, hidden concert niches, a poetry center – all tucked behind, below or above something else, and most of which we were previously unaware.

We both have found the constant change of the city as much a comfort, perhaps more so, as that which never changes: the way sounds echo or slivers of light drift through the narrow streets that snake between skyscrapers. Or the way the eastern bridges are lit by the light of the west and the west side by the morning sun. An endearing partnership between the city's transience and its endurance, although rather than see them as opposite ends of a continuum, as I do, Anna perceives them as contiguous parallel paths, a double exposure of sorts.

Nevertheless, it was the theater where our Wednesdays began and where, in the dim sobriety of Broadway's gilded antiquities, I find a perfect refuge in the enforced silence, the instant immersion into another time and place. When we emerge from those dark sanctuaries into the light of late afternoon, stepping into the bustle of rush hour, I hoist a hand in a salute to shield my eyes from the glare, as without transition, even late daylight is scathing, for me. I have never been able to shift quickly from one moment to the next, and far less so now. Only in winter months are we spared the shock, the sky having morphed to dusky blue before the final curtain, so I adjust more easily.

On all those Wednesdays, esoteric, conjectural conversations were not unusual. However the most recent Q&A stayed top of mind. Why would Anna consider the impossible notion of going back in time? There is no past for Anna, beyond the enlightenment of history, beyond the photographs that remain for reference. There is no future for that matter, the future merely hypothetical. For Anna, there is only the now – the now intrinsic to destiny.

Trained as a photojournalist, she is the lead photographer for her town's weekly newspaper. I often wonder if she derives genuine satisfaction shooting community leaders cutting ribbons and students strutting their caps and gowns at high school graduations, but I would never pose the question, and I know she makes every photograph count. They are frequently quite imaginative, given limited material. The first day of spring boating on Long Island Sound, for example, bright white sails capturing the wind in flight as if the wings of a seagull, or portraits of elders of the community in pigment as rich as the Dutch masters. She personifies the photojournalist, always seeking the story behind the scene, knowing that each individual reality changes by the nanosecond: angle, light, context and texture, matter continuously shifting form, instantly altering the view, and the view, once altered, is never the same.

Much like life: once lived, once realized, a life cannot be reclaimed. So the deliberation, even a theoretical contemplation of reversing time? Utterly incongruous.

Was it only last Wednesday we talked about going back in time? When we huddled together on a park bench, debating destiny? Now I have two points in time I might wish to return to: ten years ago or last Wednesday. Given a choice, I would go back to the day before the day I lost my family, which would also allow me to appreciate ten years of Wednesdays all over again.

Jeremy, six years-old, and Jason, thirty-six, left one balmy evening in August 2001 for a baseball game at Yankee Stadium and never returned, the victims of a drunken driver whose car hit them head-on as they strolled the sidewalk to the train station. They were pushed through a shop window, shattering the glass, but it was the force of the blow that killed them, I was told. I can only imagine the pandemonium, the thrust of a speeding vehicle out of control and the smash of glass, although I try to obliterate that sound from my imagination. A freak accident, a newspaper referred to it, as if something one might find at a carnival, like a bearded lady or a tattooed dwarf. To me, the moment that transformed my sweet life into the heartbreak that holds me hostage, and has kept me oddly tethered to the tragedy of 9/11, which happened a few weeks later.

Jeremy practically floated out the door that night, wearing his blue Yankee baseball cap and a bright white T-shirt with the NY logo emblazoned across the front, barely tucked into a new pair of neatly pressed chinos like his dad's. He was always small for his age, like me – sprite-like and energetic. However his squared jaw and bright grin mirrored his father, and his gentle nature as well. His eyes were gleaming as his scrawny arms reached around my waist to hug me good-bye, and he released a moment too soon, too excited to linger, running down the hall to the elevator, shouting back to me, "See ya later alligator!"

"In a while crocodile," I called out as the elevator doors snapped shut.

That was the last time I heard my son's voice, the last time I kissed my husband's lips.

I waited up for them. I folded Jeremy's laundry while it was warm, pressing gently into the creases and smoothing out the edges, and neatly tucking each bundle into a dresser drawer. I listened for the sound of their footsteps, expecting Jeremy to bound through the door and regale me with all the exciting details of the game. Or, more likely, for Jason to tiptoe in with his son sound asleep in his arms. I especially loved such moments, when we gingerly removed most of Jeremy's clothes and tucked him under the covers, his body as warm and malleable as a newborn.

They died instantly together. A blessing, a medical examiner told me some time later. A blessing to whom, I meant to ask, but I was rendered speechless by despair.

In those first weeks after the accident, Anna stayed with me. She slept in my bed because I slept on the couch, when I slept. She read to me, she sang to me. She gathered multiple recipes for bread pudding, what she considers the quintessential comfort food, and each week indulged us in the latest variation, the scent of cinnamon and vanilla constantly at war with the otherwise ubiquitous aroma of basil and tomato from our regular doses of pizza. I would otherwise have starved.

Beyond the near spoon-feeding and the sheer force of her presence, Anna scooped up all the family photographs I had lying around in envelopes and boxes to fill two large albums that she lined up by my bed to peruse during long sleepless nights. She served as an advocate with social workers and attorneys, and managed to secure some financial remuneration, for which I am thankful, but serves little purpose, as if a check and a signature on a legal waiver might make things right. She spoke for me when needed, because I could not, and spoke to me, nearly day and night, so that I would not be smothered by silence, and I listened, although as if she spoke a foreign language. She has held up more than her share of conversation ever since.

Over and over, she tried to convince me my husband and son had new lives in another realm. She said Jason, clearly a very old soul, was needed, and that Jeremy would return to me in another way at another time. She talked about the nature of impermanence, the cycles of the soul; rationalizations she thought would strengthen me, hoping I might see that the loss would ultimately reveal to me my own purpose.

I closed my ears: absurd talk for a grieving wife and mother. At times, fury surged in my chest and I wanted to smash Anna with her words, miserable ingrate that I was, instead turning the anger inward, becoming increasingly sullen and unresponsive.

When the towers were struck down, I might have been the lone person on the planet unaware, as I remained in a state of semi-consciousness, responding solely to fundamental bodily urges. Anna had just returned to her family and, as roads and rails in and out of the city were temporarily shut down, she was unable to come back for four days. She called a few times, but I didn't answer, and she had the good sense not to leave a message. My father called as well from Florida, and he rarely leaves messages beyond the request to return the call. Only when Anna arrived at the end of the week did I discover that my city too had experienced a tragedy and that people throughout the country grieved.

Once I watched those horrific images on television, I felt compelled to take my first tentative steps out of the apartment. The city was bathed in grief. Neighbors still searching for loved ones, flyers and photos tacked en masse on makeshift display boards all around lower Manhattan. Withered flowers littered sidewalks, occasionally tossed on the wind, as if the city itself were a cemetery. I imagined for weeks the sound of collective caterwauling carried on that wind, as terrifying as anything I've experienced beyond my own anguish.

My despair seemed to blend with everyone else's, all the widows and grieving mothers, which was oddly comforting. At the same time, I resented the sustenance they received: global outrage and commiseration, financial contributions. Why was terrorism a greater nightmare than mine? My loss was no less senseless, no less horrific, not to me. The torpedoing of buildings is no more or less outrageous than the madness of a drunken driver, and no matter how many were killed that one morning downtown, and how many more suffered, each of us grieves for our own.

Nevertheless, I feel a profound commiseration with the mourners of 9/11 and I suffer with them every year. An invisible member of their tribe, without anointment, I listen to the anniversary events on the radio as if that were the date of my own misfortune, whispering my husband and son's names as the list of names are read, in that moment where they might belong: Jason Herman. Jeremy Herman. However, there is no comfort in solidarity, rather the nominal solace that if they can survive, so can I, and survive I do, little else.

Unlike most of the mourners of 9/11 who have been able to grieve and heal, finding new loves, forging new futures, I have not. I no longer listen to rock music or read poetry. I no longer relish the flavor of fine food. I no longer look up to see the vast blue of sky, as if such pleasures have been denied to me. The beauty in my surroundings seems distant, like the sketches of a work of art that never feels the paint. I try not to think about my husband and son, but too often I think of nothing else.

Friends and family empathized. They did what they could to comfort me. However they soon drifted back to their lives, fleeing the contagion of grief. Jason's parents moved away; they never said they were afraid to live in the city, but I suspect that played a part in their decision. Perhaps they fled the shadow of their son at every turn, which I long for rather than fear.

In truth, if not for Anna, I might have ended my life soon after the accident. I often felt close to death, compelled like a snake to the call of the charmer, moving hypnotically toward the dirge, but I was in the snare of somnambulism that kept me largely immobile, physically and emotionally. As time passed, as the images of my loved ones slipped farther away, I have felt no greater desire for living, I simply no longer seem able to muster the desire for death.

Anna is the one person who has steadfastly understood I am not some sort of a freak for my inability, or refusal, to move on. From the first, she accepted my state of mind, even as she never gave up hope that I might come to a greater level of understanding. She held me close to her then, she holds me still, like a mother cradling a distraught child who cannot rest. I am beholden to her, so I would like to believe that everything happens for a reason, but for me, one day simply folds into another. I no longer believe in fate or God or any sort of guiding light; rather that some of us do better than others. No more, no less. And each of us should have the right to determine how to live with that.

On the days I work, I hunch over my computer at a small desk pushed up against a short wall between the foyer and the living room. I work as if cramming for a final exam, hours on end, often through the night, molding words and pictures into publishing software as I once molded clay. Graphic design for newsletters, brochures and annual reports meant to raise funds for schools, arts or environmental organizations, and sometimes small businesses. Scaling images to size, placing text and headlines within column guides, wrapping copy neatly into place, removing red-eyes or touching up mottled skin, trying to make flat photographs of people with cardboard smiles seem three-dimensional, and adding graphics or stock photographs or finish lines to make the pages more reader-friendly in a world where people read only snippets of information at best. Content is of no concern, not to them, not to me. Merely images that fill the screen of otherwise empty days.

I suspect my clients pity me. As far as I know, they have no knowledge of my situation; rather they can tell I am a solitary soul by late night emails and quick turn-around. I suspect they also appreciate my constancy.

When not working, I fold into the one comfy chair in the apartment to read, or sprawl out on the couch to watch endless hours of *Law & Order* or BBC mysteries, or the addictive home design and antiquities experts. Even more to my taste: classic films. However I am not entirely reclusive, not the mad lady in the attic. I go to the bank and to the market. I take walks now and then to observe the seasonal window displays. I ride the bus. Between pizza deliveries, I throw together green salads, consume large bowls of granola, handfuls of raisins and nuts, or munch on chunks of fruit, not so much seeking nourishment, rather fuel.

Now and then, I visit the nearby ABC Home store or Anthropologie, where I study the merchandise display as if to absorb color the way others seek sun in winter. I finger every quirky teacup and elegant wine glass, browse lacey skirts or picture books. I rarely make a purchase and I borrow books from the library, mostly escapist fare like science fiction or mystery. On occasion, I listen to jazz or blues at downtown clubs, squeezed into a tiny table in a dim corner, the music hypnotically soothing, and I occasionally sip Chai tea at the Rubin Museum, which, devoted as it is to the Buddhist ideal, has a holy ambiance, as holy as I can tolerate.

Anna encouraged me to relocate, but I remain in our small apartment, four square rooms blessed with high ceilings and decorative moldings, north of the hipper Soho and Greenwich Village, south of the midtown business district, a neighborhood once characterized by sweat shops and meat markets now better known for modern art and alternative lifestyles.

Jason and I preferred the inelegance of Chelsea when we first settled there eighteen years ago, colonized by an eclectic mix of immigrants, graduate students, aspiring artists, and a few preppie types with downtown tastes. Since then, gentrification has dramatically altered the landscape. Bistros, galleries, and fashionably dressed young people fill the sidewalks. Families too have settled into the neighborhood, children swooping along curbs like the pigeons.

Here, where my family was whole, I cling to what is familiar: the few remaining markets and bookstores; aging tarot readers who eke out a living on dreamers; the ruts and rounded edges of sidewalks yet to be restored. I will never leave this neighborhood.

In effect, I have resumed the lifestyle of my younger self. I was never a good desk jockey, never fond of structure and wary of unrealistic expectations. Whenever possible I worked freelance or part-time, often two jobs at once. When Jason and I were first married, I adapted my fine arts degree to a more conventional lifestyle, first as an illustrator for a small advertising agency, followed by a short stint as a window dresser at Macy's, and an even shorter stint creating centerpieces for a florist. I never lasted long at any job. My body clock was perennially at odds with the workday. I preferred to stay up late, sleep late, work through afternoons into the night, and sometimes languish for hours at a time, dawdling through daylight until sheltered by darkness.

I suppose you might say I was flighty. Restless. Anna concluded I was a seeker, although I never saw myself that way. I was not unhappy, certainly not dour. I was simply most content making pottery, losing track of time, reveling in a nearly hallucinatory state, the subtle steady hum of the potter's wheel obliterating all sound, and the sensual gush of wet clay between my fingers suiting my somatic nature.

As a young mother, I found a reason to wake up early in the morning, my motor engaged throughout the day. Once Jeremy was in nursery school, I worked three or four mornings at an artist's collaborative in an East Village loft, where I used the space and equipment to make pottery in return for profit sharing. I was befriended by other artists and enjoyed arts conversation before I rushed off to pick up my son mid-day. Through those few years, I embraced routine, delighting in my family and the satisfaction of an artisan's life, and in the evening, at that hour when most people turn off their lights and drift toward slumber, Jason and I enjoyed the pleasures of the night.

My mother told me once that most women marry either their father or the opposite of their father, their un-father so to speak. Jason was a bit of both. Even-tempered and unassuming, like my father, although my father was a tinkerer, a model builder when he wasn't at the desk of the accounting firm where he worked all his life, purposefully detached from what he referred to as the drama of daily living. Jason, far more cerebral and intimate, was devoted to his family and to me. Our marriage bed teemed with desire and we savored every moment to please one another. No one could have imagined the intensity of our lust, or the depth of our contentment. We were all we needed, all we wanted. No wonder I am lost without him.

Now, I live alone and work alone, and in some small way I try to make sense of each day. I stay in this place where, even after all this time, I imagine the scent of Jason's aftershave on the corner of a couch pillow or the slipcover of the oversized blue chair where he read on rainy nights and napped on snowy afternoons. Now and then, I hear Jeremy call to me from a distance. It is enough.

Anna's eyes were still on the sky as I approached the Plaza last Wednesday, and I watched her from the opposite corner as she studied the clouds. I had to take her word for their beauty as I never look up, not anymore, and not to look up in Manhattan defies the directional architecture. I gauge the day by shadows; however, that day, under a gray sky, I saw only soot engraved in the fissures marking city sidewalks, the same soot that tends to seep into the psyche.

She stood very still, scanning the view, setting the scene to optimum light, seeking the perfect perspective, and framing the vision with her hands, the Zoom Effect, she calls it. "Zoom out, find the focus; zoom in too close, we miss what we are meant to see."

Like the game children play, a game I once played with Jeremy, molding a sheet of paper into a cone to peer through the tapered opening to the larger end. The object always seemed magnified, the image more precise. The longer we looked, the more we noticed, detail emerging into focus, like one of Anna's photographs crystallizing in her darkroom.

I watched, knowing it would be one of those days overflowing with her determination to experience every blade of grass, every sparkle of sunshine, every billowy cloud. A day that for me is all the more painful, burdened by the pleasures of the living.

"Nell, over here," she called as I awaited traffic to pass.

The tripod for her new state-of-the-art Nikon was set up on the edge of the northwest corner of the park, across from the Plaza fountain, although a digital camera was in hand, which she uses to test the light or configure the image. She gazed upward, squinting ever so slightly against the glare, as Anna never wears sunglasses, to her mind the visual equivalent of a smudged camera lens. As a result, the outer edges of her eyes are crimped despite an otherwise smooth bronzed face that belies her age.

"Nell, you really have to see this," she announced as I approached.

"Describe it to me," I prompted.

My gaze had turned toward an old workhorse parked near the corner, his chestnut-brown mane matted like dreadlocks, his head drooped forward in a bearing similar to my own. Harnessed to a buggy that takes tourists through the park, a handsome cab they were once called, I wanted to lean my head against him in unity and rub his speckled neck.

"When the clouds move like this," Anna said, her eyes still upturned, "when they constantly move, like a cosmic clock, one might imagine there is such a thing as time."

Anna spoke to me, as she often does, as if speaking to herself, sharing her innermost thoughts without need of response. The epitome of rhetorical commentary, Jason once observed.

She went on. "Of course we know there is no such thing as time, not really, but it might be construed as nature's visual representation of the passing of time, yes?"

"And what about sunrise? Sunset? Do these not concretize time?" I asked.

"We can estimate the time of day by the position of the sun, but we cannot watch the sun tick away the moments. Imagine if we sat all day staring at the sun, what might that be like?"

"Icarus. Enamored of the sun."

"He was warned, wasn't he? Fly too close to the waves, you fall into the sea. Fly too close to the sun, your wings melt. Either way, you perish. The mythology of longing."

I nodded, unwilling to engage at that moment.

"Funny how people refer to the dreamers of the world as having their heads in the clouds, as if clouds were imaginary, or surreal, just because they are out of reach," Anna said.

I nodded again, my eyes still on the horse.

"The only true manifestation of time," Anna murmured.

I have heard this pontification more than once – the quest to comprehend the meaning of time, which, Anna contends, doesn't really exist, asserting that time is a construct humans have created in order to structure daily existence. Calendar markings merely evidence of the timeline from past to present to future, otherwise artificial and restrictive.

"You cannot capture the movement of clouds," I pronounced.

"I could stare at these clouds all day."

I knew she meant that. "Are they wispy?"

"Some."

"Drips, Jeremy called them. Like milk that drips down your chin."

"Mm. Delicious image."

Anna peered through the camera lens again as I noticed a family of two adults and two children, their jackets billowing in the wind as they excitedly climbed into the buggy. The driver flexed the reins to jerk the horse's head up. Rest period over.

"How long will you be?" I asked.

"The clouds are filling in. Gathering clouds, hard to distinguish one from the other. Harder to distinguish before and after. The moment has passed. Let's take a walk."

"Yes, then lunch, please. I skipped breakfast."

"Right," Anna responded as she gathered her equipment, giving up on the conquest of the clouds for another day.

Hard to believe it was just last Wednesday when we strolled along a path in Central Park that took us to a bench near the boat pond where we contemplated going back in time. Afterwards, exiting the park and heading east, we landed at an iconic Manhattan coffee shop, long and narrow and dimly lit, where we slurped lentil soup and munched toasted corn muffins, the contrast between sweet and salty as pronounced as clouds against sky. I don't remember that conversation, only the warmth of the meal and Anna's good company.

Less than a week later she is silent. Immobile. Her heart beating, her lungs filling and expelling air, otherwise muted.

If everything happens for a reason, what can be the meaning of this, Anna? I cried when I discovered that my dear friend had been splattered against the pavement, another victim of another random accident.

What can be the meaning of this? I screamed into the silence of my apartment when I was called to join the family in a vigil at the hospital.

What can possibly be the meaning of this?

TWO

...Into that world inverted
where left is always right
where the shadows are really the body,
where we stay awake all night.

Elizabeth Bishop

David called me first, that's what he said. What he meant was that I was the first to answer. After meeting with doctors and filling out admission forms, he scanned his watch and realized that Beth and Will were still at school and he was not yet ready to face them with the news. He left word for Anna's sister Karen in California to call. He left the same message for his brother in New Hampshire and his parents in Phoenix. He did not bother to call Anna's mother, who suffers from Alzheimer's disease and lives in a nursing home upstate, so he called the next in line.

By then he desperately needed to hear a caring voice on the other end of the phone and he knew he would likely reach me, no more answering machines to contend with.

I was on the couch, having just put the finishing touches to a glossy view book for an independent school. I had settled into the cushions with a granola bar and a Diet Coke to watch, for the umpteenth time, *The Philadelphia Story*. One of my favorites of a litany of cherished classic films. I suppose it has to do with the simplicity of relationships in those scripts, the theatrical dialogue, the lack of pretentious special effects or heavy-handed music. Or perhaps there is something about black and white film that facilitates withdrawal, as if one actually slips through a tunnel to another time.

I bolted from my seat when I heard David's voice.

"Nell," he shouted. "Are you there? Please pick up."

"I'm glad you're home," he said when I answered, his voice reverberating through the machine like an echo through a cave.

"What's up?" I asked, as casually as possible, although instantly on alert, because David never called me, and I detected at once the trepidation in his voice, a sort of dread, something I'd never heard from him before, which sounded painfully reminiscent of the tone of voice of the policeman years ago who called to report the accident to me.

"It's Anna," David said, his voice so muffled I had to strain to hear what I already suspected I did not want to hear.

"What? What about Anna?"

"She's been in an accident. She's in a coma."

"A coma?" I echoed.

I began pacing the room, a typical response to anxiety.

"Nell, are you there?" David called to me.

"My God, David," I sputtered. "What happened?"

"I don't know, I mean, not exactly. She was walking across the street…"

"Walking?" I blurted. "Not a car accident?"

"Walking, on Main Street. Near the library. She crossed against the light, they said. Or as the light was changing, something like that. There was a truck, couldn't stop, tipped over…"

A sob invaded David's throat and interrupted his narrative. Nothing seems real until you say it aloud, I know that. A crisis, once acknowledged, takes on a life of its own, a heart-wrenching, frantic life of its own.

I realized I had stopped breathing and took a sudden gulp of air. "What are they doing for her?" I shouted on the exhale.

"She's critical. Critical, but stable, that's what they said. The next forty-eight hours will tell. They've mentioned surgery as an option."

I couldn't speak. I felt the burn in the back of my eyes, the choke in my throat, that drag that overtakes the body as the motor stalls.

I stopped pacing and tried to imagine what Anna would do. "What do we do?"

"I don't know. I don't think there's anything we can do."

"There must be something," I mumbled. I took a few measured breaths and repeated more slowly, "There must be something they can do."

"I don't know," he murmured, and I pictured him, stooped in a dark corner of a brightly lit corridor, his body taut, shoulders hunched, lips pressed to the phone. A blonde middle-aged Superman felled by emotional kryptonite. Doctors, nurses and orderlies might have scurried about their business as if he was invisible. This image of David made me want to crawl back to my couch and block out the vision of Anna that simultaneously crept into my mind's eye: stony still in a sterile room with blunt lighting. Unfathomable.

"I'm coming, David," I pronounced. "I'll catch a train. I'll be there as soon as I can."

"That's good, good, yes. I'll pick up the kids at school and meet you at the hospital. Or should I tell them yet?"

"They're nearly grown. They have to know what's happened to their mother. Anna would want them to know." I paused, searching my brain for something to say, something to do. What would Anna want me to do? "Tell Will and Beth I'm coming."

"Thanks," David answered flatly as the phone clicked off.

"I'm coming," I said to no one. "I'm coming, I'm coming," I repeated aloud as I bolted to the bathroom to vomit, then slumped down to the tiled floor and sat there, longer than I should have, as if weighted down.

The last time I leaned against the cool porcelain of a toilet was eons ago, a college student retching an overdose of rum and coke. Now numbed not by alcohol, rather panic. Gradually my heartbeat returned to a steady pace and my body temperature to normal.

I reached up to flush the toilet and watched the water spin, not something generally observed from close range. Food particles and unidentified brown glop slushed from side to side, around and around, frenetic concentric circles of fluid pulled by gravity and suction through pipes and sewers to a distant place. Waste disposed. No need to see it or smell it. All that remained was fresh water sparkling in the bowl. Exactly what we do with our own lives, messes expelled, little opportunity to digest or reap their value. We swiftly banish what is vile or revolting, inconceivable or heartbreaking, preferring the sparkle.

A paramedic at the scene of the accident described Anna as a stick figure drawn in chalk against tar: body contorted, arms strewn over her head, legs tossed haphazardly across each other as if she might only be napping, hard black asphalt her mattress.

The details were revealed to us by the investigative reporting of her boss, Tim Wolfe, the managing editor of the local newspaper *The Dispatch*.

Naturally inquisitive, and never far from a police monitor, when he heard the dispatcher report a potentially fatal accident near the library, he took his lunch-time walk toward the hospital to check out what he thought might be a dead-on-arrival. He didn't know it was Anna until he got there.

Anna has been named best news photographer in the area, and like water in the desert to a small town editor, the kind of professional and creative spirit that suburban media crave, and Tim valued not only for the quality of her work, but her ephemeral approach to life, which reflected his own, so Anna told me.

Now that I know Tim better, I can imagine him standing in the emergency corridor scoping out the scene. Tall and lanky and generally a little disheveled, he has dark hair and dark eyes and large bony hands that hang low from long arms. His face is somewhat marred by the mark of adolescent acne, making him appear chiseled, like ancient stone, and with a perpetual hint of stubble along the jaw, he almost always seems weary. He told us he cornered the emergency medical technician, the son of a local businessman who advertises in the newspaper, thus more willing to share information meant to be confidential. One of the benefits of living and working in a small town, I suppose: the inside story never farther than a favor.

Tim seemed to be on a handshake basis with a lot of locals, despite having landed in the town only a year or so ago. Anna told me he tends to relocate frequently, town to town, newspaper to newspaper. Perhaps he expects a change of scene will yield a change of lifestyle, although as he always lives and works in small towns, how much change can there be? An odd sort of existence, but who am I to judge.

People seemed inclined to speak openly to him, as if he had no vested interest. Although he only occasionally penned news stories anymore, he knew how to secure the scoop, and rarely pulled out a reporter's pad or recording device, relying instead on what he claims is an unusually retentive memory. In a matter of hours he had pieced together every aspect of the accident, most of which he reported in the newspaper after he informed David of his findings.

The front-page article documented what might have seemed an unexceptional albeit incomprehensible moment in which a resident was hit by an oversized commercial delivery truck, one of those transporters with a garish blue and red logo imprinted on each side. A human-interest story lacking only Anna's companion images to bring it to life. The sort of piece that makes people hug loved ones, and one of those moments of the last decade that sparks fear of personal calamity. This town, like so many suburban communities, by virtue of the short commute, lost their share of residents who worked in the towers and, like so many New Yorkers, suffers a communal PTSD of sorts, always on guard, hypersensitive to sudden harsh sounds and startling movements.

David studied Tim's meticulous investigative notes, needing to picture exactly what happened to create in his own mind a blueprint for perspective. As a result, we all observed the event through the lens of witnesses, paramedics, police, emergency room personnel, and a young doctor who hadn't yet learned to avoid the press. I obsessed over what became in my mind a series of still photographs Anna might have taken, barely seconds apart, click, click, click, one minuscule movement to the next, so that we all might share in the unfolding of her destiny.

She left the library with a large tapestry bag draped over one shoulder, the one she purchased at a street fair on Ninth Avenue last year, filled to the brim with a hodgepodge of heavy books: a retrospective of the work of photographer Dorothea

Lange, a picture book about old houses entitled *At Home with the Past*, a local history text called *Small Town, Big History* meant to provide context for a pending feature, and an anthology of contemporary short stories for late night reading. The sort of books always piled by her bedside.

No one seems to know where she was headed. The car was in the library parking lot, a central location. She might have been on her way to visit a friend, although there was nothing written on her pocket calendar, Anna still favoring print to technology, and nothing penciled in until later that day when she was scheduled to photograph the opening of a new exhibit at the Arts Council. She might have arranged a spontaneous coffee with one of her colleagues, although there were no messages or missed calls to suggest anyone awaited her. I doubted she was shopping, as Anna is not much of a shopper, evidenced by the weathered jeans she wore that day with a navy blue V-neck sweater I've seen her wear a hundred times. She might have been en route to the cleaners, as there was a receipt in her purse for a suit of David's. She might have planned to sneak in a walk on the small strip of beach nearby; she does that more often than she admits, dropping whatever needs doing in favor of pressing her toes in the sand. She must have planned a supermarket trip some time soon, as the refrigerator was depleted of all but a few cheeses, yogurt, blueberries, left-over vegetable lasagna, a half-filled container of orange juice and two gallons of almond milk to accompany the requisite six varieties of whole grain cereals, granola and muesli, always in the cupboard for snacks or makeshift meals.

Surely she would have driven to the supermarket, as she would have driven to the beach. There were no doctor or dentist appointments scheduled. No salon, as her friend Maggie cuts her hair. She never frequented spas or dressmakers or therapists. Where was Anna going? What was on her mind when she stepped off the curb to face a speeding truck?

She might have been distracted by a particularly interesting cloud formation. Perhaps a cerulean blue sky or the first yellow forsythia bushes lined up at the corner. Anna's mind was generally somewhere else until something caught her eye, and with her camera always at hand, nestled into her bag or draped around her neck on a well-worn embroidered camera strap, she was always able to mark permanent the otherwise fleeting.

What would she have photographed at the moment of the accident? Surely not the victim, too passive. No, Anna would have been more inclined to aim for witnesses to capture their shocked faces. Perhaps she would have seized upon an expression of horror on a pudgy young mother standing on the opposite corner, accompanied by a toddler on foot and an infant in a stroller. Her name was Belinda and she told Tim she was waiting for the light to change, one hand gripping the stroller, the other clasping her son's hand. She said she leaned down to answer a question he asked just as the truck turned the corner, and she looked up because the motor of the truck was so loud, and noticed Anna suddenly step off the curb. Belinda said she wanted to cry out to her to warn her not to cross, but it all happened so quickly, she reported, like watching a scene on fast-forward.

She said Anna seemed lost in thought, a description that might be suitable at all times, although I would have said lost in the moment. Entranced by the moment, missing, or ignoring the seconds blinking on the pedestrian walk sign, green numbers flashing from twenty to zero, followed by the universal symbol of a red upheld palm. By the time she took a step, other pedestrians had gathered to wait for the next opportunity to cross the intersection of Main Street with South and North Streets, the central roads into town. Corners punctuated by the library, a stately town hall, a white-shingled historic cottage and a Mobil gas station.

Several bystanders witnessed in stunned silence as Anna stepped off the curb. They watched the truck driver, anxious to make the light, speed through the yellow warning, taking the turn too fast, too much weight shifted to one side. They all reported that Anna could not have moved out of the way in time.

Did you see it coming, Anna? I wondered.

Belinda said the truck driver tried to swerve out of the way as he turned, but there wasn't enough room. He must have panicked, that excruciating sense of being suddenly and totally out of control. To avoid hitting Anna head on, he turned so sharply the right rear fender fish-tailed and slammed into her, the force of a ton of steel scooping her up and hurtling her down the street. Loose asphalt, in anticipation of the seasonal re-paving, exploded in the truck's wake, popping like hot oil as the truck careened into the gas station, where it tipped over inches before reaching the gas tanks and idling cars, landing with a resounding crash on one side, wheels spinning wildly without benefit of traction.

The driver was bruised and shaken, otherwise unscathed, and no one else harmed. Anna was jettisoned nearly fifty feet down the road. The emergency medical technician suspected she was instantly unconscious. After all, he explained, her landing might be compared to the descent from a third story window. When I heard his description, I imagined the thud.

Anna's canvas, her camera, the small backpack she carries as a purse, and all of the library books were strewn behind her, marking her path like Hansel and Gretel, those fairy tale children who, afraid to lose their way in the forest, leave bread crumbs behind to guide them, only to end up starving.

A gas station attendant ran to the truck and pulled the driver out. Pedestrians stopped in their tracks. Drivers stepped out of their cars to catch a glimpse, some merely rubbernecking, others hoping to offer assistance. A businessman called for an ambulance from his mobile phone, and the 911 operator reported to Tim that the gas station manager, the receptionist at the historic cottage and seven motorists also phoned in the accident. An older woman standing on the far corner began to cry, her hands clutched to her heart. Another leaving the library walked briskly past the scene with her head bowed so she would not see the body lying in the street, pools of blood drifting behind her shoulders in increasingly erratic streams.

Traffic in all four directions came to a complete stop. Car horns trumpeted from a distance, unaware of the ghastly scene blocking their path. Still, despite the blare, gas station patrons shouting to each other as they extricated the driver, background voices calling out, police and fire trucks and ambulance sirens wailing toward the scene, despite all the commotion that blanketed that busy corner, the young mother said a hush fell over the spectacle the way the crowd is suddenly silenced at a bull-fight when the matador is gored.

Paramedics arrived quickly. They assessed Anna's injuries and presenting symptoms. One EMT covered her face with an oxygen mask and attached a heart monitor, while the other called the hospital for special instructions. They quickly attached an IV to begin an infusion of anti-coagulants to prevent bleeding out, and skillfully moved her onto a gurney and into the ambulance. Anna lay motionless, her body like a rag doll in the hands of the technicians, and in the eyes of most observers, likely dead. Belinda sat on a nearby bench with her son and baby, not so much watching as waiting; even without knowing Anna, she said, she did not want to leave her alone.

We discovered later they had to perform CPR in the ambulance. Anna's heart had stopped and was revived, within less than a minute, the technician reported. Still, great damage can be done in a matter of seconds. The seconds it takes for a truck to spin out of control. The seconds a heart stops beating. The seconds that forever alter a life.

On arrival at the hospital, Anna was immediately recognized as the photographer who a few months earlier had spent a day recording what would become a special series on medical care in a small town emergency room. The admitting clerk gasped in recognition. How much harder it must be, I imagine, to tend to those who are known, the occasionally familiar among the usual anonymity.

When the call came in to David's office, he was in the middle of a meeting reviewing architectural plans for a mixed-use complex in a neighboring community: a block-long office, retail and residential structure. They were sitting in his conference room on the top floor of a ten-story square building facing the downtown harbor. The surrounding floor to ceiling windows are made of a reflective glass that look nearly black from the outside, blocking the glare. From the inside, if occupants ever took time to look out, they would see sunlight sparkling on the surface of the Long Island Sound and a flurry of tiny white-caps roiling in the wake of motor boats and ferries. David and five associates were oblivious to all but the task before them, hunched over a round glass conference table at the far end of the corner space designated for the managing director of the firm of Donahue, Miller and Partners, Donahue having retired to a warmer climate years ago.

"Take a message, please," David bellowed through the speakerphone, behind schedule on the project and losing patience with interruptions.

"A personal emergency, David," his assistant responded, with a slight quiver in her voice that caught his attention. "Pick up at your desk," she added.

David told me later he was instantly wary. "I sat there, only a few seconds, yet I knew, I don't know what I thought I knew, but I knew that something metamorphic had happened."

"Take five," he said to the young architects, waving them away.

The meeting never resumed. David packed up his attaché case with sketches and specifications, as if he were going to see a client or heading home for an early dinner. Perhaps, he hoped, not yet recognizing the seriousness of the accident, he might have to sit in a hospital waiting room for a while until Anna was ready to come home. Until they carefully sewed stitches to seal an open wound or casted a broken bone, something as harmless as that.

When he first saw Anna, her left cheek was swollen and misshapen, nearly burgundy in color from eye to chin, with a deep gash under the jaw. Otherwise, her facial features were intact. That was the first thing David noticed, he said, how serene she appeared, in spite of the atrocity of her wounds, the tubes attached at various parts of her body, the artificial rise and fall of her chest via a respirator.

There was more than at first glance, of course. Her left arm was crushed, bone literally shattered, with dislocations protruding from various angles, pushing through the gauze wrap like street tar pressed up after an earthquake. Her hip too was perforated and would require reconstruction or replacement. The bruises and cuts on her arms were worse than her legs because of a thin layer of protection provided by the denim she was wearing that day, so a resident told him. Odd to think of jeans as a protective layer, David muttered, but he felt grateful for any good fortune.

"She wasn't hit at the chest or lower spine, saving the more major organs from direct damage," the resident explained. "However, she has sustained severe trauma. She may be suffering from internal injuries, the nature of which are difficult to ascertain. We're not certain if the skull is intact. She may be bleeding internally, her blood counts are already low…"

"Where?" David asked, needing a mental sketch to process the image.

"I couldn't say the source of the bleeding," he answered apologetically. "She's on her way to an MRI. Surgery may be necessary."

"Surgery?" David uttered. "How can you operate if you don't know the extent of the damage?"

"Sometimes it is necessary to directly seek out the source. Her blood pressure and pulse rate are dangerously low. However, on arrival she received an injection of Decadron, a steroid that suppresses inflammation, particularly effective in cases of systemic shock. The ventilator will ensure an adequate supply of oxygen. We will do all we can to prevent further damage."

David was dumbfounded. He said he never felt so helpless. A terrible feeling for a man who has always felt the commander of his fate. Unlike Anna, he has never been willing to accept the concept of a master plan, preferring to navigate his life along the course of his choosing, believing it was the life of his choosing, thus impatient with obstacles large and small.

He was also impatient, he later admitted, with the resident physician, as well as everyone he spoke to that first day, because no one had answers. No solutions, only speculation. They explained that Anna was in a coma, and when he answered, incredulous, that she appeared to be simply unconscious, it was explained that coma is exactly that.

"Unconscious and unresponsive," he later quoted. "As if she were in a very deep sleep."

The senior neurology resident and the chief of internal medicine were called in. An orthopedic surgeon was consulted on interim repair to her hip. Her condition was established as critical, albeit stable, and the appropriate tests ordered to determine the next steps. David was urged to sign consent forms and wait. He said he would have insisted on more information if he had known what questions to ask.

The admitting nurse took him by the arm to registration, where an emergency room intern took a medical history. David said he lingered a moment before following the nurse, listening to what she had to say while watching Anna on the gurney in a rare moment of passivity that, more than the many assaults to her body, illustrated the gravity of the situation.

"She's never been sick," he told the nurse. "In all the years I've known her, barely a cold or flu. So there's nothing much to tell, is there? I don't even know her blood type."

The nurse assured him they would ascertain such information and take excellent care of his wife. David stopped and turned and looked at Anna one last time, now barely visible down the hall. He instructed the nurse that his wife was to have a private room.

"All the rooms in the Intensive Care Unit are private," the nurse answered.

"Of course," David nodded, satisfied in that moment that at least Anna would have intensive care.

Anna met David at the King Cole Bar at the St. Regis Hotel in Manhattan, a watering hole best known for a whimsical thirty foot-long mural by artist Maxfield Parrish. Adorned in red, with a large yellow crown, and flanked by his fiddlers, the fabled monarch features the visage of its commissioner, the businessman/socialite John Jacob Astor, at his request, and likely depicted as far merrier than he.

David was there to meet with clients on one of the first architectural assignments for which he served as project manager. He was engaged at the time to a wholesome blonde with a bright smile, a good heart, and a well-considered life plan, punctuated by the attractive architect.

Anna had only recently moved to Manhattan from a rural community in Maryland. She spent several weeks wandering up and down city streets, creating her own grid within the larger grid, so that bit by bit she would learn the city like a native. The mural was one of a long list of landmarks, and that day, after many hours wandering, she shook out her hair, squared her shoulders and strolled into the bar. She perched on a stool dead center and ordered a Brandy Alexander, imagining in this way she might seem less of the bumpkin she was. There she sat, sipping slowly to nurse the one drink, entertaining herself by imagining the spirits of visitors embedded in the mural as deeply as the nicotine. She gazed around at fellow patrons and when she asked one couple if she might snap their photograph they demurred, suggesting to Anna that it might have been a clandestine meeting, a titillating idea to the small town girl with a lively imagination.

David, impatiently awaiting the delayed client, looked up from his strategically selected corner table to notice Anna chatting with the couple, and when she became aware of his gaze, she smiled. He couldn't help but smile back, appreciating the response. David is a modestly tall, modestly built man, with sandy hair and evenly spaced facial features, but not the type of man to capture the attention of a pretty woman. Not so much handsome as pleasing. Like a shirt that never goes out of style, he wears well.

He turned back to the sketches neatly piled on the table, his brand new black leather portfolio resting against an adjacent chair. He scrutinized each cross-section as if something might have been altered since his last look, checked his watch one more time with exasperation, then looked up again to Anna, her long legs crossed seductively at the knee in a pose reminiscent of Rita Hayworth. She turned and smiled again, and he smiled again, and this time he took notice of her elegant neck and large pale eyes, and a mane of dark hair that matched the mahogany bar, and if she hadn't been dressed traditionally in a cotton skirt with a cardigan sweater buttoned nearly to the neck, he has said he might have imagined her to be a high-class hooker.

David would later confess she saved him from a potentially monotonous life, although not too long after Anna and I became friends, he whisked her away to what to my mind was a predictably pedestrian existence in the suburbs. I made no secret of my disdain for the move, but Anna leveled my judgment with acceptance, reminding me there are good people and experiences to be had wherever we are, and she would of course find them.

I was comforted only that she would reside less than an hour's train ride away, permitting our friendship, and ultimately her sustenance, to remain within reach.

Anna confessed to me long ago that she knew at once she had landed at the hotel bar not so much to explore the legendary oasis as to find David, to provide the gentle nudge he needed to release his psychic limitations. However I have yet to see evidence of any profound shift in mindset, beyond his willingness to accept Anna's eccentricities and love her without reservation.

When I met Jason, I had no plan, no strategy and no sense of destiny. I only wanted to touch him. I wanted to dredge the tips of my fingers along his wrist, float my cheek against his chest, and crush my lips to his neck. I confided to Anna that my husband had captured my heart through my loins, so to speak. From the first we had a torrid sex life. Nothing either one of us had experienced in the past, thus surprising, nearly shocking in intensity. Our passion awakened otherwise repressed, humble lifestyles.

My passion was a surprise to me, as it might have been to others, because Jason was not handsome, not in a traditional way. Mid-sized and stocky, his eyes were planted a bit too close, his nose a little long, and his curly hair perpetually trailed down his neck like a scruffy construction worker. Cerebrally and emotionally, however, he was head and shoulders above anyone I'd ever met: a compassionate being with an impeccable eye for the arts and a way of consistently discovering joy in all things. To me, the most attractive man on earth.

When I told Anna about my lust for Jason, I noticed a wistful look in her eyes, as if, in contrast to my sensory coupling, she had claimed David as her husband, but without the same sort of fusion. Their union, being more cosmic than earthly, may never have kindled the desire Jason and I thrived on, having no plan or purpose but to love each other.

Perhaps there were some things Anna never quite grasped, or conquered, although she seemed to me exalted and invincible, until the moment she was struck down in the street, so I clung to this image of the all-knowing old soul in order to rely on her teachings.

In the end, this is what kept me going the four weeks she remained in a coma. Four weeks: the cycle of the moon, progenitor of the tides. Twenty-eight days, and each day another ribbon of yarn on the nearly threadbare blanket that has kept me warm.

I barely remember packing. I had no idea how long I would stay at Anna's. I wanted to believe I might be there a day or two, certainly no more than a week. Anna would come around, I supposed, maybe even by the time I got there. Or she would come through surgery triumphant, her head lifting from the pillow with that all-knowing smile.

I imagined I would hold her hand and listen to the story over and over, the way women need to repeat their tales of childbirth or lost loves, relieving while holding on to the experience. I expected to stay with the family a short time, so David might return to work, and, in some small way, repay the debt I owed Will and Beth for the many days and nights Anna abandoned them to be with me. When she was securely back on her feet, in no time at all, I presumed, I would return to my insulated life, and Anna and I would return to our Wednesdays.

I left a note with my apartment key for my neighbor's daughter, Jessica, a sweet pimply-faced 15 year-old who always seems anxious to please, asking her to feed and tend to the cat. Seuss the cat, my soul companion, an abandoned kitten we adopted as a gift for my son's second birthday. I was never a fan of cats, but we wanted Jeremy to experience the joy, and responsibility, of a pet, although we might have had the greater joy when Jeremy squealed with delight as he lifted the kitten out of the box, his small hands cradling a squirming ball of gray and white fur, and enjoying the pleasure of play all that first day. And while cats have a reputation as standoffish, Seuss from the first was Jeremy's playmate.

Six weeks after the accident, when I at last tired of the discomfort of the couch, I crept into my bed, and Seuss, who had spent those weeks dozing in corners or on pillows that Anna strategically placed for him, leaped onto the bed and curled himself demandingly into my coiled torso. I couldn't bear the touch. I tossed him off the bed so hard he was momentarily stunned, but he came back, and I pushed him away again, repeatedly, each time more forcefully, the poor animal absorbing my rage until at last he settled on the foot of the bed, licking his wounded paws, and I, too exhausted to fight with him any longer, succumbed to sleep. We have slept that way all these years and I have grown accustomed to his body heat at my feet.

Age has slowed him down, no longer nimble, so I recently fashioned a smaller bed for him on the floor out of a double-folded cotton quilt that provides sufficient cushion for his arthritic joints. He sleeps near enough to see me and hear me, and I worried about leaving him alone without the clack of the keyboard or the constant chatter of the television to keep him company. Dear Seuss, the one and only creature that still needed me.

Nothing remained but to pack and go. I searched the upper reaches of my closet for my plaid flannel weekend duffle, into which I tossed two pairs of jeans, blue and a black, both faded with age to a more perfect patina than artificially stonewashed, and a few black T-shirts. I threw in a V-neck and cardigan sweater, and shoved a handful of socks in one end, panties and another bra in the other, and grabbed a nightshirt, the one that says *Just Do It* across the front, a gift from Anna's daughter.

"Just do it," I muttered as I scoured my room for anything else I might need. What a ridiculous saying. Like *Just Say No.* Advice from the image-makers, pathetically abstract and irrelevant to the reality of human life.

As I zipped the duffle, I remembered to bury my toothbrush and toothpaste and reading glasses into the zipper pocket, whatever else I might need surely to be found at Anna's house.

I grabbed a fleece jacket and slipped into my charcoal gray mules, so old an impression of my toes are molded into the tips, and then stood in the living room for another moment to consider what I might have forgotten. I snatched an escapist mystery I was reading and tossed it into my bag, although I don't know why I would have imagined I would have the time or the inclination to read. Odd, the things you do at such moments, without really thinking.

On my way out the door, I pulled the last five packs of Marlboro Lights from the carton on the kitchen counter, a teenage habit I took up again some years ago to calm my nerves. Now and then, cigarettes soothe the savage beast, despite the perpetually nasty taste in my throat, and I only smoke out of the apartment, which is often the only reason I go out. I also picked up my vial of Zoloft and shook it close to my ear. By the clatter of tiny yellow caplets against the plastic I knew a week or so of anti-depressant benefits remained. I imagined I would be back by then and tucked the vial into my purse.

It is more than likely I would not have survived without medication. I acknowledge its power. Nor would I have survived without Anna. The thought chilled me to the bone and I stopped in my tracks, as if Anna's hands were clutching at my heart. Was there something I had forgotten? Something I was meant to remember, in fact, obligated to remember? No, not now I thought, not yet, and fled the apartment, anxiety digging into my skin, a parasite that lives within me, and now and then makes its presence known to remind me of my limitations.

I made my way down the stairs, preferring the staircase to the elevator to avoid being boxed in or forced to make small talk. I have counted the stairs many times, reassured that some things never change, and as I stepped down the twenty-six steps on each of the four flights to the lobby, I listened to my feet scrape the concrete treads and thud on each landing like the footsteps of a cripple. I shuffled through the lobby to the front door and braced myself for the afternoon air. Sunlight filtered through the haze and I lowered my eyes against the glare, lit a cigarette, inhaled deeply, settled my purse on one shoulder, the duffle on the other, and began my walk. I might have headed east a few blocks and caught a subway; even a bus would have been quicker. Instead, sloth-like, I lumbered the twenty-five city blocks, a little more than a mile, to Grand Central Station, anxious to be there, yet too anxious to rush.

We had been haunted by wet weather through the winter and future predictions were not good, attributed to El Niño or La

Niña, I never remember the difference: weather in the northern continents contrived by ocean temperatures in the Equatorial Pacific. Likely the result of the progression of the glacial thaw or atmospheric phenomena compromised by nuclear particles drifting through space, a theory I subscribe to, certain the violation of the earth's atmosphere over Japan nearly sixty years ago would haunt us. Recent months had been cold and precipitant, early spring days damp and gray. Potholes, scarred ever more deeply into the tar, were puddled with the previous night's rain, craggy pools of darkness awaiting a careless footstep or a sloppy driver.

Head bowed, an intermittent zigzag of light lit my way. I am used to this pattern of illumination between buildings. Manhattan is cavernous. Skyscrapers tower upward like stalagmites and everything about the city is like ice – solid and unwavering. A place where the lonely find companionship or the solace of anonymity, either equally well suited to the solipsistic nature of cave dwellers.

If I were living in a small town, people might recognize me. They might nudge each other knowingly as I passed. They might whisper, there she goes, poor Nell, the recluse. In this city, I pass unnoticed. No one knows my story. They might observe that my shoulders are perennially slumped, my eyes averted. That I walk slowly, no one to keep up with. Most of the time, I am largely imperceptible, neutral, like trench coats on a rainy day, and I prefer it that way. I derive nourishment from the sweet smell of roasted peppers that filters from pizza parlors, the pungent aroma of espresso wafting out of coffee bars, and the hint of vanilla emanating from bakeries.

Any time of day or night there are people about, laughing, crying, hurried, expectant or apprehensive, whispering in each other's ears as they stroll arm-in-arm or stride rapidly toward their destinations. We all navigate city streets buffered by a dissonance of sounds and scents, a sweet and sour symphony not unlike the co-existence of flora and fauna in a country meadow, nurtured by a form of photosynthesis in which by-products of human life are sucked in and transformed into psychic energy, spewed out in steadily digestible doses. Even the walking dead thrive within this vast steel and concrete oxygen tent.

I breathed deeply, lining my lungs with city air, desperate for the courage to face the coming days.

When I arrived at the station, the screen displaying departures listed a 3:40 train leaving in three minutes, which I took as an admonishment for not moving faster. I didn't stop to purchase a ticket or admire the exquisite restoration of the grand station, anchored by the iconic timepiece that ticks away moments, moments the lifeblood for every passenger rushing to make their train. I too ran for the train as if my life depended on it, sprinting down the dim ramp to the track, spurting into the rear car breathless as the bell rang and doors snapped shut.

I don't remember the last time I ran, hardly moving in more than a crawl most of the time, so I leaned against the doors to catch my breath and scan the brightly lit railroad car, down the narrow aisle separating rows of seats. I made my move as the train chugged through the tunnel toward the open tracks and slumped into an empty window seat, squeezing the duffle under my feet. My heartbeat steadily slowed to normal even as my empty stomach felt increasingly hollow. I tried to ease the anxiety by watching the scenery as the train slowed into and out of several stations along the way, but the windows were smudged and filmy, making the landscape grainy, like old film. Instead, I surveyed fellow passengers, the best way to avoid worrying about what I might find at the hospital, or, as more often on long journeys, drifting into the murky landscape of melancholy.

A typical potpourri of passengers, I thought I might describe to Anna when I arrived. Well-dressed women, chic retail shopping bags at their feet, chatting amiably on their cell phones or flipping the pages of a fashion magazine. Suited consultants who have removed their jackets and loosened their ties or the scrappier freelance artists, scribbling notes after a day of meetings or solicitations. Office workers returning home early for a doctor's appointment or a school play, perusing their tablets or catching up with the *Wall Street Journal.* Some slept, others stared at the landscape beyond their windows as if hypnotized. Nothing of note, so I closed my eyes and replayed images of frosted birthday cakes, music recitals and sports playoffs, all happy occasions when I have joined Anna's family in their milieu. I never expected to arrive under calamitous circumstances.

At last I disembarked, sluggish from the journey, and weary of my own malaise, and stood on the platform as fellow passengers dispersed, greeting family members or friends from behind the wheels of their sport-utility vehicles or mini-vans or luxury sedans, lined up in a row beside the platform like daffodils in their flowerbeds. In a matter of moments, the rush of travelers cleared, leaving only a few milling about awaiting latecomers.

I don't drive. Jason drove when necessary and mass transit takes me wherever I need to go in the city, when I'm not in walking distance. When I do venture out of bounds, someone transports me to the final destination. Even when I visit my father in Florida, I am greeted at the airport by one of his aging buddies, to whom he has bestowed the honor of transporting his only child. My father suffers from Parkinson's disease and he thankfully has everything he needs at the retirement village. My mother passed away when Jeremy was three years old, after a blessedly short bout with cancer, and I was gratified, even if she passed too young, that she lived to know her grandson and died before she had to suffer his loss.

Without a pick-up, I crouched on my knees and propped myself on the duffle to consider my options. An old man with no hair and bulging green eyes tentatively leaned out of a black sedan to ask if I needed a ride. I ignored him at first, until I realized he drove the small town equivalent of a taxi, not the garish yellow city cabs with lighted signs on top. I pulled myself up, grabbed my duffle and slid into the black leather back seat, which was spotlessly clean and saturated with the candy-coated scent of a cardboard potpourri hanging from the rear-view mirror. The door creaked loudly as I pulled it closed, like the whinny of a workhorse who should be let out to pasture.

The driver turned to face me with questioning eyes.

"The hospital," I said. "There is only one, yes?"

"Oh, yes," he answered. "A very good one at that."

On the short trip, he tried to make conversation with perfunctory questions like "Been here before? Visiting friends?"

The way a predatory male might behave in a crowded bar. I nodded without speaking and stared out the window until he stopped asking.

As we traversed neatly paved streets, I was struck once again by the grandeur of the stately older homes in town. While each had a distinct character, cumulatively they had the effect of a fortress. I imagined children spying on passers-by through lace curtains behind the tall windows of renovated Victorians, ladder-backed chairs rocking gently on their wraparound porches. Whitewashed brick Georgians hovered grandly above pitched lawns, and Colonials, the architectural senior citizens, perched proudly, as if maiden aunts at Sunday supper. Their emerging gardens stood guard. Tender pink viburnum lifted their petals from brown winter blankets, forsythia bowed golden branches like ballerinas at the bar, and on hillsides, daffodils waved in the breeze – blooms the color of sunshine, the color of lemons, and others so pale as to seem white by comparison. I hoped this seasonal abundance might hasten Anna's healing.

As I stepped out of the taxi, the driver turned to me with an expression of compassion so intense I had to turn away from his gaze. Such poignancy of emotion too often smacks of pity, which I cannot tolerate, especially from strangers. As I reached out to pay him, he grasped my hand and proclaimed, "It will be all right, Miss."

"Thank you," I mumbled, and fled up the steps to the hospital doors with a renewed sense of dread, despite or perhaps because of the old man's solicitude.

I stumbled through the large revolving doors to the welcome desk where an elderly woman sat reading a magazine, her face heavily powdered and dark eyelashes contrasting with silvered curls that sat so tightly on her head she might have been wearing rollers. VOLUNTEER was printed on a nametag attached to her collar.

She smiled when she looked up at me. "May I help you, dear?"

"Anna Miller," I whispered. "She was admitted earlier today."

"Pardon?"

"Anna Miller," I repeated, a little louder.

"Certainly," she answered, punching each of the letters of Anna's name onto the keyboard contained in a drawer beneath the desk. She peered at the screen, then pressed down on the enter button again, then again. Her smile turned to a frown as she looked up at me. "I'm sorry to say, Mrs. Miller is in critical condition. She's in the Intensive Care Unit. Only immediate family members permitted. Are you family?"

I could have said yes. Surely I would be forgiven a minor trespass to be with my closest friend. Still, I stood frozen, never one to break rules without a really good reason.

"I think I'll wait for Mr. Miller," I murmured.

I sat on an empty bench near the entry, clutching my overnight bag. Thankfully, David and the children entered soon after.

Beth looked ghostly. She had let her hair fall below her shoulders, soft curls crowding her face as if indulging her desire to hide. Tall and shapely like her mother, and solid like her father, she generally has David's rosy complexion and sandy hair, and similarly penetrating dark eyes. Yet the fineness of her features and the chiseled elegance of her jaw are unmistakably Anna's. She sat down and folded herself into me and I wrapped my arms around her. The warmth of my embrace, the feeling one has when suddenly safe, allowed her to snuggle close and I expected at any moment she would cry. She did not. She was remarkably composed, maintaining the behavior her mother would appreciate.

I would have preferred to weep, but I rarely do, compliments of anti-depressants. The medication keeps my emotions in check, but in that equanimity also makes it nearly impossible to let down. Tear ducts seem sterilized, sentiments held hostage to sanity. Now and then, a solitary tear escapes and drifts down my cheek, a fleeting remnant of sorrow, or, on occasion, I explode into hysterical crying that depletes me for days. At that moment at the hospital, I was dry. I held on to Beth and looked up at Will, who stood stiffly by his father's side. Sixteen years old now and exactly the tall tree Anna imagined he would become, taller than his father but with the face of a young boy: wide blue eyes, a ruddy complexion, and hair cropped tightly to his head in true athletic fashion.

I took his hand and he allowed me to hold on briefly, without making eye contact.

"Why are you out here?" David exclaimed with dismay. "Why aren't you with Anna?"

"They told me only immediate family," I answered sheepishly, to justify my inertia. "I thought I should wait for you."

"For God's sake, Nell, you are family. You should have said so. Come on, I'll tell them you're her sister, you might as well be."

I was so grateful at that moment for his camaraderie I thought I might collapse, but I held myself together and we all walked through the main corridor toward Anna.

The Intensive Care Unit seemed a giant fish bowl. Creatures darted around in a circular space, anchored at the center like a cluster of rocks by the nurses' station. Private rooms with sliding glass doors surrounded the center for easy viewing and access, so inhabitants loomed larger than they were. Computer screens flickered on the periphery like air bubbles.

We tread quietly along a gray-carpeted path, peering at plastic-coated name plaques mounted at each door and quickly averting our eyes to the scenes within. Some rooms were thankfully empty, others with bodies at rest connected by multiple tubes to monitors and hanging plastic IV bags. Occasionally a visitor sitting in a chair near a patient's bed looked out as we passed, despair or boredom etched onto otherwise blank expressions.

"May I help you?" a nurse asked David as we rounded a bend in the corridor.

"Anna Miller," he answered. "She was admitted this afternoon."

"Yes," she replied, glancing up at the big board above the desk with patients' names opposite room numbers. "You are Mr. Miller?"

"Yes, and these are our children, Beth and Will. And, Anna's sister, Nell," he answered, gesturing to me.

"Fine, immediate family is welcome," she said, pointing toward Anna's room. "Number 7. Two at a time, please."

We lined up outside Anna's room. A curtain was drawn so we could not see in.

"Lucky 7," Will remarked.

"You go in, David," I said. "With Beth or Will. I'll wait here."

David looked helplessly at his children.

"I'll wait with Nell," Beth said.

Will, looking remarkably at that moment like his childhood self, shrugged his broad shoulders and hung his head as he shuffled into Anna's room with David. Beth and I huddled together in the hallway, surrounded by the hum and beep of life-support equipment and the occasional squeak of rubber soles. Beth commented on the assortment of materials piled about, contrary to the orderliness one expects in an ICU: stacks of pharmaceutical samples nested into open corrugated boxes, plastic-wrapped rubber pitchers and spittoons spilling out of bins, scattered crates of latex gloves and red metallic toxic waste containers.

An elderly man and a physician in a white coat emerged from an adjacent room. "There's really nothing more we can do," the doctor said and the man lowered his eyes in desolation. At the same time, a flirtatious resident murmured into a nurse's ear, their shoulders furtively grazing. When another nurse plopped herself into a swivel chair and unwrapped a steaming sandwich from shiny foil, she looked up at us and smiled, affirming that ordinary activities go on under the most extraordinary circumstances.

Beth rubbed my hand with one hand. She might have meant to comfort me or perhaps sought comfort in the distraction. "What do we do?" she whispered.

"We wait," I answered, covering her hand with mine. "We think good thoughts."

"We trust in the plan," she said, staring at Anna's doorway as if her mother might suddenly appear.

I might have been astounded by that sort of comment from another eighteen year-old, but not Beth. She was raised to give herself over to destiny, prepared to accept even the worst. I might have been inspired, but had to take measured breaths to stay calm. My stomach growled loudly.

"I guess you need some food," Beth chuckled.

At that moment, David and Will emerged. David dabbed at his eyes with a handkerchief and Will swiped at his with a sleeve before he turned away, his hands back in his pockets, his head drooped nearly to his breastbone. He reminded me of a tree that has collapsed in a storm, twisted and distorted yet rooted in place.

"You go," I said to Beth, nudging her toward David. "Dad will go back in with you. I'll wait with Will."

David nodded, but Will turned to walk down the hallway toward the elevator. "I'll wait downstairs," he said over his shoulder.

"We won't be long," David called to him, leading Beth into Anna's room.

I waited alone with a rumbling stomach and a heavy heart. Anna would have been proud to see her children accepting their fate. They were proving, at least for the moment, to be true disciples. Her positives, she called them, in that way she had of categorizing people as the magnetic poles of old souls versus novices, and she contends that the vast majority of human beings are not so much negative personalities as neophyte souls within the spirit world, like the newest planets of ancient solar systems.

"Why else would this species be so wasteful and perpetuate such atrocities?" she frequently commented, frankly the only explanation of human madness that has ever made sense.

The first time she enlightened me on the positive-negative classification we were ambling through Central Park, Jeremy in a stroller as Beth and Will ran playfully along the path.

"Let's face it," Anna said, "personality is predetermined. Genetic and cosmic and as clearly casted as the color of our eyes. Only behavior is learned. Boundaries and principles. Otherwise, nature trumps nurture every time."

"You can tell from their first cry," I concurred.

"So true. The more aggressive personalities demand our attention, daring us to ignore them. The sensitive are more dramatic, like an opera singer without the proper acoustics. And the reserved, like Will, tentative, always testing the sound of their own voice, although deep down, a mature soul."

"Yes."

"Will is like you. Just as unwilling to intrude, quietly studying everything around and, in the end, the wisest of us all."

I laughed. "Hardly."

"Jeremy too."

"Yes, but this boy has been a squealer from the first; he is delighted by his own echo."

As if to confirm my assessment, Jeremy screeched and pointed to a squirrel scampering along the bark of a tree.

"I think we remain positives or negatives from one life to another until we evolve, or unless there is a significant, and I mean seismic shift that forces a change in outlook. Ironically, I imagine that most negatives spend their lifetimes looking for a good enough reason to switch sides and, by virtue of being innately cynical, rarely find one. These are the saddest humans, miserable with longing. Taking their heartache from one life to the next and the next. My sister Karen, remember her son Michael? All the cajoling and nurturing and coaching on earth will not encourage optimism in that dear boy. Always a half-empty glass. I'm certain he came to a bad end in his last life and cannot move beyond the most primal angst. Karen too is never satisfied with anything or anyone, although she harbors a hopeful heart. The divorce did her in. She cannot see beyond regret. A dreamer encapsulated in disappointment, poor thing."

"What purpose do they serve, the negatives I mean?" I asked. "Why couldn't we have a world of positives? Imagine what that might be like."

"Leave it to you to wish for it." Anna smiled. "The contrast is essential, like the play of light and dark. No light without shadows. No image without contrast. Although, now and then, you meet a person who is the embodiment of chiaroscuro, light and dark at once. Very special."

I nodded absentmindedly as my son let himself out of the stroller and tried to climb a low branch not quite within reach.

"Look at the children on the playground." Anna pointed to the area where young children scampered like the squirrels. "Little prigs take charge, at odds with the bullies. Adventurers want to build a tree house and naysayers list all the reasons it cannot be done. Kids with permanent smiles on their faces and others who seem thwarted before they've begun. All of them just wanting to connect. To be seen. A microcosm of humanity."

"We're lucky," Anna went on. "Beyond the course of destiny, our kids will have sufficient positive energy to deal with whatever they may have to deal with."

I remember agreeing enthusiastically, pleased that our children might live charmed lives, surrounded by an invisible shield to protect them from the dark, the dangerous and the dour, which made Jeremy's death all the more unfathomable. How could that supremely positive spirit have been felled so easily?

As I waited for David and Beth to return, I leaned back against a wall and wondered once again how we possibly explain tragedy? One can hardly formulate the questions, much less divine the answers.

"You must have faith in the master plan," Anna has said, more than once. The minister at her pulpit. "Jason and Jeremy may be lost to you, but they will surely bless other lives. You'll see them again, you will. For now, you must be grateful for your time together."

Remembering her words at that moment, I felt once again a barely repressed fury spring from deep within, which I just as quickly crushed. Anna meant for me to be comforted by such ephemerality, and in deference to her, I have tried all these years to find acceptance. Was I meant to allow Anna to slip from my life as well? To think of her as a temporary prize, without trying to hold on to her?

Beth and David stepped out of the room and as they approached, Beth fell into my arms.

"I think she needs to know you're here," she whimpered.

Anna lay still and limp, dead center in the room like a corpse rolled out of a vault and unveiled for viewing. I gasped at the sight. The silence was punctured only by the steady refrain of monitors and breathing equipment, and the barely perceptible trickle of fluids dripping through thin plastic tubes into perforated veins.

As I drew closer, a muscle in her arm flinched and I recoiled, skittish in the presence of my dear friend who seemed a ghoulish stranger. I kept a safe distance from her bed, as if she might reach out and grab me, like a skeleton in a horror movie, and I was overcome with guilt that I had yet to rush to her side and offer my unequivocal support.

"Speak to me, Anna," I murmured.

A tear rolled down my cheek. A sob restrained itself and slid back down my throat. The emotional anguish I experienced at that moment was indescribable, more torturous than anything I could have imagined at that point in my life. Who says lightning does not strike twice?

I moved closer. I wanted to touch her, take her hand, comfort her, but I felt afraid to pollute her in some way, hoping she was gathering the might of all her past lives to bring her back to this one.

I glanced at the pale green walls, marred here and there with a dark stain, and shuddered to think what might have splashed onto these walls over time. I looked back at Anna, hoping she might have miraculously opened her eyes. I peered closer and her eyes seemed to me not so tightly shut, a miniscule but noticeable space at the eyelashes. I waited for a flutter, any movement or alteration to suggest she was present.

I stepped closer still. "Why now, Anna?" I beseeched her. "You must have more to do. Surely your mission in this life is not complete. Beth will graduate in June. Will is still forming. David needs you. I need you."

Another sob clogged my throat and I slumped into the wooden chair next to the bed, watching solution drip, drip, drip from a bag suspended upside-down on a tall rod near her head. I leaned forward to speak again but, failing to find words, slumped back in the chair. I listened to the steady ebb and flow of assisted breathing, a matter only of seconds between breaths, yet each time seemed boundless, the way a bridge or tunnel reach out across space before wending back to solid ground.

"Anna," I implored. "I'm not sure what you've got in mind here, but this is not a good time. For anyone. Least of all me, I barely exist without you."

I closed my eyes, trying to transmit my message telepathically, attempting to read her thoughts, hoping for a sign, a word, a cosmic transmission. When nothing came, I opened my eyes, helpless and hopeless, and rose to leave.

Sometimes the challenges before us go unnoticed. Anna's words drifted back to me and I sat down. Words she spoke not long ago at a sidewalk cafe in the West Village. One of those quasi-European bistros she adored, certain she might have been an artist on the Parisian Left Bank, perhaps a contemporary of Gertrude Stein or Colette, taking lovers one after another and living the intellectual and artistic life now glorified as the last of a golden age.

"Perhaps I was Edith Wharton," she cackled that day. "I might have traveled the world, decorated mansions and wrote prolific portraits of New York and European society."

I was only half-listening at the time, Anna's commentaries background music.

"We have to keep the zoom effect on high," she posited, "especially at those propitious moments when the signs are there, if only we stop to see. Reach down to the deepest part of ourselves to accept completely and without question the unfolding of our destiny."

I couldn't bear another moment of my own memory, so I abruptly stood and bolted. On my way to meet David and the children in the lobby, I stopped in the stairwell to smoke a cigarette. Like a schoolgirl hiding from the hall monitor, I sucked in the potent nicotine and tobacco and exhaled forcefully, watching the smoke unfurl into nothingness. I breathed deeply, slowly, until my heartbeat returned to a normal rhythm, and, in a calmer state, smoked the cigarette down to the filter, before crushing the last ash under my foot and slipping the dead butt into my pocket to dispose of later, blowing the ashes into the crevices of the stairwell until they disappeared.

When I was a young girl, my mother kept one bedroom window open at all times. In the depths of summer, the air thick and stagnant, I nonetheless felt a profound link to my surroundings, as if tree barks and leaves, moths and butterflies, lightning bugs and bats, all shared the same scalding air that surrounded me in my little room. Without air-conditioning or shades, without protection from the elements, I was vulnerable to hot winds and heat waves, and on many long summer nights, I lay naked under a cotton sheet, perspiration the only prospect of cooling my skin. In the worst of winter, I would awaken before dawn, snugly wrapped in multiple blankets, lips chattering, nose moist and cold, rubbing my toes together and burrowing further under the coverlets. Throughout childhood, season to season, I was keenly aware of the contrasts that characterize such moments in darkness, and I inhaled from my little bed the hot and cold that defines daily living, paying dues for the safe happy life that would surely come to me. How naïve I was. So easily satisfied. Easily deluded.

Now, an open window is more habit than homily, so I automatically opened the car window as we drove away from the hospital, all of us silent, shocked, together but alone with our thoughts. A crisp evening breeze blew into the car and I imagined stars popping out across the night sky. I sat in the passenger seat, the seat usually reserved for Anna, while Will and Beth huddled against opposite rear doors, staring at the passing street scene.

David had ordered pizza for dinner and stopped to pick it up on the way home. He left the car running as he ran inside and the subtle hum of the engine muffled screams I was certain I heard from each of us simultaneously, the same muffled screams I often awaken to in the dead of night. I peered into the restaurant, a local favorite called Pizza Planet, the walls adorned with constellation cut outs shaped like pizzas with planetary toppings.

"This is the best pizza in town," Beth said, "despite the cheesy décor."

"Pun intended," Will commented.

"Mom loves their calzone," Beth murmured, ignoring Will's retort.

They turned silent again, embarrassed, I imagined, by glib conversation in the midst of a tragic situation.

A bouquet of tomato and garlic infused the car as David drove home, which under different circumstances might have been appetizing. When we arrived, the answering machine on the kitchen counter registered twenty-two messages and David and I groaned as one.

"I'm too tired for this," David said.

"You can call tomorrow," I answered. "Or they'll call back."

"I'll have to call some of them tonight."

"After dinner, Dad," Beth interjected, as she mechanically placed blue earthenware dishes and paisley fabric napkins on the table, her task every other night of her life since she was old enough to have been assigned chores.

"How about paper plates tonight?" I asked.

"Paper?" Beth derided. "In this house, what are you thinking?"

"Of course, I forgot."

Little is tossed away at Anna's house, and only if deemed unequivocally useless. No use of paper plates, plastic cups or paper napkins. Tissues are barely tolerated, paper towels used sparingly, sponges and dishcloths sanitized frequently. At the back door, three rectangular bins nestle together for cans, bottles and plastics, and a basket for newspapers neatly tied with twine for delivery to the recycling center. Leftovers are mandatory eating.

I placed the pizza boxes directly on the table, one with pepperoni and mushrooms, the second plain. Steam wafted upward when we lifted the box tops, the familiar aroma liberated like balloons let loose into the sky. Will plowed through half a pizza in a matter of minutes, chomping loudly, his head slightly bowed, his eyes on the food like a colt at the trough. David managed to swallow down a couple of slices, leaving a small pile of crust on the side of his plate, crust Anna usually nibbled, which now sat untouched. Beth and I each picked at a single slice on our plates, carving them into smaller and smaller pieces and chewing each piece so slowly we eventually tired of the effort.

As David rinsed the dishes and placed them neatly into the dishwasher, I packaged the leftover pizza slices into shining foil triangles and piled them on the top shelf of the refrigerator for breakfast for those of us who like cold pizza. Will and Beth escaped to their rooms, and David looked at me with a quizzical expression.

"They need space," I answered his unasked question.

"Will they want to go to school tomorrow? I mean, should they?"

"Good question."

David folded the pizza boxes and packed them into the compactor, which growled like a wolf as the cardboard was pummeled. "I hate for them to miss school."

"They won't be able to concentrate."

"On the other hand, perhaps it's better for them to be with their friends," David speculated, a rhetorical comment.

I had resumed a seated pose at the table, my legs dead weights, my torso once again slouched, as David continued to move around the kitchen, tidying up perhaps more neatly than usual, as if the act of housekeeping might normalize the situation.

"Who do we call first?" I asked.

"Karen, she'll want a posting. And I have to get back to my brother, he sent a message asking if I want him to come, but his classes are in mid-semester, they both teach now at the community college, you know, and the kids have busy lives. What could he do here anyway?"

I nodded. "What about Anna's boss, what's his name?"

"Tim. He was already at the hospital. He's running down the story, you know, checking the police report, so we'll know exactly what happened. He will be useful in that way."

"Would you like me to return calls? I mean, to people I know," I offered, although the thought of speaking with anyone was abhorrent as all I wanted to do was hide.

"Sure, let's check messages first."

One after another, David and I listened to shocked sympathetic voices on the answering machine. Short pained expressions of sorrow and dismay, an occasional voice choking back tears, each concluding with a piercing beep. *Let me know what I can do,* was the ending to most messages, as if people in crisis can effectively organize needs or delegate responsibility to the voices on the phone, those who, despite the best of intentions, wait for direction. I was far more grateful to friends who just showed up to offer the comfort of companionship, and those who discretely dropped off prepared food or groceries. At the worst of times, the greatest gift is relief from others' needs when you can barely manage your own.

David sank into a chair. Poor man needed a stiff drink and a sleeping pill, but it was clear the night would go long.

We split up, David on his cell phone in the bedroom, me on the landline in the den. I called Maggie first, my favorite of Anna's inner circle of friends. Vivacious and brimming with energy, Maggie is someone you meet once and never forget. Despite a small stature, compact and contoured like a guitar, she looms large, the result of a broad-toothed smile permanently etched onto full lips, a mane of streaked golden curly hair, and a colorful wardrobe that seems to attract people like bed sheets fluttering on the line. Maggie grew up in Boston and married her high school sweetheart before she finished college when he took a job in New York City. She had studied design, but found her calling in the catering business where her easygoing personality made her a favorite of even demanding clients. After years of managing a successful event space in Manhattan, she struck out on her own in the affluent suburbs, working out of her home in a state-of-the-art kitchen David designed for a professional cook. On a weekend visit several years ago, Anna and I stopped at Maggie's for a tour.

"Martha Stewart I'm not, but it works for me," Maggie beamed that day. "Of course, we can never move. Only another chef would buy a house where the kitchen is bigger than the living room." She smiled her bright smile and chuckled with a characteristic tinkle in her voice. "We're stuck here now for as long as we live or as long as I can cook."

As I dialed Maggie's number that night, I imagined her in that kitchen, stirring a pot of aromatic stew or punching out fresh ravioli from a pasta machine, a brightly colored apron streaked like marble. The image alone nourished my courage.

She answered the phone on the first ring. "Nell, oh my God, I've been absolutely frantic! The phone has been ringing off the hook. I tried to reach David, and I called the newspaper, but Tim wasn't available and no one was able to say much. Everyone is so upset. You must be devastated! Oh my dear, are you at Anna's? How are the kids?"

"Yes, I'm here…"

"Thank goodness. I would hate to think of them all alone at a time like this. How are Beth and Will? This is dreadful for them, just dreadful."

"They're doing as well as can be expected."

"And David? His cell phone wasn't on. He must be a mess, you know, men don't deal well with crises. Lord, Brian would be absolutely paralyzed if this happened to me."

"Yes…"

"I just wish men would cry. They don't you know, well, hardly any of them. Choked up like a snake with a mouse stuck in its throat. I'm so glad you're there. I'm so glad you called. I feel better just hearing your voice. The radio report was awful. I was stunned, that's where I heard about it, on the local radio station, can you imagine? I was in the car, hardly paying attention, you know, half-listening, and I heard her name. Stopped me cold. Then I wasn't really sure what happened, I had missed too much of the report. I had to pull off the road and call and, you know, I couldn't get a hold of anyone, and, oh, this is just so awful."

"I'm sorry, Maggie." I couldn't think of anything else to say at that moment, and I knew Maggie well enough to know she would do most of the talking.

"The hospital says she's in critical condition. God, I hate those words. How is she really?" Maggie took a breath, her sentences strings of words braided together like dough.

"We don't really know much. She's in a coma. It's as if she's sleeping…"

"A coma?" Maggie repeated, her voice suddenly more somber.

"Yes. She's in ICU. They're taking tests. Nothing is certain."

"This is too dreadful."

The tenor in Maggie's voice had dropped. I heard hopelessness set in. My shoulders stiffened, my spine stretched out like an alley cat threatened by a predatory stray.

"It's too soon to assess fully," I advised.

"Of course."

"She'll come out of this," I said matter-of-factly, believing my own words.

"You think so? God, I mean, what would we do without her? I feel so helpless, like the world is spinning out of control. And you know I need to be in control!"

A sad sort of chuckle emanated from Maggie's throat, a paltry attempt to inject humor into a sobering conversation, filling the emotional cavities that cry out in pain at such moments. I remember Anna remarking to me, more than once, that when she needed comic relief she phoned Maggie. Certainly this talent for turning even the most torturous of times into self-effacing humor may have assuaged many difficult moments.

"My kids are absolutely mortified. They're Will and Beth's oldest friends, you know. You've met them. This is terrifying to children, to all of us. The phone lines are buzzing; word travels so fast in this town. And there's that 'there but for the Grace of God' vibe. I know I'm talking a blue streak here, but I'm so bent out of shape. You must be as well. She talks about you all the time, not in any gossipy way or anything, just refers to you as if you are always with her, like the Lone Ranger and Tonto, know what I mean? Visiting you every week, all these years. Oh, this is horrible, so horrible. What can we do? Wait, there's my call waiting. Can you hold on, just a moment? I'm sorry, but I'm expecting calls on this wedding I'm doing next weekend and, I know I shouldn't hold you up, I'll just be a minute, hold on."

Her voice instantly vanished into a black hole and I waited, longing for the days when conversations went on uninterrupted, also wondering what there might be left to say.

"Nell?" Maggie said breathlessly, shattering the silence. "Adrienne is on the phone. Adrienne Hoffman, the pediatrician? She's been waiting for David to return her call. I'll put her on conference call. Hold on, I'm a bit of a techno-moron and I might cut you off, so call me right back if I do, okay? Okay, hold on."

I heard buttons press and the connection was set adrift, weightless and hushed. My mind returned to the image of Anna, lying on a hospital bed, suspended like I was at that moment in a murky void. I shivered at the thought and was about to hang up when all at once, Maggie's voice charged out of the distance.

"Nell, are you still there?" she shouted.

"Yes, I'm here."

"Nell, Adrienne here," Adrienne's voice chimed in. "Can you hear me?"

"Yes, I hear you."

"What have the doctors told you? I called the attending, but he hasn't called back. The nurses wouldn't comment beyond the posted status."

"What were you expecting?" Maggie asked.

"I've extracted patient information from them many times before, even when it's not my patient. Professional courtesy. Can't imagine they're certain of anything at this point, other than vitals, which are stable. I didn't have time to hassle them, Brent had a game this afternoon and Carly is waiting for me now to help practice her lines for the play, one of those spring things, probably take half the night."

Anna once remarked that Adrienne is all business all the time, more of a slogan than the description of a friend, and I've always marveled at how different she was from Anna, and Maggie for that matter. Tall and sturdy, with an olive complexion, dark deep-set eyes, and nearly black hair pulled into a bun to expose a gamine neck, she has a stern comportment and a forbidding glare, antithetical to the persona of a pediatrician.

"There's not much we can do right now," Adrienne said. "I'm sure they told you the first forty-eight hours are crucial. The longer she stays in the coma, the longer she's likely to stay."

Maggie gasped. "It's not possible she won't come out of this?"

"Of course it's possible, Maggie. Then again, she might be up for breakfast. That's the nature of this condition. I'll get to the doctors first thing in the morning, on rounds. Please assure David of that, Nell. Tell him I'm on the case; he can call me any time with any questions. In fact, he may want to filter questions through me so I can translate."

"Nell," Maggie said. "What can I do? Do you want me to make calls for David?"

"That would be helpful, I'm sure."

"I'd be happy to do that. Carolyn and Maria and Sally called. And the neighbors will want to know what's going on."

"Yes. And Diane, she left a message. Do you know her?"

"Of course. I'll call them all."

"Thanks."

"But what should I tell them?" Maggie asked.

"Tell them she's stable, that's all," Adrienne said. "Tell them we'll know more in a day or so, when the tests are completed."

"Okay," Maggie said. "Is that what you're telling people, Nell?"

Odd that someone might turn to me for confirmation. I was already wilting in my chair, desperate to rest my head on the desk and stop talking, stop listening. I felt myself hurtling toward shutdown, which I often do when faced with the least bit of stress. Slouched over the phone, my stomach churned, my heart pounded, my head felt wrapped in gauze.

"Nell, are you there?" Adrienne asked.

"Yes," I said, lifting my head, trying to stay lucid. "Tell them only immediate family can visit at the hospital. And that it might be better, at least for the next day or so, they not bother David with calls. Is that all right?"

"I suppose we can post her status on Facebook," Maggie said.

"No, Maggie," Adrienne said in an admonishing tone of voice one might use with a naughty child. "This is not a subject for the social network. Just tell people to check in with me. They can leave a message with my service. I'll selectively update."

There was a momentary silence among us, a few seconds of helplessness as reality settled over the discourse like dust.

"I guess it's better I can't see Anna," Maggie said. "I mean, well, I don't think I could bear to see her like that, you know, so still. We always have the best talks. She sits here at the kitchen counter and chops veggies or herbs or something while I prepare whatever is on the menu that day, and we drink gallons of iced-tea, sometimes wine, and we talk and laugh, God I love her laugh, so throaty, you know? And sometimes we commiserate, for the others, I mean, the people who have so little..."

Maggie stopped short, perhaps aware that I fell into that latter group. I closed my eyes and imagined Anna laughing, a cross between Lauren Bacall and Goldie Hawn: scratchy, melodic and contagious.

"Anna is a great talker, that's for sure," Adrienne said. "Wisdom spills from her lips without effort. But her silences, the listening, those profound moments of thought, those mean more. In terms of sheer output, Maggie, you, of course, take the cake."

"Take the cake, good one, Adrienne. Trés humorous, especially from you."

"Okay, Carly is waiting patiently," Adrienne responded, back to business. "Nell, please tell David I'll stay in touch."

"Thank you."

"Nell?" Maggie said as Adrienne's line clicked out. "Do you think we should visit Anna? I mean, we're not family, not technically, but, well, I worry that she's alone. I know I said I didn't

want to see her, but I'm not sure I can stay away. I read this book
once, by a journalist who had been in a coma for something like
ten days. She heard everyone around her, listening through
cheesecloth, she said, and she could distinguish one from another
most of the time. She felt things too, like the sheet on her skin, and
the respirator down her throat, can you imagine?"

"No."

"I just wondered."

"I'm sure you can sneak in to see her, Maggie."

"Maybe I will."

"David and the children will be there most of the time, I
suspect."

"And you?"

"We did stretch the truth a bit. We said I was her sister."

"Good. Anna would like that. We all have to stay close
now, hold each other up. If anything changes, let me know. I'll be
right here, up to my elbows in phyllo dough. Call me anytime,
even late at night, I always hear the phone."

"Right," I answered.

"I'll leave dinner for you all at the house tomorrow, I have
the key. Remind the kids they are welcome anytime. The side door
is always open. I never lock, and they know that."

"That's kind of you, Maggie."

"I wish I could do more. Get some sleep, you'll need your
rest."

"Good night, Maggie."

I hung up, exhausted by the one call, and wandered down
the hall. David sat on their large bed, legs dangling off the edge, his
body caved into himself, the phone cradling into his shoulder as he
scribbled on a yellow legal pad in his lap. He seemed suddenly
smaller than he is. The curly hair framing his face is turning gray,
not at the temples so much as at the tips, and the wrinkles around
his eyes are more deeply etched. He hung up the phone and looked
up at me, his dark eyes blank and pathetic, much like my own, I
imagined.

"Let me guess. Maggie must be planning our menus."

"Right."

"Adrienne has already taken over Anna's medical care."

"Yes."

David half-smiled. "They are good friends."

"How about your calls?"

"I covered the bases. I'll call the rest tomorrow. Can't listen to my own voice anymore. I'm turning in," he pronounced. "Make yourself at home, you know where things are, right?"

"I'll find what I need." There was a pained silence between us for a moment. "David?" I asked. "Do you know where Anna was going today?"

He shook his head. "I never knew where Anna was going." He smiled a wan smile, within which there was a hint of defeat. "When the kids were younger, she would forget to pick them up, remember? I can't tell you how many times I was called by a school or the Y or an irate parent to collect kids left sitting on front steps. They got used to it, more than I. Neither one of them seems the worse for wear. Family lore, we laugh about it. She'd stop to photograph a rock formation or a seascape or something and two hours later would wonder where the time went. At least, that was the party line." He paused for a moment, his brow creased like an old man trying to banish an unhappy memory. "We all have cell phones these days, we can access her more easily, and now that Beth drives, the kids are no longer hostage to her warped concept of time. We never know where she is and that's just the way it is. To love Anna is to expect the unexpected, yes?"

"True. I was just wondering."

"Doesn't matter now, where she was going, does it?"

I nodded. No, not at that moment. David stood and came toward me. We hugged, hesitant and awkward, then he trudged down the hall like a teenage boy who has lost the big game, vanishing up the stairs to say goodnight to his children. I headed back to the den to make up the sofa bed.

Agitated and anxious, I paced the worn floral carpet, trundling the fringed edges with my bare toes. The air felt heavy, like fog, and I opened a window. A gentle breeze blew the curtains toward me. Only the diffused light of a new moon perforated the darkness.

I find the silence of suburban living unsettling, more comfortable with the din of cars and sirens and the hum of conversation on the street. My white noise. At that moment, I heard a dog bark in the distance, the bark of an animal dispatched for the night. A car door slammed, followed by a short beep. All sudden sharp sounds that pierced the stillness, like a memory that surfaces at the worst possible time.

Unable to settle down, I wandered up the stairs to check on the kids. Will lay slumped against several pillows, clothes and books and water bottles scattered about. He stared up at posters of rock musicians plastered on the ceiling: Maroon 5, the Rolling Stones, others unknown to me. Percussive music resounded from his iPhone dock, a new generation of musicians with scratchy voices and discordant choruses.

"How you doing?" I asked as I squeezed onto an empty spot at the edge of the bed.

"Are you planning to sing me a lullaby?" he asked.

"*Never Never Land* was your favorite, as I recall."

Will snickered. "There is no such place."

"Perhaps not, and my voice is rusty, but, if you like…"

"I'll pass, no offense."

He turned his oversized body and buried one side of his face in his pillow, just as he would bury his fear in the days to come in an adolescent form of feigned masculinity.

I touched the fuzz of hair at the top of his head. "Sleep now," I whispered. I thought I heard a sob as I shut his door.

Beth was on the phone. "I have to go now," she said when I entered her room.

"How you holding up?" I asked as I sat down beside her.

"I'm not sure."

"Me neither."

"I don't know what to do about the play. I have rehearsal every day."

"What play this year?"

"*Midsummer Night's Dream.* Hermia."

"Good part."

"Yeah, the daughter of a God."

"Better than a sprite."

"Boring. I am so bored with classics. We always do a Shakespeare play in the spring, I guess to appease the parents, maybe the Board of Ed, but I prefer Chekhov or Ibsen. Or Mamet."

"You were great in *A Doll's House.*"

She didn't smile. "What if Mom can't come to the play?"

"When is it?"

"April 25th."

"Plenty of time."

Beth sat up and looked at me. "It's the 4th. Only a few weeks rehearsal, and we have to make decisions."

"What decisions?"

Beth sunk back against the pillow. "Schools, you know, college. Just my life."

"That's right," I said, suddenly remembering what was going on with Beth. Anna might have filled me in on the next Wednesday's visit. "All the returns in?"

"Doesn't matter now."

"Of course it matters. Tell me."

"All in. I've got choices, but now..."

"This is just a glitch, just a glitch in the plan," I said as I slipped closer to her. "She'll heal, she'll come home. Long before the play, in plenty of time to help you pick out sheets."

"My mother hates to shop, you know that."

"She might make an exception."

"You really think she'll wake up?"

"Yes, I do. I can't imagine anything else."

I patted her hand. Her lower lip quivered and she sucked it under her teeth. She rubbed her eyes. "I'm really tired."

"Sleep on clouds," I whispered as I hugged her and left the room, words I used to say to my son, every night, and an image I hold of him in my heart.

No sleep for me, certainly not on clouds. A lifelong night crawler, I was an erratic sleeper as a child and a first-class insomniac as a young adult. Only when Jason and I lay intertwined like jagged edges of broken pottery, seamlessly rejoined, was I able to sleep soundly through the night. Since his death, I have returned to the nocturnal life, and from my living room window, I often stare for hours into the shadowy silhouette of the cityscape. Sometimes I draw, charcoals mostly, or pencil sketches. Mostly I watch old movies, black and white like the night.

One takes comfort in the darkness when surrounded by the familiar; however at Anna's house, even though a second home, I felt like an interloper. Shadows seemed menacing, smells foreign. Furniture loomed as obstacles in my path. I made my way slowly to the kitchen and in the glare of the open refrigerator pulled out a beer and sipped thirstily until quenched. I scanned the postings on the refrigerator door: school schedules, a clipping from *The New York Times* about a photography show we might have seen on the next visit, and a cartoon from *The New Yorker* depicting an artist at his canvas, a nude model posed before him, but his painting a pile of rocks of decreasing size from bottom to top. The teacher stared critically at the canvas, and the caption read: *Perhaps you should try photography.*

I tossed the can into the recycling bin and returned to the darkness for an evening prowl.

Their house was originally a blacksmith's barn, a rectangular stone structure with wide-planked wood floors, vaulted ceilings and cross beams speckled with dark knots. The sort of house you might find at a historic center, crafted for modern living. Although David generally prefers to build from scratch, in the end he proudly produced a prototype of his architectural expertise and simultaneously appeased Anna's commitment to recycling. Required by historical preservationists to stay within the foundation's footprint and maintain the street facade, he reconfigured the interior for more efficient use of the space and added dormers to the attic to create cozy bedrooms for the kids. In what must have been a storage area, he placed a darkroom, because Anna has always preferred to process her own images.

Down the long main hallway from one end of the house to the other, the walls are lined like a gallery with 8 X 10 photographs in matching black wood frames with 2-inch white mats. At the front end is the den with sofa bed, which doubles as a guest room, and at the back end, David added a large master bedroom which seems even larger by virtue of a cathedral ceiling punctuated with skylights to view the stars.

It is the center of the house that provides the true architectural drama. A main living area is flanked in a half-moon shape by three bays set apart by floor-to-ceiling bookshelves: a dining area with a large oval table; a reading room with luxurious oversized chairs; and a music room centered by a rebuilt Steinway where the kids, and Anna, practice and play for each other. David, in an unusual comic turn, once referred to the spaces as the id, the ego and superego, and when Jason asked how he could tell the difference, he answered there was none, that each chamber was of equal size and thus the very essence of a perfectly balanced persona.

In the center of these three spaces, what Anna dubbed the "Common," a large plum-colored sofa is flanked by two equally plush striped upholstered chairs, and mahogany side tables, all facing the original large granite fireplace with thick stone mantel. Tall windows opposite flank the southern exposure, shedding bright light throughout the day and beckoning moonlight at night.

Extended family have often gathered in the Common at holidays, and friends on weekends, where voices tend to drift up to the rafters as if in church and, now and then, I imagined I heard the steady clang of the blacksmith's hammer, a wistful ticking of time through history. Here, children practiced lines for school plays, Anna spread out finished photographs for viewing, the family played interminable games of Monopoly and Scrabble, and it in this comfy space, lit by candlelight, Anna and I occasionally communed well into the night, debating destiny or the incongruity of happenstance.

That night I stood in the center of the room surveying the scene, not sure what to do with myself or how to make sense of being there without Anna. To settle my nerves, I opened and leaned against a door, taking deep drags of a cigarette, one foot inside, one out, and blowing smoke into the wind before burying the stub between budding azalea bushes.

When I returned to the Common, I studied the display of family photographs on tabletops, remembrances of vacations and holidays, some of which I recalled as if they were my own. Although many of these photographs were full color, Anna played with the palette, forcing images to blur, muting backgrounds or foregrounds for dramatic effect. She often used a dual color filter to produce duo-tone replicas – the sky a hazy purple meeting a ground of pumpkin orange, a stretch of boardwalk in sapphire blue against a beach shaded gold. The effect was stunning and surreal, as if Dali had used only two paints.

I sought out a favorite photograph of Jason, Jeremy and me, windblown and huddled against the bright blue summer sky of Cape Cod, taken during our first vacation together as families. I could almost smell the salted air. My heart felt once again pierced by the shard of memory and I clutched the photo to my chest like a tourniquet, as if anything could stem the persistent bleeding. I thought by now it would be easier to look at family photos, but no. Worse perhaps. The longer gone, the more excruciating the incredulity, the more pointless the loss.

My prolonged mourning is a defiance of psychiatrist Elizabeth Kubler-Ross's revered concept of the five stages of grief. Yes, I advanced in a reasonable timeframe through the denial phase, and mostly moved past anger, and I never really inhabited the bargaining stage, not much sense when faced with a senseless situation. However I have never progressed beyond what she defined as the depression period, and, while I have found a form of acceptance, the logical final phase, it is hardly the psychological dénouement that should have evolved by now. Nevertheless, I have rarely sought therapeutic support as I refuse to attempt to heal my aching heart with professionals who want to measure grief by how I felt about my parents or what trauma I might have experienced as a child. Nor do I wish to pretend that I do not feel what I feel. On this, Anna concurred. *You have to feel to heal,* she once said, and I believe that.

I moved from the family photographs in the Common to the artistic black and whites that lined the walls. Some I'd forgotten, others I don't remember seeing at all. I turned on the row of pin lights that were positioned from the ceiling toward the pictures for optimum lighting. Although these days Anna is expected to use color film for the newspaper's front-page photos and website, she often makes duplicates in black and white. More than the absence of color, such photos are metaphor: no one is black or white, rather the pigment, like hope, is concealed.

Anna explained to me once that photographers largely prefer subjects to be well lit to allow the shadows to go dark. Standard fare. However she was always drawn to the shadows, so when she wasn't playing with the lenses, she strategically placed the lighting to one side to pierce the subject on an angle, calling attention to the architecture of the image by intensifying dimension and depth. The thought occurred to me at that moment this might have been a bond she shared with David that I'd never understood, a way of assessing people and space as beyond three-dimensional.

I stepped back for further viewing as if I were at a retrospective of Anna's life and work, and stopped first to admire a shot taken from behind an elderly couple walking hand-in-hand, their bodies arched in tandem, suggesting two distinct spirits in sync. In contrast, a photo of two young girls at a juvenile shelter, their thick black hair pinned with matching barrettes, their fingers intertwined in a classic depiction of innocence. Another, an amazing shot taken while I watched, of a slight woman in a formfitting floral dress seated at a chipped table at a Manhattan coffee shop, her face striped by shafts of light, her chin cupped in one hand resting on an elbow, a cigarette nearly burned to the filter dangling between two fingers. She gazes into the distance, reminiscent of Victorian-era paintings where beautiful women beautifully dressed, or undressed, never smile, shrouded instead in disenchantment. In another favorite, back lit so the subject's face is nearly gray, a lanky disheveled man crouches over his desk, preoccupied by piles of books and printed material at which he stares as if nothing and no one else exists, evoking an acute sense of scholarly duty, or was it obsession?

I am no connoisseur of photography. I know only what I like and what Anna has taught me over the years. She regularly scanned anthologies, especially the works of Annie Leibovitz, whom she had once gratefully assisted when she first arrived in New York. She never tired of perusing the works of the controversial Robert Mapplethorpe, visionaries like Ben Shahn and Alfred Eisenstaedt, and the pioneering female photographers she revered: Julia Margaret Cameron and Dorothea Lange. I can't name photographic movements or schools or periods marked by style or content, but if photography were categorized like fine art, Anna's work might be considered Impressionism, each image an imprint of a moment in time. The events in Anna's photographs, like impressionist art, are neither momentous nor catastrophic, and rarely posed; rather the moments we take for granted. On film, they seem to me even more beguiling than on canvas, less staged, although the eye of the photographer is as great an influence as the painter, and Anna's presence in every photograph is unmistakable, like a monk who, without words, facilitates enlightenment.

I was struck at that moment by the realization that Anna would have photographed herself lying in the street that day: her skin acutely white, her blood nearly black. She would have used direct lighting that might have bounced off her body, as if the scene reverberated. Yes, Anna would have seen that incident as another dramatic moment to be captured for posterity, dismissing the following moments as inconsequential. The thought chilled me to the bone.

The next few days were a blur, muddled by false faces and false hopes, within which I loitered like a shadow cast by the glare of those around me. In this state, a condition I occupy frequently, I observe without intrusion, and, like the sketch artist I once was, I redraw moments to my liking, ignoring what I'd rather not see.

Anna looked far worse when we arrived the morning after the accident. The swelling in her face had ballooned overnight: her closed eyes puffed like a turkey and lips stretched over the respirator trailing down her throat, engorging itself as her chest drifted up and down in a controlled rhythm. Beth gasped when she saw her mother and leaned back against Will, who wobbled on his own sturdy legs, and soon after, they both fled the room, neither able to gaze at their mother in that distorted condition. Instead they waited in the hospital family room where they might use their phones or watch television.

Anna's condition was still posted as critical but stable, which might have described us all. I've never seen David as agitated as he was that morning. He paced around Anna's bed, patting her hand, withdrawing, sitting beside her, then jumping up as if he had just remembered something important, only to pace again, scanning screens in a vain attempt to decipher their meaning. He stopped at the window, opening and closing Venetian blinds repeatedly, the harsh metallic sound an echo of Anna's breathing, then turned back to her, as if he'd just remembered she was there. He simply couldn't settle down, moving about like a hyperactive child before collapsing into a chair for a while, arms and legs hanging loosely around him, head down, strumming his fingers on the chair arms until spent by his anxiety.

I watched him propel himself about all morning while I sat motionless, hardly daring to breathe too loudly for fear I might interrupt some great metaphysical bubble surrounding Anna.

Anna took me with her once to a yoga class, where she hoped I might learn to breathe into peace of mind, or at least stretch my spine. I hated it. I don't wish to be told to designate an intention or root to rise. Meditation is not even possible for me – if my mind shuts down, memory fills the void. Instead, I began to sing in my head, not chanting, rather the counter-culture lullabies I once sang to Jeremy – rock songs crooned slower and softer to soothe him to sleep. By the time he was four, he knew the lyrics of the Beatles and Led Zeppelin, Bonnie Raitt and Paul Simon. His favorite was *Stairway to Heaven*.

That day in yoga class, as I twisted by body into strange shapes and struggled to maintain balance, all the while in a meditative state, I sang the song in my head, so I thought. As it turned out, I was singing aloud, and when I arrived at the celestial guitar crescendo, the words blasted from my throat until I felt a sharp poke on my shoulder and opened my eyes to see Anna glaring at me. "Please stop," she snapped, and I was struck dumb. Looking up apologetically toward the yoga instructor, I saw that she too gaped at the noisy stranger, although I saw on her face an expression of benevolence that at last explained yoga. The only other thing I took from that experience was the instruction to breathe purposefully, paying attention to each breath as if echoes of the heart, as soothing as a Shavasana pose of rest.

Throughout that first day at the hospital, it was clear our optimism would continue to be tested. David slipped away now and then to make calls and conference with Tim, piecing together a schematic of the accident, searching for revelation only to confront improbabilities. I went from Anna's room to the lounge, trying to be more than irrelevant. Each time David returned from his distractions he would resume the pacing, glancing at Anna as he made each revolution around the room, and I knew, watching him, we were both expecting her to awaken to make everything better for the rest of us.

"We can't expect too much too soon," he commented more than once.

I nodded each time.

"She needs time to heal."

"Yes."

We spoke little through the day, between voluminous quantities of coffee or diet soda and, despite little appetite, forced ourselves to nibble vending machine junk food, our teeth grinding loudly on a handful of nuts or a stale cookie. Occasional snippets of conversation were merely an anxious smattering of small talk meant to fill the overwhelming silence; the way people talk about the weather when they have nothing else to say.

Every couple of hours, I stepped outside to smoke a cigarette among clusters of nurses, physicians and orderlies indulging their habits like teenagers lined up on the side of the schoolyard. Most chatted amiably, as grateful as I was, I supposed, for the respite to recalibrate. One nurse perched on the shelf of a retaining wall to read a fat paperback, and when her phone alarm resounded, she folded down the page with a sigh, extinguished her cigarette against the brick and pocketed the remains before heading back into the hospital to resume her day. The doctors who murmured to each other or pressed cell phones into the crook of their necks reminded me of the passengers on the train just the day before, the whole scene like sinister spaces in noir fiction. I made no eye contact, standing aside, leaning against the building like a suspicious but otherwise secondary character as our smoke blended together into a gray haze.

David took comfort in fielding the many calls that arrived from family and friends, or conferring with office staff, pacing the waiting room or the hallway with a Bluetooth receiver on his ear as if muttering to himself. When pertinent, he summarized conversations.

"Anna's sister is making arrangements to come, but first she has to settle the kids. She doesn't seem to share the urgency, convinced that Anna will pull herself out of this quickly. She said she's just resting, galvanizing her immune system. Honestly, those were her words, 'galvanizing her immune system,' as if Anna were only battling some new strain of the flu."

I smiled at the thought. "It is possible that Anna's got every ounce of energy focused on the healing process. I can imagine a flood of white cells rushing to her defense. She'll defy modern medicine and delight in telling the tale."

David perked up. "She'll only be sorry she missed the photo op."

I smiled. "Karen will come, right?"

"Oh yes. I assured her that if anything changed, if I thought she should be here sooner..." David stammered. "I'll keep her posted."

Turns out everyone seemed to believe that Anna would pull through speedily and I began to hope our collective optimism might propel her to rise up from her hospital bed like some great white unicorn, mythological in proportion, which has fallen only to catch its breath.

David might have read my mind, as he said, "Perhaps she will rise from these ashes."

"I seem to recall you referring to Anna's theories as, what was it, gobbledygook?"

David slumped into a chair. "I suppose that makes me an opportunist. I'll believe whatever I have to. Honestly, I want to see things her way, I've tried, but if our lives are totally directed by destiny, what's the point? I find it difficult to accept that everything is a matter of predetermination. I've worked hard all my life, through graduate school, and those early days, trying to make the mark, the partnership. We can never rest on laurels. I need to believe I am the master of my own fate. If Anna's right, we might as well just sit around and wait for the universe to orchestrate our future." He turned to Anna. "And it would seem that we can cop out conveniently on whatever choices we make."

I was surprised by the irritation in his voice. "I'm sure Anna never meant her philosophy to be a cop out. She just believes so completely in, you know, going with the flow."

"Perhaps she might have gone with the flow of traffic." David sighed with resignation.

At that moment, Beth and Will knocked on the door to announce they were returning to school for their afternoon commitments.

"We can't help her," Beth said. "Mom would want us to be there."

"A wise decision," David responded.

Beth turned to me for approbation.

"We'll keep an eye on Mom," I answered.

We all mustered a smile in deference to each other.

"We'll meet you at home later, okay?" Beth said, adding, "but you'll call us if, if you need us," she sputtered.

I nodded. "Of course."

"I'll just call the principal's office, right?" David asked.

"I have the cell phone," Beth answered.

"I thought you're not allowed to have it on at school?"

"They can sue me." Beth kissed her father on the cheek and waved to me.

Will nodded sheepishly and lumbered his hulking frame down the hall.

Occasionally, one of Anna's colleagues or David's partners slipped into the ICU, respectfully waiting in the hall for David to notice. He seemed relieved for the company, expressing his gratitude, assuring them, as if reassuring himself, that she would soon return to us. None stayed long and David never permitted anyone to see Anna, protecting her from view like a fine work of art awaiting the precise moment to be unveiled.

When Tim arrived that afternoon, he stepped into Anna's room as if he had a permanent pass. David barely acknowledged him, but did not stand in his way. Perhaps Tim had special privileges by virtue of his position at the newspaper, although I would have thought he was exactly the sort of person the hospital might keep out to protect the privacy of their patients. He smiled at me as if we were old friends, although we'd met only once, before conferring with David to review their joint investigative findings.

When David left the room to make a few phone calls, Tim sat very close to Anna's bedside for nearly an hour, a pattern he would repeat every day at lunchtime. He read the newspaper aloud, accompanied by a running commentary, as if they were merely talking shop. I imagined he was communicating with her telepathically as she told me he too was a Buddhist, and I might have been impressed with his devotion, were it not for the cynic in me.

The journalist has no time for tears. I learned this the hard way when a *New York Post* cub reporter hounded me for weeks after Jason and Jeremy's accident, determined to write a human-interest profile on grief. He hadn't yet had the opportunity to mine the quarry of 9/11 stories so he dug into me, a buried gem, calling repeatedly and eventually showing up at my apartment. Even when tragedy struck the city, he stayed on my case, I was never sure why. When the strain of harassment was more than I could bear, I knocked on the door of a young policeman who lived down the hall. I remember I was shaking a good deal, I must have been quite pale, and his perky wife invited me in and offered me herbal tea and oatmeal cookies. Sweet people, idealists, and I suppose I was quite a conversation piece at that time among the neighbors, although not unsympathetically at that point as the whole city was in a particularly compassionate mood post-9/11. The officer, a square-backed fellow with a military haircut, assured me he would take care of the situation. He patted my hand, anxious to make it right for me, the way the young still believe they can make things right just because they want to.

I never saw or heard from the journalist again. Relieved, and grateful for the token of kindness I needed more desperately than my reclusive lifestyle suggested, I nonetheless neglected to thank my protector. I had already tucked myself back into my cave, and I hoped people like that, the same sort of early responders who proved their mettle that year at Ground Zero, take satisfaction from the act of salvation more than accolades.

"Newsmen are newsmen first, second and third," Anna said when I told her about it. "Nothing gets in the way of the story."

Thus, I was wary of Tim, wary of almost everyone except David and the children, standing ready to blockade any intrusion into Anna's healing space. And while I might have done anything to protect her, to enhance her life as she has enhanced mine all these years, I was as yet unwilling to do the one thing she had asked me to do.

It was one of those especially beautiful autumn days: sunny and still warm, the air dry and crisp. We picked up sandwiches, and strolled into Central Park from the southern gate. Fallen red and yellow leaves lined the walkways like a Persian carpet. Children were at school, workers at work, yet the park was filled with amblers like us, drifting through the day like leaves from the trees. A scene so bucolic one might forget the park sits in the midst of a frenzied city where millions of people bustle along crowded streets and hustle each other from offices towering above the fray, all relegated to background that afternoon.

We landed on one of the rock formations on a rise overlooking the carousel and watched the painted horses twirl, organ music spinning in our ears.

As we swallowed the last of our lunch, Anna casually remarked, "I've named you my health care proxy."

"What does that mean?"

"If something were to happen to me, something terrible…"

"Anna, are you sick?" I was instantly on alert.

"No, no, nothing like that." She took my hand and clasped it between hers, although she kept her eyes on the carousel. "Each life is fragile, Nell, too often too short, you know that better than most. The the only thing we can be sure of is at some point we will pass."

"Anna, do we have to have this conversation?" I wriggled in her grasp.

"Yes, we do, to get this thing right. Please. Listen to me. This is what life is. Awareness of our mortality is what distinguishes us from the animal world."

"I thought it had something to do with cooking our food."

Anna smiled. "A technicality. Some say it is hope that differentiates humans from animals, but it is all about mortality. We are conscious of our impermanence. The mystery is only when the end will come and that is the singular impediment to a happier life. So many of us simply stop living fully for fear of dying. Instead of accepting this grand unknown…"

"Anna, please."

"Listen to me, dear friend. We are born, we die, and all that occurs between is a shadow. Sometimes the long shadow of a sunny winter day. Sometimes the shorter shadow of late spring. We live within shadows. We thrive within contrast. Those of us who embrace the contrast as the essence of life are not afraid."

"Anna, I cannot stand this talk."

Anna was not to be deterred. "Nell, please. We live in moments, moments like the new leaves that will replace these that disintegrate." She took a few dead leaves in her hand and crumbled them into dust. "Most people are attached to the supposed certainty of what is known or stymied by fear of the unknown. Death is destiny. I am not afraid, I only want it to be my destiny, not the choosing of anyone else, certainly not a stranger."

"You mean like a drunken driver? Anna, we are victims of circumstance. Whether you want to think of this as part of some grand plan or not, for those of us who have come out on the dark side, destiny is no thrill ride."

"I'm talking about professional strangers, the intruders who steal life under the guise of regulation or doctrine. Doctors. Lawyers. Politicians. Whoever might make that decision for me if I am incapable of making the decision myself."

"What about David?"

"David can't execute my end-of-life directive. David will never let go."

"Neither will I."

Anna gazed into my eyes.

"You underestimate yourself. When put to the test, my friend, you will do what is right. You will honor my wishes and, in accepting my destiny, you will accept your own."

"Anna, just put your wishes on paper for David. I'll witness if you like, and you can notarize. He will have to comply, that's the law, I believe."

I tried to pull my hand away, but she held on as she turned back to face me, her eyes beseeching. I thought I would do anything for this woman, anything, but how could I possibly make a decision related to life or death?

"There is a force to our fate, Nell. I wake up every day certain of very little and it is absolutely exhilarating. Control, or the attempt to control, is stifling. You know this, you won't, perhaps you cannot admit it, but you know it."

"I know what is out of our control," I answered, jerking my hand from her grasp. "It is all out of our control and it is not the least bit exhilarating."

"You confuse powerlessness with acceptance. You have yet to accept that there is a purpose to not only every life but also every moment of life. Up to and including the last."

"Enough, Anna! No more."

"I need you to do this, for both of us."

"But you are asking me to take control of your life. Makes no sense."

"Not my life, Nell, my right to die. Won't you please take this on faith? I might live another forty or fifty years and die peacefully in my sleep one night, after I've taken one more roll of film of my great-grandchildren playing in this very park, with an incredibly exquisite sunset on the horizon, the likes of which I have never seen, not even in my wonderfully long life. Or, fate may have other plans. The dice must be permitted to fall where they may."

I felt myself folding. There was no way to argue Anna out of her will.

"I thought, because you more than most understand the fragility of our mortality, I thought you might help my passing to be as natural and unencumbered as my life. I don't ask much, do I? Please, do this for me."

We sat in silence, only a thin strip of air separating us.

That was the final argument. Anna asked nothing of me, as a rule. "I still don't know what you are asking of me. What do you want me to do?"

Anna pulled from her purse printed papers with an official looking cover page.

"I have a declaration here that will suit, although I really had a good laugh when I read the template. Pure mumbo-jumbo. Living wills, health care agents, immunity from civil and criminal liability for removing or withholding life support... Get the picture? Legal-speak. It's all about liability. Litigation, not self-determination. Listen to what they have to say about life support." She read: "The conditions under which my wishes go into effect, through a health care proxy, are a permanently unconscious condition, meaning that I am in a coma or a persistent vegetative state, which, without the administration of life support systems will, in the opinion of the attending physician, result in death within a relatively short time." She laughed at this, harrumphed actually, as if she were reading the comics. "The life-support systems they stipulate are artificial respiration, cardiopulmonary resuscitation and artificial means of providing nutrition and hydration. And then it adds, in a separate paragraph, that I do not intend any direct taking of my life, only that my dying not be unreasonably prolonged. That line really made me screech. Of course one cannot appear to be taking one's own life because that would be against the law!"

She shook her head in exasperation and went on. "I drafted my own addendum. You can read it when you need to. Far more palatable language. After all, if I do find myself in some sort of persistent vegetative state, which I think I would find fascinating, like twilight sleep, when you see and hear everything inside of yourself that is generally repressed by daily living. You know? Like sitting on a plane, lulled into a stupor by the hum of the engines, you suddenly remember things you have long forgotten, you visualize ancient images, you hear music in the air above the clouds. I love that place, endless possibilities there. So perhaps that sort of state might be wonderful for a time."

I shook my head, confused by her rambling.

"Then there's the transition period, from one life to the next. An existential serenity until the next presence is revealed.

And the people I might encounter there. A thrilling thought! Whatever comes to me, I want to move forward unimpeded. The only jurisdiction that matters to me are the angels who will escort me to my next life."

I shuddered.

"We are all so busy holding on, always holding on, instead of learning to embrace the letting go. Anything else is like trying to commandeer a cloud. Don't fear for me, Nell. The life support system I need, I have. We all do." She opened her arms wide to present the park to me. "Artificial life support is just that, artificial. Natural life support, that's all that matters. Fresh air and water. Love. Friendship. Memory. Faith."

Anna stopped to take a breath, intoxicated by her vision, I imagined at the time. Or was it the prospect of another life? Perhaps she'd had a premonition of her demise, which she might have shared with me had I not squandered the moment with resistance.

"We are blessed, you and I, and those closest to us," she went on that day. "Whatever the losses we have known, and yes, some have been truly tragic, and whatever the disappointments, the wasted moments, we have had the privilege of living our lives largely unencumbered. This is the only way I wish to live, and die. Freely. In my own way."

"Anna, I beg you, I am having a really hard time here. There must be a better choice."

"There is no better choice." Anna moved closer to me, our knees touching like college girls confessing secrets. "We might live to be very old ladies together, enjoying our Wednesdays, taking long walks in the park, comforting each other as old friends do. I cherish all of it. On the other hand, these might be our last moments together. We never know."

I nodded. We never know. "Tell me something I don't know."

Anna smiled. "You know but you don't believe."

"Oh Anna..."

"My dear friend, I ask only that you facilitate my fate. I trust no one else to do that as unselfishly as I believe you will."

"You expect too much of me."

"No, I do not expect too much of you. I believe in you."

I gave up. "And I believe in you."

"Thank you." She took a deep breath, sniffing the breeze, while I sat as immobile as one of the carved carousel horses, having quickly repositioned the curtain that protects me from feelings I do not wish to feel.

Anna continued, buoyed perhaps by her resolve. "While I seem to have evolved over many lives, I have so much more to learn, so when the time comes, whenever that time comes, I will be ready to move forward, closer to the final release."

"Release?"

"The awakening. Buddha suggested the true purpose of life is to attain freedom from the cycle, but only for those who are truly worthy."

"Like you."

"Oh no, I am deeply flawed. I have too often failed to be present."

"How can you say that?"

"Nell, the very act of photography, the attempt to capture the moment for eternity, is anathema to the purity of presence. I understand my weaknesses. I look forward to the lives ahead. And I will be waiting for you."

"What makes you so sure you will be first?"

I remember now that Anna did not answer that question. She only gazed at me as she so often did with the serenity of a spiritual mentor, waiting for me to answer for myself.

She handed me her version of the living will. "Signed and witnessed, perfectly legal and enforceable," she said with aplomb.

"I have the only copy?"

"There is one other."

"With your lawyer, what's his name?"

"Bruce Russell. No, for now, I would rather keep it out of the hands of the professionals and in the hands of the people I trust."

"So official," I muttered, running my finger over the raised seal of the legal stamp and, fixed in the seriousness of that moment, I neglected to ask who might have the second copy.

Anna pulled a plastic Ziploc bag out of her purse and placed the folded document into it, pressing the closure together until the seal snapped into place.

"I suppose you could keep it in the freezer for safekeeping," she quipped.

I remember laughing at the absurdity of that idea, yet the blueprint for Anna's life and death was tucked away, as suggested, in the freezer, the edges of the plastic bag encrusted by ice crystals, thus nearly invisible, waiting for me to do what I was asked to do.

Time in the hospital passed as slowly as a sluggish summer day, despite oversized wall clocks ticking away moments. Those first two days felt like two weeks.

The floor nurse made the mistake of approaching David with a request for a DNR [Do Not Resuscitate] to be placed in Anna's chart, and when he nearly took her head off in anger, she slunk back to her desk, although she would ask again, each day, as she was obligated to do. I attempted to ameliorate David's hostility by reminding him that she was only doing her job, although as I spoke I felt the shame of hypocrisy, having betrayed my promise.

Maggie arrived that second afternoon with a basket of sandwiches, like little red riding hood gliding through the forest, but with yellow hair and an orange sweater.

"I'm sorry I'm late," she said breathlessly. "You must be starving. Where are the kids?"

"At school," David answered.

"Oh. For the best, I guess. Well, what would you like, dears?" she asked as she rummaged through plastic-wrapped offerings. "Roasted chicken salad on a spinach tortilla or grilled vegetables with pesto on pumpernickel?"

Her good cheer was incongruous, as if she had parachuted into our drab world from a lively planet, and had it not been for her good intentions, might have been irritating.

"Well you have to eat," Maggie responded to the surprised silence. "You have to keep up your strength. Vending machine food will not do, not at all. Nor will a hospital cafeteria, I assure you, not while I'm around."

Properly scolded, we devoured sandwiches, delicious and hearty, working their magic on our energy levels like a drug.

Adrienne showed up several times to confer with the nurses, who jumped to attention when she came down the hall as if school children in the presence of the headmistress. Even David took notice, commenting that she had a way with the nursing staff.

Adrienne stood so erect she might have had a book on her head and she wore black-rimmed glasses with lenses that automatically shaded in brighter light, so even indoors her eyes were overcast, making her seem all the more formidable. However she was patient with nurses, she conversed in a quietly commanding voice with all of us, more so than the practitioners who came and went all day, scanning machines, placing fingers at Anna's pulse points, lifting her eyelids, examining her wounds, and scribbling notes on portable gadgets that magically translated them onto an electronic chart. They offered only perfunctory remarks, nothing meaningful to report.

David was repeatedly crestfallen, and all I could think was what I used to say to my son: a cloudy day can go either way.

When we returned home at nightfall, a full meal was warming in the oven, with serving instructions written by hand in block letters on a page from a notepad with *Maggie* scrawled across the top. The aromas that greeted us were rich and tantalizing and terribly welcome to noses stifled all day by stale hospital air.

Nevertheless, home was not a welcoming place. Without Anna to ground us, we drifted almost aimlessly. Even inconsequential tasks – sorting mail or making beds or taking a morning shower – required Herculean effort. Although Beth and Will were surrounded by day by the vibrant safety net of their friends, at night, even their façades wore down. As if some sort of sacrifice to the Gods, the remains of Maggie's meals piled up in the refrigerator, wholesome offerings for eccentric breakfast habits.

What does it mean to be unconscious? The question haunted all of us, but it was Will, true to his generation, who actively sought out answers. His curiosity was admirable, although I might have advised him that consciousness is abstract, a construct defined more by Freud and Einstein than physiology, and not well illuminated by search engines.

I watched him that night from the doorway of the den. He sat bent over the desk, so focused on the computer screen he was at first oblivious to my presence. The long pointer and middle fingers of his right hand hovered over the touch pad, flicking repeatedly like the tongue of a lizard, and his face was lit by the screen as if the glow of a full moon.

Jeremy might have been just like him at this age. He might have studied at the computer late at night. He might have grown too quickly into a man's body, muscles pushing through his skin, a thick neck tanned from afternoons on the playing field, hair tousled and in need of a trim. He might have had too many questions unanswered, the constant quest for information ravaging his brain as intensely as hormones storming his body.

As I watched Will, melancholy rose to the surface, taut and curdled like old milk. Will seemed a vision of my lost boy and I sighed so loudly, he turned, his eyes glazed with fatigue, and confusion.

"I looked up coma," he said, as if he were working on a school project.

"And?"

"Lots of links, mostly medical papers, hard to read."

"Anything comprehensible?"

"Some. The biological explanation is pretty plain really."

"Is it?" I stepped into the room, closer to Will.

"Most comas, not something like a diabetic coma which is different, the kind of coma brought about by trauma, comes from, like, damage to the cerebral center of the brain. Damage or shock. Usually the functions of the brain stem remain intact. You know, where things like respiration and circulation are controlled. See?" He pointed to an image on the screen.

"I always thought the brain stem looked like a mushroom," I said.

"Looks like an atomic bomb blast to me, you know, like those pictures in text books about Hiroshima."

"Yes, Hiroshima." I wilted onto the couch.

"Maybe that's what happened to Mom. Sort of an atomic blast. When the truck hit her, the force might have been, I mean in human molecular structure, like the force of a bomb on the surface of the earth. Like, pow!"

I took a long deep breath and exhaled slowly, audibly, to still my nerves.

"If the brain stem has been damaged, that's when a person goes into what they call a persistent vegetative state. I mean, it's kind of spooky how simple that part is." He peered closely at the screen. "'A state of unconsciousness and unresponsiveness,'" he read, "'distinguishable from sleep in that the person does not respond to external stimulation.' You know, like shouting or pinching. Although, there is an example here of a woman who had an advanced case of tetanus, like, everything shut down. No response to external stimuli," he read, and then turned again to me. "Then they showed her a series of cards, which she remembered when she recovered."

"Showed her?"

"Yeah, some people in comas open their eyes a lot, or jerk around and stuff. Sometimes they mumble, like talking in your sleep, I guess. Has Mom moved?"

"I haven't seen her."

Will shrugged. "Sometimes, like, Saturday mornings, I sleep like nothing could ever wake me. Does that mean I'm in a kind of coma?"

"I don't think so. You would awaken to startling noise or a poke in the arm."

"I guess."

I heard the apprehension in his voice. "There's much more to it, Will." I sat up taller. "It's not just external stimuli, you said so yourself. Breathing, digestion, elimination. All suspended in part. Not at all like sleep. Sleep is restorative."

"Yeah, that's what it says. 'The coma comes from disturbance or damage to areas of the brain involved in conscious activity or the maintenance of consciousness. In particular, parts of the cerebrum, upper parts of the brain stem, and central regions of the brain, especially the limbic system.' Whatever that is."

He wrote the word limbic on a pad on the desk, where several other words were scribbled in a column like a list to be memorized for a spelling test, some marked with oversized exclamation points. "It says that the damage should be visible in brain imaging."

"Right, the scan. They did that."

"Yeah, but this article said the damage may not show up for weeks, unless it's like really nasty, you know, like a tumor or brain abscess. He turned to his notes. "Or intracerebral hemorrhage," he read slowly, articulating each syllable. "They didn't see any of that, did they?"

"I don't think so. But there are other things that cause coma, the doctor said."

"Yeah. Autonomic disturbances, anoxic conditions." He read again from his notepad. "Where the blood flow is interrupted for too long."

"I'm confused by the medical lingo. I have a few clients in the field but I never pay much attention to the text in their newsletters. Over my head I guess."

Will turned silent with a particularly pensive expression. He clicked the touch pad several times, abruptly exiting the Internet, and in that moment, the screen exploded into a wallpaper montage of clouds against a pale blue sky. I was stunned by the vision of sky I have denied myself so long and the cluster of white cumulus clouds reminded me of the conversation I had with Anna just last Wednesday. I felt once again the astonishment one feels when everything changes in an instant.

"The doctor, the neurologist I think, said it was like a prolonged sleep. So, then Saturday morning is like a little coma for me?" Will asked.

"A deep sleep."

"When I sit in Spanish class sometimes and, like, completely zone out, I don't hear a word the teacher is saying and I'm not even aware of my friends or anything and then, like, suddenly the bell rings, like I have been unconscious for a half an hour, is that a kind of coma?"

"A classroom coma, I remember those. A daze, yes, but not unconscious."

"Kind of like a computer in sleep mode."

"Good comparison."

"But if a person is unconscious, in a deep sleep or something, I guess that is the opposite of consciousness."

"Literally, yes."

He sighed. "Mom used to tell me to be conscious of everything around me, not just everyday things, like people in my path or steps or sharp objects and stuff, but the things we don't always pay attention to. Like the way the wind changes before a storm, or how a squirrel scurries up and down the branch of a tree, like he has a definite plan, although he looks crazed."

"Jeremy and I used to watch squirrels in the park for hours sometimes," I said.

Will shook his head sadly. "I look up at the stars at night and search for constellations. I check out sunsets and harvest moons. I hear the music in birdcalls. I give my seat on the subway to an elderly person. I always look both ways before I cross. I'm conscious of everything around me." His voice grew shrill. "So why wasn't Mom conscious? Why wasn't she paying attention?"

He abruptly slammed shut the lid of the laptop, staring at it for a moment as if it might speak to him, then stood and crossed the room to leave.

"Will," I grabbed his free hand. "Something must have been on her mind, or in her view. Mom wasn't always as conscious of the little things as she was the wonderful things."

"I guess," he said and pulled his hand away. "And now she's just unconscious."

"Will," I implored.

"Night, Nell." He leaned down to kiss my cheek. "Sleep tight."

"Don't let the bed bugs bite," I whispered as he lumbered down the hall.

As the days passed, we grew more accustomed to each other's habits and rhythms, despite the absence of Anna, our missing link, and, for me, the added stress of displacement. Still, people are known to quickly establish a routine to meet the demands of even the most difficult situations and I began to observe us as if through Anna's lens, a narrative sequence of photographs, decidedly black and white, documenting a family in the throes of a crisis.

Almost seamlessly, we managed to eat and bathe and dress and organize ourselves each morning, the kids off to school and David checking in with his office before we drove to the hospital for the day. Even I awakened early to their sounds and got myself moving more rapidly than I usually do, invigorated by human energy, or simply unwilling to be left behind. Although we were bound by circumstance, we were also separate, the way so many live in tandem, every day, leaning on one another only as needed for protection from further disharmony.

Hospital time was monotonous and predictable. Maggie appeared with food, Adrienne attended regularly, Beth and Will arrived after school but stayed only a short time in the lounge before heading back for sports practice or play rehearsal. Tim visited during lunch hour and returned, I discovered, late evenings. Throughout the day, a medical regatta sailed in and out of the room, and each time one approached, I feared them like a wind that whips up stormy waters. David however jumped to attention in their presence, always anxious for new information, although there was none.

A diminutive round Hispanic woman who mopped floors and emptied waste pails stopped each morning as she departed to whisper in Spanish what I assumed was a prayer. She smiled at me with great kindness, an odd sort of kinship expressed silently as I lingered on the sidelines, blending as best as possible into the background. A persona she seemed to understand.

When a nursing aide arrived to give Anna her daily sponge bath, I watched again from the doorway. A black woman, darker in contrast to her patient's sickly pale skin, she lifted and turned her limp body, one arm or leg at a time, as if Anna were as light as a rag doll, moving quickly and skillfully, wiping each limb with a washcloth before enveloping the exposed skin in a towel to keep her warm.

She described each task aloud as she went along. "You're doing fine there, yes you are, that's it, I'm just going to lift this arm a bit, wash you underneath, don't want you feeling sloppy, do we? You have a good strong body, you must have a good heart in there, keep you going."

The aide moved steadily, having mastered her technique by who knows how many years of experience, slipping a damp cloth between Anna's fingers and toes, and turning her onto one side to wash back and buttocks, and, when the torso was clean, lightly pressing a new cloth into the folds of her neck and along her jaws, working around the tubes protruding from her mouth, the IV attachments to her arms, the catheter, then gently sponging her forehead and brushing her tresses behind her head before wrapping her hair into an elasticized paper cap, leaving her patient sanitized for another day of sleep that might have awaited only the kiss of a prince.

"There now," she said as she tucked Anna's sheet and blanket tightly at her shoulders, leaving her arms exposed at her sides. "You rest for a while. Plenty of exercise for one day."

David paced the hall, talking on his cell phone, while I alone observed the cleansing ritual, inspired by the aide's capacity to care for strangers, one after another. She gathered her equipment, tossed the towels into a bin, glanced at the monitors and looked up to meet my gaze.

"You can come closer now," she said.

I followed her heed.

"You know, when I talk to coma patients, I feel the heat rise under their skin. An electrical current zips through their muscles. They hear us, for sure. Talk to her. Read to her. Read the news, all that nasty stuff will make her want to jump right up and cover your mouth."

She stepped toward me. Nearly black pupils floated in the milky whites of her eyes.

"Hold her hand. If she's coming back, you'll make a path. If not, you'll have time together." She patted my hand as she left and I did not pull away, snared by her kindness.

I felt weak in the knees, assaulted by her reprimand, I believed, to do more for Anna than I had, so I sat down and grasped her hand. I stared at her freshly washed face, tiny freckles dotting her cheeks and nose, and under those closed eyelids, the eyes that had watched out for me all these years, eclipsed now like the moon in daylight.

"Anna, you should see the food supply at the house. Maggie has been cooking. The best ingredients, beautifully presented, wrapped for leftovers, which I promise we will eat. She pops in and out of our lives the way the sun peeks in and out of the clouds, and just as welcome."

Anna's chest swelled and depleted with air, otherwise still.

I took a breath. "You would be proud of the kids. Beth is remarkably stoic. She remembers everything she is meant to remember. And Will, he is an inquisitive truth seeker, as you knew he would be. He reflects in a very existential way. One fine little philosopher he is."

I waited for a response, and, realizing the stupidity of my expectation, felt a flair of anger, tempered only by the chronic inability to express any sort of animation, neither hostility nor happiness. I suppose I might be described as inhabiting a persistent emotionally vegetative state.

I stood to pace around the room as I spoke, as if on stage. "You should see us, Anna. Theater of the absurd. Maggie is catering your coma, Will is studying your coma, Beth is bravely accepting your coma, Adrienne is monitoring your coma, nurses are tending to your coma, doctors are analyzing your coma, Tim is reporting your coma, David is, well, David fluctuates between dealing and denying, hard to read, and me, God, I'm doing what I always do, I am drifting through all of this. I am drifting through your coma, Anna."

I slipped back into the chair by the bed.

"What does it mean to be conscious?" I asked aloud, as if we were seated across from each other in a coffee shop. "Will raised the question. He said the very essence of coma hinges on the essence of consciousness, or being conscious, he said, which perhaps is not the same. Very deep thoughts here, my friend. Lots of medical terms for coma, but consciousness? Far more difficult to define. If you breathe and digest and eliminate, are you conscious? If you are cut, you bleed, you trip, you fall, is that all there is to it? If someone calls your name and you turn, are you conscious? What about feeling the warmth of the sun on your skin, do you have to be conscious for that? What about joy? Can you be in a state of consciousness without joy? If you've deracinated yourself from optimism, are you conscious?"

I saw Anna's eyes flicker beneath her lids.

"Wake up, Anna!" I cried, and when she remained motionless, I lay my head on her shoulder, my upper body rising and falling in sync with her breathing. Even in that controlled state, she comforted me.

"I don't have the answers to Will's questions," I whimpered. "And I have failed you, I failed to do what you asked of me. I can't. It's too soon. We all need you."

I remained in that position for what must have been several minutes, until I felt David's hands tugging my shoulders, gently pressing me back in the chair.

"What is it? What's wrong?"

"No, nothing's wrong. Anna is fine."

A doctor stood at the door, watching us, waiting respectfully for us to notice him. I hadn't remembered seeing this one before, although they had all come to look much the same – another surprisingly young man with a sincere expression and studious eyes.

"I'm sorry to disturb you, Mr. Miller. May I have a moment?"

I stood to leave.

"Stay," David said.

"We are moving Mrs. Miller to Telemetry, South Wing," the doctor reported.

"Telemetry?" David asked

"Used to be called Continuing Care."

"I don't understand."

"It's a contemporary term. Continuing Care is a step-down unit for patients who require constant monitoring. The reason we call it Telemetry now is because patients are connected at all times through cellular technology. Even if a patient is ambulatory, monitoring equipment constantly transmits vital measures to the nurses' station, so they can be observed continuously and carefully, with less intrusion."

David stared at him in confusion. "Ambulatory? What are you talking about?"

The doctor, realizing he had answered the wrong question, nodded apologetically. "What I mean is, Mrs. Miller has been stable for three days. Her readings are steady and the scans are inconclusive. The critical period for a coma patient is forty-eight hours, but scans often will not reveal the full damage for as long as two weeks. We reserve the ICU for patients who are in crisis or immediate danger. Telemetry is the better place for a coma patient of this type."

What type? I wanted to scream.

"I see." David said, apparently resigned to the vagaries of medical lingo.

"We'll arrange for her move as soon as possible."

"What type?" I heard myself say.

"Pardon?" the doctor asked.

"What type of coma is she in?"

The doctor looked at me, then at David, as if for reassurance that he was permitted to respond to my question. Or did he need time to construct an answer? David looked back at him with the same inquiry on his face.

The doctor cleared his throat first. "Mrs. Miller is in a continuous unarousable unconsciousness. There is no response to verbal stimuli and no localizing or appropriately resisting motor response. As you can see," he stepped close to Anna to flicker a penlight into her eyes, "her pupils do not respond to the light, although her eyes do blink on occasion when touched. That's a good sign." He touched Anna's eyelids with a piece of gauze, but no response. "On the Glasgow coma scale, she registers a six, which is borderline."

"Meaning?" David interjected.

"Meaning the potential for recovery cannot be predicted." He paused for a moment, recognizing that we were desperate to know more. "The duration of the coma is contingent on brain damage. If brain cells have died due to lack of blood flow, then the coma is irreversible, but we cannot know this yet. If the brain cells are merely injured, there is a greater possibility for recovery, maybe even function."

"Merely injured," I murmured.

"We cannot read the damage to the cortex, not fully, and the truth is, even extensive damage to the cortex will not necessarily impair consciousness. The cortex must be aroused by signals from the reticular activating system. Right now, her scans show nothing indicative. No blood clots, no clearly delineated abnormalities, no lesions. However, the longer the patient stays in this state, the more likely that other, perhaps multiple areas of the brain, have been affected. For now, she is stable. She may even be able to breathe on her own, but I suggest we table the discussion of life support for now."

He looked down at the chart again. "I don't see…does she have a living will?"

"No." David barked. "My wife didn't believe in that sort of thing."

I said nothing.

"Her fate may be in your hands," the doctor answered. "However, we don't have to make that decision now." He pursed his lips briefly. "I realize the uncertainty is difficult, but we've covered all the bases. For now, we will keep her comfortable. A room in Telemetry is available, so we'll check her vitals one more time and release her there shortly."

"A private room please," David demanded, the only control he might exert even as we both begrudgingly accepted the next step in the master plan.

David stayed with Anna that afternoon while I waited in the lobby for Beth and Will to explain the room change. I sat on one of those benches meant to be sturdy for those feeling unmoored, shifting position repeatedly to ease the pressure on my back and wishing I could sink into something softer, perhaps achieve my own form of unconsciousness. Adrienne, striding toward the elevators, saw me and stopped.

"What's going on?" she asked.

"Anna's been assigned to another wing. Telemetry they call it."

"Yes." Adrienne sat down next to me on the bench and I slid over to create space between us. "They don't keep patients in ICU for long. She'll get good attention there."

"Doctors are confounded by coma," she went on. "I sometimes wonder if the very reason for the condition is to force us to question our efficacy. So little is yet known about brain functions, or, more importantly, how to repair them when damaged. Or even how to fully read the damage." She looked more closely at me. "I'm sorry. The last thing you need to hear is the frustration of a physician. Why are you down here anyway?"

"I'm waiting for the kids. I don't want them to discover an empty bed in the ICU."

Adrienne glanced at her watch. "I've got a few minutes. Let's have a cup of coffee."

I was about to object, assuming Adrienne did not understand my intent, when she charged into an office off the waiting area, returning with a perky adolescent in a pink striped uniform. "Meet Allison. She's a volunteer, and she knows Will. She'll sit right here and wait to escort them to Telemetry."

The girl smiled warmly at me. She reminded me of a beauty pageant contestant: blonde, bright-eyed, perfectly aligned white teeth and an earnest expression. I didn't really want to leave, but I didn't know how to reject the gesture.

"Okay, but please tell them that everything is fine, just a room change."

The girl nodded and sat, her spine perfectly straight, on guard duty.

"This way," Adrienne said, leading me down a wide flight of stairs toward the cafeteria, which was a little noisier than the lobby, but not much, as if the obligatory hush had migrated down the stairwell. We moved along the beverage line in silence. Adrienne poured coffee into a Styrofoam cup and added milk. I filled a tall plastic cup with ice and Diet Pepsi from the fountain, plunging a straw through the perforations in the lid, slurping most of it so quickly I had to refill before we reached the checkout. Adrienne paid for our drinks and ushered me toward a separate area for physicians.

"It's quieter here," she said. After a sip of the steaming brew, she studied me through her shaded glasses, the way an ophthalmologist studies a patient head on.

"How are you, Nell?" she asked in a clinical voice.

I almost laughed, the whole scene seemed ludicrous at that moment, and I wished once again that Anna were there to observe the charade. I lowered my voice. "Compared to what?"

She smiled. "I know all about you. Anna talks about you all the time."

I sipped my soda in self-defense. "That cannot be of great interest."

"Quite the contrary. You are a fascinating person."

I shook my head no.

"Anna so admires your creative spirit. Your passion. Your constancy."

"Constancy." I snickered at the description. "Like a pet."

"That's not as Anna sees you. She sees you as a great mystery really, perhaps the only one she has never been able to solve. You'd be surprised how much she admires your fortitude."

"Fortitude? Her word?"

"My interpretation. I don't think she sees you as the tragic figure you see yourself."

Stunned by her audacity, I gulped more soda rather than attempt a response. The cup in my hand shook noticeably and I felt the ice rattle within.

Adrienne went on. "You'll have to forgive me. I'm not one of Anna's disciples. I do not buy into the theory of predestination. I think it's mostly an excuse for poor choices, or for those unwilling to take responsibility for their actions. There might be a path, I get that, and we might not have total control over our fate, I see that every day. And yes, our lives meld into a larger context, what Anna considers our personal orbital path. However, we make choices. Every day of our lives, we make choices. We choose, if not our destiny, the route to it, and our response."

"Did Anna choose this?"

"In a way. She stepped off the curb. She clearly wasn't paying attention and a truck driver chose to speed through the light. Accidents are the consequence of choices."

"A truck driver takes a turn too tight and keels over on Anna, or a drunk plows into innocent people on the street, these are merely outcomes?"

"Listen, I grapple with this all the time. Dear children come into my office, innocent, unencumbered by bad habits, yet they face disease, deformity, sometimes death. Are they victims of some loftier destructive force? Perhaps. However I cannot believe it is completely out of our hands. What did their mothers drink or smoke during pregnancy? What drugs are in their fathers' systems? What pollutants have we allowed in our groundwater or spewed into the air in favor of convenience or cheaper prices? We collectively make choices, too often thoughtlessly, or for the wrong reasons, which affect so many others. Even Anna plays a part in the chain of events."

Adrienne sipped her coffee. "Ugh. I hate tepid coffee, I need a refill. You?"

I shook my head. She returned moments later with steaming coffee, this time black.

"I don't mean to be ornery," she said as she sat. "Anna was extremely tolerant of my tirades. We were forever kicking around the existential dilemma." She smiled, a smile only on the lips, no other muscles seemed to move. "We all play a part, Nell. I play the part of the healer, Anna, the chronicler, perhaps the sage as well. You, I guess, a reminder of how suddenly and irrevocably life can change, for better and for worse."

"The part was chosen for me."

"Perhaps your part was fated more than most. And in a sense my whole life was scripted for me. My mother directed my childhood, almost every move of it, determined for me to have everything she did not. My father was busy working and my big brother played the big brother. I thought I had it made when I got a scholarship to college, finally the master of my fate, but there my faculty advisor made all the important decisions and my roommate made the rest. I think the only choice I actually made for myself was that I wanted to be a nurse."

"A nurse?"

She nodded. "Yes, a nurse. I decided to switch out of liberal arts into nursing school, and my advisor stepped in and urged me to transfer into nursing at Johns Hopkins, a combined BS and RN degree. He wrote me a stellar letter of recommendation and, when I was accepted, bragged to fellow advisors as if I had nothing to do with it."

Adrienne paused for a moment, a nostalgic expression on her face. "I loved nursing school. I love nurses. The squeak of their rubber soles. Their starched whiteness, their persistent calm. I wanted to steep myself in that selflessness. I wanted to go home at night, as I imagined, to soak my feet or plunge my whole body into a hot tub and soothe my tired sinews with enormous satisfaction. I wanted to live the law of Tikun Olam, it's the essence of Jewish life, to give of oneself to others. I had the whole thing mapped out in my mind and I was completely exhilarated by nothing more than my own personal plan. Well, that didn't last very long. Ira changed all that. My husband, you've met, yes?"

"Yes," I nodded, remembering the tall, swarthy, overbearing husband, holding court at dinner parties.

"He was in his last year of medical school. We met at a diner, a whole bunch of students celebrating the end of final exams. I was a good student, but never better than the year I studied nursing. By the end of the second semester, Ira and I were a couple, and he convinced me I shouldn't sell myself short. Nursing wasn't good enough for me, oh no, he insisted. I should go all the way and become a doctor. He even suggested my specialty, pediatrics, because there were so few females studying pediatrics in medical school then. How could I possibly disappoint him? After all, it was the nineties. Between the media and my husband, the message was clear: I was not to be ordinary or predictable. I was to have it all."

She paused again to stare down at her feet. "I never wore the white shoes."

I was confounded by her confession. "But you are a physician. You protect children's lives. Surely you see that as a noble purpose?"

"Anna told me you were a potter, is that right?"

"I was," I said, gazing down at my own scuffed shoes.

"So if someone suggested you become a sculptor because pottery wasn't quite good enough, and you became a fairly successful sculptor, but you never really thought you were as good at sculpture as you were at pottery, would the success matter to you? Would you embrace the marble as the clay, even though the clay felt soft and silky and the marble hard and cold?"

I looked directly into Adrienne's eyes. The darkness there seemed less foreboding, more sorrowful. Anna must have recognized her disenchantment from the first.

"True," I replied. "I could never sculpt in marble."

Adrienne smiled, this time with her whole face. "But here's the thing: I always had a choice and I chose not to object, not to anyone who loved me. I was convinced to reach higher for myself, although even then I knew that more isn't always better. I wanted to care for people directly, not cure them, heal them. Impossible to explain to someone like Ira. Or my mother or my brother, who were over the moon when I became the first female doctor in the family. By the way, my brother's a cardiac surgeon." She sighed. "On occasion, I save a child's life, and yes, I take satisfaction in that. Most of the time, I tend to sprains, ear infections, STDs. I prescribe too many antibiotics, immunize against diseases that are thankfully almost obsolete, and wait for the cures to the diseases that scare the shit out of me. I occasionally nurse the battered emotions of over-achieving mothers and try to convince budding adolescents to stay away from drugs and dark places. I suppose that has to be enough."

"It sounds mundane when you describe it, but it isn't. You must know that."

"Yes, but what you know and what you feel, they don't always jive, do they?"

I nodded. They rarely jive.

She gulped down the last of her coffee and crumbled her napkin into the cup.

"However, do something right or don't do it at all, that's our family mantra, so I do it well. When Anna moved into town, she seemed to sense immediately that I would be the best because I have to be the best. She inherently understands the difference between success and satisfaction, between mastery and passion. Do you know what she said to me the first time she came into my office? 'I have put my children in your care. Do your best for them.' Mothers around here don't talk like that. I decided that first moment we would be friends. And now, more than ever, I wish I were a nurse. I can't save her, but I might have brought comfort to her."

I touched Adrienne's arm and she patted my hand, although her smile had faded. Without another word, she stood to leave, as if an inner alarm signaled she had let down her guard long enough, and I silently followed, happy to shut back down myself.

When I returned to Anna's room, Tim was sitting by her bedside, reading the newspaper in a hushed syncopated voice, the way a parent reads one last book to a nearly sleeping child. I was surprised to see him at that hour.

"Where's David?" I asked as I tiptoed into the room.

"He had to go to his office. I'll drive you home."

"Aren't you working?"

"Paper has gone to press."

"I'll wait for the kids," I said.

"David said Will has a game and Beth has rehearsal. I'll drive you."

"Well, if you don't mind…"

"I don't mind."

"I can take a taxi."

"It's not a problem, Nell."

With that, the conversation ended briefly, until I asked, "Why do you read the newspaper to her?"

"Anna read the paper cover to cover, every morning, although I accused her of only perusing the pictures. She likes to know what's going on, you know that."

"I do know that."

"I don't mean to sound confrontational," he said, turning to me with a sheepish grin.

I walked to the window and peered out to the darkening sky as Tim continued flipping through the pages of the newspaper.

"Slow news day," he reported to Anna. "Ellen wrote another flat fiction on the Board of Ed meeting last night. The City Council report is the usual nonsense. Old Henry Mason passed the hat to help preserve the northwest parkland the gang of five is trying to save from the developers, and sure enough, he pulled in $683. I bet he'll be down at the Town Line Tavern tonight whooping it up with the boys. Oh, and sweet Mrs. Turner passed on. Otherwise not much. Nothing's going to happen until you pull the pixels, so you better get back here soon."

He stood to leave and waited for me at the door while I took another glance at Anna and pressed her hand. We left and walked silently across the corridor and down the stairs.

I lit a cigarette as we came out of the hospital. "Do you mind?"

"Not my place to mind."

Tim's car was parked almost directly in front of the main door. In answer to my thoughts, he said, "I've got a press pass, I park anywhere."

"Is this a story for you?"

"What?"

"Are you following this story?" I repeated.

He stopped to face me, so I had to stop as well, and we stood a moment awkwardly confronting each other. "No," he said, with an amused expression. "Anna is not a story."

I nodded, slightly ashamed for my suspicious nature. Tim unlocked the passenger door of an old Saab convertible, a benign counter-culture car for grown-ups who haven't quite grown up. As I sat, I noticed the backseat was covered with newspapers and file folders and a faint scent of cologne filtered through the mustiness.

"This Saab has seen a lot of mileage, in all ways," Tim said as he settled into the driver's seat and fastened his seat belt.

"Is that how you ended up here?"

"By here you mean this town?"

"Yes."

What else might I have meant? I wondered.

"Sort of. I tend to move around a lot. Might have to do with a youthful fondness for hallucinogens." He chuckled.

"Hallucinogens?"

"LSD. Peyote. Opens the peripheral vision, unlocks the inner eye. What seekers do, because it seems like a good idea. Not much any more, for me, by the way. I might have seen once too often what I wasn't prepared to see."

I was too flummoxed to respond.

"For the most part, the Zen put an end to that. Mind altering interferes with presence. What they call mindfulness these days. Besides all that, I'm a bit of a stumbler by nature."

"Stumbler?"

"I stumble around, that's how I travel through life. Constantly shifting perspective."

"How often do you change locations?"

"Every couple of years or so. The duality of the universe, you might say. Natural bifurcation. I get itchy. I've lived in big cities, rural towns, high and low elevations, I rather prefer the high, geographically hallucinogenic, so to speak."

"Isn't all the moving around hard on a career?"

"Might be, sure, but seems wherever I go I was meant to be because I've picked up a newspaper gig pretty much the moment I land. And these days, I can work in cyberspace if I need to. In fact, some of the best journalism is online, and that makes it possible to be just about anywhere, and everywhere, all at once. Very heady."

He turned to smile at me, then returned his gaze to the road, and even as I engaged in the conversation, I kept my eyes straight ahead, anxious to return home and have a little quiet time before the gathering of the clan.

The car weaved along back roads as if on autopilot. Tim turned on the radio and the gentle notes of a classical guitar blanketed the silence.

"So why this place?" I asked, surprisingly curious.

"I was headed toward Philadelphia, from a town in Rhode Island where I started up their first weekly paper. Everything is on a smaller scale in that state, cozy and contemplative. I liked it, but it had run its course. Always liked Philly, but when I got this far, I decided to spend a night here, and take the morning train to the Big Apple for a few days. Get myself a museum fix. I walked around town first to take it in and, I don't know, something about the setting appealed to me. The pace maybe, not as slow as an authentic New England community, and not too small. A touch of sophistication, I suppose by virtue of the proximity to Manhattan. Of course meeting Anna may have had something to do with it."

"That first day?"

He smiled, keeping his eyes on the road ahead. "Yes, that first day. I watched her take photographs of boys skateboarding at the park on Main Street. You know the one?"

I didn't remember the park specifically, but I nodded nonetheless, to speed the telling.

"Kids were zooming this way and that, randomly zipping along pathways meant for strolling, hurtling themselves up the rocks, back down, up again. Another shooter might have moved with them, in that handheld cinematic way favored by hip photographers these days, but Anna perched her camera on a tripod and stayed put, shooting stills as they passed. So there was a sense of movement, almost an animation in the final series. She also captured their expressions at the very moment they were least on guard. Most photographers would focus on the obvious, the angle of bodies, maybe the speed, but she got their concentration. And their elation. You know, you learn an awful lot about kids in the throes of sport by the look on their faces, more than the physicality. I watched her and realized I knew her. In another life, I mean. So the next day, instead of the city, I went to the library and read a few months of the newspaper's back issues, and learned enough about the lay of the land, and the editorial viewpoint, so Monday morning, when I strolled over to the *Dispatch* office, the retiring editor nearly jumped with joy when I presented my credentials. And here I am."

"You've settled in then?"

"For now. One adapts. You make peace with a perennial sense of dislocation. Less likely to become complacent. I imagine you feel displaced right now."

"Anna's home is my home away from home."

"Comfortable guest room?"

"I don't sleep very well anyway."

"Ah, a fellow insomniac."

I looked over at him as we paused for a red light. I noticed swollen bags beneath his eyes and craggy edges at their corners. His rugged good looks only partially offset the slightly disheveled attire, slumped shoulders and downcast eyes. He reminded me of someone, but it was much later when I realized that someone was me.

"So much for Buddhism," I commented.

"How so?"

"I would have thought all that inner peace makes for a good night's sleep."

"If only that were true." He laughed loudly.

"Sorry, I missed the joke."

"People have bizarre impressions of Buddhists. We are not monks, not most of us. We are hardly humorless. I mean, the Dalai Lama laughs gleefully. We appreciate humor because we don't get caught up in propriety. We don't attach to the right or wrong way to live. We accept the struggle and resist suffering. It's really that simple."

"Nothing is that simple."

"Even Anna has sleepless nights. She spends many a late night in the darkroom, so she says. Might have done her best work in the wee hours."

"I thought of checking the darkroom, to see what was in process, but I'm hesitant to enter the sanctum."

"As far as I know, no one is permitted."

Neither of us commented and I suddenly tired of talking. I watched the parade of homes and, as pretty as they were, with perfectly tended lawns and shapely specimen trees, I longed for gritty sidewalks. I would never have dreamed of living the sort of nomadic lifestyle Tim embodies, and even short-term adaptation is clearly not my strong suit.

Tim pulled into the driveway and I thanked him and started to slip out of the car, anxious for solitude, but he reached over and grasped my wrist.

"I'm around any time, if you want to talk. We can have a drink if you like."

I didn't answer at first, shocked as much by the suggestion as his touch.

"We have much in common, you and I," he said.

"How so?"

"We both love Anna. You might say we are connected, through her. Rather an intense connection, wouldn't you say?"

I was surprised by his use of the word love. "Not everyone who cares about the same person is connected."

"I beg to differ. Some people serve as lifetime links, and Anna is that much a force of nature. Certainly she connects us now."

"A little too new age for me."

He smiled. "If you open your mind to it, you'll see that these people who bind us, they are the hub of the wheel, and we merely the spokes. If a connection is broken, the wheel wobbles, might even collapse, and that may be harmful to the connector."

"Wait, are you suggesting that someone in Anna's personal orbit, or whatever you choose to call it, has failed her in some way, and may cause her further harm?"

"I wasn't saying that, although it is a provocative thought."

"Sorry, I prefer to live in the real world."

"All I'm saying is Anna brought us together and we should honor that."

"By having a drink? Do you expect me to suddenly become your friend, just because we both have a relationship with one particular human being? Like Facebook or something?"

Tim peered at me head on, a piercing gaze, not unkind.

"Anna has mentioned you now and then, but I had no reason to feel connected to you until you arrived."

"Now and then?"

"I suspect your tether to Anna is more securely fastened than hers to you."

I took offense at that statement, although true, and peered at Tim to gauge his intent. I saw nothing in his dark eyes beyond a desire to understand. The eyes of a seeker. A stumbler.

"Thanks for the ride," I said, as I extricated myself and headed toward the house.

I imagined Tim watched me for a moment before backing down the driveway. Likely trying to figure me out. I chuckled at the thought as I opened the front door, and once he was out of sight, I stood outside to smoke. Dusk had descended, taking with it the warmth of the sun, so I puffed quickly and returned inside, snapping the door securely to block the chill.

In the kitchen, I followed the instructions Maggie taped to the packages of food she left for us, welcoming the heat emanating into the room as the oven warmed. I poured myself a glass of red wine, sipping as I set the table. David arrived, and with barely a nod, poured himself a glass and put the wine bottle on the table, which we drained over dinner.

Will and Beth joined us as the steaming meal came out of the oven, and after dinner, with a modicum of small talk, we all watched an innocuous PBS travelogue on Istanbul, the images foreign enough to take us out of ourselves for a little while, and then bid each other good night.

I cleaned up, put on my nightshirt, opened the window in the den, and discovered a steady shower saturating the air. I lay down on the sofa bed, aged mattress springs bouncing with the weight of my body, but I couldn't get comfortable, so I rose and walked the halls for a while, staring again at Anna's photographs, as if searching for some buried truths, some sort of revelation that might bring Anna back to life. Nothing was revealed, and nothing soothed the frayed edges of my equilibrium, so I turned in again, hoping raindrops might lull me to sleep. I missed the sound of cars sloshing along damp city streets, the timbre of rain splattering on sidewalks and windshield wipers skimming back and forth. Here at Anna's quiet suburban home, raindrops never quite landed at all, instead nearly silently absorbed into the landscape.

Beyond the raindrops, I heard the steady stream of Beth's late shower and imagined hot water washing away her tears. I heard soft classical tones on David's radio and the insistent bass of Will's playlist, the two euphonious sets connected in spirit. I pictured Adrienne sitting up in bed reading while her husband slept, unaware of her discontent. Tim sitting silently in the dark meditating and Maggie wiping a smudge off the marble slab on her kitchen work-island, caressing the stone like a jewel.

I suddenly felt a slow stream of tears on my cheeks. How I wished Anna were home safe and sound. Dear Anna, oblivious to us all, even as we all are connected through her: a human form of telemetry.

While Intensive Care had seemed as turgid and foreboding as heavy fog, Telemetry seemed as lively as a country tavern. Classic rock music played at the main desk and nurses dressed in pastels bustled about like waitresses who might have been taking orders for dinner as amiably as tending to the sick, and, though they recurrently popped in and out of Anna's room, there seemed no sense of urgency, as if resignation had taken the place of anticipation.

Anna's room was spacious and bright and thoughtfully appointed with a small chest of drawers and a closet, both finished in dark wood that matched the wainscoting. Gleaming tile floors were hardly scratched, a couple of innocuous landscape paintings were hung at eye level, and the windows were so tall that even from just the second floor, aided by the hilly terrain below, the view was surprisingly vast. A room meant to provide comfort, although totally lost on Anna. A comfort to visitors, I supposed, if there was any comfort to be found.

I stood by a window for some time and gazed across the pitched slate and shingled roofs of modest in-town houses and the tarred flat tops of the commercial core. Downtown streets spread their tentacles to winding tree-lined roads leading to what local residents referred to as the back country, where large homes on large parcels were set back from view, establishing both primacy and privacy.

More signs of spring had emerged from the oppression of winter. Tulips joined daffodils in ribbons of reds and yellows. Elms, oaks and maples spread new branches to the sky. Aged hemlocks reached fingers to the sun from bushy bases and the first tiny buds of magnolia trees speckled their barks.

Within all that fresh growth, a tall tree with nothing but barren branches soared toward the clouds, still trapped in winter: no hint of green, no new shoots. Dead or dormant, I was uncertain of its role in the ecological balance, and simultaneously admired its natural stoicism in the face of possible demise.

I appreciate anomalies. As a small-scale potter, I too am limited somewhat to shape and size. Whatever begins at the wheel can go just so far before straining the form. My bowls fit within my frame of vision and within my grasp. Perhaps I was drawn to pottery because the outcome is functional as well as aesthetic. I mold, which is not the same as to construct, or for that matter, to create. For other ceramicists, a fine work of art, elegant and decorative, but for me, the simple fashioning of an amorphous substance into something of value. At best, a still life versus a Pollack; a nursery rhyme versus Homer.

Anna and I are alike in this one way. The potter and the photographer manipulate what already exists. Both challenged by inherent limitations. In those first few days at the hospital, however, I was increasingly aware of how different we are, even if dependent on each other, to some extent, for completion. Our relationship might be defined as a form of symbiosis called commensalism in which two organisms rely on each other, although one, usually the smaller, benefits fully from the association, while the other neither benefits nor is diminished. I discovered the term in one of the newsletters I designed for a scuba diving club and was stopped cold by the similarity to our friendship. Like a tiny fish, I swim tentatively close to the stinging tentacles of sea anemone. Anna is my coral, intimate and obligatory, yet she exists fully without me. Her life would be unimpeded by my absence. It has always been so.

So why was Anna in a coma? Why does damage to the brain transcend damage to the heart? It should have been me in that hospital bed. After all, I have been effectively comatose for years, although, according to the young physician, merely injured.

David stopped to see Anna that morning and left soon after. He no longer paced the room, favoring the seclusion of the visitors' lounge, where he took calls and worked on his laptop an hour or so at a time between brief visitations. He had arranged a staff meeting there that morning and I was offended for Anna, perhaps for myself, to have been swatted like an insect in favor of the mundane matters of the day.

I reached through the bedrail to touch Anna's hand. She felt wonderfully warm, wrapped like a mummy in a robin's-egg blue cotton blanket and matching hospital gown. Her facial wounds were less egregious, her skin less pale, her lips nearly red in contrast. Under other circumstances, I might have expected her to be smiling, pleased to be ensconced in Telemetry, which she would embrace as the next step on the great journey.

I had a flicker of memory of the two of us, last summer, when she convinced me to join her to play hooky for the day. We lay on a blanket on the beach, buoyed by the sound of the surf and the warmth of the sun.

"How can something as glorious as the sun be bad for us?" Anna asked that day, her skin tanned, hair sparkling with lingering salt-water droplets. "I hate all this hype about sun damage and skin cancer. Is there nothing sacred?"

"Not to the media."

Anna smiled. "Ah, Nell's favorite target, the media."

"I'll hold my tongue."

"The media is only the message. It's the scientists, the doctors, the pharmaceutical companies who ruin a beautiful day like this."

"Ah, Anna's favorite target, capitalists. Seriously?"

"In the name of marketing they take all the spontaneity out of life. They desecrate the pleasures of the natural world. They would have us ingesting synthetically produced supplements instead of oranges and pumpkin seeds, and running on elevated treadmills instead of country roads. And they want us to hide from the sun. How is something so essential for living as bad for us as they would have us believe? We revolve around the sun. Most of the animal world and the plant world cannot exist without sunlight. Yet they would have us cover our bodies, heads, windows… Not me. If the sun that warms me to the core kills me, so be it."

"Can we at least wear sunblock?" I asked.

Anna laughed. "You are not listening to me, my friend."

"Anna, I am always listening to you," I said that day.

"I am always listening to you, Anna," I whispered into the silence of her hospital room, as I ran my fingers through my hair, freshly washed and soft to the touch, clinging to the enchantment of sand in my scalp and sunshine on my face.

When Adrienne and Maggie stopped in at noon, and Tim soon after, we adjourned to the lounge where David was just concluding a business call. Maggie extracted more than enough sandwiches for all of us out of a black suede backpack while Adrienne secured sodas and water bottles from a staff supply closet.

We were all dressed in gradients of gray: me in a black T-shirt and black jeans; Adrienne's black turtleneck peeking above a white medical jacket; David in a charcoal V-neck sweater and black pants; and Tim in a white shirt tucked into black khakis. Only Maggie stood out, wearing a lemon-yellow tunic over black suede cargo pants, topped with a faux emerald necklace that sparkled as she moved about, brightening an otherwise dreary palette.

Anna once described Maggie as the package under the Christmas tree everyone would open first, the gift of a charming ornamental object meant only to beautify the surroundings. By comparison, we all seemed like the packages opened and discarded for something better.

We chomped sandwiches and gulped drinks, but spoke little, the black and white tableau infecting our moods. At last the hush grew onerous and it was Maggie who spoke.

"Maybe we should have dined in Anna's room."

"The scent of your food might appeal to her," Tim said.

"Next time I'll bring Pad Thai, her favorite. That might bring her back to life! Oh, my God, I'm sorry, I didn't mean…" Maggie stammered.

"We always think about whether the comatose can hear or feel, but scent is compromised as well, I believe," Tim said, directing his remark to Adrienne.

"Damage to the skull can obfuscate the sense of smell, sometimes completely," Adrienne answered. "Anosmia. When we cannot smell, taste is also altered."

"I know what that's about," Maggie said as she swiped a tissue at tears bubbling at the corner of her eyes. "When I have a cold, even my food tastes bad."

"Everything is connected," Tim remarked as he swallowed the last of his coffee. He smiled up at me to remind me of our conversation, as if I might have forgotten.

Adrienne wiped her mouth with her napkin and crumbled up the few last bites of her sandwich in the foil. "The truth is, more people are in long-term vegetative states today than ever before, yet we still know precious little about what they experience. Few reports of recovery have been published in the last twenty years."

Everyone stopped chewing or drinking, and I think we collectively stopped breathing for a few seconds, until Adrienne realized the portent of her words.

"Patients recover, of course, they frequently recover; however there has been little documentation on the experience while in that condition."

"I take a metaphysical view," Tim pronounced and we all turned to him. "Medical intervention is about arousing the person from this so-called vegetative state. We're disappointed if they do not awaken immediately or respond visibly. However Anna does not seem to be in distress. We are the ones suffering, but suffering is optional. I prefer to think she is in a sustained dream state. Perhaps she sees and hears and smells whatever is within her dream. She may be mentally surfing in Maui or skiing in Aspen. She might smell the salty froth or feel the icy air as if she were there. Just like the dreams we have when we sleep, but more vibrant because they are prolonged, even if in another temporality. We assume she is an empty vessel of sorts because she seems that way to us, and we project our anguish onto her, but she may be quite content."

Tim must have perceived our stunned expressions as fascination, or a tacit appreciation of his theory, so he continued theorizing. "What if someone in a coma has unconsciously, I mean subliminally, perhaps purposefully, sought out the chance to go deep inside themselves, to slip away from the stress of everyday life? Sort of a physical-emotional sabbatical? Maybe Anna is in a subdued state of consciousness for the sake of psychic renewal? I might even go further to suggest that this is not a random happening, rather a critical juncture in Anna's destiny. She may have divined her own demise as a way of re-balancing herself, a preparation for the next step, or to get back on track in this life. If you imagine her situation this way, you would be less distraught. And less fearful."

"Where are you getting all this, Tim?" Adrienne snapped. "Too many hours in meditative states or one too many lunches with Anna?"

"Pure speculation on my part, although certainly the situation is ripe with possibilities, having no concrete answers to the question of the spirit's path."

"This is not about destiny, that's not what we are talking about. We're deliberating the manifestations of brain damage. And while we still have much more to learn, outrageous hypotheses do not serve any purpose," Adrienne retorted.

Tim was not easily deterred. "What if trauma to the brain triggers a metaphysical response we cannot begin to diagnose because it is cerebral in the truest sense of the word? Even you might agree, Adrienne, there is a mind-body connection, and we cannot underestimate the power of cognitive conditioning, or the realm of spiritual healing. Don't be so quick to condemn what may be beyond your comprehension."

Adrienne stared at Tim with a heavy dose of hostility and if I had been on the other side of that glare I would have flinched, but Tim showed no fluster at all.

"You do sound like Anna," Maggie said.

"Thank you," Tim responded with a slight bow of his head.

"We do Anna a disservice by not facing reality for her," David said, and I noticed he too gazed at Tim with contempt. Clearly I was not the only person for whom Tim was an irritant.

"Perhaps we have to think like Anna in order to do what is right for Anna," Tim said.

"*We* don't do what is right for Anna," David bellowed. He stood, angrily dumping the remains of his lunch in the trash. "The doctors do what is right for Anna. Or *I* do what is right for my wife."

"David," Maggie said gently, "We are all concerned for Anna, that's all. This is really very healthy for us to share our feelings."

"Please Maggie, spare me the touchy-feely psycho-babble!" David barked. "Far more than I can bear right now."

"I just think we all need to support her as best we can at this crossroads," Tim said. He stood to leave. "I meant no offense."

"We're all a bit edgy," Maggie cajoled.

"Thanks Maggie. And thanks for lunch. I'll just say a word to Anna and be off."

I nodded, but no one said good-bye to Tim as he left.

Adrienne's beeper went off and she too prepared to leave. "Coffee later?" she whispered as she passed.

"Okay," I answered, reluctantly but without good reason.

"I'll meet you in the lobby at four."

Maggie picked up and tossed the remaining cups and cans into the trash, and zipped up her backpack. She kissed David on the cheek and smiled at me. "Come to dinner tonight," she said. "We can… oh, wait, I've got Gemma's team dinner tonight. Almost forgot. Cooking for twenty and they eat like it's their last supper! How about tomorrow night? I picked up a terrific Argentine Malbec the other day. Will pair well with a hearty meal."

"Sure," David answered with a grateful smile. "Thanks. I'll tell the kids."

"Great."

Maggie patted my shoulder as she passed. "Hang in," she whispered.

David and I were left in the lounge. He stared out the window briefly, then pulled out his cell phone, and as he dialed, he looked over at me. "What?"

I shook my head in puzzlement. "I just wonder if we should consider every possibility. I like the idea of Anna surfing in Hawaii."

David punched the phone to stop the call and stared at me in dismay. "Honestly, I don't know what's worse, the coma or the commentary. I can't stand not knowing, but I despise that sort of abstract positing, even the benign Buddhist variety. I just want to know what's happening and what we can do about it. That's not so much to ask, is it?"

Even as David asked, he knew the answer. There was nothing to know and nothing to do. An impossible situation for those who need to know and need to do. Impossible even for those of us who accept that most everything is out of our hands.

I returned to Anna's room and sat by the window enjoying the warmth of the mid-day sun on my face, although before long, the heat was magnified so intensely by the glass, I had to close the blinds. I sat in the chair and dozed. David, the nurses or doctors might have stopped in while I rested, but I didn't notice, until I suddenly awakened to find Will sitting in the chair opposite me.

"Are you all right?" he asked.

"Fine, just needed a nap I guess."

"Must be hard hanging here all day."

"How was your day?"

"Same old, same old."

"No game? No practice?"

"I skipped."

"Where's Beth?"

"Don't know. I thought she was here."

"Why?"

"She wasn't at play rehearsal. Didn't see her around the student center either. She must be at the library, I rarely go there."

I smiled. "So how did you get here?"

"Walked."

"That's quite a way, isn't it?"

"Just three miles."

"Well, if you're not at your work-out, at least you're getting exercise."

"I don't think the coach will see it that way."

"Are you in trouble now?"

"Season's nearly over." He walked over to the window and stared out.

"Maggie invited us to dinner tomorrow night," I said.

Will shook his head. "I love Maggie, but she makes such a fuss. Do we have to?"

"We'll have a really good meal."

"She sends leftovers. Or I can live on pizza, all the key food groups."

We both chuckled, momentarily shattering the solemnity, then Will stood, embarrassed I supposed, and anxious to remove himself from the continuing fright of his mother's state. Or was there something he wanted to say?

"I'm going to get a ride home," he said.

"I'm happy for your company if you want to stay a while. And Dad will be back soon, I think. He can drive you."

"Thanks, no. It's fine, I'll get there."

"Will?"

"See you later, Nell."

He was almost out the door before he turned to Anna and called to her, "Bye, Mom."

I looked up at the wall clock. Nearly four o'clock, time to meet Adrienne. I kissed Anna's forehead the way a mother kisses the forehead of a child. Her temperature felt a little cool without the benefit of sunshine and her skin tone slightly gray.

Adrienne suggested a walk instead of coffee and I was relieved to stray beyond the confines of the hospital. The landscape was gray, the air chilly and damp. I zipped my jacket and stuffed my hands in my pockets, walking slowly at first, gawking at the stubble of new growth on bushes and trees. Adrienne maintained a brisk gait so I increased my pace to keep up with her, too soon short of breath from the exertion.

"I thought New Yorkers were quick walkers," she said.

"I've got short legs."

Adrienne nodded and slowed her stride just enough to be kind, still leading the way. We paced each other in silence for a time until we passed a nearly barren tree like the one I had seen from Anna's room. I stopped to look more closely.

"What is it?" Adrienne turned to ask.

"I noticed a tree like this from Anna's window, maybe this one. No sign of life yet."

Adrienne stepped forward to touch the bark. "The trees that bloom late often last longer into the fall."

I glanced up the trunk, not all the way to the top, but far enough to see that the tree was even taller than I imagined. "Looks old. Do you know what it is?"

"Maggie would know, she's big on trees. Food, fashion, nature. Boundless energy that woman." Adrienne stared at me for a moment before she remembered the question. "I'm no authority, although might be a mulberry."

"Mulberry? So old-fashioned."

She examined one of the branches more closely. "Mulberries do come in later, although they tend to be more amorphous, as I recall."

"Do you think anything in nature is truly random?" I asked.

"I don't. I tossed a bunch of wildflower seeds into the yard one spring, thought they would sprout into a perfect English cottage garden, and discovered they need far more tending than expected."

"Anna would photograph this tree," I said.

"She would like the stark image of a naked tree amidst the bloomers. Great contrast."

"Perfect for black and white film."

Adrienne smiled and I sat down at the base of the tree, leaning against it to draw upon its fortitude. Adrienne stood in place, and when her phone pinged, she checked in with her office and then with her children. She mouthed "sorry" to me, however I was content to sit quietly. I lit a cigarette, ignoring the disapproving look she sent my way, inhaling deeply and gratefully, although I had been adapting to long abstinences.

"I have to get back," she said as she pushed the phone into its holster on her waist. "Too much going on today, too much," she muttered.

"Anna and I saw an exhibit a few months ago at a gallery in New Haven," Adrienne remarked as we started the walk back. "We happily passed the time there while Beth had her interview at Yale. All black and white photographs, they're trendy again, although I suppose they always are, the way vintage clothing is never out of style. I commented that people like to look at shadows of the past and Anna said all photographs are shadows of the past. 'At the very moment the lens shutter snaps, the present becomes the past. Not yet memory but past.' Something to that effect."

I nodded. "I've heard that refrain. I think I prefer black and white because the gray blurs the distinctions a bit, sort of smooths out reality."

"Did you know that before the Civil War photographs were considered unsuitable for recording events because they captured only a split second in time. Photography was in its infancy and lithographs were preferred, to better interpret, as original art can do. By World War I, photographs were considered the best presentation of fact, and still, even in the era of Photoshop."

I was aware once again that Adrienne tended to lecture, even casual conversation presented like a professor, and she continued the lesson.

"Anna tried to teach me something of photography. I've never been one to compose an image. I look, I see, I move on. My husband yells at me all the time because we have so few photos of the kids." She chuckled. "School photos document the timeline well enough, to me, but Anna wanted me to appreciate the elegance of composition. I mean, these days, we just aim our phones and click. Post to some form of social media. Documentary visuals, that's all. Not like the masters, or like processing in a different key. You know about that, yes?

"Some."

"Fascinating to me. The dominant tones are high key or low key, like a piano keyboard; black keys the counterpoint to white. A major component of black and white composition."

"Have you always been interested in this?"

"I took a couple of classes. I gravitate to photographs in high key, like a snow-covered landscape, where the horizon is outlined subtly against the white, so the darker images, like trees, bleed into the lighter. The image appears eerie, but also more innocent."

"You're a good student."

"I thought I might understand Anna better."

"And?"

"I wonder if Anna is meant to be understood."

I had no response, Anna being, to my mind, a person to be admired, without understanding.

"Nudes tend to be photographed in higher key as well," Adrienne went on, "and even the most seductive nude seems virginal, have you noticed that?"

"Now that you mention it."

"I imagine you prefer photographs in a lower key."

"Why?"

"Accentuated reality."

"What makes you think that?"

"Something Anna must have said. You certainly don't seem to relish her existential chatter, or Tim's for that matter."

"I may not buy into it, but I try to keep an open mind."

"Not me," she said sharply, and I recalled how harsh she had been with Tim. "Take Anna's photograph of the young woman all dressed in black. The very air around that woman is intense. You can feel the birth of her sensuality. She absolutely cries out for attention, like the child in the posters to feed the hungry. A very effective technique."

The children in those posters are not so much starving, I might have said, rather languishing for lack of interest.

"And that other photograph she loves? I forget the photographer, shame on me. The one of an apple orchard after the harvest? Graceful branches stripped of their fruit, set against a nearly colorless sky? I'm sure you know it. As barren as a forest after a fire, and a very different depiction of harvest, as if Mother Earth the destroyer rather than giver of life."

"Odd," I said, "how the void of color in living things suggests death, while the absence of color in a photograph emphasizes life."

Adrienne did not respond, rather shook her head slowly, side to side, in that way that suggests confusion, or regret.

We parted at the hospital lobby and I went back to Anna's room. More than any other of the many emotions I experienced that day was apprehension. Fear of facing the future without Anna, fear of what she had asked of me, and the unforeseen terror of remaining buried in the past like a faded photograph, bereft of color or contrast.

I slept through the night fitfully and long past dawn, awakening just in time to wave good-bye to Beth and Will as they left for school. David was on the phone in the kitchen and pointed me to the coffee pot as he paced, nodding or shaking his head vehemently, as if the person on the other end of the conversation might interpret his body language. I slipped quietly into the kitchen, discovered the refrigerator empty of Diet Coke, poured myself half a cup of coffee, filled the rest with milk, sugar and ice cubes, and quickly moved into the dining area to sip cold caffeine, my preference no matter the season.

David hung up the phone and growled. "We've got system problems." He slugged the last of his coffee before pouring another cup into a sealed car mug with a black rubber casing and an aluminum rim. Like David, I thought: neat and functional.

"I have to go to the office, I'll meet you at the hospital as soon as I can."

"Can you drop me on the way?"

David looked at his watch. "I really need to get going," he said, eyeing my crumpled sleep shirt and boxers. "Call Henry, he'll drive you."

"Henry?"

"The taxi driver, Anna's favorite. She must have mentioned him. Quite the character."

"Oh yes, I remember," I said, glancing out the window, wishing for a city street to walk. David came toward me as he put on his jacket. "I'm sorry to take off, Nell. I just have to take care of this." He wrote down the phone number of the taxi service on a yellow post-it note by the phone. "Call ten or fifteen minutes before you're ready to go, he'll be here." Our eyes met for a moment and he might have seen the panic in mine. "Are you, will you be all right?" he sputtered.

"Yes, fine. Go. I'll see you later."

As soon as I heard the door slam behind David, I reached for a cigarette, wrapped myself in a throw blanket, and sat on the back patio inhaling smoke and morning air as if nourishment.

Soon after, and not long after the call, the taxi arrived and the driver called out to me as he pulled into the driveway.

"Sit up front, Miss," he entreated, as he reached over to push open the door. "I've got to deliver these packages downtown after I drop you off, didn't realize they were so big." He gestured toward two corrugated boxes that filled the rear seat.

I nodded and slipped in, the seat sagging noticeably under me like a feather pillow. The driver stared at me.

"To the hospital," I said.

"As soon as you buckle up. Buckle up for safety," he sang in a scratchy voice.

I fastened the seat belt as he released the hand brake. The radio was on, but so softly as to hardly be heard, and I turned my head to the window hoping to preempt conversation. Old men seem to hunger for dialogue, seizing an opportunity to talk to those who have no choice but to listen: at airports, on buses and trains, at the counter of a diner. I notice this on rare visits to Florida where there is a preponderance of older men who especially enjoy repartee with young women, as if momentarily plunged back in time to a romantic encounter.

"How's Anna?" the driver asked.

"Are you Henry?" I turned back to face him.

"The one and only," he pronounced as he navigated the car from the driveway to the street. "I drive dear Anna around now and then, you know, when the car is in the shop, when she's tired or just wants a little company. Yep, Anna and Henry, we're old friends."

I stared dumbfounded at this odd little man who spoke of Anna as if an intimate, although she had a tendency to adopt all sorts of characters and bring them into her orbit.

I turned to the window again and watched the houses as we made our way to town and I had the sensation, as I often do, that the vehicle was stationery and the landscape moved around us, like the images on the screen of an obstacle course in a video arcade. Henry drove quietly for a while down South Street and I thought I might have been spared any further conversation, but as soon as we turned onto Main Street, he launched into a monologue.

"We slaughtered hogs in the winter," he bellowed, the way older people speak when they can barely hear themselves. "On my grandmother's farm, right where the Carvel Ice Cream is now. Can you imagine? Right where Route 1 winds up to town, that was all farmland."

I turned to face craggy leathery skin and green eyes glistening in deep sockets. There wasn't a strand of hair on his head to soften his face, his dome gleaming as if polished, and a bulbous nose protruded all the more for lack of framing. He smiled broadly to reveal a few teeth missing among the yellowed remains, yet I saw clearly at that moment how handsome he must have been when he and the town were still young.

"We raised chickens and pigs, and when we slaughtered those pigs, absolutely nothing went to waste. Nothing. Not even the blood. I know, I know, sounds awful, but it was a good time. Good food. Good work. Good sleep. Yeah, you sleep real well when you put in a hard day's work. Of course the Great Depression hit us hard. I was just a tyke, but I knew what was going on, hard not to know. Back then, we were all in it together, you know? All together. The whole country. Every family here knew each other up and down these old roads, across open acres of farmland, at the country store. And here we are now, stuck in all this nasty traffic. Nobody hardly knows anybody any more."

He waved his hand toward the street in a grand sweeping gesture. I looked over at him and half-smiled, then turned my eyes back to the window.

"Anything you want to know about this town, you ask me," Henry said. "I'm just passed eighty now. Seen a lot of changes, and I know just about everyone, at least the people who are worth knowing. Anna has heard all my stories. She loves to learn the history, and Anna, she takes the time to know people."

He stared straight ahead, beyond the traffic. He might have been peering directly back in time, seeing only what was, whereas I saw nothing of interest beyond the mass of cars.

"How you holding up?" he asked and I turned to him in surprise. "I know," he said. "Not my business, you think." He smiled again. "The truth is, driving a taxi is like being a bartender. Everybody eventually tells you their business, whether they mean to or not. Anna used to check in with me when she was researching a story. Many a time she got the scoop from me. Yep, Anna and me, we're kindred spirits. Must have traveled together in another life, maybe a few I'd say, but you must know all about that," he said, his eyes twinkling.

I sighed with dramatic effect, tired of the talk, the wishful thinking that nothing ends and that people find each other again and again.

"I wish you could have seen it back then," he said, this time speaking more to himself than to me. "A beautiful place it was."

"It's a nice town," I responded.

"Oh, sure, and pretty high-falutin nowadays. Coffee bars, gelato shops, Apple store. Can't hardly afford to eat at restaurants. Used to be grain and feed stores. Dry goods, liquor, a few saloons, fruit stands, the mercantile. You could see clear down the main street, that's about when they named it Main Street, clear down to the water."

I listened lackadaisically, and as we pulled up to the hospital entrance, I reached into my purse searching for bills. I pulled out a $5 dollar bill.

"Enough?" I asked, and glanced more directly at Henry, realizing that he was the driver who had delivered me from the train station just days ago.

"My pleasure," he said, waving away the bill. "Any time you want to know more about this town, ask me," he said with pride, like a museum docent who stands at attention, ready to share details with the inquisitive. "I'm the keeper of history, the keeper of secrets." He winked.

"Thanks," I said as I pulled the handle on the door.

"Nice to meet you, Nell," Henry called to me.

As I ran up the steps and through the hospital's revolving door, I realized I had never introduced myself, and when I looked back, Henry was gone.

Maggie sat next to Anna reading to her. She was dressed in purple, head to toe, like the hyacinths in vases in the corridors, and with her golden hair, she might have made a spring bouquet. She held in her hands a book so old the binding was unraveled at the edges. I stood in the doorway listening to her voice, lilting and sweet.

"*How do you suppose I know about all these things that took place so long ago?*" she read. "*I don't. I'm only guessing about them. But there are different kinds of guesses. If I hold out my two closed hands and ask you to guess which one has the penny in it, that is one kind of a guess. Your guess might be right or it might be wrong. It would be just luck. But there is another kind of guess. When there is snow on the ground and I see tracks of a boot in the snow, I guess that a man must have passed by, for boots don't usually walk without someone in them. That kind of a guess is not just luck but common sense.*"

I was as attentive as a kindergarten child, fascinated by the strange text, and wondering what it was Maggie hoped to convey.

"*And so we can guess about a great many things that have taken place long ago, even though there was no one there at the time to see them or tell about them. Men have dug down deep under the ground in different parts of the world and have found there – what do you suppose?*" Here Maggie's voice turned into a question, the way a teacher speaks to a youngster. "*I don't believe you would ever guess. They have found the heads of arrows and spears and hatchets. The peculiar thing about these arrows and spears and hatchets is that they are not made of iron or steel, as you might expect, but of stone.*"

Maggie looked up over her reading glasses to Anna, and I too peered at Anna in the hope she might be smiling back. Despite our optimism, she remained inert; a tabula rasa on which Maggie's words might be imprinted.

Maggie turned back to the book and read again. "*I guess that's why they call it the Stone Age, don't you think?*" She laughed and when she noticed me, she laughed louder. "You must think I'm a lunatic."

I shook my head and smiled. "You read beautifully."

"Oh, it's this wonderful old book, I read it to each of the kids when they were little." She closed the cover and caressed the faded cloth. "It's called *A Child's History of the World*. It was first written in 1924, this is a later edition, published after World War II." She turned to the title page. "1951. And the last line reads..." She flipped to the last page. "*And so on – World without end – Amen*! That's it! I just love it. Every chapter covers a period in history. It starts at the very beginning of time, and goes through every age, every phenomenon, kings and prophets, wars and plagues. Packs quite a lot of detail into short chapters. Sort of an old-fashioned Twitter." She chuckled again. "Written so children can understand. They need to know what came before, you know? Gives them a sense of continuity. So, maybe, I mean, if Tim is right, if Anna is restoring herself in some way, maybe she needs to be reminded of her place in the timeline, especially right now, so she can return."

Tears sprang into Maggie's eyes, the rims instantly reddened, and she swiped her cheeks with the sleeve of her sweater before reopening the book and beckoning to me to look at the table of contents. "The chapter headings are so clever. The one I was just reading, about the Stone Age, it's called *Umfa-Umfa and Itchy-Scratchy*. Get it? Cave people! Just look at these titles. *The Puzzle Writers, The Tomb-Builders, Kings with Corkscrew Curls, A Light in the Dark Ages...*"

"Very clever."

Maggie nodded appreciatively. "The nurse said to talk to her, and I tried, but even I, if you can imagine, can't talk without someone talking back, not for long. So I thought reading might be better, and then I spent half the night trying to figure out what to read. A classic? *Jane Eyre*? *David Copperfield*? Hard enough to follow when you're awake! So I thought maybe something risqué, like *Lolita* or *Lady Chatterley*, but frankly, I couldn't imagine sitting here reading that kind of thing aloud." She giggled like a schoolgirl. "And then I thought about reading Nancy Drew to her. In fact, I dug out the first one, figured I would start at the beginning and go from there. We all read those, right? And when we read that series we were maybe nine, ten? Just at the age we thought we were hot stuff."

I nodded with a smile, charmed by Maggie's thought process, and my own memory of hunkering under blankets to finish one more episode in the life of the iconic girl-sleuth.

"I've had talks with Adrienne about this, this coming of age thing. My oldest, Gemma, I named her that so she would always feel like a jewel, she's twelve now. So hard for girls. Boys get taller, a bit of stubble on their chins, a little chest hair, a few muscles in their arms, their abs, they think they're cool. Their voices change, that's cool too. They just seem to grow into their manhood. But girls, they go through changes in fits and starts. They can't hide what's happening. They get fat, or they think they are. They bleed. Moods go wild. I remember it all so well, don't you?" She didn't wait for an answer. "Nancy Drew seemed invincible. Like maybe being a girl could be powerful, before reality sets in, before, well, before we seem not such hot stuff anymore." She sighed the sigh of disappointment but continued, inured to some extent to past hurts. "So I thought, I know this is a stretch, but I thought if I read Nancy Drew to Anna, she would feel powerful again. She would, like, surge up out of this state she is in and drive off in her little blue roadster. Triumphant!" Maggie raised her hand in a fist as a gesture of victory.

"So why the history book?"

"Well, I came across this one on the kids' bookshelves and realized Anna would see herself in any number of these chapters. I mean, she believes she was present at them all."

She turned and lifted a stray hair from Anna's forehead and tucked it back into place as if she were only adjusting an hors d'oeuvre to fit the plate. "I guess it doesn't really matter what we read to her. It's the sound of a familiar voice that matters. I used to read recipes to my kids when they were babies, what did they know?" She shrugged her shoulders. "Anyway, the only other books I have are cookbooks. I'll leave this one here, if you feel like reading."

"Thanks."

She stood and came so close to me I instinctively stepped back. "How are you?" she inquired, peering into my eyes inquisitively.

"All right."

"It's so good you're here."

"Where else would I be?"

"I don't mean for Anna, I mean, well, yes, of course it's good for Anna, but also for you. No good to be alone at times like these. Better to be with family." She kissed me on the cheek and gathered her things. "I've got shopping to do. I'll be back at lunch, and we'll have our dinner tonight. I'm glad we'll be together, but you're going to be guinea pigs. I'm testing recipes."

"Lucky for us."

"Well, at the very least there will be plenty. See you later."

Maggie disappeared down the hall and seemed to take the little bit of warmth in the room with her. Even so, I wondered if perhaps there might be a downside to over-stimulation and, as I needed a bit of quietude for my own sanity, I selfishly sat in silence, staring alternately at Anna and out the window toward the barren tree. A nurse dropped in, nodding politely to me while talking to Anna as she checked monitors, and nodding again before disappearing. Around noon, Tim stopped by and read the newspaper to Anna while I fled to the smoking area, eavesdropping on the chatter of nurses who puffed in sync as they complained about one indignity or another. On my way back, I noticed that Maggie had left sandwiches for us, which David gobbled at once. Adrienne too devoured a sandwich when she made a brief stop to review the chart before speaking with the floor nurse. Will came by after practice.

Between visits, in the occasional moments alone with Anna, I scanned the history book to decide what chapters I might like to read. The contents were a delineation of firsts: first life forms, first weapons, first gods and emperors, philosophers and demons, and the discoveries that define humanity.

"How about you become the first photographer to come out of a coma in the Telemetry Unit of this hospital?" I announced to Anna. "What do you say? We like firsts."

I thought about all our firsts together. The first chance meeting at the maternity ward. The first play date with the children. The first afternoon browsing an exhibit at the International Center for Photography. The first dinner with our husbands, the first Christmas, the first photography hunt, the first family weekend at the beach. The first time I looked up after those early days and nights of grieving to discover Anna there. The first day I left the apartment, my legs wobbling like a young colt. The first client project I completed as a graphic designer, after which Anna came to celebrate with a bottle of wine, a fresh baguette and chunks of cheeses, which we ate and drank every bit of until we thought we might explode. The first Wednesday.

Is this all that remains? Photographs and firsts? Memories created, captured in photographs or stored in cranial memory centers like canned goods in the basement? Is it all in the end random and unforeseen, or is it, in truth, part of a grand plan?

No point to speculation, and, torn from my comfort zone for a time, I suspected I had already lost what little perspective I had.

I opened the book to the marker to read the last passage in the chapter on the Stone Age. I discovered that the book was not only about firsts, but also lasts, the two irrevocably connected. All that mattered, in the end, was the time between, as Anna prompted us so often.

"But I have only told you part of the story. The cave would have been cold and damp and dark, with only the bare ground or a pile of leaves for a bed. There would probably have been bats and big spiders sharing the cave with you... For breakfast you might have had some dried berries or grass-seed or a piece of raw meat, for dinner the same thing, for supper still the same thing. You would never have had any bread or milk or griddle-cakes with syrup, or oatmeal with sugar on it, or apple pie or ice cream. There was nothing to do all day long but watch out for wild

animals…And then some day your father, who had left the cave in the morning to go hunting, would not return, and you would know he had been torn to pieces by some wild beast, and you would wonder how long before your turn would come next."

We never made it to Maggie's for dinner as Anna's sister, Karen, arrived at last from California.

"I can't sit here any longer waiting for Anna to be roused from this nightmare," she told David when she finalized her plans, as if an admonishment to the rest of us for not attending properly to her sister. Karen is self-congratulatory enough to believe she alone might lure Anna back to consciousness as she once coerced her little sister into tea parties or teenage pranks.

She had reluctantly parked her two adolescent children with their father and new stepmother and snagged a seat on a flight that would route her through Chicago into the nearby Westchester County airport, where she expected David to meet her.

Will spent the afternoon cloistered in his room, consumed, he said, with schoolwork. Beth fled for play rehearsal, a granola bar in hand and a fresh coat of blush on her cheeks, after she'd taken a call in the den in the flirty giddy voice an adolescent girl uses only with a crush. She called later to say she would be spending the night with a friend and would see her aunt the next day. Perhaps the play held more than thespian appeal.

Maggie, capable of disappointment but not recrimination, delivered a steaming paella in an iron pan overflowing with orange rice, chunks of vegetables and seafood, tossed with herbs and olives and accompanied by crusty bread, mixed greens, and a bottle of wine. "Got to eat, darlings," she said as she plopped the food on the counter and waved good-bye.

The spicy aroma was intoxicating and I could barely refrain from diving into the meal at that moment. My appetite had improved considerably because of Maggie's cuisine, as if I had subsisted on gruel for years.

David left a message he would collect Karen and stop by the hospital, so when Will followed the scent of paella down the stairs, we sat at one corner of the long pine table to feast. Will filled his plate to overflowing, his teenage body starved for nourishment at all times, while I slowly savored the mix of flavors. Now and then he glanced at me, a smidgeon of tomato dangling from the edge of his mouth or chin and, as if reading my eyes, wiped his face haphazardly with a napkin that would forever hold the stain of this dinner as well as those before.

"Know anything about trees, Will?" I asked.

"Sure."

"Really?"

"If you didn't think I knew anything about trees, why did you ask?"

"Good point." I smiled.

"What do you want to know?"

"Well, I noticed this tree, outside Anna's window…"

"Here?" he pointed his fork to the side of the house, beyond the master bedroom.

"No, at the hospital."

"What about it?"

"Well, it was tall, mature I suppose you would say, with a thick trunk and pointed branches, you know, one of those old trees that seems refined and orderly, but when you look at it from a bit of distance, seems more like a painting by Pollack or Kandinsky."

"I don't get modern art."

"Not the best comparison."

"But I get what you mean. Lots of trees like that, especially old ones. Like rivers that wander beyond their embankments into, what are they called? Oh yeah, tributaries. A little like those Etch A Sketches we drew when we were little."

"I remember those."

"You can scribble like that on my phone, but mine always look like a Rorschach test."

I chuckled and took another mouthful of paella.

"So what do you need to know about this tree? Like, why is it important?"

"Well, most of the trees in view from that window were budded, some of them leafing, but this one looked, almost, dead…" I stumbled over the word.

"Barren?" Will asked, also uncomfortable with my choice of words.

"Yes, barren, like it wasn't going to come back from the winter. Didn't seem to fit with the other trees, out of place somehow."

"Maybe an ash."

"Ash?"

"Yeah. Lots of them around here. In the olive family, I think. A favorite of the gods."

"Ash," I murmured.

"Symmetrical, the leaves I mean. They bloom later. In fact, they look, like, lifeless, way past when all the other trees are coming back."

"Sounds right."

"They use the wood for baseball bats. Really solid, but you can shape it. Maybe that's why they take so long to leaf, maybe they draw their strength, you know, like, through the bark. Takes longer, but ends up stronger."

He smiled at his rhyme, as he munched another generous mouthful.

"When did you become so interested in trees?" I asked.

"I think when we lived in Manhattan. We were always playing in the park. I was just a little guy then and the trees were so tall, gigantic to me. Like superheroes. Towering. Mighty. Superman or the Incredible Hulk." He grinned sheepishly at his confession.

"I remember the Halloween costumes."

"Yeah, but the trees were even more awesome to me. Almost holy."

"And now you can identify them? Know their names, their families?"

"Did you ever notice all the streets here are named for trees? Elm, Spruce, Maple, Oak. Walnut, Sycamore. They even extend the names, like Mapletree Drive, Oakwood Lane. I'm surprised they didn't go all the way to Norway Maple and Sugar Maple." Will snagged another portion of paella. "You know Mom, she makes everything a lesson. We read the street signs wherever we walked, then tried to find the tree to match the name. I think we took out every book in the library about trees. And I think she saw them as sort of superheroes too."

"How do you mean?"

"Like an elder or a spirit. Protecting the earth, keeping the air clean. She goes crazy when people take down trees. Every time someone in this town clears land to make room for an addition or a pool, I swear, Mom gets so mad, you can see the steam coming out of her ears. One of the only things that makes her mad." He chortled. "She really simmers."

Will wiped his mouth and sat back. "Sometimes she cries. Really. I hardly ever saw my mother cry, but she cried for the trees. Last year, she took amazing photos of a bunch of trees that were marked for cutting, you know, with the red band around the trunk."

"Red band?"

"The town puts a red band around trees that have to come down. To make sure they cut down the right tree, I guess. Anyway, she was carrying on about it at dinner one night and the next morning, at sunrise, she drove around town and took pictures of all the trees with the red bands and all the stumps of trees that had already been cut down. One tree nearly drove her mad, a huge maple, maybe two hundred years old, near the library. She made Tim publish an article about it, and she played with the processing so the trees and the landscape were black and white, but the bands were bright red, like blood. The old maple made the front page. In some of the close-ups the red band looked like an armband on a Nazi soldier. Tim titled it Arbor Fascism."

"I missed that story."

"And she's right. I mean, when people buy a house, they buy the property, but only for a while. Like, they don't really own that property, not forever. Trees belong to all of us. Trees are like life. I mean, we can't live without trees, not people, not birds or insects. A tree is a whole ecosystem. Take down trees, we're cooked."

A flush moved from his neck to his cheeks and his voice grew strident. "She's right you know. And that whole night after she photographed the trees, Mom muttered over and over again, 'How are we supposed to breathe?'"

Will sat very still as the color faded from his face.

"I didn't mean to get so loud," he apologized.

"Impassioned. A nice kind of loud."

"I have homework," he said, rising to clear the table.

"I'll clean up," I replied. "Thanks for the dendrology lesson."

"Sure," he answered as he trudged back to the sanctuary of his room.

I placed the paella in the oven to keep warm and washed and dried our dishes before folding myself on the couch in the Common with a cup of chamomile tea. I replayed the dinner discussion in my mind, contemplating the future of the ash tree as if my own. Anna as important to me as trees to the ecosystem.

How am I supposed to breathe?

I must have dozed off and snapped awake when Karen plopped herself on the edge of the couch, the ripples of her weight as startling as a bad dream. I heard David fussing in the kitchen, unwrapping hot crinkled foil and cursing at the steam that singed his fingers.

"Nell kept the dinner warm. Come and eat," he called.

My eyes met Karen's. "Hi," I said.

"Long time no see."

"How was your flight?"

"Exhausting, and then I saw my sister."

"How is she tonight?"

"Awful, just awful. I can't believe this."

Strips of mascara streaked her cheeks and her eyes were blotchy. She smelled faintly of a fine perfume, Chanel or Odalisque, a fragrance for women who want to be noticed.

Karen patted my feet as she rose to join David for dinner. I was struck by the gravity of her demeanor. No diatribe. No ballistic remarks. The sight of Anna in a coma must have been more than even her declamatory personality could endure.

"Come," she instructed.

"I've eaten."

"Sit with us."

"In a minute," I said, needing to brace myself.

Karen and Anna are as different as sisters can be – Anna the lithe stallion, Karen a cheetah: shorter, squatter, and frequently ferocious. Her eyes are large and oval like Anna's, but dark, with eyebrows severely arched and chin rounded like a child's drawing of an adult. Her brown hair is always fashionably cut, and never beyond the nape of her short neck, with auburn highlights increasingly prominent over time. Large diamond stud earrings adorn her ears, and that night, several necklaces embedded with colorful stones hung from her neck. On her right ring finger she wears a large square diamond, her former engagement ring. She is always fashionably dressed and accessorized, from red leather belts to high-heeled boots, although she is quick to say she found this on sale and that at Target for pennies on the dollar. When the dollars add up, she whines about insufficient alimony.

A realtor before marriage, she chose to stay home with her children for over a decade, dabbling now and then only to retain her license. After a vitriolic divorce three years ago, she joined a prestigious agency in Palo Alto, not only for the financial security, she told Anna, but for the opportunity to match elegant habitats to affluent clients, and, in that way, influence their destiny. I often wondered if she chose this wording to rebuke Anna, whose Buddhist philosophy she does not share.

"Join us," Karen called to me and I rose from my comfy sprawl to the kitchen.

"Any change?" I asked David as he forked into his food as hungrily as his son.

"Nothing, not a thing."

"She looks like an angel," Karen said, and we all held our breaths for a second at the thought. "Something has to be done."

"I think we are doing, and the doctors are doing, all they can, as I explained," David mumbled as he tore off a chunk of bread and slathered it with butter. "We have to be patient."

"Maybe, but the truth is, you know, he who hesitates…"

"I would prefer to think that patience is a virtue."

"Not one of mine," Karen answered. "Nor yours either, brother-in-law."

I smiled to myself. Karen goes beyond impatient to irascible. She begins every other sentence with "the truth is" and frequently arrives at what she calls "the bottom line" long before the discussion suggests a conclusion. She rarely stops talking to listen, exhausting her companions by the constant punctuation of her commentary with sarcasm laced with rage, or misery, and whatever the conversation, she brings it back to what ails her.

"You have to hover over these doctors day and night," Karen garbled through a mouthful of salad. "American medicine is in the dumpster. You cannot rely on physicians to do what is best for a patient anymore. The bottom line is, they don't care about Anna; we do. We must be her medical advocates."

David dug his fork into the plate perhaps more forcefully than he intended, the clang startling and emphatic, although he did not directly answer the reproach. They ate their last bites in silence, David chomping, Karen nibbling with little enthusiasm.

"What could we do?" I asked and David looked at me in surprise.

"I've been reading everything I can get my hands on and there are some experimental medications, maybe herbal alternatives or physical therapies we should look into," Karen proclaimed. "Treatment alternatives Anna would prefer."

David sat back in his chair. "You surprise me, Karen, seeking the unconventional route."

"Any port in the storm."

"Hmm." David gulped his last forkful of food. "I've got calls to make."

"I'll clean up," Karen said, perhaps to make amends.

I sat at the table as Karen made small talk and ate a few more bites. When she rose to clear the table and rinse the dishes, I wrapped the leftovers for Will's breakfast.

"As I recall, you are a night owl, right?" Karen asked.

"As a rule, although we get going early around here."

"But I am still on California time. Want to have a drink somewhere?"

"There's more wine," I answered, pointing to the rack.

"I'd rather go out. I'm too fidgety, I need a diversion. Don't you?"

"It's more comfortable here."

Karen groaned and snatched a bottle of cabernet, scanning the label before she pulled the cork. She grabbed a stem glass from the overhead cupboard.

"I hate hospitals," she muttered, as she poured the dark red wine into the glass and swished it around aggressively. She held the bottle up in my direction.

"No, thanks."

"Gruesome places."

She marched into the Common, expecting me to follow, which I did, although my inclination was to flee, and she flopped onto one end of the couch, dropping her shoes on the floor with a thud and stretching out her legs as far as they would go, leaving little room for me. Her toenails were as red as the wine. I sat on one of the oversized chairs beside the couch.

"I'd rather see her in hospice." She looked up at my incredulous expression. "What?"

"Hospice is for the terminally ill, I thought."

"All I meant was that a hospital is not always the best place for the holding pattern she is in. Too easy to fall between the cracks. Hospitals these days are dangerous. This one calls itself a Wellness Center, did you notice? As if they're really in the business of making people well. Hah! The truth is, they're in the business of doing the least possible for the least possible time so they can realize the full return on every patient and justify every penny they jack out of insurance companies. Most hospitals are so busy marketing themselves, I'm not sure they are even in the business of medicine anymore."

"Honestly, Karen, Anna gets a lot of attention. Adrienne watches over her as well. The place is state of the art. There just doesn't seem to be a whole lot to be done."

Karen sipped wine so slowly and silently she made me even more uncomfortable than I generally am in her presence.

"Please," she pleaded, bolting upright. "I cannot stay here right now. I get cranky when I fly. And I keep expecting my sister to walk into the room. Don't make me go out alone."

I reneged. Karen brushed her hair and applied a coat of lipstick before grabbing the keys to Anna's car, and within moments we were on the short drive into town.

"Do you have any idea where you're going?"

"I know how to get to Main Street, must be some sort of saloon there."

I checked to make sure my seat belt was tightly fastened and gripped the edges of my seat so tightly Karen laughed.

"I'm from California, we're drivers. I'll get us there and back in one piece."

Karen zipped the car into the first available spot, which happened to be in front of a cafe named The Grill, and when she peeked in the window she raised her thumb to me exultantly.

"Perfect," she announced as she flung open the door.

We were greeted by soft lighting, a low din, and an adolescent hostess who waved her arm toward the bar tables when Karen told her we were there only to drink. One long exposed brick wall matched terra cotta stained concrete floors, and dark wooden bar stools with red leather seats echoed the banquettes opposite, illuminated by hanging lamps with low wattage.

"It was a fire station a hundred years ago," the waiter recounted in a monotone voice, weary of the required commentary.

"A little like a New York neighborhood joint," I answered.

"If only," he answered. "What can I get you?"

Karen ordered a bottle of red wine for us both, as if I were a fledgling sorority sister in need of sophistication. Within seconds, the young waiter dutifully presented the bottle to ensure that the label was to Karen's liking and pulled the cork with surprising ease, pouring a sip into her glass for tasting before filling our glasses.

Karen clinked my glass to toast, without speaking, her eyes perusing other patrons as though she expected to encounter someone familiar.

"I think we've been here before with the kids," she commented. "You?"

"I don't recall."

She sipped again. "There's a guy checking us out at the bar," she reported with a smile. "Not sure which of us, maybe both."

I turned reflexively to look.

"Oh, very smooth, Nell. I can see you're out of practice."

I bristled. "Tim Wolfe," I said, as he raised his beer glass toward us.

"Anna's boss?" She looked up to meet his gaze. "She never mentioned how attractive he is. Only that he showed up from nowhere and got the paper into shape."

She waved him over and Tim pulled up a chair.

"Karen, I presume?" he asked, extending his hand.

"The one and only," she answered, holding his hand a moment longer than one might expect, and I noticed that Tim seemed touched by the gesture, like a young boy grateful for a bit of kindness at a school dance.

"When did you arrive?"

"Hours ago. Had to be here, of course, just took a bit of scheduling."

"Of course. And how are you doing tonight, Nell?"

I nodded without answering.

"Glad you stopped by, it's a friendly neighborhood place," Tim said.

"Any friend of Anna's is a friend of mine," Karen smiled.

Karen and I sipped our wine, Tim his beer, the ambiance settling over us like a warm fire on a cold night.

"Ironic that Anna would be in a coma, don't you think?" Karen observed, and without waiting for an answer, she went on. "The ultimate paradox, my sister. I mean, really, isn't it just like her to conveniently drop out while the rest of us are mystified? The one who usually has all the answers kind of left us in the lurch, didn't she?"

She gulped the wine and poured a refill. "The absent-minded professor," she muttered and sat back against the padded banquette. With the hand not gripping the wine glass, Karen anxiously rubbed her thumb over the edge of each of her dark red nails from the pointer to the pinkie then back again, as if buffing the tips.

"That's what my sister is. Wacky and brilliant, all at once. She was ready to argue capital punishment when she was fourteen. She can quote Proust and Plato and expound on mythology at the drop of a hat. She was always delighted to debate existentialism over brownies and ice cream, and while she was still in high school, she engaged my college friends in her discussions of destiny. But ask her what day it is or what time or where she is supposed to be? Not a clue."

I smiled and noticed out of the corner of my eye that Tim too was smiling. Yes, Anna might be seen as an absent-minded professor, the type whose class is always full.

"She watches the world and takes gorgeous photographs…well, you know better than anyone, don't you?" Karen asked Tim, again without waiting for an answer. "You would think, I mean, it would seem, she sees the same world she photographs, but I wonder what she sees. What was she looking at the other day? How could she miss a truck coming right at her?"

I interjected. "She might have been looking at a tree."

"A tree?" they responded in unison.

"At dinner tonight, Will mentioned an old tree she was enamored of, near the library. I don't know if it was in her line of sight, or even if it's still there, but maybe she was looking for that tree. I, I don't know," I stammered. "It's a stretch, and we won't know for sure until she wakes up to tell us."

"She did a great piece on trees last year," Tim said.

"Arbor Fascism," I said, as if I'd seen the piece.

Tim smiled and nodded.

Karen stared at us both for a moment with an expression of exasperation. "A tree," she muttered. "Well, that would explain it, of course. My crazy sister, no cause for concern because her destiny is resolute. Why not just step off the curb and tempt fate? Makes me want to scream."

Karen sipped more wine and shifted her position to lift her legs under her on the seat like a child. She had dropped her shoes to the floor. "Where the hell was she going anyway?"

"No one seems to know," I said.

"Figures." She sighed. "Anna's journey to enlightenment, what a joke."

"Why is that a joke?" Tim asked.

"Because she is the most enlightened person on earth. That's what I am trying to tell you. She is my little sister, but she always knew more than me, more than anyone I knew. She was born enlightened. So while we all struggle to make a life, she has the secret to some sort of inner peace that she has had from day one, and she ends up flat out on a hospital bed breathing through tubes. Does this make any sense?"

Karen poured more wine into my glass, despite my raised hand in protest, and topped off her own glass.

"Can we smoke in here?" she asked, knowing the answer.

I shook my head, wanting a cigarette but refusing to confess my own jitters. Tim grabbed a candle from the table adjacent and placed it on our table. "Breathe in a little smoke, it helps."

"A fellow smoker? I know Nell is guilty," Karen said.

"Just a fond remembrance for me," Tim answered.

Karen swept her palms over the candles to pull the smoke toward her before leaning back again. "I'm a bit pissed," she giggled. "I'm pissed in more ways than one. I had wine on the plane as well." She stared at her glass, swirling the wine into concentric circles like the stirrings of a tsunami. "Just like Anna to ignore her responsibility to the rest of us. The truth is, she has been stepping off the curb to challenge the fates all her life."

Tim watched her, silently, like a psychiatrist or a priest, while I focused on steady breathing, longing to hide.

"She just expects all of us to fall in line, accept her reality as our own, and we are supposed to idolize her because she never gets angry and she's always there for us and she is so goddamned mellow all the time that we know for sure she has it right and we don't. I mean, if you relinquish your whole life to fate, you are by definition not responsible for your actions. When you think about it, she's just like a man that way."

I was unable to restrain a smile. Karen never passes up a chance to malign men, men as an extension of her ex-husband Philip, who represents the species badly. Whenever I've been with her, conversations invariably disintegrate into a diatribe about men. She begins with Philip, who, she laments, with some justification, betrayed her trust, abandoned his children, and, the ultimate travesty, married the younger lover. From this, commentary expands to men as a breed, uniformly defined by the same values, or the lack of.

"No offense," she added for Tim's benefit.

"None taken."

"They're having a baby, did you know?"

"Who?" I asked.

"Philip and Felicia," she pronounced with disdain, impatient with my ignorance. "Sounds like a ballroom dance duo. Can you imagine? He's fifty; she's thirty-five. He's got two kids he still needs to spend time with, and now he's starting over? Recycled fathers they call them. Recycled my ass. That would suggest they had fulfilled their purpose the first time, highly debatable, and have residual value in the world, like glass or plastic. Hardly! Oh," she whimpered. "I need to get past this, I know, but how the hell does that happen when his life is in my face every single day? And now, Anna in a coma! Damn."

I nodded with compassion, understanding more than most her inability to move on, although I found the wallowing at that moment hard to take. Tim made eye contact but said nothing, and I was suddenly more conscious of the low pitch of homogenized chatter that wafted around us with the candle smoke, which should have been soothing but rattled my nerves in light of Karen's rancor.

"She reminded me of my mother today," Karen grumbled. "My mother might as well not be there either, although at least her eyes are open. Alzheimer's is like a waking coma. Eyes open or closed, neither of them conscious." She looked up at Tim, then at me, her eyes beseeching, her body language suddenly less forbidding. "I've never felt so alone in all my life."

Tim reached out to touch her hand and she grabbed his and clung to it like a plank of wood on the open sea.

"I've come to accept Mom's condition. I might even accept my divorce one of these days. But my sister? Maybe the most important person in my life, even though we don't see each other often enough, but we talk, every week, sometimes more. The only connection to my childhood, the only connection to me, I mean, the person I thought I was, the person maybe I was, before…" She inhaled and exhaled heavily, the long day, the wine, the anxiety, threatening to turn her into a simpering child. "She is the only human being on earth who loves me unconditionally. Even my kids look at me differently now, as if I've failed them." She began to weep, her lips quivering dramatically, and abruptly let go of Tim's hand to rummage through her purse for a tissue. "We have to do something!"

"All we can do is be there, every day, as she has been for us," I said.

"Talk to her," Tim added. "She'll know you're there."

"I know, I know." Karen wiped her face and blew her nose loudly.

"Excuse me a moment," Tim said as he stood to greet a couple at the bar.

Karen leaned toward me conspiratorially. Her voice dropped a tone and her breath was sour with wine. "Do you think Tim's right? I mean, about waiting Anna out? David told me what he said. He's another enigma that one. Nice looking, and a good enough boss, I suppose. I've never heard Anna complain, although she wouldn't, would she? Do you think he makes any sense? Think she is, you know, taking a breather? Was she upset about something? She's not sick or something, is she? My God, maybe…" Karen's voice turned louder and more strident.

"Karen, I don't know of anything wrong with Anna. She would have told me."

She grimaced. "You think she would have told you but not me?"

"That's not what I meant. It's just that I was with her last week, she seemed fine."

Karen lifted the candle, peering into the flame; her hands shook ever so slightly.

"Maybe it was just a stupid tree," I said, hoping to ameliorate her misery. "That would be just like her."

Karen nodded. "Yes. Just like her."

Tim returned to the table. "Sorry, the mayor. Always have to check in with him. He asked about Anna, by the way. Everyone is wishing her well."

He studied us in turn, realizing the conversation had come to an end.

"We all need some sleep. May I drop you?" he asked, and I was grateful for the closure.

"We drove," Karen answered.

"Perhaps…" I started to say, uneasy with Karen's inebriated state.

"I'm fine," she said with startling acuity. "I can get us home, don't fret."

Tim turned to me. "I don't drive," I admitted.

He raised his hand and called for the check, which he insisted on paying. "I'll drive you home. Just pick up the car in the morning before nine, when the meters kick in."

"Good idea," I answered with relief.

When Karen objected, we both shrugged her off. Even she was too tired to argue and leaped into the front seat of Tim's car as if she were on a date as I climbed into the back and mouthed the words thank you through the rear view mirror.

After Tim dropped us off, Karen and I smoked a cigarette in the driveway before stepping into the house where she collapsed on the couch, folding herself into the pillow cushions and flopping around to get comfortable like a fish out of water.

"I know I have to find closure," she whimpered. "How will I ever do that without Anna? I need my sister. She cannot leave me alone with all this."

My back suddenly spread out like an alley cat. How dare she slump into self-pity? She has two children, a husband who may be an ex-husband but still alive, and plenty of life in her if she would only look forward. I could not at that moment bear the self-indulgence.

"Just find your own way," I groused, surprised at my interjection into a losing argument. "All you can do is accept your losses, and your limitations. You think one last farewell is all it takes? *Good night sweet Prince, parting is such sweet sorrow.* This isn't Shakespeare. There is no end to this play."

Karen stared at me in shock. "I'm sorry, Nell. I guess I struck a nerve."

I stood to escape to the den but Karen grabbed my hand.

"Really, it's the wine. Mea culpa."

I turned back to her. "I'm not sure there is closure when you lose your life. Not closure, just whatever follows."

"So who gives your life back?" she asked.

"No one gives anything back."

Karen sobbed again, a drunken pathetic weeping for which I had no patience. Closure? Closure is merely a concept created to force people to conform to a generally accepted pattern of behavior. An artificially constructed timeline to which we are meant to adhere. Some of us cannot fall in line. We absorb our losses like water spilled on a scorched summer sidewalk, the longing stored under the surface as if another subcutaneous layer meant to slowly wither with age. Time is not closed-end. Time is neither the measure of love nor the measure of destiny. Each of us merely a tree: barren or flowering or felled.

Some time in the middle of the night, Karen slipped into my bed and pressed her back against mine as she pulled the quilt to her shoulders for warmth. I awakened with a start and jumped up, wrapped myself in the spare blanket and slowly eased down the dark hall to the couch. I slid into a hard sleep and awoke as morning light filtered into the Common to find Beth seated beside me.

"Why did you sleep here?" she inquired.

"Karen commandeered the den," I answered as I sat up, and then collapsed back against the cushions, bones achy and stiff, the stale taste of Karen's acrimony still in my throat. Had I been at home I would surely have turned over and shut down.

"You could have slept in my room, on the rollaway."

"Rollaway?"

"Under my bed, we keep it there for sleepovers. I'll make it up for you for tonight."

"Thanks." I sat up. "Are you sleeping home tonight?"

"Not sure yet."

I searched for sunlight through the tall windows that bordered the room, but glimpsed only the first shadows of morning bouncing off the lower branches of trees. I found myself wondering what type of trees they were.

"What time is it?" I asked Beth.

"Ten or so."

"Why are you home?"

"It's Saturday, although I have play rehearsal, actually, right now," she said, glancing at her watch with alarm. "I'm late." She rose to go.

"When are you going to see Mom?"

"Later."

There was more than a hint of disinterest in Beth's voice. I had noticed it before. Or was it that I rarely saw her at Anna's bedside. She seemed to come and go at the very moments I was on the back stairs smoking, having coffee with Adrienne, or gaping at trees.

I pulled on jeans and crept into the kitchen where David and Will were munching on waffles. A large pool of syrup sat on Will's plate, perfect for dunking. Freshly brewed coffee smelled better than usual, so I poured myself a cup.

"Morning," I mumbled and they mumbled back, their mouths filled with breakfast.

"Up late?" David asked.

"No more than usual."

"I guess Karen is on California time," David commented, acknowledging Karen's absence. He and Will had scheduled a few rounds of tennis, he said, and would come to the hospital in the afternoon. In response to my expression of surprise, he remarked in an unusually terse tone of voice that after long days of bedsitting they needed to work off steam on the court.

Tenacity may be the most essential quality of a builder, beyond vision or skill, and Anna occasionally cited David's tenacity by referring to his astrological sign: Taurus. The bull. Resolute, indefatigable and yes, frequently obdurate. However, all the tenacity and vision in the world are inconsequential when patience and compassion are required.

Anna too might have been described as persistent, in her way. Perhaps she too often looked only ahead. More acute peripheral vision might have saved her life. Perhaps the steadfast adherence to destiny is its own deterrent, I thought. So much so that an out-of-control truck compromised her spiritual path. Or was that too destiny?

My brain ached from trying to make sense of it all and I sat down at the table to rest my head on my arms while I awaited Karen, who emerged soon after David and Will took off. She trudged into the kitchen in a pink rumpled T-shirt and purple plaid boxers, pale and dehydrated, chugging multiple glasses of water from the fresh water barrel on the counter, droplets scattering down her chin as she glugged. She poured herself the last of the coffee, took two sips and tipped it into the sink with a moan before turning to me.

"The Bucks," she muttered.

"On the way to the hospital, I guess."

She nodded. "First a shower, I won't take long." Her words dissipated with her as she sprinted down the hall toward the master bedroom's larger shower.

I was in and out of the guest bathroom and dressed before Karen had even toweled off, so I slipped out the side door for a morning smoke, eavesdropping on a tirade of chirping from a flock of small birds flittering around an ornamental cherry tree teeming with pink buds. Their behavior was mesmerizing: blind instinct decidedly blissful.

Karen finally emerged wearing a tight-fitting sweater over slim-fit jeans that hugged her girlish figure, hair styled, make-up applied, and last night's sparkly jewelry replaced with a simple silver pendant. She glanced reprovingly at my frumpy black T-shirt and plain jeans. As she trotted down the hall to search for the car keys, we simultaneously realized the car was on Main Street.

Karen dug out the keys from her bag and shrugged her shoulders. "I'll call a cab."

"The number is on a post-it in the kitchen."

As Karen made the call, I noticed the keys to the darkroom on the hook and decided that some time soon I would slip into the sanctuary. Perhaps chemicals needed to be drained or a photo rescued from its alkaline bath. Certainly I would not be invading Anna's privacy, not much privacy to be had at a time like this. And I might discover the last facet of the jewel that is Anna – perhaps a message to assist her recovery or to assuage my guilt over failing to present myself as her proxy.

Moments later, we stepped outside as Henry pulled up.

"Welcome, Karen," he called out the window. "Good morning, Nell."

Karen laughed. "Henry, you old coot, how nice to see you." She scrambled into the back seat. "To Main Street, please. Starbucks. Don't spare the horsepower."

"Buckle up," I instructed Karen as I climbed in, eliciting a grin that spread from Henry's parched lips to his bulbous eyes.

Karen traded small talk with Henry, who waved off our offer of coffee with thanks as he took off for his next assignment. With Starbucks coffee cup in hand, Karen drove to the hospital, where she eased into a cavernous underground parking area. We circled three levels until we found a spot for Anna's Mini Cooper, what David referred to as her mid-life crisis car.

"The poor woman's sports car," Karen said as she zipped into a space marked for compacts. "Drives like a bumper car at an amusement park."

I remembered so well the day Anna acquired the car. Her ancient Honda, at 260,000 miles, had finally succumbed to age, jerking and sputtering each time she shifted gear. David had hounded her for years to drive a newer model, but Anna wouldn't hear of it.

That year she turned forty-four years old, a number she considered especially auspicious. She hosted a birthday party with giant balloons, a heavily spiked punch bowl with chunks of fruit floating in it, and a game of pin-the-tail-on-the donkey, which, after a few rum punches, was quite rowdy. At the cutting of Maggie's six-layer chocolate cake, Anna made the toast.

"Take this to heart, dear friends. Age is a prize, reserved only for the young at heart and the oldest of souls. We will be pals forever."

The next day, on her way to a photo shoot, she noticed brightly colored sale flags strung across the façade of the BMW dealership, and drove home that afternoon in a silver Mini Cooper with a black top, honking wildly to attract our attention. I was still there, having been pressured to linger a few days after the party, and we all stood at the front door astonished.

"What can I say?" she answered our incredulous faces. "I saw the signs!"

It was almost noon by the time Karen and I entered the hospital, where we ran into Tim at the elevator. "I'm glad you're here," he said, as if we were invited to an exclusive party.

Karen smiled. She glanced appreciatively at the length of his body, his rugged frame, and the broad shoulders beneath a corduroy jacket. "Nice to see you again so soon," she said, extending her hand, which Tim shook warmly. "Anna says the nicest things about you. Wish I had a boss like you."

Tim smiled as the elevator doors opened and he stepped aside to usher us ahead. Upstairs, as we made our way down the hall, Karen walked along with him, her hips nearly skimming his legs, and I followed slightly behind, so that as we entered the room, Karen in the lead, Tim had to turn to converse. "David around?"

"They'll be here a little later today."

"You're on duty?"

"If you want to see it that way."

"I have to get in early today, but maybe later we can chat."

I neither confirmed nor denied, not particularly interested in more existential banter, and walked ahead to the nurses' station for a posting on Anna's progress.

"How are you holding up?" the lead nurse asked.

"Holding," I answered. "How is she doing?"

"I checked her this morning. No change. Usually there is a little bit of variation, but Mrs. Miller's measures do not alter from day to day."

"Should they?"

"Not necessarily. No rules in these conditions. I just, she just..." The nurse wrestled with the words. "She seems so calm. Different from coma patients I've tended to. Not nearly as passive a pose as you see in the movies. But in this case, no deviation, statistical or anecdotal. It's like she's at rest, in the truest sense. Maybe more resigned than most. Hard to explain."

"Accepting," I explained to the nurse. "Not resignation, acceptance."

"Hmm," she mused. "What a rarity."

She smiled and resumed her paperwork as I made my way outside for a smoke. When I returned, Tim was gone.

"He said to tell you he'll catch you another time," Karen remarked as I entered the room. She sat in the chair next to the bed, pulled as close to Anna as possible. "You know him well?"

"Not at all."

"Anna doesn't mention him often."

"But you said…"

"Oh, well, seemed like the right thing to say. I wonder if he's been married? Probably screws around."

No answer was needed, clearly a rhetorical comment.

"He's quite attractive, don't you think? In that Marlboro Man kind of way."

"I hadn't noticed."

Karen peered at me. "Seriously?"

Not wanting to engage in that conversation, I changed the subject. "The floor nurse thinks Anna is completely at rest."

"Hmm. Wonder if she's dreaming. She used to tell me her dreams sometimes. I never remember mine, if I even dream. Made my shrink crazy."

She chuckled as she turned to take Anna's hand, and we sat for a few moments in silence, our own breathing nearly in sync with the respirator's steady ebb and flow.

"You know," Karen exclaimed, "Not sure why this popped into my head, but I was remembering when we were, I don't know, maybe ten and twelve, something like that, we were walking home from school one day, it was early fall, a little colder than expected, so we were hustling along to get warm, racing maybe. I always wanted to race home, actually fast walking, that was our rule, because her legs were so much longer, even then she had the advantage. Anyway, we were trotting down this residential street and suddenly this dog, this huge gray mongrel, I never was good at breeds, fangs fully exposed, blocks our way on the sidewalk. A broken chain leash hung off his collar, I swear he looked like a gang leader or something, and there was no one around, I mean not a soul, and we stopped dead in our tracks. He was growling at us, ready to pounce. A real standoff. Terrifying. Anna just stared at him. I remember I whispered to her, what should we do? And for a moment she didn't answer. Like she wasn't really there or something. Then she whispered, 'don't move.' I was shaking, not trembling, shaking like crazy, because I thought for sure we would be attacked. I remember wondering which one of us he would go at first. And then, suddenly, an older woman, a hag, the dog's owner as it turns out, charges out of the house and calls to him, sharply. 'Caesar, come!' And the mutt just turned and walked to her, tail wagging, incredibly docile. She grabbed his chain and led him around the house to the back. I fell down on the sidewalk. Literally! I couldn't stand I was so shaky. The woman came back and apologized, babbling that nothing like that had ever happened before, something about the leash stand giving way, yanked too often, blah, blah, blah. The bottom line was, she was negligent, I know that now, but then, I couldn't make any sense of what she was saying. I think I was really in shock. Anna stood there politely taking in what the woman had to say and told her we were okay. She made it all right. But it wasn't, not for me, and ever since, I cannot be around big dogs without feeling fearful. Here's the clincher: as we walked home that day, all Anna said to me was, 'it wasn't our time.' Can you imagine? She's a kid, and she's telling me it wasn't our time." Karen sighed, that unmistakable sigh of melancholy. "Oh, I almost forgot the best part. So Anna goes home, grabs her camera, her first good camera, my dad bought it for her birthday that year, oh yeah, that's right, she was ten, her tenth birthday. And went back to the house to ask permission to photograph the dog. Do you believe her? She took a whole role of film of this dog, chained in the backyard, growling at her the whole time. Yet, I don't know, in the pictures, the dog didn't seem so scary. He seemed lonely. Sad. You see things differently in Anna's photos, right? Anyway, she put all the pictures into a little album and printed by hand on a sticker on the front cover, *Beware the Dog*. Her first photographic essay."

Tears filled her eyes. "She really is something, my sister. I can't stand to look at her like this," she whimpered. "Maybe she's willing to accept this, but I can't. We have to do something. There's, like, no sense of urgency around here. Who's actually in charge?"

"The nurse will know. There's a resident, I can't remember his name, he's here every day. And the Chief of Staff, Adrienne has been in touch with him."

"That's who I need to talk to, Adrienne. There must be some sort of advanced treatment or intervention. We need to call in the cavalry."

I reached into my jacket pocket and pulled out Adrienne's card to hand to Karen, who whipped out her cell phone and stomped out of the room to find a quiet place to make the call.

I sat down in the chair and held Anna's hand. Temperature comfortably cool. Eyelids smooth, only an occasional ripple. Peaceful. I picked up Maggie's history book. The bookmark protruded at a chapter called *Blood and Thunder* having to do with the eruption of Vesuvius in 79 A.D, with a simplified description of the volcanic fires that destroyed Pompeii and its residents, stunned into sculptural remains for all time. And, as after all previous eruptions, the Romans erected a new city over the old, without knowing the remains of Pompeii lay intact below. Another place Jason and I had hoped to visit.

"*There are houses of the Romans who went there to spend their vacations,*" I read aloud. "*There are shops and temples and palaces and public baths and the theater and the market place or forum. The streets were paved with blocks of lava, once melted stone. They still show ruts, which were worn into them by the wheels of the chariots that the Romans used to drive. Stepping-stones were placed at some crossings, so that in case of heavy rains, when the streets were full of water, one could cross on them from curb to curb. These stepping-stones are still there. The floors of the houses were made of bits of colored stone to form pictures. They are still there. In the vestibule of one house, there is in the floor a mosaic picture of a dog. Under it are the Latin words, "Cave canem." What does that mean? Can you guess? It means, 'Look out for the dog!'*"

Karen returned at that moment just as the phone in her hand rang, loud and jarring. I dropped the book, startled in part by the sound, in part by the juxtaposition of Karen's childhood anecdote to the ancient message in the chapter on Pompeii.

Karen was talking to Adrienne, but staring at me.

"You're as white as a sheet," she said as she hung up. "Are you all right?"

"Fine, I was just reading, and I was startled by the phone."

"Are you sure?" She picked up and examined the cover of the book, then handed it back, without further inquiry.

"Yes. I'm sure."

In truth, I was not sure of anything, and less certain as time went by.

Another week passed, nearly two since the accident, the days repetitive and indistinguishable. Chitchat was all we could muster most of the time and each member of what Tim had dubbed Anna's clack, her cheering section, dealt with the situation in our own way, even as we melded into one entity with an increasing degree of despondency.

Karen was the most vociferous in her disappointment but, to her credit, she was equally persistent, determined to save her sister. She lobbied doctors by phone. She hounded them during morning rounds. She made contact with all the neurological physicians in the area, the Chief of Staff, even the infectious disease expert who, she insisted, was often the best source of "out of the box thinking." She pestered Adrienne to distraction about everything from unorthodox practices to rehabilitation options. She discovered from a naturopath that high potency compounds of vitamins B and C have been known to stimulate nerve cells and increase the blood supply to the brain, although only in patients who have emerged from the comatose state. When she argued for giving that a try, the physicians denied her on the grounds there was no comparable protocol for Anna's condition.

"Protocol" she sneered. "What's the point of protocol when someone doesn't fit any mold? What's to lose?"

David removed himself more and more from her queries, unwilling to deal with her bellicosity, or distress, which inflamed his own. How frustrating for the architect who can always find a stronger material, another bearing wall, a deeper foundation.

To my surprise, no one mentioned a living will. Each time a nurse or physician suggested a DNR, David dismissed them with a wave of his hand. All of them – her husband, her sister, her dearest friends – all assumed that Anna would not concern herself with legalities, preferring to allow destiny to manifest. I never spoke of it, instead cowering in their shadows, deferential and sympathetic, loath to betray myself as protector or obstructionist.

Under cover of silence at night, I lay awake deliberating what action to take. It was unthinkable that I should have found myself in a situation where I might have dominion over life and death. No one, not even those of us most battered by loss, can fathom what the end of life means, and I took consolation only in that I had fervently expressed my reluctance to be her proxy. On a more practical level, it seemed too soon to intervene. After all, people have been known to emerge from comas after months. Years sometimes. The situation was out of our control, and, in truth, I hoped whoever else knew of the existence of the living will would eventually come forward and absolve me of confession.

I convinced myself that Anna's fate lay not in artificial respiration or liquid food drips or alternative treatments, but in the realization of something beyond our comprehension. Perhaps, as Tim had suggested, she was internally restoring herself, waiting for a signal from a higher power. Or, as the thought too frequently slipped into my mind, despite her steady breathing and even body temperature, perhaps she was already gone.

Sunday morning, Karen awakened early and went from room to room like a town crier exhorting everyone up for church. Beth had slept out again and wasn't home. Will reluctantly agreed, and David, coffee cup already in hand, seemed eager for the comfort of community.

Half asleep on the rollaway in Beth's room, I murmured regrets, as I had the previous Sunday, and once they were gone, nestled back under the covers, drawn into the drowsy repose of the morning nap. I was awakened by voices in the living room.

"Are you sure no one's home?" a boy queried.

"Anyone home?" Beth's voice cried out loudly.

I was too startled to answer, and embarrassed to be the only one still in bed mid-morning. The door to Beth's room was ajar, and had she come upstairs she would have seen me.

"They must be at church," she said in an unfamiliar seductive tone of voice. "I'm too much a sinner." She giggled.

After a moment of silence, I heard the unmistakable shuffling of clothes being removed, neither too quickly nor too slowly, suggesting this was not their first sexual encounter. The house was so hushed I heard, or imagined, exploratory affectionate caresses. Halted breaths. I tucked my head under the pillow, ashamed to listen, although not surprised.

The stories of sexual escapades at funerals and wakes are legendary, and not without truth or reason. Mourning provides only a brief respite from grief; sex offers a place to flee from one's memory and despair, as well as a blessed foray into visceral release. Stolen moments of physical pleasure supersede sorrow, alleviating briefly the vise of desolation. The void is always there, but for a time, less of a black hole. There is nothing like that feeling and I too occasionally seek the hedonism of a sexual tsunami, until the waves recede.

As Beth found her way to soar above the images of her comatose mother, and her wounded family, I found myself aroused by their passion, a quiver from my breasts to my toes, and when I heard their moans of pleasure and cries of completion, I sighed with satisfaction for them, appreciating Beth's fidelity to self-preservation.

What followed their surprisingly brief liaison was a round of giggling, ruffling of clothes, fluffing of couch pillows, and the flush of a toilet. I heard them go down the hall to the kitchen, chatting amiably now, while I huddled in bed, thirsty and hungry, anxious to rise but unwilling to betray my existence. When the boy finally left, I waited a few moments before descending the stairs in my nightclothes, stretching my arms out for effect as if I had only just awakened.

Beth stared at me in amazement. "I didn't know you were here. I called out when I got home, no one answered."

"I guess I was in a deep sleep. I went back to bed after everyone left for church."

She breathed a noticeable sigh of relief.

"So it's official, you are a heathen," Beth said, smiling broadly as she combed her fingers through her hair to straighten the mess.

"I am no good in the mornings."

"I noticed." She chuckled.

Especially Sunday, I might have added, and Beth might have concurred, which has been a mixed message in this house. Anna, as spiritual as she is, has generally refused to engage in religious ceremony. She opined that whatever god one chooses to believe in is within us and therefore not to be found within any one structure or doctrine. Monotheism was simply not in her vernacular. However she stopped short at declaring herself an agnostic. Her belief system was the sanctity of the individual, preferring to postulate ideology more mystical than godly.

For David's sake they were members of the Congregational Church and, although Anna only occasionally attended a service, she said she prized the tranquility and the sense of history, the church having been gathered in 1705. The family attended Christmas Mass with Maggie at the Catholic Church and Rosh Hashanah services with Adrienne at the Jewish Synagogue. Anna also took Will and Beth with her to march for the liberation of

Tibet and read to them from the Quran. By the time they were in high school, they had a solid education in comparative religion, including a look at lesser known denominations like Seventh Day Adventists, Unitarians, Hassidim, and, of course, Buddhism, which Anna believed less a religion than a way of life.

Each year, some time around Easter, Anna and Adrienne's families join Maggie's for what they have dubbed "Eastover" dinner: a Passover Seder filled with ceremony and song, followed by Mass at St. Mary's Catholic Church. The long-standing tradition for the three families bonded their mutual celebrations of renewal. Easter Sunday was approaching and I supposed the families would gather, with or without Anna, knowing she more than anyone would want them to preserve the tradition. I felt a sudden hopefulness that Anna's internal clock might recognize the season and awaken her for the festivities.

"Want to go to the diner for breakfast?" Beth asked. "It's a madhouse after church, everyone ends up there, and you know there are like seven churches within a mile of each other, but if we go now, we might avoid the mob."

"Sure."

"I could go for pancakes. They are pretty ordinary diner pancakes, not filled with nuts and fruit the way Mom makes them, but they're good. Gushy inside, crispy out."

"I'm a purist, plain pancakes are perfect."

Beth drove Anna's car and we arrived in moments. She was right – the diner was full but not to the brim and we slipped into a booth in the back. A short brown man with a tired smile poured hot coffee the moment we sat down and the aroma jolted me awake, although I ordered a Diet Coke chaser. We scanned the massive menu: four plasticized pages of largely starchy comfort foods. A similar waiter passed by shouldering a perfectly balanced tray piled high with large dishes.

Beth craned her neck to check out her options. "Maybe I'll go with the waffle. Strawberries and powdered sugar on top, looks yummy."

"Sounds good. I'm going to stick with pancakes."

"Short stack or the real thing?" Beth asked.

"I think I'll go all the way on this. You can help me if I can't finish."

"Count on it."

A pale-skinned waitress with blue streaks screaming atop nearly black hair wore a starched white uniform with a black apron: Snow White gone punk. When she stopped at our table to take our order, she took a pencil out of her ponytail, a move that might have been scripted for her, and I felt as if we were extras in a low-budget film. She never made eye contact as she took our order.

Beth waited until she was out of hearing range to say, "Another in a long list of jobs I don't ever want to do."

"Waitress?"

"Waitress in a diner."

"The uniform or the food?"

"The whole thing."

"Do you have a list of what you might want to do?"

"No, not yet. Only what I definitely don't want to do."

"What else?"

"Toll taker. I would die of boredom. House cleaner, no way. Accountant, I hate math. Nurse, doctor, no thanks, no blood. Trash collector, for obvious reasons. And I don't think I ever want to be a teacher, I would feel caged."

"Good to know what you don't like."

"But I don't know what I'm going to do or what I'm going to major in."

"You don't have to know yet."

"What about you? Did you always know what you wanted to do?"

"No. Still not sure."

Beth smiled. Another waitress suddenly appeared to refill my coffee cup. She too had a pencil in her thick locks.

"You know, being a waitress can be a good experience." I sipped from a cheap china coffee cup, no mugs or cardboard at the diner, nothing fancy.

"Why?"

"Well, you encounter all kinds of people. You learn to be quick. And you learn to listen."

"You mean take orders."

"Well, more than that, to really listen to what people want. A good lesson."

"I suppose, but the tips are lousy."

"That's the truth, but look at the bright side, you get to keep a pencil in your hair."

Beth beamed a quick bright smile and just as instantly sobered.

"I'll probably end up a waitress anyway. I can't even decide where to go to school, much less what I want to do."

"When do you have to decide?"

"We have to send the hold-the-place check May 1st."

"What's the choice?"

"Well, a week ago I was pretty sure about Michigan."

My heart stopped for a second. "Jason went to Michigan. Undergrad. He loved it there."

"Really? Ann Arbor is so cool."

"Very cool."

"Did you meet there?"

"No, we met in New York, when he was in graduate school. New York is cold enough."

"I don't mind. I like bulky sweaters and boots. But now, now I don't know."

"Why?"

She looked at me as if I had two heads. "Well, if Mom, I mean, if she doesn't get better, or if, well, if..." She stopped, unable to complete the thought.

"Your mother would want you to choose the school that suits you."

"I know, I know."

"And it must feel great to have choices."

"I almost wish I got into only one school, no decision, you know? If I had applied early like some of my friends, I would know by now."

"Just choose whatever feels right."

"But it wouldn't be right, to go so far away, I mean, leave Will and Dad. Yale might be better. New Haven is on the train line, so I can get home more often, and Will can drive my car for a year."

"Recycling," I said with a smile.

Beth nodded vigorously. "You know it."

I reached for her hand. "Listen, don't decide just yet. A lot can change before May 1st."

"Only a few weeks."

I tried to think of something encouraging and wise to say to help her with her dilemma, but nothing came to mind. Fortunately, at that moment, the waitress arrived with large white plates filled to their edges with food, and placed two pitchers of syrup on the table. We forked in, the meal the perfect diversion.

"Is Sunday the start of the week or the end of the week?" Beth mumbled as she munched her waffle. "I was never really sure. Like, according to Genesis, God rested on the seventh day, what churches view as Sunday, so that is supposed to be our day of rest, right? But it always seems like somehow Saturday is the end of the week, and Sunday starts the new week. Although, when you think about it, for people who go to school or work, Monday is the first day of the week. So that leaves Sunday sort of in limbo."

"I see what you mean."

"Since people pray on Sunday, are they praying for the past week, like, settling their debts, or are they praying for the new week to be better? I mean, Jews pray at the end of their week, on their Sabbath. That makes more sense to me."

I swallowed a bite of pancake and looked up at Beth. "If you were in church today, what would you pray for?"

She shrugged, her shoulders and eyebrows lifting together. "I don't know."

"I think you do."

She sipped her juice and I saw in her eyes the look I so often see when Anna turns philosophical, a look equally divided between wonder and bewilderment.

"Guidance, I suppose. I mean, I know what I'm supposed to do. I'm supposed to accept my fate. Learn the lessons I'm meant to learn. And I've tried, I've really tried. I've thought about everything Mom taught me. I know if this is her destiny, if she is meant to go on to another life right now, I should be grateful for the time we had together. Permanence is an illusion, you know? Just a few weeks ago, we were talking with Will about this project he's doing, and Mom reminded us that two hundred years ago there were a billion people on the planet who no longer exist. Their descendants do. We're all descendants, right? We live, we pass on, we return."

To my dumbfounded expression, she continued. "Most of the time my mother has been a grown-up companion anyway, like a governess in the old days, except she's my mother, and not like anybody else's mother I know. So I must be grateful and not expect more."

She wiped a bit of syrup from her mouth. "I should be glad for her, I guess, because, well, she will go on to a whole new life somewhere, and see people who are no longer here, and I will remember everything she taught me. I know all this. I do. So I shouldn't pray to have her back. That's selfish."

I had stopped chewing, staring at Beth, likely with a deer in the headlights look. How could one so young possibly accept the most profound loss of her youth without some desperation or despair?

"You are wise for your age, Beth. Very wise," was all I could say.

"Mom taught me well. I know that longing is a fatal flaw."

"Excuse me?"

"You spend enough time with Mom, you know the drill. Attachments, longing, this is self-serving. Leads to envy, anguish, the emotions that limit our potential for fulfillment." She spoke as if she were reciting a poem she memorized for a performance on parents' night at school. "Compassion is all that matters, compassion and forgiveness, actually not forgiveness, kindness. Forgiveness suggests judgment. This is the one true path to enlightenment. I think that's the way it goes, at least what I remember. I feel like I've been studying for a test. Did I get it right?"

She gulped down the last of the juice and ate a large mouthful of waffle. Her eyes were red but there were no tears.

"I guess I should pray for acceptance. Still hard for me sometimes. To accept the fact that if my mother really is gone, I can accept her absence without longing for her, without suffering more than I have to. I guess all this is practice; maybe that's the intention. Like play rehearsal, you know, learn the lines, hit the marks. Before the real thing."

I had completely lost my appetite. I watched Beth eat the remains of her waffle and each of the large red strawberries on her plate, dropping the stems into a tiny pile.

"Are you done?" she asked, wiping her mouth with a crumpled napkin.

"I've had enough."

"You eat like a bird, but I'm too full for more. Take it home for Will."

"Too soggy."

"I guess." She dipped her index finger into the last of the syrup on her plate then sucked it off with delight.

"Beth," I said tentatively. "Is there anything else you want to talk about? I, I don't have all the answers, but maybe we should..."

"No, I've got it."

"I mean, anything in your life that needs talking about. Not just Mom. I'm happy to listen and, well, I'd be happy to help, in any way..."

"No, thanks. But maybe..."

"Maybe what?"

"Want to go over to the steeple?"

"Steeple?"

"At the church, where Dad and Will and Aunt Karen are probably singing the final hymns about now. Last year the church opened the steeple to the public after the restoration and they keep it open around the holidays. You can climb all the way to the bell tower. Amazing view. Mom was the photographer on the committee to restore the steeple, remember that? Dad talked her into it. In fact, they had quite a row over it. Mom, naturally, did not want to take pictures to glorify any one religion, but Dad convinced her she was preserving the history. That got to her, but not until they battled it out a bit. It was great."

"Great?"

"You know Mom and Dad hardly ever argue. Nice, most of the time, but now and then I'd like to hear a loud voice besides Will and me. And even we tend to go easy on each other." She sighed. "Sometimes I feel like we live, oh, like, like we don't feel things the way other people do. Dissension is a good thing, right? For the right reasons. So when mom and dad duked it out over the steeple, it was cool. In the end, Mom must have taken a hundred pictures for the brochure to raise money for the restoration, and some of them made the newspapers, even the *New York Times*. The photos were gorgeous."

The waitress passed by, tossing the check on the table with murmur of thanks, and I dug out a $20 bill to cover it.

"You have to pay at the counter," Beth said. "Thanks."

"My pleasure."

"So, anyway, Mom took pictures every hour for days, waiting for just the right light to make it look especially holy, you know, the kind of picture that makes you stop and look and wonder if God doesn't really live there. Like some of those medieval paintings where the light is shining only on Mary, or Christ, and everything else is dark. They raised a lot of money to clean and repair the stone and modernize the bell tower. The bell is huge, bronze I think. Really heavy metal." She chuckled. "The bells used to go off every hour, all day and all night, but I guess the neighbors complained, so they put in a computerized mechanism. Now the clock chimes at seven AM and every hour until ten. They can set it to go off like twenty times when there's a wedding, you can hear it at the house, that's how far the sound travels. Sort of like a steel drum with pitch. And the stone! Wait till you see. Dad was on the building committee. Fieldstone I think; maybe limestone? Used to be kind of shoddy, and now it is so clean, honestly, it sparkles in the sun. Dad told me the top of the steeple is the tallest point between New York and Boston."

"Really?"

"Yeah. Sits high on a hill and towers over everything. Two hundred and twelve feet up. Last year, mom and I climbed to the top. 'So close to heaven. Stretch out your hand, you might touch the clouds,' she said. I wish I could. Maybe I'd feel better."

"Let's go," I said, as enthusiastically as I could muster at one of those moments when I would have much rather climbed back into bed.

"It's not far. We can walk," she chirped as she slipped out of the booth to lead the way.

The congregation was dispersing as we approached the church, scattering in the shadow of a steeple that rose like a mountain peak. Sharply pitched roofs tiled in slate added height to the two intersecting smaller structures that pointed like arrows to the central spire. Manicured lawns sloped to the corner and tall maple trees fenced a graveyard perched on the hill, where I imagined many stories of past lives etched into aged headstones.

As we approached the entrance, Beth pointed out Henry shaking hands with an older couple. I almost didn't recognize him. He wore a crisply starched white shirt, striped blue tie, and a pale gray suit, quite distinguished in his Sunday best as an elder of the congregation, in contrast to the eccentric taxi driver.

"What brings you here?" he asked as he came toward us and gave Beth a hug.

"Beth wants to show me the steeple."

"Ah, a great experience."

"You've been to the top?"

"Last year, just the one time. These old legs don't go quite so far anymore."

He motioned us toward the side entrance and we walked together on bright green grass, freshly mown and tightly woven. We passed a large bronze statue mounted on a beveled stone plinth, where Henry stopped to launch into a description.

"His name was Josiah Henry Mason, the man who convinced the congregation to build the steeple. Leopold Eidlitz, a famed church architect, designed the original church in the 19th century, but without a steeple. Such an undertaking cost a lot of money in those days. Even years later, in 1856, when they added the steeple, thirty thousand dollars was a lot for the congregation to spend. Doesn't sound like much now, does it?" He winked at Beth. "Josiah here convinced them to build the tower by offering to act as general contractor, even though he wasn't a builder or an architect. He was a banker, from a long line of bankers, although the Masons were originally farmers, arrived in these parts in seventeen hundred thirty seven with a land grant to much of the county. They were not very good farmers, I'm afraid, so they sold off the land bit by bit and accumulated sufficient wealth to open banks. I guess old Josiah's treasury was good collateral, so the congregation agreed and, when the money ran out, he financed the completion himself. Imagine that?"

"When did they do the restoration?" I asked.

"This most recent one? Just a little more than a year ago. The congregation had quite a celebration when it was all done. Even the Governor was here."

"Is that when they put up this monument?" I asked.

"No. That was in 1919, in honor of the steeple. Stone by stone, all the best masons in the county worked on it. Took them years."

"Did you work on the steeple, Henry?" Beth asked.

Henry laughed heartily. "No child. I'm old, but not that old. I was just a sparkle in my daddy's eye back then, but he worked on the steeple."

"Your father was a mason?" I asked.

"Actually, my father was a farmer, masonry was sort of a hobby. You know, in those days, people had to know how to do a lot of things. Necessity being the mother of innovation, or is it invention? I never get that right."

He laughed and I couldn't help but smile. No wonder Anna had a fondness for Henry.

"My dad was the only one of five sons not to go into the family business. He was a man who liked to work with his hands."

"And what was the family business?" I asked.

"Banking." Henry said. "Josiah Mason was my grandfather."

"The keeper of history," I said.

"You remembered." He smiled. "You know, once completed, congregants climbed on open ladders from scaffold to scaffold until they reached the circular capstone." He pointed to the top, although I did not look up. "Only eight feet in diameter up there, that's all, just eight feet, but they sat there with their picnic baskets and ate supper, apparently undisturbed that they were more than two hundred feet above ground!"

"Awesome," Beth said.

"And, this is the God's honest truth, while still under construction, they got a letter from Thomas Edison about how to protect the steeple from lightning strikes." He pointed up again and Beth peered upwards with him. "We still have a kind of weather vane up there, looks like violin strings hanging in mid-air with a cross at the top. Very clever that Edison."

"Did you know him too?" I asked.

Henry chuckled and shook his head. "Never had the pleasure."

We stood at the monument looking at Henry's grandfather, a sturdy man with a square set chin and broad shoulders, more like a revolutionary than a banker.

"Si monumentum requiris, circumspice," I recited the words on the capstone. "If you seek his monument, look about."

Henry nodded, pleased that I recognized the same inscription on the tomb of Sir Christopher Wren at St. Paul's Cathedral in London. Jason had read it aloud to me once from a treatise on architecture he had edited. Wren, he learned, had great plans to rebuild London after the fires, hoping to replace the city's narrow alleys and byways with broad sweeping boulevards like Paris, and open up the old city to light and air. Instead, King Charles had him rebuild the churches, his life's work.

"Christopher Wren," I told Beth. "An English architect."

"I've heard of him."

"He built something like fifty churches," I added.

"Fifty-one to be precise, in forty-six years," Henry said.

"My husband particularly admired St. Paul's."

"Ah, yes, but the chapel at Cambridge… very special."

"I see you are a student of architecture as well," I said.

"Historical architecture," he answered.

"Must be nice to have a monument erected to a family member," Beth said. "Everyone knows who you are forever."

"Tell me, dear," Henry asked with a professorial expression. "There's a monument down at the post office. Do you know who it is?"

Beth shook her head no.

"Monuments are nice, but they are merely markers. People forget, monuments are ignored, or decay, but the meaning is in the legacy."

"You think maybe Josiah Mason was a descendent of Wren?" Beth asked. "Like, maybe there is a connection."

"Don't know about that," Henry said. "Interesting question. We do hail from England."

"Or maybe…" She stopped speaking, a quizzical look on her face.

"What?" I asked.

"I was just thinking, maybe they knew each other in another time."

"Could be. Yes, indeed, could have been great friends."

Beth began to move toward the doorway to the steeple, waving me on, and calling over her shoulder, "Thanks for the lesson, Henry."

Henry gripped my arm to hold me back a moment. "Nearly one hundred years this steeple has been a town beacon, Nell. Seen our boys go to war. Seen planes fly overhead and turnpikes built below. Lit by fireworks in the sky every Fourth of July and wreaths on doorways at Christmas. The bell chimes through good times and bad because time goes on and time heals."

He squeezed my hand and turned to stroll down the hill toward town, leaving me to absorb his message, although I had little time, Beth shouting to me to move along.

She led the way through an iron door rounded at the top, like doorways in medieval castles, which led to a tiny dark entry, then to another door to the steps where we began the climb. The stairway curved, increasingly narrow and winding as we climbed, room only for single passage near the top. The stone steps had a short rise, thus more steps for the distance and harder on the feet. No windows, only increasingly dank air. A dim refracted light emanated from the top so the passage felt more like a tunnel into a mine than a stairway to heaven. As this was the only route, footsteps came from behind as well as descending from above, as if simultaneously forging through time from past to present to future, and back again. Three times we had to squeeze ourselves against the outer wall to make room for passersby and I had to stop twice to catch my breath. Beth skipped up the steps ahead of me and I used the sound of her footsteps as my guide, until she landed with a sharp thud.

"Just look at this view," Beth cried to me as I emerged into the light. "You can see the whole town, and up and down the coast. See the tops of all those buildings? They seem so much bigger when you're on the ground. It all looks like one of the models in Dad's office. Little boxes with tiny windows and outside, tiny cars. You can hardly see people."

She moved about from one narrow viewing panel to another around the perimeter of the circular platform, as if revolving on a carousel.

Beth was right. Everything below seemed tiny. Insignificant. Tall trees reduced to twigs, streets to paths. I scanned the vista for something familiar to set my compass. I found the hospital, the largest building in view, seemingly inches away, and the library not much farther, marking the corner where two weeks ago Anna lay bleeding.

To the south, along the coastline, the harbor shimmered in the mid-day sun, tiny sails fluttering like whitecaps. To the north, sleepy country roads meandered like pencil drawings. Residential rooftops faded near Main Street, replaced with flat commercial roofs and shop awnings. Hardly an open plot of land remained and I pictured the once lush farmland that occupied the expanse of Henry's memory. From this vantage point, the town seemed a blueprint for the modern life of a once provincial hamlet, the steeple towering above it all, prodding the community to cherish its heritage, and, at the same time, a reprimand that no one person, or edifice, was more important than another.

There we stood, nearly in the clouds, equally insignificant, no closer to God, no closer to heaven, certainly no closer to enlightenment. Nevertheless, as anxious as I felt to be so near the sky, I was not uncomfortable, preferring in that moment to soar above the banal.

I turned to see Beth clutching a railing, gazing below, tears pouring down her face.

"I can't look at her, Nell," she cried. "I can't look at my own mother. I'm a terrible person. I haven't been at the hospital for days. I tell Will I'm at play rehearsal. I tell the drama teacher I have to leave early to go to the hospital and then I go to the park. I stay at a friend's house, his mother's away, no questions asked. I've told Dad I just missed him in the lounge. Aunt Karen too. I've lied to everyone. I can't bear to see her this way. It's just too awful." She swiped the back of her hand to her tears. "How could she leave me now? It's too soon. I can't accept this, I can't."

Sobs shook her body, yet, as I stepped closer and reached out for her, she pulled back, unwilling yet to be comforted.

"It's too soon!" she shouted. "It's too soon." She hid her eyes in her hands as if to obliterate the vision of her comatose mother. "I'm not ready for this!" She screamed now, loudly, angrily, to the heavens. "How can my mother not be at my graduation?" she implored, removing her hands from her eyes and spreading them out in front of her as if arguing before a judge. "I know it's selfish. I know it's wrong to feel this way, but I want my mother! It's too soon."

This time, when I reached out my arms, she crumpled against me and I held her as she wept, weeks of anguish bubbling to the surface. An occasional visitor stopped at the landing and quickly shifted to the opposite side to leave us in peace. Beth's convulsive sobs, her impeachment of her mother's destiny, her anger and desperation, echoed off the iron bell and stone walls and resounded through the stony hollows of my own heart.

Longing becomes craving; craving becomes anguish. Anna recited this mantra to me only once. Perhaps she knew better than to preach to me the very essence of loss. Only words to Anna. Only words to someone whose life has progressed without serious complications – nothing more than an occasional misstep, a minor disappointment. Even when her mother was diagnosed with Alzheimer's, she accepted the dementia as essential to her mother's journey, and her own, pleased, she said, that her mother would not suffer, and, more to the point, she would no longer long for what was long gone.

Anna the goddess, protected by the camera lens, sheltered by existential philosophy, never truly attached to more than an allegory, thus exempted from human suffering. Her role in life, her purpose, to witness, to guide, perhaps illuminate, without the agony the rest of us experience.

How did I not see this before? How did I not see that Anna remained largely detached from the living, looming above us like this very steeple, her head in the clouds, forfeiting personal pain as an oblation to an obscure and unrelenting master plan?

If we do not allow ourselves to feel the longing, to crave what we love most, to suffer the agony of loss, are we of this earth? Are we fully conscious?

I meant to visit Anna that afternoon, but for the first time I can remember, I did not want to see her. And, on the verge of an anxiety attack, I opted instead for a walk. A blanket of mist soon settled into a steady spring shower and by the time I'd walked a short distance, my clothes were soaked. Shivers set in, despite raindrops warmer than the air.

All day I felt the heat crawling up my back. My cheeks were surely ruby-red, my breath shallow, and as I raced back to the shelter of the hospital, I realized I had run out of antidepressants nearly a week ago. This has only happened twice before, with nearly disastrous results. I stopped in my tracks. Every bone ached and a rush of tears descended too quickly to contain, the anesthetic effect of the medication having fully worn off and my nervous system heading toward mayhem. Much as I had to focus on deeper breathing and remaining in one piece, the truth is, liberation from psychotropic constraints is also exhilarating. There is no serotonin uptake or hormonal inhibitor capable of shielding me forever, not without relinquishing all connection to reality.

I reached out my hands to capture the rain and sip nourishment from the clouds before I began the return walk to the hospital, using its roofline to navigate. I paced steadily and breathed evenly, the gasp of each breath like the metronomic rhythm of a church organ, or a respirator.

Perhaps it was the rain that afternoon, perhaps Maggie's delicious meals or regular sleep in a homey place, but I began to appreciate the release from the chronic rumbling of psychic lava. As if depleted and restored simultaneously, like Edgar Allan Poe, one of my favorite writers, who was said to suffer manic depression and who, in high states, saw through walls and into people's hearts. I have never felt that sort of jolt, never experienced the joy or rage of mania, but in that moment, I felt more acutely the sensory and the surreal. And I heard Anna's voice, the only voice that mattered. Her voice, like Poe's telltale heart, screaming to be heard.

No matter my disillusionment, no matter my disappointment in the Anna she suddenly seemed to be, I owed her my life. I owed her fidelity to the promise she had exacted from me.

I stopped when I encountered the tall ash tree and stood before it, breathing decisively and evenly, waiting for the rain to pass. I could not hold back the tears and allowed myself the indulgence of weeping, licking from my lips salty tears and raindrops all at once. Rain bounced off the still largely barren branches of the tree, however, on closer inspection, I noticed a few subtle shoots of green. Renewal, even late in the season, is possible, and I took this as a sign to continue to wait for Anna to revive. Although the thought was ever-present that she was waiting for me.

Tim was seated by Anna's bedside when I returned.

"Had a little encounter with the storm, have you?"

I must have appeared like a Dickensian waif, bedraggled and brackish.

"I rather like a walk in the rain now and then," I replied.

He sighed, as if fondly remembering similar walks, but said no more on the subject. Instead, he stood and strode beyond me into the bathroom, returning with a towel, which he tossed to me. While I patted down my exposed damp skin and rubbed the towel through my hair, Tim talked to Anna, including me in the conversation as if we three were hanging around the Common on a rainy afternoon.

"You know, Anna, I think we've waited long enough. Time for you to strut your stuff, one way or another. Let's get on with this show, before everyone's nerves are completely frayed. Time to spill the beans, don't you think?" He turned to me as he said these words.

"What beans would those be?" I asked.

"The beans that Jack planted, you know, the ones that grow overnight into a giant stalk leading to heaven."

I stopped toweling my hair and stared at him. "What makes you so sure she's ready to climb that stair?" I demanded.

"Being in limbo doesn't suit her at all."

"Seriously? Anna was forever in limbo, she likes transitions."

"Yes, but transitions of her choosing. Look at her." He raised his arms toward Anna, with his palms upwards, like a magician who lures a body to levitate. "An artificial holding tank: no sunlight, no fresh air, no human interaction. It's just plain wrong. She should be set free."

"Of course you would believe that, Tim," Adrienne proclaimed as she entered the room. She must have been listening to our conversation from the doorway.

"Adrienne," Tim nodded.

Adrienne positioned herself at the foot of the bed, facing us on either side. "Anna requires sustenance until she regains her strength."

"That's one way to look at it," Tim answered.

"Makes sense to me," I said, hoping to curtail the animosity.

"Isn't this late for you, Tim? I thought you were the mid-day shift," Adrienne remarked.

"Late press tonight, thought I'd stop in now. Anything new here?"

Adrienne shook her head no and turned to me. "You need a ride?" she asked.

"No, thanks. I'm, I'm going to hang around a little while," I said, although even as I spoke, I shivered, and knew I should get out of my damp clothes sooner rather than later.

Adrienne left without another word to either of us, and we both turned to stare at Anna.

"Do you really think she should be released?" I asked.

"I wonder if the body shuts down in self-defense against all this artificial intrusion, the way the metabolism shuts down when we fast."

"Without life support, Anna would have no nourishment, she might not be able to breathe. How could she even begin to restore herself?"

"I don't know, but she's been pricked and poked like a pincushion for long enough. She doesn't bleed, but she may well be wounded."

I felt as if a pin had been pressed into the chest of a voodoo doll likeness of me.

"If we take her off life support, we might sign her death warrant," I pleaded.

"Someone may have to eventually. I'm surprised Anna left no directive."

"Why do you say that?"

"Well, she talked a lot about death in the last year, after she did that piece on hospice, did you see that?'

"I heard about it."

"Phenomenal photographs of people at Queen Anne's Hospice, on the outskirts of town. Anna made dying with dignity seem nobler than living. And after that, didn't you notice? She became sort of obsessed with death. She took photographs at funerals, not on assignment. Sometimes she read obituaries aloud as if she were reciting a eulogy in a chapel."

"Was she worried about something, Tim?"

"Not that I know of. And she's the healthiest person on the staff. I used to tease her that if she ever called in sick I'd know she was playing hooky." He smiled. "No, I think she became preoccupied with death as her version of manifest destiny. She seemed, well, she seemed…" He paused in contemplation.

"What?"

"She seemed almost determined to find out more about death first-hand."

I was too stunned by that thought to respond.

"We all flirt with the ogre of death every day, don't we?" Tim added. "Every time you smoke. Every time I speed through a yellow light. We invite death to come for us."

"No," I said, shaking my head fiercely, a few droplets of water scuttling along the floor like ants. "Anna lived in the moment, she did not manifest an end game."

"I'm not saying she did anything deliberately. I just suspect her obsession with all this might have colored her judgment. She had come to see death as elegant, her word. Her natural sense of caution might have been compromised, that's all."

I slumped into a chair. "This talk is wearing me down."

"You really should get dry," Tim said. "Can't afford to get sick, Anna needs you."

Need. I let the word filter through my mind. If Anna needed me now, it was only to do what I promised to do.

"I live nearby, why don't you come put your clothes in the dryer, I can find something for you to wear for a while. And I always have red wine on hand, will that do?"

"I should get back," I stammered.

"Karen stopped in and said she was having dinner with an old friend. David and the kids need their own space. Give yourself a break. I'm not dangerous. I won't hurt you."

I shivered. You can't hurt me, I might have said, as we said good-bye to Anna.

"You are impenetrable, Nell," Anna remarked once. "I wonder, if pricked, would you bleed?"

I was stung by the remark, believing that she of all people would know better, although she had perfectly good reason to suspect I had wrapped myself so tightly the seal was now inviolate. Nevertheless, even in a state of suspended animation, passion exists, if no longer in the heart, or the soul, certainly in the body.

To that end, I spend time, now and then, with a special friend. Danny. A fireman once married to a watercolor artist named Lynne who shared the communal studio where I potted for a time. Jason and I often dined with them, last-minute dinners in which Lynne and I concocted hodge-podge salads or stir-fries from whatever was edible in our fridges. Our husbands never complained. We consumed vast quantities of wine and jabbered late into the night.

Danny was raised in Queens and came from a family of firefighters, yet he was also a classically trained pianist, an attempt by his immigrant mother to free the youngest son from the dangers of the family business. Despite her efforts, the heroic call appealed to him, and solidarity with fellow firefighters sealed his fate. When they were first married, Danny worked the day shift at a firehouse on the Lower East Side and supplemented his income playing back-up bass guitar at one of the downtown jazz clubs. When Lynne began lobbying for kids, she lobbied even more aggressively for Danny to give up the firefighter's life, contending he might make a decent living as a musician. He refused, resigned that his identity was irrevocably tied to the world of first responders. They argued often and without resolution for years.

Danny survived the fires of 9/11 profoundly altered. One person before the catastrophe and quite another after. One of his brothers died, his father was disabled, and half his unit perished. In spite of this, or because of it, he became more obstinate in his refusal to quit. Within a year, Lynne left him to marry a former high school sweetheart and move to the suburbs, disappearing from the lives of her city friends, and I lost touch with both after

Jason and Jeremy were killed, as I did with most everyone with whom I had spent time, dismissed, over time, like an old car with no residual value.

A few years ago, I ran into Danny on the street and we started spending time together. We walked, we sipped beers in dimly lit bars, we shared pasta in tiny Italian restaurants. He is an easy person to be with and pleasing to look at: olive skin, hazel eyes, curly brown hair. His knobby nose has been broken in two places and, as he almost always has a serious expression, when he smiles he truly lights up. His arms and hands are thick and he is always warm to the touch. It was inevitable we would sleep together and comfort each other, without obligation.

On nights when I feel bold enough to indulge desire, I wander down to one of the clubs where he plays and slide onto a barstool. Under cover of darkness, I watch him strum his instrument, eyes closed, droplets of sweat on his brow, plucking the strings and gently tapping the tempo on the shaft as if making love to the music.

After the set, with a knowing nod, we take a taxi to his studio apartment in the East Village, a sparse open space where all his belongings – clothes, shoes, books – are stored in milk crates stacked against one wall. A full-size mattress and box spring lay on concrete pilings in the center of the room, covered with white linens and a faded quilt. Under the windowed wall is a substantial record collection, on top of which sits a nearly antique turntable and speakers and several boxes of replacement needles stashed in preparation for their obsolescence. A small table, a couple of chairs, one oversized comfy chair, that's all there is, all purchased at flea markets, Danny being the type to take home all kinds of strays, including old friends.

We do not engage in foreplay beyond a touch of hands, a hug, and the accompaniment of the kind of music you might expect in a sexually charged relationship – Miles Davis, Nina Simone, Etta James. We rarely kiss, we make little eye contact, we whisper no endearments. Instead, we stroke, we nuzzle, we writhe in a primitive coupling with the urgency of animals in the mating season, which allows me to dissociate, responding only to primal urgings and existing against a black surround that obscures memory. And reason. I know Danny does the same. However we never rush, preferring to prolong the fleeting climax in a nearly tantric tango, as once worn out, we revert to mutual discontent.

I don't know if Danny sleeps with anyone else; he likely knows I don't. He never asks questions, he never makes demands, he never needs to do more than press me tightly to his body, sometimes so tightly I feel as if I might fuse into him and vanish from this earth altogether. He always offers to take me home, but I prefer to leave alone, and sometimes I walk all the way, roughly two miles, to hold onto the pleasure without the guilt I invariably feel when I am in the apartment I shared with Jason. I never invite Danny to visit me and he understands that he has no place in my sanctuary.

Whatever one calls this sort of thing, it works for us both. You might say he is my version of life support, he and Anna, from which eventually I will be disconnected, I suppose.

Tim lived on a modest tree-lined street in town in a cottage with a picket-fenced, postage-sized lawn, and a porch punctuated with two white ladder-backed rocking chairs. The setting seemed as essential to his position as newspaper editor as his drab car and jaded bearing.

In contrast, the interior of the house bore no resemblance to its façade. Minimally furnished, nothing upholstered or plush, the unembellished décor made the place feel like an ashram. In the middle of the room, four mix-matched rattan chairs fringed a low round table covered with an Indian mosaic fabric, topped with several squat candles in various stages of burn and an incense tray embedded with ash. The scent in the air was so pungent it took my breath away for a moment. No shades or curtains affixed to windows and no artwork on the walls, the only adornment a couple of middle-eastern rugs in hues of vermillion, reflected by wall sconces that cast a shadowy glow. Many books were piled in built-in shelves, but no videos or DVDs, and no television. Only one concession to technology: a Bose iPod dock, which he turned on as we arrived, the strains of Indian music leaping into the room. Despite, or because of the monastic ambiance, I imagined more than one seduction took place there, women so easily enticed by men who seem to have no need of them.

Tim motioned for me to wait while he ran upstairs and returned with a plaid flannel shirt that smelled of a dryer sheet, and a pair of sweatpants he held up against my frame and pronounced might stay up if I pulled the drawstring really tight. He showed me to the laundry room to toss my clothes into the dryer, which contained still damp laundry awaiting a tumble.

When I emerged, a bottle of red wine was open on the table and Tim was puttering in the kitchen beyond, searching, he said, for something palatable to eat, returning in moments with a container of hummus and a bowl of olives.

"So, where were we?" he asked as he poured the wine.

I took a cracker from the box and dipped it into the hummus. As the garlicky flavor coated my tongue, I was suddenly ravenous, grateful to line my stomach before the alcohol landed.

"I don't remember," I replied, swallowing another mouthful. "Wait, I do, you were saying Anna had grown obsessed with death? That perhaps her judgment was impaired."

"Yes," Tim said as he snatched an olive, popping it into his mouth like a pill. "She told me not long ago that she felt she had failed the Buddhist tradition because she had allowed herself to experience longing. She had become convinced she had not moved far enough along the continuum and would require many more lives."

"Strange."

Tim looked at me the way a lawyer studies a potentially hostile witness. "I wondered if she had ensured her desire to pass unencumbered with some sort of directive." He shook his head in puzzlement. "You know as well as I do, David will take every possible measure to keep her alive, likely indefinitely, and tabloid tales of miraculous survival years down the road make the decision that much harder."

"You would let her go?"

He drained his wine glass and, with an oddly sad expression, reached across the table to cup my hand with his. "Nell, she's already gone."

I shook my head no and yanked my hand away. "You cannot know that."

"This is a woman who could not possibly be so still, not with an ounce of life left in her."

"You said yourself that day at lunch, you thought she might be deep within herself."

"I was hopeful then. Look at her closely now. Touch her. No life. No spirit. Blood merely drawn through veins, air pumped through lungs. Anna has moved on."

"No." I shook my head more vehemently. "This is what coma looks like."

"Listen, for the last year, Anna and I were very close. Hardly a day went by without contact. I felt her presence in the office before she came into view, as if an invisible electric filament quivered when she arrived. We talked about everything, we shared everything. She was the closest thing I'll ever have to a truly intimate relationship."

I sat up in my chair. "What are you saying?"

"You really don't know?"

"What?"

"We are lovers, Anna and I. Throughout many lives, we were certain of that. Centuries perhaps. When I arrived here, we found each other again."

I was dumbfounded although as Tim stared at my shocked expression, a memory came to mind. A little over a year ago, Anna surprised me with a visit on my birthday. A Friday. She charged into my apartment at noon and we took off for a walk. I remember I was especially glad to see her as she had skipped the two previous Wednesdays, claiming an especially heavy post-holiday workload. It was one of those blisteringly cold February days and a steady wind blew dust and debris from one corner to another as if small bands of hornets. We bundled up and headed to Serendipity for hot chocolate, slurping down to the bottom of our oversized mugs like children, before spending a few hours browsing books at Rizzoli, after which we dined on mussels and fries with a split of champagne at the iconic Brasserie on Madison Avenue.

While waiting for a table there, I noticed a man sitting at the bar watching us. I assumed, as I do now and then, he was a compatriot; another New Yorker mired in prolonged mourning. We often recognize each other by the shroud of grief on our shoulders. One of the throng Thoreau once described as living lives of quiet desperation. Our eyes met momentarily before he turned away, and now I realized the man was Tim. No wonder when I met him some months later he seemed familiar, although I couldn't place him. He must have been waiting for Anna that night, who told me she planned to take the late train to be with the kids the next morning.

I swallowed hard the last of a cracker and sighed. "Seems to me the transmigration of souls and the trek of everlasting spirits is occasionally terribly convenient."

Tim smiled, pleased, I supposed, to have sparked enmity, although he continued as if I had slid open the window of a confessional booth.

"It was impossible to resist. The pull was too strong. We were lovers in the truest sense of the word. We enriched each other spiritually and intellectually. Our relationship transcended the physical. What Anna and I had, that was something most people never know. No demands, no expectations, no role-playing, only a profoundly metaphysical connection. And because of that, I think I would know if she was still with us."

"For the most part, she had no regrets," Tim went on, as I was too stunned to respond. "She would never leave David. I knew that. However lately, I don't know, she seemed remorseful, not so much because of her transgression, but because she had violated the tenets of her beliefs. She reached for more, no longer fully accepting."

"How could I have been so easily deceived?" I sputtered.

"Innocents are easily deceived. Besides, let's face it, you are the center of your universe. You don't see much beyond your circumstance."

I was struck dumb by his words, their condescension as well as truth.

"You mustn't think less of Anna," Tim implored. "She's not like anyone else, you know that. She's a goddess. Well above we mortals, yet she needs human connection the way we need air to breathe. An epiphyte."

"Epiphyte?"

"Air plants. They grow on other plants, not soil, using their stems as the medium, so to speak. No damage to the host; in fact, the host is enhanced by the relationship."

"I pictured us as a form of commensalism, is that what you mean?"

"No, the opposite. She feeds on you, not the other way around."

"I don't think I've ever seen an epiphyte."

"Sure you have. Ferns. Orchids. Bromeliads. They hover over branches or tree trunks. They mean only to derive what they need to exist, without harming the environment. In fact, they beautify the environment. That's Anna. She takes what she needs and does no harm. And oh, what she gives in return! A human orchid. I was happy to be her host in this life. Her colleague and her confidante."

"David would be devastated by this," I said.

Tim lowered his eyes, the first evidence of shame. "David knows."

"What?"

"He's no fool. Denial works for men like David. He won't compromise what he has."

"And Adrienne," I muttered, putting all the pieces into place. Likely the reason she was always so hostile to Tim.

Tim nodded. "Yes, Adrienne. I always suspected she leaked to David."

"Why?"

Tim shook his head. "I've never been sure. Adrienne's marriage is less than satisfying, so she leans harder on friends, and Anna had less time for her, so maybe old-fashioned spite?"

"But she forgives Anna."

"Of course. We all forgive Anna."

"I'm not sure I do, not because she had an affair, that's not my business, and Anna should have known that."

"Why then?"

I don't think I have ever felt the ambivalence I felt at that moment. My stomach churned and I shivered openly, emotional leeches sucking dry what little psychic stability I had left.

How often in the last year had Anna used me as camouflage for her trysts? In my naiveté, I had assumed she had at last tired of my state of being. I never expected loyalty, not really, not to me, but honesty, yes, and I never imagined she might betray her marriage.

"All that high-minded talk," I said. "All the existentialism, and she turns out to be an ordinary human like the rest of us."

"As we all are."

"So Buddhists are not obligated to the Golden Rule?"

"Good Buddhists, yes."

"Who ever heard of a bad Buddhist?"

Tim laughed. "Every religion operates in gradients. True Christians, observant Jews, good Muslims. Buddhists however have little latitude in other people's eyes, although we don't strive for perfection, quite the contrary, we embrace our humanity. We accept our vulnerability. We only mean to learn. No self-flagellation, no confessions or penitence."

"And apparently no guilt."

"And that is exactly where it might have fallen apart for Anna. Perhaps too many Sundays in church. Or trying to be all things to all people."

"Which transgression was the greater challenge? Marital infidelity? Deceitfulness? Let's get real. She fell for another man and convinced herself it was exalted, or predestined, or whatever crap rationalization to justify your behavior!"

I wasn't at all sure whether I was angrier with Anna for her adultery or for not sharing her secrets. I wasn't sure if I was angry with Tim for confessing to me more than I could bear or jealous of him for the intimacy he shared with Anna.

He seemed to read my thoughts. "I'm surprised she never told you. She trusted you."

"Obviously not. Besides, I think you've got it backwards. We are the epiphytes, you and I. We lean on Anna for sustenance."

"Visit the bromeliads at the Botanical Garden some time. You'll see yourself, stolid and still, while Anna floats above you, reaching out for the sun, eclipsing your beauty with her own."

"Tim, Anna is not an orchid and she's not a goddess. She's a human being, just like the rest of us. We just thought she was better than we are."

"And this is exactly what she was feeling, that she had betrayed trust, that she displayed human flaws she hoped by this life to have resolved."

"Humans are flawed!" I shouted.

"Nell, when you take time to think about it, you'll realize she lived more fully than most, but you're right, she's not a nun. We all ascribe perfection to her, which is a terrible burden, far too difficult to live up to."

I drained my wine glass and stared at Tim, who seemed, in the shadow of confession, terribly forlorn.

"You're wondering what she saw in me, aren't you?" he asked.

"No, well, yes, but more than that. What is it she wanted from you that she didn't have?"

"Listen, we were the perpetuation of a life force; this thing had existed between us forever. And I am completely mortal. I never learn my lessons, thus I am condemned to repeat them, lifetime after lifetime. I don't think I ever move forward." He shook his head and poured more wine for us both. "I always want more than I have. Perhaps the only satisfaction I have ever known is my commitment to her. She has enhanced my life by the simple reassurance of her existence. Hasn't she for you?"

"Yes," I acquiesced. "At least, I thought so."

"She loved you especially, Nell, perhaps because you asked for so little. She felt she had failed to bring you beyond grief to acceptance. She so much as told me so, not long ago."

How could Anna ever believe she had failed me? I felt tears welling up and knew I would be unable to contain them for long. "Why are you telling me all this?"

"Because you more than anyone can urge David to take her off life support and let her spirit fulfill her destiny. That's what she would want, I know that for sure."

"What makes you so sure I will ever let her go?"

"I guess I thought you would understand something about accepting the cards that are dealt to us."

Our gaze met and in Tim's eyes I saw genuine compassion, an understanding of loss and grief that few have, something in this life, or in the accumulation of lives, he might have encountered too often. No wonder Anna was drawn to him, another among the walking wounded.

"I need to know, I don't know why, I just need to know…" I stammered. "The day of the accident, was Anna on her way to meet you?"

"No, not that day. Our day was Wednesday. When she cancelled with you. I am the culprit. I demanded equal time now and then. Sometimes Wednesday nights, on her way back from the city. David assumed she stayed late with you. The paper publishes on Thursday so it's out of my hands by then." He paused. "I'm sorry. We shared the day."

What secrets we all keep. All this time I believed I was the one feeding on Anna, never imagining for a moment Anna was breathing our air, feeding on our moisture, and holding on to us all the more tightly by way of emotional symbiosis.

What is the meaning of all this, Anna? Did you place yourself too far above ordinary mortals? Or did we place you there, reverent followers that we are? Maybe you were meant at last to discover that destiny does not convey in a straight line and the twists and turns can throw you way off course. That may be the simple truth you've never comprehended.

Now you know.

Late that night, as everyone slept soundly, I slipped into Anna's darkroom and the door closed slowly behind me like portals in a gothic horror film. I groped in the darkness for the light switch, placed farther from the entry than usual to avoid the intrusion of light at an inopportune moment. When I flicked the switch, a low light filtered across the room from an opaque glass fixture on the opposite wall and I heard a fan whirring from the ventilating system David had installed so the small room, tightly insulated against illumination, would have breathable air.

That little bit of air, however, retained a hint of the chemical stench one would expect in a processing lab, which brought to mind the hurried preparations for Jeremy's birth – that terrifying moment when the doctor's eyes met mine and the nurses leaped into action, swerving around the room with aluminum tables of emergency equipment. Cold antiseptic was slopped across my bloated belly like swaths of paint on canvas, and I recoiled from the smell, never more frightened, but Jason's hand gripped mine, his assurance my strength, until, moments later, my squirming baby boy was elevated for viewing, safe and whole.

I forced myself to return my attention to the darkroom, my eyes slowly adjusting to the limited light. What was I expecting to find there? Sneaking around like a private detective, searching for clues to destiny, I nearly laughed aloud at myself. One thing was certain: Anna had tidied the space to perfection, everything sealed and stored with precision, as if a summer home shuttered at the end of the season, although Anna is not known for neatness.

The room reminded me of a chemistry lab, populated with piping, double sinks, storage shelves and processing tanks, all empty and sparkling even in low light. A wall clock displayed a second hand steadily ticking around its face like the larger versions marking time at the train station. A small refrigerator contained bottled water as well as temperature-sensitive liquids and a few ice packs to ensure the optimum temperature of the finishing baths. On an overhead shelf, a pile of printer paper and bottles of wetting agent, fixer and developing liquids, and on a larger shelf, a tall rectangular receptacle with three stacked trays for negatives. In a drawer, a pair of rubber gloves, a sponge, a lens, a brush and a metal pen: tools of the trade. In the center of it all, an enlarger, shaped like a microscope, adjacent to a light box. All the artifacts of a photographer's life frozen in time like the remains of Pompeii.

Only the cameras were missing. I had noticed a pile of them on the bed stand in the master bedroom, clustered like a shrine, and without them, the darkroom seemed the inner workings of the brain, without a heart.

As I sat down on the small stool between workstations, grateful for an anchor for my wobbly legs, I pulled the chain on the overhead safelight, which emanated a direct colorless beam, not at all the soft natural glow of sunlight or moonlight or even the extended glow of camera light. Odd that a photographer relies so completely on light to capture the image, then contrives desperately to seal in darkness to protect it. Photography suddenly seemed to me an odd vocation for a person who believed in the spontaneity of life's journey.

Stacked on one of two long shelves mounted high on the back wall were a number of manuals on photographic technique, materials and processing, and a blue paperback written by Susan Sontag, which I pulled down. An old train receipt bookmarked an underlined passage:

To take a picture is to have an interest in things as they are, in the status quo remaining unchanged [at least for as long as it takes to get a "good" picture], to be in complicity with whatever makes a subject interesting, worth photographing – including, when that is the interest, another person's pain or misfortune.

I pondered Sontag's words briefly before replacing the book to examine the line-up of black canvas albums that filled the second shelf. A handwritten white sticker affixed vertically to the bottom of each spine identified their contents and I leaned forward and cocked my head to read the labels. To my surprise, instead of collecting photographs by year or period, events or subjects, Anna had labeled her albums either Living or Dying.

I suppose I shouldn't have been shocked, in light of Tim's commentary. Still, such a macabre means of organizing one's life's work was unsettling and I scanned them closer, in the hope of some sort of explanation, but all read the same: Living or Dying #1, #2, #3, #4 and so on.

I tentatively opened Living #1. A series of 5X7 photographs were compressed in plastic sleeves. The first contained an image of David, long ago, taken from behind his coiled body stretched out on a mattress on the floor of what must have been their first apartment. He was stark naked, his marbled body a horizontal Michelangelo's David, and the photograph seemed to depict a young man at rest from his own masculinity. Next, a photo of Beth as a newborn, nestled into a gunnysack, its thick burlap folds acting as a shield against the elements, set onto a large dense pile of multi-colored dried autumn leaves awaiting disposal. I thought perhaps these would all be family photos, but the very next was of Tim at work, huddled in conversation with staff, their faces filled with expectation. Another of a regatta of boats near the harbor, brightly colored sails fluttering like the serrated fringes of a celebratory banner, with a sharper focus on one solitary, barely visible figure leaning into the wind. A color photo of nine or ten year-old boys playing soccer, Will dead center, their legs and uniforms mud-splashed. Another of David dressed in jeans and work boots, wearing a hard hat and standing atop a scaffold, a broad smile on his face, one thumb raised in a gesture of accomplishment. A photograph of Maggie in her kitchen, her work island covered completely with aluminum cookie sheets filled with exquisitely formed and lightly browned phyllo dough-filled appetizers, perhaps still warm. Other friends, other settings: unconventional portraits of ordinary acts of living. As they were taken over several years, I wondered if Anna may have only recently gathered them together into these albums, obsessed perhaps with mortality, as Tim suggested.

I took down each album in turn, all without apparent sequence. One contained several photographs of Karen and her ex-husband frolicking at the beach when they were younger and of the two families together on Christmas morning. A recent photograph of Will leaning against the car, reeking of adolescent arrogance like James Dean, followed by one of Henry leaning against his taxi in the same pose. A heart-stopping photograph of Anna's parents, when they were much younger, her mother dressed in a blue silk gown, father in a tuxedo, dancing among others as if no one else were in the room. One of Adrienne in her medical garb but barefoot, sitting in a lotus position on a shiny linoleum floor in what seemed the children's ward, an intense expression of concentration on her face as she pasted a wooden popsicle stick to a dollhouse roof.

I discovered a photograph of Jeremy tantalizing Seuss with a tiny stuffed mouse on a string and touched the page as if I might pull him from it, staring at this image far longer than the others before continuing to the next collection.

Each album was filled with similar portraits of family and friends, neighbors and colleagues. Some contained duplicates of framed photographs hung in the hallway, and I felt that flush of recognition one feels at a museum when you see a work of art you have viewed previously only in books. One album consisted entirely of the spiritually infused photographs of the steeple, as well as scenes of the restoration in progress. Another with photographs of the trees marked for destruction: old elm and oak, sugar maple, and an ancient copper beech with red bands around their trunks. And the series taken at the hospital emergency room: patients and doctors desperate for life.

Everyone in Anna's orbit was captured among the living – David and the children, Adrienne and Maggie, Karen, Tim, Henry – as well as Anna's favorite newspaper photos. Taken together, a retrospective on life. However not one image of me. Not that I like to be photographed, although Anna has snapped a few over the years, yet none were there. Nor any other photographs of my family beyond the one of Jeremy.

Hesitant, I turned to the first album of the dying. I was afraid to look and started to put it back unopened, but held on to it, succumbed to curiosity.

The first image was of Anna's mother now, who, although alive, has no memory and little consciousness of living. I was struck by the sense of continuity behind her eyes, a sort of light in the distance, like the soft glow emanating from an old house on a hill, so far from everything else one wonders how to get there and who might reside within. The photographs that followed were similarly shadowy and restrained, stunning in their artistry: a reflection of dying as homage to living.

I opened another album to find Anna's father on his deathbed, his eyes closed, likely moments after his spirit had drifted gently past her cheek the day before we met at the hospital. Her elegant grandmother, dressed in a red dress and wearing a slightly tilted felt hat, slumped in a wheelchair. An elderly skeletal neighbor lying on a chaise lounge with his eyes closed to the sunshine on his craggy face. The photograph of a family at a graveside service that I had admired in the hall, and when I recognized Henry standing at the center of the mourners, I realized the funeral must have been for his wife. There were several images of headstones in the church cemetery, stones tall and short, curved or squared, as if a panorama of a community. In another album, a photograph taken at the hospital morgue, a dead body draped in white fabric and, despite the morbidity of the scene, there was the same sense of serenity that permeated all the photographs on dying. This album contained no one familiar to me, only image after image of strangers coping with death, some with a greater sense of peace than they might have experienced in life.

The last album contained an extraordinary grouping of photographs taken at the hospice. A white woman, with a freckled, wrinkled face and hair the color of polished silver, had eyes as clear as a mountain stream, despite a body twisted and hunched. Several images of a woman with remarkably smooth, dark brown skin that contrasted sharply with snow-white hair; she never looked directly into the camera, rather into the distance, beyond the narrow parameters of old age. One man with sagging skin and wispy hair, his eyes sunken into his sockets, who in each picture smiled in a flirtatious way, grateful for a bit of attention from a pretty woman.

All three had accepted their impending death: no tubes, no hoses or machinery, taking comfort in kindness, their last lingering memories, and the opportunity to die gracefully.

The next to last photograph in that last album on dying stopped me cold. I felt myself sinking toward the floor, as if I might faint, so I tipped my head forward to my knees and breathed as evenly as possible to restore equilibrium. At last, I sat up to face a black and white photograph of me, dressed in sweatpants and Jason's wrinkled plaid pajama shirt, curled into a fetal position on the floor of Jeremy's room. A photograph Anna must have taken during those first weeks after the accident. I stared at that pitiful image for several moments before turning to the last in the collection, another of me, some time later, asleep on the couch, Seuss curled at my feet, still in Jason's clothes, so worn out and disheveled I was hardly recognizable.

The camera had captured my grief, detected not with kindness but with the detachment Sontag described. Misery dramatized for effect. I stared at the woman in those photographs, bereft and cadaverous like hospice patients, but without the acceptance I had seen in their eyes. Ten years later, I remain that wretched creature, no longer worthy of the camera. Anna grouped me with the dying, and rightfully so, as I am a mere proxy to my own life.

Was it no wonder she withheld from me her secrets? Why would she choose to share her stories of living with the dead?

I closed my eyes and recalled the litany of life supports Anna listed that day in the park. All were there in her albums. Love. Friendship. Sunshine. Family, faith and memory. And the willingness to accept one's destiny. Had Anna fulfilled her purpose to remind us of this continuum of living and dying? The albums were full and clearly labeled, basins washed and emptied, darkroom spotless and ready for light.

You were my crutch, Anna. The fractures to my psyche so incapacitating I could barely walk without you. Nevertheless, I never imagined you pictured me a cripple, crawling toward death.

As I replaced the last album, I noticed one smaller album tucked in the back that I almost missed. Worn and dusty, with a cover unlike the others, the label was printed in a child's hand: BEWARE THE DOG. Anna's first foray into photojournalism, featuring a lonely dog that might have represented both living and dying, as we all do.

THREE

They never forgot
That even the dreadful martyrdom must run its course.

W. H Auden

Throughout that night, seething with indignation unaccustomed and repulsive, I paced the den so feverishly I carved a path in the rug. Like all the feelings I have held at bay these ten long years, hardly an ounce of emotion spewed, even without the shackles of antidepressants. At last, as if one final indignity, my body convulsed in spasms in a decisive retreat from medication, aided and abetted by rage. I collapsed to the floor.

I lay there, shaking uncontrollably, wondering whether I would at last fall apart. No medicine, no Anna, nothing to lean on. At the same time, I bristled at the betrayal of trust. The tether that bound me to Anna had snapped in my hand, a tether within which she concealed her true self on a supposedly divine path to self-actualization. Was I so self-absorbed to not see Anna as she really is? Directing her future even as she allegedly relinquished herself to destiny, and all the while perceiving me not as a special friend trapped in grief, rather a miserable, nearly comatose creature, worthy of weekly visitations, unworthy of a compassionate lens.

As dawn light peeked over the horizon into the little room, I knew I had to leave Anna's house. No matter the comfort of familiarity, or the nourishment of friends and the sense of being once again a fuller participant in this ritual we call living. I was desperate to return to my cocoon, resume my quiet life and regain control of my emotions. And I needed a breather before fulfilling my responsibility as Anna's proxy, which I realized, no matter my abject feelings at that moment, I must do. I rose from the floor to face whatever was to come next.

"I have to go back to the city," I informed David and Karen, who sat at the kitchen table opposite each other sipping hot coffee until cool enough to slurp. They looked up at me with eyes ringed with dark circles, both rumpled from what I imagined was their own fitful sleep, and I had to stifle the inclination to confess the secrets of the darkroom. My disillusionment had no place in that kitchen.

"Must be things that need attending," David replied. "You will come back? I mean, your being here has meant a lot to the kids. To all of us."

Karen, who sat floppily on the kitchen chair, elongated her spine like a cat whose turf is threatened. How crucial it was for her to feel essential, and I momentarily considered asking her to take on the task entrusted to me, what a relief that might have been, but a deal is a deal, and Karen would be even less willing than I to fulfill Anna's wishes.

"I'll be back, very soon." I touched David's shoulder and he patted my hand with genuine affection. "Hang in," I whispered.

"Have a good trip," Karen called to me as I fled to the den to stuff my duffle with dirty clothes and personal belongings.

Will suddenly appeared in the doorway "I heard you're going to the city." He slouched against the doorframe with an ardent expression suggesting he had something on his mind. "Need a ride to the station?"

"Since when do you drive?"

"Won't have my license until fall and I haven't driven in two weeks. I need the practice. Want to take a chance?"

In the midst of mayhem, we had forgotten one of the most crucial moments in a suburban teenager's life: learning to drive. What else, I wondered, had been forfeited, or yet to be, by a prolonged vigil.

"How many lessons have you had?" I asked.

"Enough. And Henry let me drive the taxi once; that was cool. At the end of Driver's Ed, we get a few hours behind the wheel with a pro, but for now, I'm on the permit. The next train is at noon," he added as he checked the time on his cell phone.

"Don't rush," I cautioned as I gripped my bag.

Will grabbed the keys to the BMW wagon, the car David generally drives. On the back seat were rolls of blueprints bound in thick rubber bands that rolled back and forth now and then when Will's pressure on the brake pedal was too sharp. Once in town, we were stuck behind a line of cars held captive by the upturned hand of a traffic cop and while waiting, Will strummed his fingers on the steering wheel to a tune on the radio.

"I can't stand the traffic lately," he muttered.

"You sound like Henry," I answered, forcing a smile.

"He goes on and on about it, I just get bothered. Mom never seems to care a whole lot, unless she has a shoot, but she always has time. I mean, even if she's late, what's the problem? They wait for her."

We all wait for her, I thought, as the traffic slowly merged before breaking out again to a more even flow.

"You're doing very well," I said.

"Nothing to it."

"Maybe not for you."

"You don't like to drive?"

"Don't need to."

"Maybe I'll never live in the city. I would always want to have a car."

"There you go. All about priorities."

He nodded and as I turned to face him, he appeared to me the small boy he was, navigating a tricycle. He kept his eyes on the road as he pulled into the station driveway, carefully easing the wagon into a slot at the designated drop-off area.

"You'd better hurry back," he said. "Mom will wait for you."

I was dumbfounded by that thought, wondering what I might say to Anna when, or if, the opportunity presented.

"When your mother opens her eyes, it will be you, you and Beth, and your Dad, that's who she'll want to see."

I leaned over to kiss him on the cheek and he wrapped one arm around me and hugged me tight, a simple gesture that nearly destroyed what little emotional vitality I had left.

The short wait for the train seemed interminable. I patrolled the platform and puffed on my last cigarette, and when the engine rumbled into the station, slipped into the nearest window seat. I inhaled the familiar scent of mildew and newsprint and closed my eyes, overcome with exhaustion. I had been away just over two weeks and felt as if I had been gone for months.

Once at my apartment, I found a note from my neighbor that Seuss was lonely and lethargic but otherwise fine. The same message was on my phone answering machine, which I had failed to check remotely as I so rarely have messages. I stepped into the hallway, felt for the spare key my neighbors keep tucked into a crevice between our apartments, and let myself in. Seuss was sleeping on a pillow on the floor in Jessica's room. I watched him for a moment until his radar alerted him to my presence and he opened his eyes. Slowly, with great effort, he rose. How feeble he seemed, age often settling over animals and humans all at once.

I gathered him in my arms, carried him home, and placed him on a couch pillow. I put on a teakettle and moments later returned to sit beside Seuss, staring out the window that faces the dark space between apartment buildings, mindlessly dipping a bag of Darjeeling tea in and out of a mug until the steaming water turned the color of copper. I sipped the warm brew until my body felt limp. Beside me, Seuss's chest undulated with each breath, just like Anna. The two of them, my two precious companions, struggling to breathe, made me wish I could relinquish my air to them, as they had so generously given to me all these years, and just as I had that thought, I remembered Anna's duplicity. We so often do not know people as well as we believe we do, even this one person I assumed I knew best, and thought I could trust, who apparently felt the need to hide her true self.

Anna's motives may not have been as existential as she professed. Having held herself up so long as an archetype of constancy, perhaps Tim was right, perhaps she dreaded the revelation of her own frailty. Or, seeing me as a pathetic creature, barely living, she believed I might never let her go, whereas David, the wounded husband, could not be trusted. Everything seemed topsy-turvy, yet nothing explained why she stepped off the curb that day, why she remained in limbo, or why I was destined to facilitate her fate.

The phone rang suddenly, loud and shrill through the hushed apartment, and I scrambled to answer it, assuming it had to do with Anna's condition, grabbing the receiver just before it went to voice mail.

"Hey, babe. Your cell phone's been turned off for days. Where you been?"

I sighed with relief to hear Danny's voice. "Out of town."

"Your dad?"

"Anna's."

Danny didn't wait for elaboration.

"Want to come over tonight?"

"I can't."

"Okay."

"Danny?"

"Yeah, Nell?"

"Will you come here?"

"To your place?"

"I've been away too long, Seuss needs company. Will you come?"

"Twenty minutes."

"Thanks," I murmured gratefully.

This was the first time Danny and I would be together in my apartment, and even though I needed to be with him, I could never take him to my bed, so I piled two thick quilts on the living room carpet, where I might also keep an eye on Seuss in a deep sleep on the couch.

The satin of the quilt cover and the soft pillow of down filling made a comfortable mattress, the hard wood floor beneath a reminder of the temporal quality of passion. With Danny, on our makeshift bed, I drifted far from the dismal landscape of Anna's world. I inhaled a warm breeze drifting through the open window, and, radiating with longing, left all else behind.

We clung to each other at first, grateful to be reunited. Danny wrapped his long legs around my body more tightly than usual, as if he understood I needed fortification. I felt a force between us even beyond the clutch of limbs, the probing of lips and fingertips, until the moment when I pulled him into me, frantic for that union, my body arching to him and erupting with passion. We climaxed quickly, sorrow and arousal once again in harmony, and I clasped him to me until well after our breathing and body temperatures returned to normal.

When at last we separated, Danny curled himself around me with such tenderness, I felt I might tell him anything, so I described what happened to Anna, her infidelity, the revelation of the darkroom, her apparent obsession with eternity, and her perception of me among the dying. I also confessed my terror of collapsing completely, any day now, once and for all, under the weight of my best friend's pending demise and my part in facilitating that possibility.

He listened. He steadied my trembling limbs and gently stroked my cheek. No questions or answers or expectations.

It was the middle of the night when he left. The city was as close to silent as it can be, only the distant timbre of nightlife. I slugged the last of the cold tea and slipped into stained black sweatpants and a faded gray sweatshirt with "Cape Cod" embroidered in large scripted letters across the front. I outlined the words with one finger. The sweatshirt was a memento of a summer vacation ten years earlier, the summer we celebrated Jeremy's sixth birthday, and our last summer together. The calendar for that September still hangs behind the door of Jeremy's room, I never took it down, and a brown stuffed bear he won at a carnival still sits on the windowsill, watching me through green glass eyes that glow in the dark.

I flicked the switch and the room was suffused with bright overhead light, the direct opposite of Anna's darkroom. The space is mostly empty now, all of Jeremy's furniture donated years ago to a homeless shelter. Only my potter's wheel is perched dead center on a jute rug, as if a sculpture. Dusty remnants of dried clay clung to the edges, making it seem especially eerie, and reminding me once again of the remains of Pompeii.

The magic of potting is the taking of inanimate material and molding it into something unique. The wheel itself becomes an extension of the potter, so much so that it takes on nearly human characteristics – energy, intimacy, motion, and response. We used to dance together, the wheel and I: dance and sing and delight in the rush of conception.

I felt the need that night to try again. Seuss' breathing was labored but steady, so I filled a bucket with water and pulled packets of old clay out of the closet, gently punching out air pockets to break down clumped particles. Materials at hand, I crouched down at the wheel, right foot poised above the motor control pedal and the left pushed to the floor for support. I sunk my body securely into place and hugged my arms to either side of the wheel, welcoming the familiar musty scent and sighing with the pleasure of the ritual.

I piled fresh clay onto the center plate and sprinkled water along the top until it was supple to the touch. I felt the pull of leg muscles grown stiff from disuse as I pressed my toes to the pedal, slowly, cautiously easing my way back into the process. I closed my eyes and fell into the trance, pacified by the gentle hum of the wheel. For an hour or more, I kneaded and caressed the clay, taking in the nourishment of pulverized plant life and minerals, adding droplets of water, and increasing or decreasing the speed of the wheel as needed. Cold wet particles clung to my fingers and my slippery hands cradled the contour in an effort to recreate life out of water and clay and loneliness.

A midwife to memory, I closed my eyes and saw Jeremy and Jason frolicking in the park. Anna laughing, her pale eyes bright and caring, and Seuss a precious kitten chasing her tail. A sob seeped from my lips. Salty tears fell from my eyes onto the clay and I lost control of the wheel, whirling wildly at first before wobbling in place like a flat tire, steadily slowing until the momentum was lost. I tried again, to no avail. Clay crumbled in my hands. Nothing left for the potter: no shape, no substance, no life.

When I sat up, I saw Seuss watching me from the doorway, gasping for breath. I crawled to him and lifted his fragile body into

my lap, smoothing his fur, infusing into my touch all the affection
I had.

"Dear, dear Seuss," I chanted. "Sweet friend," I
murmured, holding him close to my chest as I rocked him to the
inner rhythm of the wheel. I thought he might be all right when his
body and breathing seemed to relax; however, all at once he heaved
a deep spasmodic breath and looked beseechingly up at me.

"It's all right, Seuss," I whispered. "It will be all right."

He closed his eyes and went slack in my arms.

A flicker of light seeped through the blinds and I heard the rumbling of early morning delivery trucks. I wrapped Seuss in his favorite blanket and nestled him into a black plastic garbage bag. Before I sealed the bag, I tucked Jeremy's bear under the edge of the blanket to keep Seuss company, perhaps to return to Jeremy wherever they might encounter each other again. Tears streamed down my cheeks as I sealed the bag and bolted from the apartment, nearly sprinting to the veterinarian's office and muttering all along the way a feckless repetitive prayer: "Goodbye Seuss, Goodbye Seuss, Goodbye."

His body quickly grew stiff and heavy, and I had to stifle an overwhelming urge to throw the bag like a javelin off a rooftop, gripping the handle so tightly my own life might have depended on it as I dashed through early morning traffic, knowing that if I stopped, even for a second, I might not go on. I must have made quite a sight in my stained sweat clothes, crying and clutching a black trash bag containing the last remnant of my family.

A technician rushed to my side when I pounded on the door, but as he reached for the bag, I pulled it back.

"What can I do for you?" he inquired.

I couldn't speak and he stood silently, knowingly, then turned and returned with a cup of water, which he placed into my hand as he gently extricated the bag from my grip.

"Seuss Herman," I sniveled. "I'll want... I'll want the ashes."

"Of course, Mrs. Herman. Do you want me to call someone? A taxi perhaps?"

"There's no one to call," I answered.

I returned to my apartment, pulled all the dirty clothes from my duffle and filled it with a fresh batch. I wiped down the last bits of clay on the potter's wheel and rinsed the dishes in the sink. I turned off all the lights in the apartment and closed the living room window. I wrote a note of explanation and thanks to Jessica and Ruth and returned the key to its hiding place.

Before I left, I retrieved from the freezer Anna's health care proxy, and tucked it carefully into the zippered compartment of my purse. Fearful of finality, I nonetheless pressed on, making my way back through city streets to the train.

Henry was waiting for me on arrival.

"Karen called a meeting at the hospital," he said as he took my bag and opened the door to the taxi. "You'll want to be there."

"A meeting?"

"The big enchilada. They want to move Anna to another facility."

"Why?"

Henry shook his head. "It's a small hospital. I imagine they prefer these patients to be treated at nursing care. Or hospice."

"Okay, to the hospital," I pronounced.

"Perhaps we'll stop at Anna's first. You might want to freshen up."

I looked down and saw that I still wore my potter's clothes, streaked with clay, nearly matching my tear-stained face.

"Thanks for looking out for me," I said as I parked myself on the front seat and scanned the increasingly colorful landscape.

At Anna's house, while Henry ran an errand, I lingered in the shower longer than usual, welcoming the torrential scalding water to strip away the last of the city's soot and encrusted clay. I used a loofa sponge hanging from the showerhead to scour my body, then scrubbed my scalp until tingling, rinsing with an almond-scented conditioner. I stood under the showerhead until the heat made me woozy and emerged spent and purged.

I dressed quickly and gulped down a can of soda and half a blueberry muffin I found in the fridge, mustering the energy I needed to face Anna's caretakers. If Henry had not been waiting, leaning on his taxi like a chauffeur, like one of Anna's photos of the living, I might have curled myself on the couch to hide, but when I peeked out the window, there he was, conscience and ally, and so, renewed and ready as I might ever be, I grabbed my purse and headed back out into the light of day.

At the hospital, the players were seated opposite each other at a U-shaped conference table, no one at the head, and the assembly felt from the moment I arrived like an inquisition, or one of those nasty congressional hearings where everyone attacks the person in the hot seat to serve personal agendas. Clustered on one side were the attending physician, the neurologist, and the resident in charge, nearly indistinguishable by virtue of white jackets and steely expressions. A short round woman with tight curls and a practiced smile was introduced as the social worker, sitting nearly shoulder to shoulder with a hospital administrator, a tall lean woman, with stylishly short cropped hair and designer glasses hanging on a chain around her neck, who assured us by way of introduction she was in attendance merely to be of assistance. Adrienne stood near the door, straddling sides, I guess, prepared to facilitate or mediate. David and Karen faced the hospital contingent and David motioned for me to sit to his side when I arrived, although Karen scowled at my late entrance.

The hospital was determined to remove Anna from life support or move her to another facility. She was no longer a candidate for continuing care, not, as the doctors repeated, parenthetically but emphatically, under the present circumstances.

My jaw clenched, my stomach churned, and I'm certain I must have cringed noticeably now and then, but I said nothing, waiting for the right moment to intervene, if I had to.

Karen argued that Anna needed more intensive treatment and the doctors countered there was nothing further to be done, that all measures indicated a persistent vegetative state and there was every reason to believe Anna would remain in that condition until death. This was the first time we had been given that dour a prognosis. We sat agape for a time. Poor David blanched, before turning red in the face. The social worker said a few words, platitudes largely, meant to ameliorate the tension. The administrator took notes. Adrienne interjected now and then. David, maintaining his stoicism, argued that Anna was not the typical sort of patient and the hospital should not make the mistake of giving up on her too soon. I remained paralyzed, as if masking tape had been placed over my mouth, even knowing my authority might settle the dispute, foolishly awaiting divine intervention.

At the close, the hospital administrator confirmed that Anna would be moved in forty-eight hours. We all silently exited the meeting room and our contingent adjourned to the lounge, where Maggie had just arrived with sandwiches. We settled into chairs to eat like factory workers who, responding to a bell, fall into place without expression or energy. I opened the window and a welcome gush of air blew into the room. The mid-day sun shed no direct light, so I turned on a few lamps as if to ward off evil spirits. We ate nearly in syncopation, digesting the situation with our food.

Karen continued the charge, and I admired once again her temerity. "Adrienne, is there anything else we should know?"

Adrienne shook her head no. "They need a DNR or David's permission to remove life support. Otherwise, she will be moved, and you will have to make other decisions at that point."

"Makes me so damn mad I could scream," Karen roared.

"Karen, keep in mind, there are just so many beds. Post-operative patients require intensive nursing care. Senior citizens are in distress and sick children need attention. All patients must be considered."

"Why doesn't Anna deserve the same attention? That's what I don't get."

"Anna needs maintenance care now. She should be in a facility that deals in long-term patient care, not a hospital. Frankly..." Adrienne stopped mid-sentence.

"Frankly what?" David asked.

"They would have moved her already had I not interceded. And they will move her, unless she is removed from life support."

"Then she can stay?" Maggie asked.

"Yes," Adrienne answered. "Not indefinitely mind you, but a while longer, because at that point, she falls into a different category..."

"Extortion, that's what it is!" Karen interjected.

"Karen, please," David said. "Condemnation doesn't help."

"But David, this is medical politics. We cannot fold…"

"I know, I know," David muttered. "Everything is politics. The hospital has rules, the insurance company has rules, but everything is negotiable. They cannot force us to do anything."

"Actually, they can," Adrienne remarked.

"What is wrong with you, Adrienne?" Karen asked. "You sound like you would like to pull the plug."

Maggie uttered a cry.

"For God's sake, Karen, must you say it that way?" David cried out loudly.

"I asked Adrienne a question," Karen repeated, ignoring David and Maggie.

"I am not ready to concede defeat for Anna," Adrienne answered. "But I am a realist and I know what will happen next."

"Why is removing Anna from life support conceding defeat?" I ventured. The group turned to me as one, having just remembered I was there.

"What do you mean?" David asked.

"I mean, well, perhaps the next steps are preordained, and the best option is to proceed with minimal intervention."

"Oh, not you too," Karen muttered.

"Nell, I know you think she is the master of her own destiny," David argued, in a distinctly patronizing tone, "but we're not talking about the flu or pneumonia. We're talking about potentially life threatening brain damage."

"Yes, I know that," I answered, refusing for once to be deterred. "I am suggesting the diagnosis or prognosis may no longer matter."

"Really. And what does?"

"What matters is what Anna would have wanted under these circumstances, and Anna would never have permitted artificial life support, certainly not for long. You know that."

"No, I do not know that, Nell. Neither do you, even if you think you do," David snapped.

"The point is moot," Karen said. "These sorts of discussions are absurd because we never know exactly what circumstances might bring us to this moment in our lives. It's all well and good to say we want to live, or die, without interference. We don't want feeding tubes or respirators or what not. Purely theoretical. It's kind of like childbirth. We all want to deliver naturally, you know, focal points and shallow breathing, but the truth is, when the pain is completely unbearable and not likely to subside, we beg for drugs. And if there is any danger, we are ready to rip that baby right out. We don't really know how we will react until we get there."

"Whatever," David pronounced soberly. "In the absence of a living will or an alternative power of attorney, the spouse makes these decisions. So let's get back to the real question at hand."

"Anna expressed her wishes to me," I said, my voice so feeble I was hardly heard.

"What did you say?" David asked.

I breathed in deeply and exhaled slowly, aware that all of them were staring at me in confusion. "I am Anna's health care proxy."

"What are you talking about?" Adrienne asked.

"Anna made a living will and asked me to represent her."

"That's ridiculous," Karen bellowed.

"She would have told me," David said, in a measured tone of voice that suggested to me he suspected otherwise.

"Whether or not she asked you to be her health care proxy is, at this point, irrelevant, Nell," Adrienne said, calmly but contemptuously, the way a Dickensian headmistress might belittle a student into believing she is ignorant and unworthy.

"How so?" I asked, inserting calm into my shaky voice.

"You have no legal grounds. These things have to be executed officially. A casual discussion between friends does not supersede spousal authority."

David leaned over to pat my hand and said, "I'm sure you mean well, Nell, but let me handle this."

His smug dismissal riled me enough to inspire greater resolve. And, recognizing at last my commitment to Anna, I no longer intended to disavow my place in the discussion.

"Excuse me, David, but you may have to let me handle this, because I have an official living will and I have the responsibility to execute based on Anna's wishes."

Karen shouted, "Who the hell do you think you are?"

"Oh, please," Maggie pleaded, "please, we're in this together. Maybe this is just a misunderstanding…"

"Stay calm, Maggie." Adrienne's eyebrows were nearly strung together in a dark furrow over the bridge of her glasses. "You actually have legal documentation?"

"Not possible," David muttered. "Let me see what you have."

They all glared at me as I unzipped my purse and withdrew the Ziploc bag containing Anna's health care directive. I snapped open the plastic locking and handed the papers to David. "There is another copy, with the witness."

As David unfolded the papers, Adrienne asked, "Who is the witness?"

Unwilling at that point to surrender one ounce of my carefully constructed composure by admitting my ignorance, I casually remarked, "It's all in there, Adrienne. I assure you, it is legal. More importantly, it is what Anna wanted."

"Let me see it," Adrienne demanded, stretching out an upturned palm.

"Just a minute," David answered as he scanned the document.

The silence, as they say, was deafening. I peeked up at Maggie, the one person I hoped would retain equanimity under those conditions, but saw only dark flecks of anxiety in her eyes as she awaited David's response.

"David, I can tell you if this is legitimate," Adrienne pestered.

"Just a minute, Adrienne," David growled, turning the page and glancing down to the signature lines.

"My Lord," David bellowed. "Henry Mason!"

"Henry?" Adrienne repeated.

"The taxi driver? What's he got to do with it?" Karen snapped.

"Henry Mason, Esquire," David pronounced.

He handed the papers to Adrienne, leaning back in his chair in defeat.

"Esquire?" Karen asked, rising to peek over Adrienne's shoulder at the paperwork.

"Yes. Henry was a lawyer, for the bank, the family bank. Some fifty years or so. He handled trusts and estates," David muttered.

"Driving a taxi is his retirement thing," Maggie added.

At that moment, Tim stepped into the room. "Any sandwiches left?" he asked Maggie as he moved toward the food basket on the table by the chair where David sat rubbing his forehead, silently pondering the surprising turn of events.

"What's going on here?" Tim asked.

"It seems," Karen piped up, "Nell is Anna's health care agent, which she has failed to mention until today."

"Really?" Tim asked. He smiled, cocking his head as he turned to me. "Well, well, little Nell. What a nice surprise."

"What's so nice about it?" Karen grumbled.

"Someone has to speak for Anna," Tim answered.

"Why Nell?" Karen snapped, grabbing the papers from Adrienne.

"Because Nell is the only one here who completely and unequivocally cares only what Anna would want for herself," Tim declared.

I turned away and slouched in my chair, easily fatigued by conflict.

"That's ridiculous!" Karen exclaimed.

"You are out of line," David barked.

"Really, Tim, you think you know Anna better than you do," Adrienne countered.

A smirk filtered across Tim's lips and he pointed one finger at Adrienne as he clucked, "We all think we know Anna better than we do."

Adrienne groaned as she reclaimed the papers from Karen.

"What do you think?" David asked her.

"Why did you not show us these papers from the first?" Adrienne asked me, her way of endorsing the legitimacy of the living will.

I sat stolidly still for a moment before I spoke: a criminal caught in the glare of interrogation.

"I suppose I could tell you that I forgot, but I guess I chose to forget. The day of the accident, I simply couldn't allow myself to think that Anna was in a life or death situation. And then, everything happened so fast, and she was already on life support, and, well, you hope for the best, and I lost track of time… Let's face it, I failed to live up to my obligation. That's the truth. I failed her. Now I have to make good." I scanned the room, searching for a glimmer of understanding and found none except Tim. "I never wanted this responsibility, but Anna begged me to do this for her, so I agreed. I never imagined I would ever be put in this position."

"And what position is that?" Karen asked.

Adrienne answered for me. "Nell has the power, in fact the responsibility, to fulfill Anna's wishes regarding life support. Anna's fate is in Nell's hands."

I felt at that moment as if we had all been thrust into the theater of the absurd, or, more likely, one of Anna's augmented photographs: everyone reduced to background while I might have been lit with a bright direct light.

"My obligation is to fulfill Anna's wishes." I hoped the plea would sink in, and, as I spoke, imagined that our stage came back into focus and we were once again level players, all equally desperate for a reasonable resolution.

"And what are your wishes?" David asked, leaning toward me as if in supplication.

"My wishes? Does it matter?"

"Yes, I think so. We need to know what it is you want for Anna."

I stared into David's eyes, eyes equally imploring and irate.

"I want exactly what all of you want. I want Anna to be well, of course."

"I am not questioning that," David answered. "I just think we can work this through to our advantage. Right now, only those of us here are aware that this proxy exists. Even Henry hasn't come forward."

"He might have forgotten," Maggie said.

"I doubt it," Tim responded with a snort. "Henry doesn't miss a trick."

David ignored Tim. "Anna was placed on life support as soon as she arrived at the hospital, her wishes have already been violated. I'm not sure these papers are valid at this point."

"That's a legal question," Adrienne answered. "Medically, the existence of a living will and a health care proxy will at the very least place a DNR in her chart, so if any life-preserving medical treatment is in question, the hospital must withhold. However, removing her from life support systems requires specific instruction."

"Unless, unless…" David stammered. "Unless Nell agrees to put it aside."

I stared in astonishment at David. Could he possibly be so facile in his disregard for his wife's wishes? Perhaps Anna's concerns were legitimate.

"You cannot be serious," Tim said.

"Stay out of this," David ordered Tim before turning back to me.

"Nell, let's talk about this," he said in the tone of voice a parent might use to assuage the pleas of a demanding child.

"There is nothing to talk about," Tim interjected. "Henry would tell you that."

"Henry is not here," David retorted. "And this is between Nell and me."

"This is between Nell and Anna," Tim quipped.

"I think you should leave now, Tim," David snapped. "And if you print one word of this, I promise you I will sue you and the newspaper. This is none of your business."

"Surely you know by now I am only concerned with Anna's welfare. I am not a journalist in this room, David, but I am a witness, keep that in mind."

Tim circled the room to pass me as he departed, leaning over to touch my shoulder with one hand and whisper, "Hang in, Nell. And thank you."

I was moved by his unanimity, and grateful for an ally in what was clearly becoming a more adversarial situation than I could have imagined.

David contemplated his options. Karen started pacing the room as Maggie picked up the remains of food and drink to discard. I noticed tears on her cheeks and tried to make eye contact with her, but she didn't look up.

"Nell, let's talk," David said.

"I need a cigarette," I answered.

David nodded. "Let's take a walk."

David followed me to the smoking area at the side of the hospital, but as there were several nurses and orderlies milling about, we moved to a nearby patio. Clusters of young trees and bushes, their roots mounded in dark fresh earth, bordered the flagstone, reinforced with wires attached to stakes. I could have used similar support at that moment. A family of four huddled nearby, swiping at tears, and we kept our distance as if we might be contaminated by the obvious irrevocability of their situation. We sat down on a stone bench set among fledgling birch trees with white bark and dark green leaves and the promise of a long life ahead. Anna would have liked these trees, I thought, and even in the midst of that surreal situation, I felt the comfort of her companionship, letting go of my disenchantment in favor of the challenge ahead.

I smoked a cigarette in silence, down to the filter, lighting another from the stub, nicotine essential at that moment to fuel my psychological stamina. David watched until ready to speak.

"I'm sorry if we were hard on you," he began, his words evenly paced, as if they had been quickly rehearsed in his head. "You can imagine how shocked we are."

"Yes."

"We don't want to lose Anna."

"No, we don't."

"What shall we do then?"

"I've done what Anna asked me to do. I should have done it sooner. I was just so confused and frightened. I know I should have spoken up right away, but I couldn't. I didn't know how to deal with any of this, can you understand?"

"So why bring it up now? You could have let it go."

"Henry knew."

"Did he ever mention it to you?"

"No."

"Maggie may be right, maybe he forgot. He is over eighty after all."

"I don't think so."

"Why do you say that?"

"The way he talks to me, the way he looks at me at times, as if he's waiting for me to act. Besides, whether he remembers or not is of no consequence. I know, and now we all know what we have to do."

"We cannot let her go. People come out of comas long after this. Christ, Nell, she has been there for you every single moment. Ten years! She never gave up on you. She is your goddamn lifeline. Do you even have a life without Anna?"

I lowered my eyes, shaken by the rebuke.

"Did it ever occur to you that you owe us something, the children and me? All the days and nights Anna was in the city with you and wasn't with us. Tending to your wounds. Protecting you. Countless Wednesdays! Don't you owe us something in return? Maybe you owe Anna just a small ration of the years she has given to you."

I thought about the conversation with Anna that day in the park. Whatever secrets she may have kept from me, whatever choices she made for her own life, she was the best friend I ever had and I was indebted to her. To her, not to David, not even the children.

"You're right, David. I owe Anna a great deal. I owe you and the children the deepest gratitude, I know that. But that is all I owe to you. And the only way I can repay Anna is to be the same kind of friend to her as she has been to me. Besides," I continued, surprised by my audacity. "You and I both know I was not the only way she passed her time on Wednesdays."

David glared at me. "You are speaking of Tim."

"Yes, and for the record, I was in the dark on this. I've only just discovered where she was when she wasn't with me. Turns out I was a convenient alibi, easy to deceive."

"It doesn't matter," David muttered.

"No? Maybe you've made your peace, but I need more time."

He didn't speak.

"How did you know?" I asked. "You said yourself you never knew where she was?"

"You forget that while I do not always see the big picture, I'm all about the details. I notice right away when something is amiss, and something wasn't right with Anna for some time. While this scenario is the last thing I would have imagined, neither was I surprised."

"Why not?"

"I never imagined for a moment I would be enough for her. I just took what I could for as long as I could."

"But you accepted this? Allowed it?"

"I hoped it might peter out."

"You're not angry? She betrayed you, and me for that matter. I don't especially like having been a cover for her indiscretion."

David looked at me with pity in his eyes.

"It's not about you, Nell. I'm her husband. I'm the injured party here. But right now, my priority is to protect my children." He shook his head sadly. "What might be gained by letting this come out now?"

I nodded. Nothing to be gained, although I needed to make sense of it. "Whether you think so or not, she let me down. Makes me mad, that's all."

"Mad enough to pull the plug?"

"How can you say such a thing?"

"Then why now? Why can't you wait longer?"

"David, that day, the day Anna talked to me about all this, she talked about what truly sustains us. Whether we understand every word she says or can accept her way of life, she has the right to make these decisions. Tim called her an epiphyte, and she certainly shares those characteristics. I may be angry with her, but I love her, as I know you do, and, yes, I may be extremely dependent on her, yet she asked me to facilitate her wishes. *Me.*"

David winced. "Listen, Nell…"

"No." I shook my head, galvanized now with the righteousness of the moment. "We have no authority over her life. Not me. Not you. We have only the obligation to respect her wishes, and not just when convenient. We have to be prepared to let her go. That's all any of us can do."

My whole body was shaking; however my heartbeat was surprisingly steady, my breathing evenly paced. Perhaps I was not going to fall apart after all.

"Honestly, I don't know how I will go on without Anna. I wish I didn't have to, but I will do as she asked."

"Nell, you will kill Anna if you do this. Do you understand?"

"That is a terrible thing to say!" I turned to leave.

David grabbed my arm and held it firmly. "I cannot let this play out this way. There have to be other options. We need more time. Don't make me take this to court, Nell."

"You would do that?"

"Yes. I am absolutely unwilling to let my wife die without more time to live."

"David, you do not let Anna live or die, nor do I. We only allow her life to fulfill itself."

"What about Beth and Will? How will you explain this to them?"

I shook my head, stymied by the inability to make my case.

David stood and cowered over me. "I suggest you think about this before you act. You can make this easier for all of us."

"I will fulfill Anna's wishes. Perhaps you should consider doing the same."

The look on David's face made me fear he might slap me, but he just stood there scowling at me another moment before scurrying back into the hospital. I turned and sprinted toward the main entrance, where Tim was waiting for me.

"Are you all right?" he asked.

"Define all right."

He smiled. "Good girl. Don't let them wear you down."

"This isn't about me."

"Well, in some way, I think it is."

"Please, Tim. No more."

"I don't envy you this."

"Don't you? Seems people are as upset that I'm the chosen agent as with the next steps. What's that about?" I sat down on a stone bench, grateful for the grounding.

"In an odd sort of way, we are all Anna's disciples, vying for priority."

"I never asked for much."

"Perhaps that's why you are the chosen one."

"This is all giving me an awful headache," I moaned as I lit another cigarette.

Tim sat down next to me on the bench. "I confess, I wish it had been me."

I hung my head. Nothing made sense anymore, least of all my silent friend, a peaceable woman, surrounded by chaos and animosity.

"Don't be too quick to judge." Tim had read my thoughts.

"She used me. She's using me now. Anna is not nearly the ephemeral epiphyte you describe. More of a woman who got what she wanted under the guise of living in the moment."

"Nell, you're angry, but…"

"I am angry. And oh so tired. I definitely don't want to hear any more Zen-talk."

"Honestly, she never meant to hurt you."

I held up my palm to stop him. "We're done. I'll work this out for myself."

"Do you need a place to stay?"

"A place to stay? You think David will throw me out?"

"Maybe, or you might feel uncomfortable with them now."

"I'll cross that bridge when I get there."

"Be brave," Tim said as he walked away.

Brave. Not part of my lexicon, I thought, although I felt unexpectedly self-possessed, not at all the dependent bromeliad I am.

FOUR

Then I heard my own voice again,
as if discovering some marvel
in her face, the knife-edge of a consummate
unlooked for joy as she turned to go
where we could not follow.

David Whyte

Jason and I were too poor to take a proper honeymoon, so we took the week off from work after our small wedding and pretended to be honeymooners on holiday in Manhattan. We spent many languorous hours of bliss on the new mattress his parents purchased for us, a step up from the hand-me-down double we had previously squeezed into, although even in a queen bed we pressed our bodies close together because, as Jason often said, why would we want to be farther apart? We took in a couple of foreign films and a very off-Broadway play that turned out to be far too avant-garde for our taste, but which provided fodder for more than a few laughs. Afterwards, while the sky was still light, we walked hand-in-hand up and down tree-lined crosstown streets, stopping frequently to admire the city's architectural pageant and, when dusk fell and interior lights lit, peeking into brownstone windows to admire elegant lifestyles.

Jason, although not professionally trained, was a life-long devotee of architecture, and ultimately produced several photograph books on classical and modern icons, esoteric tomes that ended up dusty on university library shelves, but of which he was especially proud. One of those honeymoon nights, he whispered architectural terms as foreplay, which, as it turned out, proved to be, like almost anything he said or did, highly erotic to the young bride.

"Parapet," he crooned.

"More," I murmured.

"Pilaster. Modillion."

I swooned in mock adulation.

"Flying buttress," he chortled. "Crowstep gable," he murmured as he ran the tips of his fingers over my breasts.

That was the last straw of our tantric linguistic tryst, as I recall, and I smiled now as I remembered, the pleasure of memory and residual longing spreading through my body, and bolstering my nerve for what was yet to come. Jason, even in absentia, my rock, my inspiration, and all the more crucial without Anna.

Some time after that nasty conversation with David, as the day was coming to an end, I took the stairs to the Telemetry wing and, after peeking down the hallway to ensure no family members were there, stepped into Anna's room. I imagined them caucused in the lounge, or in the Common at home, contemplating next steps, and was relieved to be alone with her. Gray light filtered through the slats in the blinds. The room seemed especially sterile, all the vases and baskets overflowing with bouquets and well wishes gone now, the last wilted petals swept away.

I stared at Anna quite a while before I spoke. "I guess I know everything now. Well, I think I do. And I could kill you for this." I laughed aloud at the absurdity of that statement. "Literally, Anna, I could kill you. Your life is in my hands. Although you might say you have orchestrated this as well, haven't you? You assumed that because you kept me ignorant of certain important truths I might never be the wiser. That I was so neatly tucked into my insular blankets I would be easily deceived."

I sat back and closed my eyes and behind them saw Anna's face, that broad smile she reserved for moments of conquest, like the finale of a photography hunt. I opened my eyes again and pulled the chair closer to the bed, metal legs scraping the linoleum and spoiling the solemnity. "I suppose you might have been right after all. Even knowing what you've been up to, I could never punish you. You of all people who opened your arms to me, the weakest among us, and never shut me out. Not once. Even this betrayal is no betrayal at all. You were entitled to your privacy."

"Was Tim the first? Was he really the centuries-long connection? Is that why I'm here? Did you fear David might take his revenge? Was I meant to preserve your stay of execution? You needn't have worried. David loves you too much to let go. And I will do as you asked." I sighed. "As you knew I would, although, really Anna, in the end, it is you who are impenetrable, you who imagined you would not bleed."

I lowered my voice. "But you are just like the rest of us, aren't you? Just one of those jelly doughnuts we used to gobble down when no one was looking, all gushy on the inside. As soon as I get back to the city, I'm going to find myself a fresh doughnut and wash it down with a champagne toast to you. For now, I will do what you've asked of me, although maybe not as easily as you imagined. David is preparing to wage battle. And, as I guess you expected, I am not the weakling he imagines. A surprise to me as it will be to him."

Anna, of course, did not respond. Tiring of my monologue, I flipped open the history book and read the chapter entitled "Bibles Made of Stone and Glass" about the evolution of churches and their architecture. I suppose I should have been surprised, once again, by the confluence of thought, but nothing surprised me in that room. The chapter included a sketch of Notre Dame, labeled for its flying buttresses, props of stone used as a brace for arches, characteristic of the earliest churches in Europe. Jason would have loved this book.

"The people in Italy thought this a crazy way of building," I read. *"They thought such buildings must be shaky and might easily topple over – like a house of cards. The Goths who had conquered Italy in 476 were wild and ignorant and after that people called anything wild and ignorant Gothic. So people called all buildings such as I have just described Gothic, although the Goths had nothing to do with the buildings, for they had all died years before. Gothic churches had beautiful spires or arrows, which have been likened to fingers pointing to heaven. The doorways and windows were not square or round at the top, but pointed, like hands placed together in prayer."*

Fingers pointing to heaven. Perhaps Anna had sent a message after all, although I preferred to believe it was Jason. Only last week, I stood at the peak of the Maple Avenue church spire, nearly touching heaven, yet unwilling to look up.

In the midst of my musing, Adrienne entered. She stared at Anna as if I weren't there.

I could not bear the passive aggression. "Adrienne, what is it you are so angry about? So Anna had an affair with Tim, why is that your business? And she named me her proxy, why does this irritate you?"

She turned to meet my eyes. "We are all more dependent on Anna than makes sense. Odd really, the power that woman had over us."

"If, in fact, Anna had power over us, we've given her the power, that's what we do."

Adrienne's eyebrows ticked up in surprise. "So you've got us all pegged now, have you? You sound like Tim."

"Am I mistaken?"

"No, although the word power is perhaps too strong. Influence perhaps."

"Choreography?" I snapped, entitled, I believed, to a bit of righteous indignation.

Adrienne hung her head in resignation, just as David and Karen resisted defeat and the children would feel powerless. Everyone in Anna's midst was suffering and I couldn't help but feel that it was up to me to put an end to it.

"She made me believe in myself and in my own potential, not as a physician, or a wife or mother, but as a human being. She convinced me, without ever saying so, that I might have options of my own choosing, not something I've ever really believed."

Adrienne waited for me to respond, her eyes turned downward, one hand running up and down the edges of her white coat and coming to rest on one button, which she circled repeatedly with two fingers in a rare display of disquiet. I said nothing, waiting her out.

"She never judged and she never skipped a beat in our friendship, no matter my resistance," she said.

"Resistance?"

"To change. To redirecting my own destiny."

Did Anna believe all along that we might reset our own course? "I thought Anna was all about acceptance."

Adrienne sighed. "Right now, I am concerned about Beth and Will. There is no greater trauma for a child than the loss of a parent. I presume you understand that without the respirator, Anna will breathe her last breath.”

While I found her certitude unsettling, I merely nodded, needing to believe, and take consolation in that belief, that an ending to this life would be the beginning of another.

“Whatever you all think of Tim, he seems to be the only person who understands my position,” I said.

“You misunderstand me. My fault, I always come across as a technician.” She stared at me with a more benevolent expression. “I speak as a friend as well as a physician, and I can tell you that when the dust settles, they will realize you did them a favor. All of them. You kept her alive long enough to come to terms with this. And long enough to say good-bye.”

“Have you? Said your good-bye?”

She nodded. “She’s gone. Only machines pumping air. You’re not pulling the plug, Nell, you’re putting an end to the deception.”

We stood silently together on opposite sides of Anna’s body, as if sharing a moment of mourning.

“Thank you,” I said, and left the room. When the desk nurse approached me with a pen, I signed the DNR with only a slight quiver in my stroke.

Henry was waiting for me in his taxi outside the hospital and motioned to me to sit up front. When I climbed in, I noticed my travel bag on the backseat.

"I think perhaps it's best you reside elsewhere right now. The hostility at the house will be unsettling and you've been through quite enough." He started the engine. "I also had a chat with Beth and Will. Better coming from me. David won't be pleased; however, I too must honor Anna's wishes. She asked me to serve as mediator, if needed, as well as attorney, and she asked me to keep an eye out for you."

"Where are we headed?" I asked nonchalantly, even as I wanted to weep at the thought that Anna had arranged for someone to watch over me in her absence.

"I know a nice quiet place to stay for a while, right in town."

"You always seem to turn up at the right moment, Mr. Henry Mason, Esquire."

"Like a bad penny."

"Thank you."

"You're all right," he stated, rather than asked, and patted my hand. "You just need a good night's sleep."

"I don't think sleep is in the cards for me."

"We'll see about that."

I closed my eyes for the few moments it took to drive into town, mostly to obliterate the image of Anna as one of the people in her own album of the dying. As the car slowed, I opened my eyes to a small white colonial with a wrap-around porch, one of several similar relics on an in-town street in walking distance of the train station and not far from the larger vintage homes that had welcomed my arrival a few weeks ago.

"Nights and weekends, it's still pretty quiet on this street," Henry said as he pulled into a short driveway. "Most of these houses are offices now. I'm one of the last holdouts."

The house itself, the shutters and pitched roof and front porch, were the structural equivalent of a plain Jane. Only the gingerbread trim and rows of hanging flower baskets, recently planted with red geranium, hinted at the resident's pride of place. A couple of old wood rocking chairs, freshly painted, and a slightly rusted tin milk box by the front door, suggested the owner was elderly, certainly old-fashioned.

"Welcome," Henry said proudly as he parked the taxi in front of a freestanding garage.

Tall maple and oak trees surrounded the property, ringed within an exquisitely irregular stone wall. I felt as if I had been transported into another era, the street scattered with survivors of the unrelenting onslaughts of modern life. Much like Henry himself.

"My wife, Margaret, was an inveterate collector," Henry explained as we entered the main room, which, like those that followed, was filled to the brim with furnishings and accessories. "She just loved stuff, may she rest in peace."

The house was small, solid, a place one might expect to smell musty. Instead, the scent was fragrant and the space as cozy as a magazine spread on the creature comforts of early America. Constructed with narrow doorways, plastered walls, and tongue and groove wood floors, thick crown moldings surrounded doors and windows and cropped the tips of the walls to the low ceilings. Two fireplaces were filled with nearly white ashes, and iron fireplace tools with burnished edges rested against decorative tiles, capturing the scent of the previous winter, perhaps hundreds of winters.

One living room wall was decorated with iron and bronze keys dangling from rope or braided yarn, below a wide wall shelf filled with pitchers of various sizes in pink Depression glass, porcelain, or slightly tarnished silver. Hurricane lamps on every table were half-filled with yellow lighting oil, awaiting darkness to be useful, and candlesticks were abundant, the molten edges of partially burned tapers dripping down the sides in abstract one-of-a-kind shapes.

Henry's home might have been an antique shop or the storage space of a flea-market vendor who has taken in his wares for the winter, as Margaret obviously had a passion for things other people discard, rescuing useless artifacts from obscurity and presenting them as a testament to endurance. I imagined she must have been as much an original as her collectibles, and as much as Henry. What luck for them to have had a long life together.

"This is a wonderful place. Did you grow up here?"

Henry's chest swelled with pride. "My great uncle owned this house. I grew up on the farm, not far." He pointed into the distance. "When that land was sold for an office complex, my mother moved here, and when she passed on, Margaret and I moved in."

"Did you raise your children here?"

"Never had the pleasure," he said. "Great sorrow for Margaret."

I felt so deeply saddened for Henry never to have experienced the pleasures of a child.

"The house is a bit worn these days, but it's rock-solid. Nothing fancy, mind you. I patch things up when they need patching. My neighbors, they would like to tear it down to the foundation and start over, but I will never do that. Margaret would not be pleased."

He pointed to a photograph on the wall and even before I approached I knew by the familiar framing that it was one of Anna's: a portrait of a sturdy woman with a bright smile on her face, her arms wrapped around bunches of flowers from the garden. One of the living.

After dinner of warmed-over meatloaf and mashed potatoes, I slept tightly tucked into sheets that felt as old as the house, washed and air-dried on thousands of sunny days. I imagined them flapping on the line, softened by warm winds to a perfect patina. The moment I closed my eyes, I fell asleep and stayed asleep through the night, awakening to the caw of crows and the thump of coffee into the glass cap of an old-fashioned percolator, accelerating steadily until brewed, then haltingly reverting to silence, an entreaty to withdraw from the warm bed.

"Smells wonderful," I said, a little groggy from the long sleep, as I tramped into the kitchen, wrapped in a cotton throw blanket previously folded at the foot of the bed.

"Maxwell House, good to the last drop," he recited, "and a bit of bacon."

I sniffed hungrily at the bacon sputtering in a pan on the stove.

"Sit," he said, pulling out a chair from a square oak table in the center of the kitchen.

We crunched toast and bacon and slurped coffee, almost in unison.

"As good as the diner," I said.

"High praise." He smiled.

I poured Henry more coffee. "What happens next?"

"David will counsel with his lawyer, Bruce Russell, and they will seek a temporary restraining order to prevent you from executing Anna's living will."

"Can they do that?"

"Temporarily, sure, based on the probability of life-altering consequences."

I cringed. "I haven't actually asked for Anna to be removed from life support."

"They will assume that is your intention. Bruce won't have a problem finding one of the judges to sign the order, if you know what I mean. A small favor, and legally justifiable."

"How long?"

"Until a judge hears arguments. Usually within seventy-two hours, especially in a case like this. We will likely be at Surrogate Court Monday morning. No later than Tuesday."

"Surrogate Court?"

"That's where custodial issues are heard."

"What will the hospital do?"

"They will be bound by the restraining order, so they can't move Anna just yet."

"What then?"

"Well, my guess is that Bruce will argue the living will was not executed as written, therefore it is moot. He will assert that the spouse is the inherent conservator."

"Conservator?"

"The person with the final authority over such matters."

"Is that a valid argument?"

"Well, there is something to be said for the fact that the living will was not presented at first; however this does not void your position as the health care proxy. If Anna had wanted her husband to be her conservator, she would not have appointed you. She made a very conscious choice that David has power of attorney over her finances and property, but not her medical care. I will petition the court to confirm your position as the final authority."

"Final authority," I muttered. "Anna would have a good laugh at that."

Henry chuckled. "Yes, I know, Anna would argue only destiny carries authority."

"I see you've had that conversation."

"Many times."

"Will I have to go to court?"

"Once the restraining order is signed and I file the petition, there will be a hearing."

"Can I just, you know, sign a deposition or something? Or, can you speak for me?"

"No, dear. You will have to answer the questions directly, but I will be with you."

I wrapped the blanket more tightly to my body. "What do we do now?"

"Wait. You can only wait. I'll get the schedule of the hearing, and I'll find out which judge will preside. Any one of them will hear this fairly, although I have my favorites, and I have no doubt your conservatorship will be upheld."

"Whatever the court decides..."

"If Anna wanted the court to make the decision, she wouldn't have gone to the trouble of designating you her agent. You are Anna's voice in this. Don't you back off for a second."

"Yes, sir," I nodded and feigned a salute.

"Besides, we're partners now."

I smiled and took Henry's bony hand. "Thank you."

"My pleasure," Henry answered, a flush moving from his cheeks to his shiny dome.

He rose to clean up the dishes for us, motioning to me to stay seated, and I allowed myself the indulgence.

"By the way, Henry, do you know where Anna was going that day?"

"Don't think so."

"The library is near here. Was she coming to visit you?"

"Maybe."

"Did you have plans to visit?"

"Anna never really made plans," Henry mused. "Not unless she was on assignment. Every day was an adventure. Maybe she was in the mood for a good sandwich, she especially liked my peanut butter and jelly."

I began to accept that I would never know where Anna was going that day.

"I have a few chores this morning, and my regular barber appointment," Henry said, as he rubbed his hand over barely noticeable stubble along his jaw and smiled. "You make yourself at home. Peanut butter in the cupboard, made from fresh Virginia peanuts, and grape jelly in the fridge if you get hungry. Sandwich bread in here." He pointed to a hammered tin breadbox on the counter. "I'll leave my cell phone number if you need anything. Yes, I do have one!" He chuckled as he scribbled on a note pad by the phone.

I was afraid to go to the hospital, afraid to run into the family, to have to defend myself against their distrust. Henry was right; I needed time to rebuild equilibrium. I opened a window in the spare bedroom before wandering the house, examining some of the knick-knacks more closely, running my fingers over their odd shapes and smooth edges as if rubbing them for luck. I rummaged through dusty bookshelves and found several classics, many first editions, their cover illustrations wonderfully old-world, papers thick, and typeface rounded and elegant. I read the first passages of *Moby Dick*, the first chapter of *The Age of Innocence*, the first pages of *A Tale of Two Cities*, rediscovering the pleasure of classical prose.

It was the best of times, it was the worst of times… it was the season of light, it was the season of darkness. It was the spring of hope…

Was it possible to be all things at once? Anna thought so.

I reclined comfortably on the couch, reading more of the Dickens, wrapped in the soft blanket to which I had become attached. The ambiance was as soothing as snow on Christmas morning, which was especially meaningful to me, as anxiety had taken command of my nervous system, so much so my skin felt fevered. Another sign of the absence of medication. I downed a tall glass of water and ventured outside to smoke a cigarette, enjoying the in-town noise of traffic and muffled voices.

The chimes of the church steeple marked the hour. Was it nearly a week ago that Beth and I communed with the spirits there? Before long, I would have to leave this safe place and champion Anna's right to die. As I thought about it, I realized I would more likely have to defend myself. A familiar gnawing sensation floated into the pit of my stomach, the way I felt as a child when I had to speak in front of the class or when I waited for spelling test results, never confidant I had them all right.

Late day, as the sun descended through a clear blue sky and I dozed on a rocking chair on the porch, Will drove up.

"How did you know where I was?" I called out in greeting.

"Where else would you be?"

I smiled and stood on my toes to hug him and we lingered in that embrace longer than either of us might have expected, the comfort of our affections a tonic.

"I didn't think Henry would have any of these lying around," he said as he withdrew and pulled a Diet Coke from his backpack. "And I've read up on living wills."

I squealed with delight and flipped open the can to gulp thirstily. "What have you learned?"

"You really don't have a choice. Dad thinks you do, but you don't. You have to do what Mom asked."

"Did you read the living will?"

"Dad gave it to the lawyer, but Henry explained it to us. Sounds just like Mom."

"She made me promise, Will. I didn't want to, but as you say, I have to. I have to honor her wishes, especially now, because that's what she wanted."

"I tried to explain that to Aunt Karen, but she won't listen."

"She's upset."

"I know. Dad too. He got a restraining order, do you know?"

"We were expecting that."

There was an awkward silence for a moment. "Did you know that the rules governing living wills are different from state to state?" Will asked.

"No, I didn't know," I said, restraining a smile at Will's consistently animated curiosity.

"One of those states' rights things," he said. "Never made sense to me. I mean, if something seems right or legal in one state, why not another? Living wills, gay marriage, school vouchers… It's supposed to be one country."

"Do you really want to talk about federalism?"

"No."

"Why don't you tell me what's really on your mind?"

He lowered his eyes and sighed. "I've been thinking about Jeremy."

The sound of my son's name caught in my breath. No one ever spoke of him. As if he never existed, not to anyone but me.

"He was my little buddy, my city buddy."

"I know," I whispered.

"And then one day he was gone. Vanished. I was just seven. My first experience with death. Mom was very clear about what happened. I mean, she wanted us to understand, you know, without treating us like babies, but all I wanted to do was be there. With you and Mom, those weeks she stayed in the city with you. Dad wouldn't let me. He said I had to go to school."

"Oh, Will…"

"Every day, when everyone else went to lunch in the cafeteria, I sat in the stairwell. I just felt like I had to do something, you know, like, I had to feel bad. If I'd known the term, I would have said I needed to mourn. So I sat on the stairs eating my lunch alone and thinking about Jeremy." He shook his head at this image of his young self. "I had to say good-bye, but I didn't know how. I still don't. Sometimes I still feel awful."

I took his hand. "I'm so sorry, sweetheart."

"I don't mean to…"

"It's all right to talk about it."

"Is it? After all this time."

"Of course. In fact, it's good for me. It's terrible that people won't speak of the dead, especially children who have died, as if it might hurt my feelings. Open the wound. Hurts more that they've been obliterated from consciousness. The whole point of memory is to keep them with us in some way. No matter how much time goes by."

"I just seem to be thinking about him a lot lately. Like it's happening all over again."

"Yes, every time we lose someone we love, we feel the loss of all the others again."

"I wish… I wish…" Will stammered.

"What do you wish?"

"I wish Mom would wake up and straighten things out."

"Me too."

"But she's not going to, is she?"

"No one knows for sure."

Will looked at me skeptically.

"I'm not sure anymore," I admitted.

"Beth doesn't think so, but I know she's wishing the same thing."

"Of course she is. We all are. And we will go on wishing until the last possible moment."

"Beth says I am supposed to let go."

"You don't ever have to let go. Not the way people say, and not if you don't want to. There's nothing wrong with holding onto someone you love in your heart. The thing is…" I faltered, the wrong person to explain grief I imagined, but I wanted so much to help Will understand. To articulate what no one has ever invited me to explain. "You can accept the loss without forgetting. You don't have to detach, you don't have to sever the connection. You never stop loving."

"Forever?"

I saw the tears in his eyes and felt my own ready to spill. "Memory lasts forever."

"Like tradition, maybe."

"Yes, tradition. Like Eastover dinner."

"I wish we hadn't bothered this year. Better you weren't there, it was kind of terrible."

"That's the whole point of tradition. You go on, no matter what."

"I guess." He paused contemplatively. "We're all getting together again. A vigil sort of, at Maggie's. Will you come?"

"I think I had best keep a wide berth, give everyone time to get used to this."

Will nodded. "I probably need to get home. Beth will want the car and I've got a project for school. A report on the Holocaust for my world history class." He looked at me with an expression of exasperation. This was not the moment to be immersed in the enormity of death.

"Talk about loss," was all I could muster to say.

"I know, makes these things seem small. Like 9/11 makes everything, I don't know…"

"Will, every loss hurts. Take politics and religion out of it, and its heartache, that's what it is. Just plain heartache."

"Yeah."

The course curriculum, Will explained, covered the first half of the twentieth century as compacted and homogenized as Maggie's children's history book. They had previously studied World War I, what the students would come to know as "the war to end all wars." Then the second world war, what Will referred to as the ellipsis, meaning the war that led to the three subsequent wars in Korea, Vietnam and the Middle East. So like Will to connect the dots. He explained that he planned to write his report on the non-Jewish members of the Eastern European community who perished in concentration camps. Less was written on this subject, he said, and he hoped to learn more at The Museum of Jewish History in downtown Manhattan.

Facing the Statue of Liberty, this institute is neither as large nor as renowned as other Holocaust museums throughout the world, yet, on a small scale, another powerful appeal to never forget. Anna and I visited once, attempting to comprehend what force of destiny might have brought so many to the same devastating end, and I imagined Will too trying to make sense of the untimely deaths of so many innocents. He might wonder, as young people do, what kind of God would permit such an atrocity? He might wonder what takes some of us to concentration camps or the burning inferno of a bombed out building, while others pass unscathed, or end up the victim of a runaway vehicle.

Where might the spirits of six million Jews or nearly three thousand downtown workers migrate nearly all at once? If souls transition quickly, where do the spirits reside of friends and loved ones who have passed too soon, not enough births to compensate for the deaths? Is it possible to remain in limbo indefinitely? These questions, forever unanswered, like those many souls, like Anna, haunt those of us left behind and cursed to wonder.

Will looked at his watch. "I've got to catch a train and get the car home first."

"Do they know you're here?"

"No. I'm not supposed to drive alone on the permit. Only with an adult."

"But you also drove back from the train station that day."

"I know. I cheat now and then."

"I'll drive with you."

"Don't bother. That might be, like, creepy for you."

I grabbed my bag and left a note for Henry.

"I'll deal with it."

Karen stood in front of the house puffing on a cigarette and chattering into her cell phone. Her eyes enlarged in astonishment when she saw me get out of the car and then narrowed in an exaggerated glare of intimidation so farcical I almost laughed. She reminded me for a moment of Madame LaFarge, the old hag in *Tale of Two Cities* who cackled as the revolution shattered the politics she despised, stitching her contempt into shrouds for her enemies.

"What are you doing here?" she snarled.

"Will needed a co-driver."

Karen glanced at Will in confusion before turning back to me. "Obviously, you have found someplace to stay," she said in a staccato voice reminiscent of Bette Davis in one of her evil roles.

"Can you drive her back to Henry's?" Will asked.

"Henry's? Certainly not." She punctuated her indignation by dropping her cigarette and mashing it angrily into the ground with the point of a shoe.

"But…" Will began to respond.

"That's all right, I'll find my way back," I said, with a polite smile meant to irritate Karen even further.

Beth stepped out of the house, slamming the door behind her, tossing her hair across her head to one side in that way adolescent girls do, and didn't notice me at first. "Where did you take the car?" she barked at Will, and when she saw me, she stopped in her tracks. "Nell?"

"I wanted to say hello," I said, stepping toward her.

"Hello?" she mimicked.

"Shall we have a chat?"

"No, she doesn't want to chat," Karen answered for Beth in a similarly mocking tone of voice. "In fact, none of us should be talking to you. This is going to court you know."

Apparently, the prosecution had already begun, so I chose my words carefully.

"Karen, we are not at trial. There are no gag orders. The lawyers will do their thing, but we can still talk to each other. We should talk to each other."

"I beg to differ, Nell. We are past discussion. We are on opposite sides of a legal argument and we had best leave it at that."

Will shook his head sadly as he trudged into the house.

"You see, you've upset the boy," Karen said.

"He has many reasons to be upset and bickering doesn't help."

"Why didn't you tell me?" Beth shouted. "Don't you think we had the right to know what Mom's wishes were? I spilled my guts to you at the church. You knew what I was feeling, you should have said something right then and there."

"What difference would it have made?"

"What difference? Maybe a big difference. Like, maybe I needed to know exactly what my mother wanted us to do."

"You knew what your mother wanted. You certainly knew what she expected of you."

"The girl is not a mind reader," Karen retorted. "Beth, honey, let us take care of this. You don't need to concern yourself with legalities."

Beth ignored Karen's remark. "If you were uncertain about the living will, how can you expect us to be so sure?"

"That's fair, I've had more time to deal with it," I answered.

Karen stepped toward me menacingly. "The bottom line is, you wallow in your own life and you don't really care about anyone else, even your supposedly best friend."

"That's enough," I exclaimed, raising my palm in a halt, as threatening a move as I make. "Enough!"

I turned back to Beth. "Yes, I should have responded immediately. I should have told you all what she had asked of me. I'm sorry. Your mother trusted me to speak for her and I promised her I would, but it took me a while to find the courage. I'm not as strong as she is, not even as strong as you. And I couldn't bear the thought of losing her."

"Now you can?" Karen shouted.

"No. Now I've come to my senses, that's all."

"I don't know anything any more," Beth cried. "Is this my mother's destiny, or mine?"

There was no answer to that question, certainly not from me. I inched closer to Beth and spoke softly, hoping to ameliorate the tension.

"We all seem to intersect in this place. Our destinies converge. Your mother knew…"

"She knew what?"

"Somehow she knew what was coming, for all of us I suspect."

"This is absurd," Karen said. "We are talking about free will. Why would Anna have made these plans? I'll tell you why. When push comes to shove, she knew choices must be made. She just made the mistake of entrusting her wishes to you."

I turned to Karen with venom in my eyes. "You live across the country, Karen. You took a while even to decide to come, did you not? Anna knew I would be here in a flash, although intervention at that point was premature. Now sufficient time has passed and her wishes must be recognized. That's the only course of action. Antagonism serves no purpose. None at all."

"I suggest you stay away from the family until this is settled," Karen responded, as if I hadn't even spoken. "Perhaps you ought to stay away from the hospital as well."

"You cannot keep Nell from seeing Mom," Beth said.

"Well, we should at least alternate visits, maybe set up a schedule, so that we don't have to, what was it you said, intersect?" Karen said.

"It's all right," I answered. "I've made peace with Anna. I'll leave you to do the same."

"I'll drive you back to Henry's," Beth said.

She called to Will to hurry up to make his train. He emerged instantly, likely listening from behind the front door and we climbed into the car without speaking. I sat in the back and Beth made certain there would be no conversation by turning the radio volume high. I wanted so much to find words of comfort, to bridge the divide, but the seatback between us seemed as formidable as a brick wall, and, in truth, I was already exhausted by the conflict.

Will hurriedly said good-bye at the station and although I moved to the front seat, Beth and I drove on in silence. Only when we arrived at Henry's house was I able to find my voice. I turned off the radio.

"Listen to me. You are a remarkable girl. A person of compassion and maturity. Your mother would be so proud of you right now."

"Thank you," she said, and pulled the lever into reverse as the signal for me to depart.

"Beth, go see your mother. Say what you want to say. Cry. Shout. Please, I know what I'm talking about. You have to connect with her, now, while you can. Tell her you love her, say it out loud. Hold her hand while it is still warm. Kiss your mother good-bye."

Tears fell from Beth's eyes and she buried her face in her hands.

"Please, sweetheart, don't hold back. She never meant for that. Acceptance does not mean hiding from your feelings, or from people you love."

"I'm not sure you are the expert," Beth whimpered as she raised her head from her hands to look at me defiantly.

"Actually, I am," I answered.

There was little more to say. I let myself into Henry's through the back door. I inhaled the fragrance of vanilla-scented candle wax and called out to Henry to let him know I had returned, but the house was silent. I curled up on the living room sofa in a fetal position and felt the embrace of history as I slipped into another deep sleep, awakening only briefly when Henry covered me with a quilt. Even in that state, I savored a new resolve, a potency I had not tasted in ten years, ten long years, and the flavor, to my surprise, was sweet.

Tim showed up Sunday evening to take me to dinner, as if he had been assigned the shift. Henry had a regular poker game and said it was especially important to be there. I imagined judges might be at the table, allies to be cultivated or to provide counsel.

I tried to demur but Tim insisted. "You deserve a decent dinner, what would you like?"

"I've been the fatted calf since I got here," I answered. "Compliments of Maggie and Henry. I don't remember the last time I ate so well. There's no need, really…"

"We need a civilized meal, without fuss, without the onslaught of the tribe. A dose of comfort food, so to speak. What's your preference?"

"Tim, I don't like to go out…"

"Nell, I miss her too. I would venture to say that you and I miss her the most, there feels the greatest absence for us."

"Tell that to her children."

"They have a father. They have a future. They have multiple surrogate mothers. You and I, we're on our own."

I reached for a cigarette, desperate for nicotine to fill the vacancy of anti-depressants. Tim grabbed the lighter from my hand, striking a flame with dramatic emphasis.

"Listen, Karen is on my tail. She's all over me to get more involved, not knowing about Anna and me. She wants to meet for a drink and I told her I was busy, so I have to be busy."

As much as I would have liked to reject his plea, the thought of beating Karen at this game was tantalizing.

"Perhaps a coffee?" I offered.

"A glass of wine and a burger," he answered. "Or whatever your personal equivalent of a burger is. Thai food? Pasta?"

"A burger is fine," I reneged, as a burger suddenly sounded delicious.

I took a moment to splash cold water on my face and grab a jacket. Tim drove down the Post Road toward the next town and, to my inquiring expression answered, "I thought I'd take you to a spot where Anna and I used to go. A gastro pub where we never expected to run into anyone we knew. Our hideaway."

"Are you sure you want to go there?"

"You'll like it."

Pointless to argue and if it didn't bother him, why should it bother me? However, when we arrived at the restaurant, we were guided to a booth near the back, a place where lovers might hide, and I bristled at the notion.

Tim ordered a bottle of Pinot Noir. "Oregon, great vintage," he pronounced. He sipped the sample offered by an insouciant waitress who might not be old enough to drink, and nodded satisfactorily. She poured first for me, clumsily resting the neck of the bottle on the rim, and then filled Tim's glass nearly to the brim.

"You are an oenophile?"

"I just know what I like. And I like a good wine, not too often though."

"Why's that?"

"I'm not an alcoholic, if that's what you mean, although there were times when the bottle seemed too friendly. I just believe in moderation."

"Got it."

"And you? What are your vices?"

"I'm boring."

"Go ahead, confession is good for the soul."

"The short list? Simple. I smoke, I drink way too much diet soda, the caffeine will kill me one of these days if the chemicals don't. I'm a night owl. I down anti-depressants to stay sane. And I, I… well, let's just say, I spontaneously satisfy the needs of the flesh." I was stunned at my free admission.

"All sounds pretty benign to me. I guess Anna had a penchant for benevolent sinners."

"I suppose so," I said, sipping the wine, enjoying the velvety mouthfeel.

Tim held up his glass as if to toast. "Here's to benevolence."

We clinked our glasses and sipped. "And to the kindness of the court," I added.

"What's Henry's take at the moment?"

"I would imagine you're as up to date as I am."

"We don't have to talk about it if you don't want to."

"And we're off the record, yes?"

Tim laughed. "Yes."

"Even so, there isn't much to say. David has his temporary restraining order. Henry has filed a petition to make me conservator. We go to court Tuesday. That's it."

Tim mulled the status report and perused the menu. The waitress returned promptly to report the specials and to our joint request for burgers, asked how we wanted them cooked. We responded at the same time, "rare."

Tim smiled. "Does that make us bloodthirsty?"

"Anna would suggest we come from a long line of carnivores. Blood type O."

"Not good vegetarians, like her."

"Type A."

"You mean blood type, not personality." He smiled.

"Definitely not. You might say she's the antidote to that type, or so I thought."

"No one I have ever known lives in the moment as well as our Anna."

I sipped the wine. "To a fault."

Tim ignored my judgment. "Most people I know are mired in the past or obsessed with their future."

"Which way do you lean?"

"I try to stay in the moment, but I tend to look forward, and that's where Anna and I were in conflict. Only lately, she seemed to be more future oriented, sort of like a dog with a powerful scent, although most of the time she relished the mystery, right? More than any of her charming character traits, it was the sheer delight with the unknown that made her most enchanting."

I nodded. "A character misalignment I'd say. When you think about it, only those who care little for others, even for themselves for that matter, truly live in the moment. Kind of Ayn Rand, what was that called?"

Tim nodded as he sipped the wine. "Objectivism. Being true to oneself and only oneself, without allowing outside influence, what she saw as a moral imperative."

"Hm. Never seemed right for me."

"Maybe because the philosophers of the time made it more than that: reality existing separately from consciousness. Totally laissez-faire in principle"

"Seems metaphorical at this juncture," I said.

"Yep, maybe Anna's version of Objectivism. Still, I find it impossible to think of her as so self-absorbed, although… I mean, there were times, for sure, maybe this is one of them, she was so busy living in the moment there was no concern for the ramifications of her actions."

Tim poured more wine for us and I sat back more comfortably in my seat, enjoying the first feel of the buzz.

"She told me recently that she had come to imagine death as going home," he said.

"Home?"

"The way she might think of home, reunited with people we love."

"She never talked about it that way to me. In the zillions of hours of discussion, she never talked about death. Not after those first weeks, you know, after I lost my family." I took a deep breath, the words still so hard to say aloud. "She tried to cast an existential spin at first and finally gave up. The only other time was last year when she asked me to be her proxy."

"I can tell you it has been very much on her mind."

I peered into his eyes. "Are you angry with her?"

"A little, sure, although I'm not exactly sure why, or what to do with it."

I nodded. "I hear you."

"I'm still surprised she never told you, about us, I mean, although I know she meant to keep our relationship private. We were very selfish in this." Tim took a long slug of wine. "Although we had little to confess. We never fully consummated our affair."

I couldn't hide my shock. "Excuse me? Consummated? What a ridiculous word."

"Have you got another?"

"I'm thinking of when I was a girl, you know, we called it going all the way."

Tim smiled. "Oh, don't get me wrong, I've had my fingers and lips on just about every inch of her body, just not the home run."

"Rather Clintonian," I said with a heavy dose of sarcasm. "Whose choice?"

"Ours, although I would have done whatever she asked. In the end, I feel as if we rose above something, and, I know this seems pretentious, but it made our relationship more sacred."

I stared at him in disbelief. "Seriously? I'm so weary of this holier-than-thou pretext. If you betray a marriage and risk a career, not to mention the impact on children, what's the point of holding back? Sacred my ass. This resist attachment Zen thing, it's merely a form of protracted foreplay. People who want each other that badly ought to fuck. It's that simple."

"My, you're quite irreverent when you want to be."

"Well, if you inhabit the land of the living, you ought to live. These are among the things that make life worth living." I paused to reset my tone and took a deep breath. "I'm starting to wonder if Buddhists are lousy lovers."

"Well, some of the women in my life might agree with you."

He smiled so openly I too found it hard to resist a smile, even as I said, "It's not at all funny."

"Actually, if you pay attention to what goes on in this crazy world, as I do, if for no other reason than my work, one has to laugh rather than cry. I don't take too much too seriously."

The wine began to settle over me like mosquito netting. Lights around the room flickered in my peripheral vision and my body felt heavier in my chair, as if I might drift away to play with Anna in a distant place, the place where old friends and loved ones wait for us to find them.

A little tipsy, and in the confessional nature of the moment, I relayed in great detail what I discovered in the darkroom. Tim listened attentively, without reaction or comment, not as astounded as I was by Anna's odd curating, although tears gathered in his eyes, which he deleted with a swipe of his fingers. I reached for that hand in a show of solidarity and he grasped mine gratefully. We sat silently in that way for mere seconds when, as if the period to any further narrative about living and dying, our hamburgers arrived, so large they overflowed even oversized buns, their burgundy juices seeping from the edges, surrounded by an abundance of perfectly browned shoestring potatoes.

Tim smothered his with ketchup while I crunched one fry after another, licking the salt off my fingertips. The restaurant had begun to fill and the background din made it possible to dine without feeling the need to fill the spaces of silence.

We savored our food without conversation, for a time, until I pronounced, "Apparently, I can never be truly angry with Anna, not for long, although there have been moments, for sure, I wanted to slap her."

Tim nodded.

"It's beautiful, her world," I said. "Also infuriating. I think of her as so honest, so grounded, but she then betrays her marriage, and our friendship, and she expects, well, I don't know what she expected. How did she reconcile all this?"

"We simply embraced fate."

"Very convenient. You know, if you set aside the Buddhist bullshit, you might say Anna is a hedonist, maybe a narcissist. Not that other people aren't important, I can vouch for that. But her own passions and interests trump most everything else. Or am I spouting sour grapes?"

"No. The same could be said of me."

"And I'm sure Adrienne would, given the chance."

Tim chuckled.

"She must assume you would rather lose Anna permanently than give up your relationship."

Tim sat back for a moment in a pose of contemplation. "I suspect Adrienne sees herself as maybe the whore to Anna's Madonna. When she found out about us, and I'm still not sure how, she accused Anna of hypocrisy, and Anna asked for her forgiveness, which seemed to me ridiculous, but she wanted to maintain good will."

"I don't understand. Adrienne seems to me to be more fully self-possessed than most, despite regrets."

"I suspect this is integral to some extent to being a physician. A godliness of sorts; at the very least, a fixer."

"I thought surgeons were the godly ones."

"So they say, but Adrienne is determined to protect every child and save every life. Even in a first world town like ours, kids get sick, kids die. Must drive her berserk." Tim looked up at my pained expression. "Sorry," he said.

I nodded. "Seems an odd persona for Anna to befriend."

"Adrienne was in awe of Anna. Perhaps she hoped some of Anna's existentialism might rub off on her. Instead, I think her need to manipulate might have rubbed off on Anna. I feel sorry for Adrienne, really I do, although I've always been convinced she was the one who let it slip to David about us."

"Really?"

"Of course, although he never spoke of it, and never let his pride get in the way."

"I call that denial."

"Denial is sometimes a powerful antidote to what ails us."

Yes, I thought, but did not say. "Did Anna defend herself to David?"

"I think she was relieved that he blinded himself to the situation. We debated not seeing each other, but we couldn't stay apart. Adrienne must have been humbled by David's response. She forgave Anna, of course, but she has always made it clear to me, with that piercing look of hers or the superior tone of voice she uses with me, she believes I am the culprit. Anna was absolved of her sins."

"You don't seem to mind."

"I don't really care what people think of me. I just have to recalibrate my future right now because, well, I expect I'll return to a monkish existence. I'm a quintessential cave dweller at heart. Resisting the light in favor of the dark. Maybe you can advise me on how to resume a solitary lifestyle." He paused a moment. "Sorry, the journalist in me always comes out."

"I would rather you talk to me like a human being than tiptoe around me like most people do. If I've proved anything all these years, it's resilience."

"I see that."

"My way is not for most. One must be reclusive by nature."

"That would be me. Anna took me out of myself and now I need to go back."

"It will be hardest on Wednesdays."

"Yes," Tim said somberly. "Wednesdays."

"Coffee or dessert?" the young waitress appeared to ask. She snatched our nearly empty dishes and wiped a few crumbs to the floor, handing the ketchup and mustard bottles to an even younger busboy who materialized to assist her.

"Coffee for me," Tim answered.

"I've had enough caffeine today," I said. "Decaf cappuccino?"

"Perfect," the waitress chirped. "And all our desserts are homemade."

"We should have a sweet," Tim said.

I half-listened as the waitress recited a surprisingly long list of sweets, picturing Anna seated between us, enjoying our conversation and observing other diners with her photographic eyes, envisioning herself in their past lives or imagining a convergence of destinies, even as she relished the prospect of a confection.

"What do you say, Nell?" Tim interrupted my reverie.

Tim seemed far away, a little blurry, and I squeezed my eyes to bring him into focus. "Ice cream," I said, and gulped down a large glass of water to help quell the impact of the wine.

"With hot fudge," Tim instructed the waitress, and we both smiled. Anna's favorite.

The coffee and cappuccino arrived first, steaming hot and aromatic. I sipped too quickly and burned my tongue.

"Ouch" I whined more loudly than I intended. "Ice cream will come in handy."

The sundae arrived soon after in a large glass pedestal bowl with whipped cream sliding down the sides. We dipped our spoons simultaneously. Hot fudge coated my tongue, sugary sweet, and I was reminded of late night deserts with Jason and summer cones with Jeremy. Memories as delicious as the chocolate. Oh how I wish I could live every one of such moments over and over again, going back in time as Anna suggested. Then again, one might say that's exactly what I do, every day.

Anna was mostly right. I may not be at death's door, but I have not been living.

"Anna and I had an ice cream dinner once," I said, as I tasted another spoonful, laughing suddenly so uproariously that a bit of whipped cream slipped down my chin, which Tim instantly wiped away with his napkin.

"It was one of those horrifically hot summer evenings. We had been in and out of galleries all afternoon and were headed back to my apartment. We thought we might break for an early dinner, but Anna said all she really wanted was ice cream, so we stopped at a Haagen-Dazs. I had chocolate-chocolate chip and she had dulce de leche, you know, the caramel swirled in the vanilla? We spooned in all at once, voracious, and so grateful for the cooling effect, and then we wanted more. One scoop was simply not enough. We walked on a bit and found a Ben and Jerry's on Eighth Avenue. I had Cherry Garcia and she had Chunky Monkey, both chewier, like a main dish."

Tim chuckled.

"We were a bit giddy, probably a sugar rush, wickedly devilish, but still not full. We kept going and landed at Oscar's, a neighborhood place, where we shared a three-scoop sundae – Tahitian vanilla, dark chocolate, and pistachio – with tons of hot fudge. We ate every bit of it, our lips browned like little kids. We even scraped the sides of the bowl. Then we moaned all the way back to my apartment. Anna fell on the couch and I plopped into Jason's chair and we tried to remember what had possessed us to eat so much ice cream!"

"Sounds fabulous. Decidedly hedonistic."

I leaned back and smiled, filled to the brim with food and wine, and fond memories.

"I can never be truly angry with Anna," I sighed. "She saved my life."

"No one can save anyone else, you can only save yourself. Keep that in mind when you face the judge."

Tim sipped the last of his coffee and looked up at me with inquiring eyes. "Is this what it's like now, Nell? Every meal, every restaurant, every scene, a memory? Every sound, an echo? I strive to make each day a new day, but I feel as if I'm walking backwards in my own footprints. Is this the new normal?"

"Time will tell." I spoke kindly. "Not normal, as in not the norm, and not for everyone, but not terrible either. Not for me."

"I'll take your word for that."

I asked Tim to drop me at the hospital that night. He would have liked to come in with me, and I suspect he would have liked me to come home with him, but I banished him with a peck on the cheek and a nod of finality. Perhaps, at another time, in another life, we might have meant more to each other, but in this life, we were merely spokes of Anna's wheel.

Although after midnight, I strode into Telemetry with an air of authority, the late hour my chance to be alone with Anna once more before whatever happened next. A night nurse glanced up at me as I approached before returning to her reading, and I relaxed into a confidence I rarely possess. If nothing else, Anna had bestowed on me an exalted place in the hierarchy of responsible parties and I wanted to embrace that persona, despite the persistent churning in my stomach.

I stopped short at Anna's door when I noticed a chaplain at her bedside. He wore a gray full-length robe, its wide hood splayed against broad shoulders, reminiscent of clergy in medieval England. He leaned in close to Anna, lips nearly pressing against her cheek, murmuring in a steady stream as if chanting. I was not surprised to see him there, only surprised by the timing of his visit, as I had previously observed members of the clergy wandering the corridors of the hospital, stopping in to see if a patient or loved one needed comfort, a special prayer, perhaps last rites. Sooner or later, one of them was sure to attempt to minister to Anna a spirituality with which she was already more saturated than most.

The room was intensely silent, even the monitors and respirator seemed subdued, and an incredible tenderness enveloped what I could see of the chaplain's face, all the hardness of age softened in Anna's presence, as if he were another person entirely, perhaps a loved one from another time in her life, and likely one of her eclectic circle of friends, like Henry.

When he stood to leave, I took refuge in the room next door, dimly lit by a muted television, where the patient slept soundly and snored loudly. I counted sixty seconds before I snuck back to Anna's sanctuary. A thin shaft of light emanated from a fixture mounted above her bed, illuminating her face with nearly heavenly rays. I felt I should kneel to her and pray. Pray for hope. Wisdom. A sign.

I hadn't seen Anna in forty-eight hours. Two days had passed since the confrontation with her family. Three weeks since the accident, nearly four weeks since our last Wednesday together. Memory seemed all that was left of her: the furrows in her brow when she examined something of interest, the creases like tiny whiskers around her mouth, the elegant timber of her voice.

This is what happens when loved ones are lost. Their essences dissipate too quickly, insistently. Over time, we cannot recall their laughter or picture their smiles. We cannot imagine their touch.

I should have advised Tim that memory centers require props. Pneumonic devices. Photographs. Without them, no matter how hard we cling to the shadows, shadows fade. What irony: Anna, the keeper of memory, rarely included in her own photographs, thus doomed to vanish more rapidly than most.

I pictured Will wandering the halls of the Holocaust Museum meditating on the meaning of consciousness. I thought about Beth, so determined to fulfill her mother's ideology she denied her most basic emotional needs. Karen and Adrienne certain they might manipulate the outcome of another person's life. Maggie avoiding hard truths by appealing to softer senses. And David, still believing he might out-maneuver providence.

Searching for enlightenment, I turned to the last pages of the history book to read what was written about the Holocaust. Chapter 80, the first of two chapters devoted to World War II. Mussolini was described as small potatoes compared to Hitler and the Nazis as even more horrible than *Alaric and his Goths or Attila and his Huns.* The Holocaust was depicted in startling simplification as an effort by the Nazis to annihilate Jews.

In the final passages, a new weapon known as the atomic bomb was briefly cited, reporting that just two were dropped from American airplanes onto two Japanese cities, but they had caused so much destruction only two were necessary.

If spirits perpetuate from life to life, as Anna believed, where were the millions of innocent casualties of perpetrators armed with their manifest destinies? Were these the walking wounded among us, psyches forever bleeding, determined to search through lifetimes for loved ones? Doomed to gloom? How is it that some people are able to resume full lives while some of us are at best malfunctioned, at worst, shattered?

I lay my head on Anna's chest, hoping for a sign of life. At first, a few silent tears dripped down my cheeks until, at long last, I couldn't hold back.

"Why? Why, Anna? Why now?" I yelled, weeping in that way women weep in documentary footage on war. The shrieking of mothers in concentration camps as their children were marched to gas chambers. The howling of the mothers of Nagasaki. The wailing of eight million New Yorkers in the aftermath of terrorism. The monumental mourning of parents who have lost their children to senseless violence. I howled for us all in an explosion of heartache, ten years of grief unleashed on my friend's lifeless body.

"What is the meaning of all this?" I moaned, fighting the sobs that seemed never ending. Of course, no answer.

When I finally composed myself, I made my way through the hospital's hushed corridor, down the stairs, plodding through impending dawn into town. Henry was already awake and preparing coffee.

"Are you all right?" he asked as I entered the kitchen.

"A little too much wine."

"Would you like a hot bath?"

I leaned my head on Henry's shoulder and wrapped my arms around his chest. "Did you draw a hot bath for Margaret when she was tired?"

"Yes. She liked lavender-scented bubbles. In the last weeks of her life, the bath was the only thing that eased the pain."

"I'm sorry for your loss, Henry."

"Thank you, dear. No need. We had a good life together. That's all there is. Whatever you have, that's what you have, for as long as you have it."

Early Tuesday morning, showered and dressed and jittery, Henry insisted on a good breakfast before we went to court. Happy to forestall the inevitable a little longer, I nibbled at billowy scrambled eggs atop an English muffin oozing butter, and even as I munched, I heard the roiling of my stomach and felt anxiety coursing through my nervous system. I wished I had refilled my prescription for Zoloft when I had the chance, but that train had left the station. And, in truth, in recent days, the more I allowed myself to feel, no matter the weeping and apprehension, the more I preferred feeling whatever I was meant to feel; in effect, re-framing my own image in a higher key.

As we drove toward the government building, I watched the landscape scroll past the taxi's glistening windows like a convicted felon on her way to prison. For a moment, my gaze drifted upwards, but the habit of averting my eyes from the sky prevailed.

The county courthouse was suitably stately, a building of white stone with tall arched windows and Corinthian columns across the façade. We entered through a security checkpoint where an expressionless older man in a brown uniform peeked into and squeezed my bag as if he might conjure the contents. He nodded for me to pass, reserving his smile for Henry, who greeted him with a pat on his shoulder. As we stepped into an imposing marble lobby, I trembled, noticeably I imagined, and sought a ladies' room to douse my face with cold water. When I emerged, I stopped at a vending machine to consume in nearly one gulp a can of Diet Coke, caffeine leeching into my bloodstream instantly, providing a much needed energy jolt.

Over the doorway to the courtroom, a plaque read: *The law is reason free from passion. Aristotle.*

"Free of passion," I murmured. "Can there be reason without compassion?"

"No, but passion is another thing. Got to be rational in the court. Reason must prevail."

"I suppose."

"On the other hand, Aristotle was also the philosopher who believed that the most striking aspect of human nature was change. He spent a lifetime searching for order amidst what might otherwise be chaos."

I suppose the principle of order in the court should have been a comfort. We had come to this revered setting to determine in an orderly fashion what is rational and logical and acceptable, when all we needed to do was to accept that we know very little of life, and nothing of dying.

"Ready?" Henry asked, and when I nodded, ready as I would ever be, Henry cupped his hand at my elbow to guide me through the double doors.

I had never seen a courtroom other than on television or film, where they appear to be cavernous, a judge looming over the space like DaVinci's Jesus at his last supper. In fact, the space felt more like a college lecture room, and the judge's chair sat on a platform only elevated by one step, hardly looming or menacing. The witness seat was set to one side, slightly lower, and the court stenographer's desk on the other side, adjacent to a jury box with two rows of empty chairs. Opposite, tables for the plaintiffs and defendants faced the judge, and behind these, six pews for watchers. Dark wood paneling around the room enforced an impression of austerity and intractability, and recessed lighting cast no shadows, incongruous in a place meant to argue contrasts.

I began to imagine the background voices of a thousand disputes – feuding families, venomous spouses, siblings fighting wars that began in the cradle – and became increasingly nervous, as if another sheep to be thrown to the lions.

Henry gestured to me to sit at the table across from where David sat conferring with his lawyer, Bruce Russell, a tall man with broad shoulders and a thick neck, around which his tie seemed so tight he might choke. A lush crown of salt and pepper hair provided the essential gravitas and wire-rimmed glasses greater severity. David wore a navy suit and tie and appeared more somber than I had seen him since the first day at the hospital. Karen sat behind them with her legs and arms crossed in prototypically defensive body language. She wore one of Anna's sweaters I've seen many times and my heart ached for my missing friend.

Will and Beth sat to Karen's side, their heads bowed, texting or tweeting, I suppose, to ignore the surreal situation into which they had been thrust. They looked up as I entered and nodded to me, without expression, although Will's eyes held the gaze a moment longer. I imagined their stomachs were as queasy as mine. I wished they weren't there, wondering if David had brought them to the courtroom to use them as a form of coercion, and that made me irate, an anger that began to gnaw at me more than fear, preparing me for battle.

A few moments later, Adrienne entered the courtroom with Dr. Brunnell and four others representing the hospital. Maggie slipped in accompanied by her husband Brian, a short stocky man with curly brown hair and a tightly cropped beard, who reminded me of a cuddly stuffed bear. I noticed the day nurse sitting in the back row and she smiled at me. Two other women I did not recognize also sat in the rear, as well as a few of what Henry described as regular court watchers. Tim rushed in a moment later and positioned himself directly behind me. I was uncomfortably aware of his presence as a reporter rather than casual onlooker, or ally, although he had every right to be there. Beyond the estate proceedings and local lawsuits that typically occupied the court, we were an unusual local news story.

The judge entered, a small man with rumpled gray hair and the hint of stubble along his cheeks, dressed in the iconic black robe, and we all stood and sat in in one fluid movement. He seemed to me like a turtle that has stuck his head out from his shell to assess the terrain. I might have felt better if he had seemed a wise old owl perched on the top branch of a mighty tree.

I steadied my breathing and imagined the courtroom tableau like one of Anna's avant-garde layered photographs. She explained once that multi-layered images depict what's known as an aesthetic continuum, meant to convey the perennial human longing to bring order to our existence. Just as in the courtroom, where multiple, often incompatible realities co-exist. All of us fit neatly into that composite: observing through veils, seeing what suits us and fashioning end results accordingly, as if in the darkroom processing one image into contradictory portraits.

I had a vision of Anna standing right in front of me, bathed in soft light but scintillating with color, like an exquisite orchid floating atop its nest of green leaves, and I before her, a wilted leaf, as pale as if my blood had been siphoned. But it wasn't Anna who had browned my withered edges, nor the drunken driver who destroyed my family. No, I had muted myself, unwilling to be seen, less likely to hurt, so I thought. Now, nowhere to hide.

Bruce Russell opened the proceedings by arguing that the living will was moot because it was not executed in a timely fashion, presenting deposition statements from various parties and insisting that without power of attorney, or bloodline, I had no authority to make decisions of such magnitude after the fact.

Henry responded. "I would like to remind the court that we are not here today to determine the course of treatment for Mrs. Miller, nor a conclusive prognosis. We are here only to establish conservatorship. We are all going to die, surely the court will grant us that truth. It is only a question of when. As for how, well, most of us would rather die peacefully in our beds, but that's like waiting for the hen to lay that golden egg." Henry paused for a moment for the message to sink in. "Anna Miller wanted to have a voice in the how of her final days and she appointed her best friend, Nell Herman, as her health care agent, to facilitate her preferences. If she had wanted that role to be assumed by her husband, she would not have taken legal action to ensure otherwise. She was quite clear. She was equally clear in expressing her wishes in a life-threatening situation without the expectation of an immediate recovery. I call your attention to her living will, the use of the term immediate, which she qualifies as without 'either immediate recovery or the expectation of a clearly impending recovery.'" Henry pointed to the opening paragraph of the document in his hand. "Mrs. Miller stipulated that no measures be taken to prolong her life artificially. And, as you know, your Honor, the law on this subject specifies that a living will deals with withholding as well as removing life support systems, so the fact that the proxy was not immediately executed is irrelevant. I would also like to remind the court that in this state, statutory conclusions must give due weight to the opinion of the health care agent."

Henry pointed to me as if I were expected to do something. "The official health care agent is Mrs. Herman."

"Mrs. Miller knew exactly what she was asking," he went on. "The timing of implementation has no bearing because Mrs. Herman waited a suitable period to evaluate the expectation for recovery. According to the hospital affidavit, in a case like this the full extent of the damage may not be evident for two weeks. Or more. Mrs. Herman was prudent to wait until an informed decision could be made. Was she also in a state of shock? Of course. But she arrived only hours after the accident occurred, I can attest to that, I drove her from the station." The judge smiled. "She has been with the family ever since. She took stock of the situation. She conferred regularly with Mr. Miller, with Mrs. Miller's sister, Karen Linton Lewis, and with Mrs. Miller's children. She has been at the hospital every day since and has attended conferences with medical professionals. Until she was absolutely certain the prognosis fit the terms described by Mrs. Miller, she did not take action. She understands now that she is impelled to fulfill her responsibility by discharging the living will. To this end, your Honor, Mrs. Herman is the only person designated to act on Mrs. Miller's behalf. Mr. Miller holds only the power of attorney. Do I need to recount the areas of responsibility of the durable power of attorney?" Henry went on without waiting for a response. "Real estate transactions, chattel and bond, share and commodity transactions, banking…"

"That's sufficient, counselor," the judge interrupted. "The court is familiar with the boundaries of the durable power of attorney."

Henry nodded. "Yes, and it is explicit that the durable power of attorney does not supersede the health care agent,"

Henry asserted in a louder and sterner voice, as stern as I'd ever heard him speak, before resuming a normal tone to conclude his statement. "Mrs. Miller made her wishes crystal clear in a carefully worded health care directive that I witnessed and my firm executed. She knew exactly what she wanted. There is no vagary here, Your Honor. Nothing capricious. Mrs. Miller expressed her belief that Mrs. Herman, and only Mrs. Herman, should represent her wishes. I respectfully request the court to confirm Mrs. Herman as conservator."

Henry stood very still for a moment, staring into the eyes of the judge as a form of punctuation to his argument. Bruce stood to speak but the judge motioned him to sit.

"The other witness is present?" he asked Henry. "And the presiding attorney?"

"Yes," Henry answered, and pointed to the two women sitting in the back.

The judge acknowledged their presence but did not call them to the witness chair.

Dr. Brunnell was the only witness to be questioned, describing Anna's condition, and the current dour prognosis, in painful detail and a deafening monotone, closing the lid on the possibility of any further medical intervention unless something changed.

"Is it possible for Mrs. Miller to recover?" Bruce asked.

"No two cases are ever the same. I would say highly doubtful, " Dr. Brunnell answered somberly.

"Nevertheless, a recovery is not impossible, correct?"

"Nothing is impossible."

"Of course nothing is impossible," Bruce repeated. "What would you say is the probability of recovery?"

"I have seen several cases where patients are removed from a ventilator to breathe on their own for some time. However, Mrs. Miller may not be able to breathe without assistance. Her brain functions have gone from marginal to nearly non-existent. Without nourishment, she will likely perish."

"How long might she live without life support?" Bruce asked.

"I cannot answer that question."

"Would you agree, Doctor, that the ventilator and feeding system are sustaining Mrs. Miller's life?"

"At this time, yes, I would agree with that statement."

The doctor was excused and I felt the burden of his testimony on all of us, even without making eye contact, the depiction of Anna's condition simply too horrific.

"Is there anything else?" the judge asked.

Bruce stood and said, "Mr. Miller would like to be heard."

The judge looked over at David. "Mr. Miller, I recognize that you and your family are in distress and I sympathize, I do. However, unless you have a legal argument or crucial new information to be brought to the attention of the court, I have to rule only on the facts."

David blanched, visibly disappointed, and I felt badly for him, also grateful that family sentiment would not unfairly influence the outcome.

"Your Honor," Bruce said, resting his hand on David's shoulder. "We respect your concerns. However, I must raise the issue of whether or not Mrs. Herman is competent."

Henry jumped from his chair quicker than his age might generally permit. "Mrs. Herman is not on trial here."

"No, she is not," Bruce answered, "however, if she is to act as conservator, the court must establish that she can fulfill the living will in the spirit in which it was established."

"You have some concern of this?" the judge asked.

"Yes, we do."

"Your Honor, this is posturing. There are absolutely no grounds…"

Henry was cut off by a wave of the judge's hand. "The issue of competency is relevant. Short and sweet, counselor," he instructed Bruce.

"Of course."

"Mrs. Herman, will you please take the stand?" the judge asked.

Henry sat down and whispered in my ear. "This is not a trial, Nell. You do not have to answer any question that makes you uncomfortable. And when you do answer, take a breath first and answer only the question. I'm right here."

I nodded and steadied myself as I stood and stepped up to the witness chair. I was asked to state my name and spell it for the record. I was asked my address and stumbled over the zip code. A bailiff appeared and asked me to raise my hand and swear to tell the truth, so help me God. No bible, just a raised hand, surprisingly disheartening, as if anything I said was therefore inherently questionable.

The judge reiterated that this was a hearing, not a trial, and I was free to answer or not answer any question that was put to me.

"Do you have any questions?" he asked. He had hazel eyes and a grandfatherly face, and when I looked over at him, I was no longer afraid.

"No, thank you."

The judge nodded. "Proceed."

Bruce stood at the table as he spoke. I was unable to look at him without seeing everyone in the courtroom. All eyes were on me; every one of Anna's loved ones staring at me with expectation, and, I believed in that moment, a smattering of condemnation. Anna would have gleefully taken the shot.

"Mrs. Herman, I understand that ten years ago you suffered the tragic loss of your husband and son."

I felt as if I had been hit head on by another speeding truck. My breath caught in my throat. What was to be asked of me?

"Is this true, Mrs. Herman?"

"A matter of public record," Henry bellowed. "What is this?"

"Not a matter of court record. I only wish to clarify the context of the relationship between Mrs. Miller and Mrs. Herman," Bruce said to the judge.

"Go on."

"I am sorry to speak of this, Mrs. Herman. I know this must be difficult, but it is my understanding that you have had a very hard time adjusting since then. Is this true?"

"How do you mean?" I asked, and out of the corner of my eye I saw Henry smile.

"Well, is it true that on a number of occasions it was Mrs. Miller who found you in a debilitated, shall we say, nearly catatonic state, in your apartment in Manhattan."

I inhaled and exhaled slowly before responding. "Yes."

"Is it true that you attempted suicide on more than one occasion?"

I repeated the breathing. "On one occasion."

"Only one?"

"Yes. Many years ago."

I looked over at Henry, who nodded his encouragement.

"Are you employed?"

"No."

"You do not earn a living?"

"I work freelance."

"What do you do?"

"I am a graphic artist."

"You work from home?"

"Yes."

"Do you have any other family?"

"My father, in Florida."

"Do you have any friends?"

"A few."

"Is it not true, Mrs. Herman, that Anna Miller is your only real friend."

"Anna is my dearest friend."

"Let me ask this another way. Is it not true that Mrs. Miller, by virtue of her friendship and attention, is the one person you've leaned on the ten years since the loss of your family?"

"Yes."

"Do you suffer depression, Mrs. Herman?'

"Yes."

"Do you take medication for depression?"

"Most of the time."

"Would it be fair to say that you are agoraphobic? You do not leave your apartment?"

"I go out to do what I have to do. I also visit the Millers here, now and then. I've been here for all, well almost all of the family's most important events. And I visit my father at Thanksgiving. I have never been diagnosed as an agoraphobic."

"Your Honor," Henry stood. "I repeat, neither Mrs. Herman nor her medical condition are on trial. This line of questioning is not relevant."

"All right, all right," the judge said, motioning to Henry to sit. "Let's get to the point."

"I am getting to the point, your Honor. Mrs. Herman's mental state goes to competency."

"And, I repeat, Mrs. Herman is not on trial," Henry exclaimed.

"Competency is the issue. The court has been asked to confirm Mrs. Herman as conservator and we question her ability to fulfill that role."

"All right, go on, but please, show some respect for the witness, and the court."

"Yes, Your Honor." Bruce Russell turned his attention back to me and I saw the steely gaze in his eyes, the hunter ready for the kill.

"Mrs. Herman, I want you to think carefully before you answer this question. Can you honestly say, given the trauma of the loss of your husband and son, and that you rarely go out, and you are frequently depressed, and rely on medication, and that you are dependent on Mrs. Miller in large part, so much so that you must have been in a state of shock since her accident, can you honestly say that you are of sound mind and capable of acting on her behalf?"

I heard Maggie utter a cry and saw Adrienne shake her head as if embarrassed for all of them. I glanced at David who maintained a poker face, but his eyes seemed to me a little less severe, perhaps even apologetic.

I stared at the lawyer with as antagonistic an expression I could muster, even as my composure wobbled like a renegade tire. I was well aware he might have spoken for everyone present and he had good reason. Yes, I live a diminished existence, hardly what most people consider a normal life, if there is a paradigm for normal. But it is the role I chose, as Adrienne pointed out to me early on, however pathetic to Karen and David and people like Bruce Russell.

I forced myself to sit up taller in my chair and steady my nerves. Henry was wrong. I was on trial.

"Are you all right, Mrs. Herman? Do you want me to repeat the question?"

"No," I answered, leaning forward and looking directly into his eyes. "Once was quite enough."

I saw Henry and Tim smile. Beth and Will, Maggie and Adrienne looked straight at me and I wondered if they might have been waiting for me to stand up for myself all along. I imagined Anna once again in the courtroom, watching, urging me to rise to my own defense as well as her own.

"May I speak, Your Honor?" I asked the judge.

He nodded and indicated with his hand for the attorney to step back.

"Thank you," I said, gulping ever so slightly to control the quiver in my voice. I took a deep breath and then I began to say what needed to be said.

"I saw the quote of Aristotle above the doorway when I came into the courtroom. I learned a lot about this philosopher when my husband produced a book that connected his writings with ancient art. Aristotle was grounded in logic, a syllogistic approach to reason, and I wonder if there's a syllogism for me? All human beings experience loss. I am human. Therefore I suffer loss. Humans who lose loved ones grieve. Therefore I grieve. Loss, sorrow, grieving… these are natural to the human experience, yet, somewhere along the way, in this culture at least, we stopped permitting ourselves to assimilate our losses. We are only concerned with our gains. In this age of hyper-induced optimism, I am a painful reminder that we bury grief so deeply in our collective psyche we never fully mourn. I am perceived to be unbalanced; in the view of some, many perhaps, I am without reason. So what would be the syllogism that might apply here? All people who are sad are defined by passion, passion being in opposition to reason? I am thus without reason? Does this make sense? No. And I resent the dispassionate attitude of Mr. Russell, and others here as well."

I raised my voice a notch and went on, a truck out of control careening through the courtroom. "People who have never experienced such a sudden profound personal loss assume that one mourns and moves on. After a suitable period, maybe a year, we must be brave soldiers and bury, or at least bypass, what we feel. Snap out of it, people think. Some of them dare to say it. Those of us who remain in the grip of grief, for however long, are presumed to be emotionally unbalanced. Frankly, I think there is something unnatural about the pretense of forgetting. My life took a terrible turn ten years ago, and it is my decision, only mine, how to live with that."

Will was staring at me intently, as he might stare at a professor in class, so I used him as my focal point.

"I suppose, if I had other children, I might have come through this differently. Anna and I talked about that. Or, if I were a different kind of person to begin with, I might have responded differently. But I am solitary by nature and without anyone to tend to, or responsible to, for better or worse, I live as the introvert I am." I paused a moment and took a very deep breath. "There is a Psalm that reads, *To live in hearts we leave behind is to live forever.* Those words are engraved on my husband's headstone. Of course we should go on living the lives we are meant to live, whatever lives we make for ourselves when we are left alone, but there is no statute of limitations on grief. Ask the mothers of the Holocaust. The orphaned children of Vietnam. Women of Bosnia, Ethiopia, Argentina, the Middle East... Gather together the refugees of a thousand civil wars and suggest to them that they just get on with it. Tell that to the families of the World Trade Center. Or turn around and tell that to Will and Beth Miller. Tell them they must be a brave little boy and girl and move on."

I paused, but did not look at Beth and Will, afraid to lose my composure.

"Ironically, they will do well, better than I, because Anna raised them to accept life's joys and sorrows equally. If there is anything wrong with me, anything at all, it is that I allow sorrow to trump joy. That's all. I am neither disturbed nor unbalanced. I can assure you, I am completely competent. In fact, never more so. Anna trusted me to do this for her. That trust should be the only endorsement I need."

I inhaled deeply and allowed the air to filter slowly through my lips in a loud exhalation, as if blowing into frigid winter air to make steam, and just as Bruce stood to comment or contradict, I continued my remarks, so he resumed his seat.

"I maintain a vigil, in my heart, for my husband and son. Anna understood this because she knows that reason and passion are not mutually exclusive." Tears began to burn the back of my eyes, but I held them in check. "I am more grateful to her than words can express for the sustenance she has provided to me all these years. It is because of her friendship that I was able to live as I choose. And it is because of our friendship that she chose me to represent her, which I fully intend to do, so that she can live and die as she wished. I never intended for this situation to be antagonistic, quite the contrary. I would prefer that all of us, Anna's family and I, acknowledge her intentions as one."

Henry sat back in his chair and nodded appreciably. Tim feverishly took notes. Beth held her head down and I saw her shoulders shake with sobs. Maggie rested her head on her husband's shoulder and Adrienne stared at me with an expression of bewilderment laced with awe.

Bruce Russell stood, but the judge motioned to him to remain seated.

"Thank you, Mrs. Herman. I appreciate your perspective. Perhaps you also know Aristotle argued that the soul is defined as the perfect expression of a natural body. I believe he referred to the body as the realization of the soul. Both, he suggested, are unified, like an impression stamped on wax. My question is, will you be able to let go of your friend? Will you fulfill Mrs. Miller's wishes, knowing the outcome may be death?"

I am sure I stopped breathing. The judge's words blew around my head like shriveled leaves in a blustery wind, and I hesitated for a second before I answered.

"Anna believed in a naturally evolved, unobstructed life. She trusted me with her intention, Your Honor, and I must do as she has asked. I will do what she has asked."

He nodded, apparently satisfied with my answer. "Thank you. You may step down."

I stood and took the hand of the bailiff, who had quickly stepped forward to offer his assistance, as if he knew I might stumble on my own. The few steps back to my chair seemed endless, my legs like rubber, but I made sure to sit as if fully in control.

"Anything else, gentlemen?" the judge said to the attorneys.

They both stood.

"No," Henry answered.

"Not at this time," Bruce said.

"Well, this is going to be the only time, counselor, so I gather your answer is no."

"Yes, Your Honor. Nothing further."

"Good, be seated." The judge spoke softly but his words echoed off the walls. "This is of course a difficult challenge. Not the first time a proxy dispute has come before the court, surely not the last. There is no crystal ball when it comes to the phenomena of consciousness. That is not the issue. Mrs. Miller was very distinct in her wishes. She designated Mrs. Herman to be her health care agent and I see no reason whatsoever to alter that. Mrs. Herman, you are reaffirmed as conservator. However, I am asking Mr. Mason, on behalf of the court, to act as co-conservator, to ensure that Mrs. Miller's wishes are fulfilled as expressed, without bias, and without interference. And one more thing." He turned to the plaintiff's table as he spoke. "This will not be taken up by a higher court. And don't even consider a media circus. The health care proxy is upheld and inviolate."

As the judge banged the gavel on the desk, our eyes met. The turtle, it turns out, was a wise old owl after all.

No one moved at first, gradually coming to the recognition that the decision had been made and we had been dismissed. I was equally speechless, even when Henry whispered, "Anna chose wisely."

We filtered out of the courtroom silently. David and Karen ushered Will and Beth with them to the exit. Adrienne, Maggie and Brian, even Tim, seemed to disappear, as did the other observers. There was no triumph in the determination of the court. No forgiveness. Only a course of action.

Henry and I sat for a few moments on a bench near the main entrance of the courthouse. It was an especially bright afternoon, new leaves on the surrounding trees fluttering in warmer spring air. I smoked a cigarette, without a word, while Henry gazed out at the landscape he had watched change so dramatically throughout his long life, from boyhood to husband and lawyer and now, for me, and for Anna, liberator.

"Penny for your thoughts, Henry," I said, linking my hand through his arm and leaning my cheek against his shoulder.

He patted my hand. "I have no special thoughts today, Nellie. Only the pleasure of another day."

A constellation of blue jays bounced along the upper branches of a tall maple tree. I watched them flitter noisily from branch to branch until they took off and my eyes followed them to the sky. This one time, I did not look down. I looked up. I stared into the vastness of that remarkable blue heaven I have denied myself all these years, mesmerized by the splendor of scattered wisps of clouds drifting across the dome. Exquisite.

"Yes, Henry. The pleasure of another day."

FIVE

There is a land of the living and a land of the dead,
and the bridge is love,
the only survival, the only meaning.

Thornton Wilder

Today is the day. Anna senses it at once. Something has changed. A difference in the way the early light floats across the microscopic space between her eyelashes. The way the hospital room air warms ever so slightly to the first rays of the sun through her window. Even the chattering of early morning birds is sweeter today.

Today, new voices. None recognizable. No Maggie reading. No Nell or Tim pleading, or Karen griping. No murmurings from David or Will.

Suddenly, penetrating the bubble, there is a flurry of activity. Not the usual attendants or typical examination. One male voice speaks in the clipped monotone of the physician, and two alternating female voices respond. Nurses. Adrienne was right: nurses make everything better.

Hurried fingers press against pulse points and lift her eyelids. Nothing else. No longer the suspense of recovery. No, today they are taking the last measures for the dossier. They are here to record her final moments.

At last! She has awaited this day. For how long, she cannot say. If ever she believed time is an illusion, she is certain of it now. She might have lived another life entirely while physically hostage to this state. Perhaps more than one existence between the Anna before and the Anna to come.

She has been aware all along of the shift from daylight to darkness, morning to night. However she cannot be certain if she has detected every 24-hour cycle. She may well have lost track. She may have been in a deeper sleep, a prolonged trance, or the occasional deadening loss of consciousness. She may have lost whole days, weeks perhaps. No way to know for sure. Nevertheless, it seems three, perhaps four weeks since she stepped off the curb and once in this condition, she never expected to wait quite so long to move along.

Nell must have finally raised her voice. Of course she would have been reluctant. Giving Beth and Will the time they needed to adjust. To say goodbye, because even when one accepts each life as one among many, farewell is essential.

Will, she is certain, will do his part to shepherd his mother's destiny. Solid as the deepest tree roots, that boy. He will honor their conversations about Buddhist burial traditions. He will ensure fidelity to his mother's ideals.

Beth, however, seems to have wavered. Her voice has been noticeably absent. Perhaps she slipped into the background among the others, she tends to do that. Or she might have refused to visit, unwilling to expose her uncertainty or seek maternal wisdom within Anna's silence. Even to speak to her muted mother would suggest the painful truth that Anna had vanished, that such conversations might never happen again. There is also the possibility that Beth is angry. Yes. There is anger. Will is going to respect his mother's teachings, whatever the hurt he feels, and Beth will resist. No matter how often they spoke of acceptance, Beth has yet to fully assimilate the lessons. She will understand better with time. Too soon now.

Nell on the other hand needed more time than even Anna imagined, although Anna was confidant she would do what was asked of her. She would always do the right thing, in the end.

Anna would have smiled if she could have. She felt a smile within, as she has many times in recent days. She wishes she might have shared her contentment with the others, especially today. Today is the day she will move on and Nell will begin again.

Oh my! A striking pain in her chest, as if she were a vampire, staked through the heart. The breathing tube. That horrible hose, slinking from her windpipe like the intruder it was. Ah, sweet liberation, although oh so terribly painful. Her throat parched, raw, nearly impossible to swallow and she would so much like a sip of water right now.

She coughs unexpectedly, the discomfort nearly takes all her breath away, so she inhales slowly through her nose, natural air like a cool evening breeze after a sweltering summer day. She delights in breathing on her own, although suddenly she gasps for breath, as if she cannot get her fill of oxygen. Out of practice, she imagines. She feels her chest rise and fall more naturally. Repeatedly. Without assistance. What a marvel! We never appreciate this phenomenon, the simple inhalation and exhalation that sustain us, until it slips out of reach.

She focuses on the breathing as if she is at yoga class. Steadily, slowly, with intention. Blood flows, electrical impulses connect, life force surges from the depth of dormancy. She has yet to vacate. She cannot move her extremities or open her eyes or speak, yet she is alive. She hears, she feels, she intuits, albeit suspended in this form, in this spirit, in this place. But why? She was certain she had gone through what the Buddhists call the Bardo, the stages of spiritual existence between lives. She should be ready to move beyond this body. How much longer must she wait?

She explained all this to Will not long ago. They had attended Margaret's funeral, and after the gathering at Henry's house, they took a walk. They talked for hours about the eternity of the spirit and the cultural rituals associated with burial. He recalled stumbling upon a funeral in a cave during a family vacation in Hawaii, the cadaver's hands and feet tied and covered with cloth made from the bark of a mulberry bush. No wonder so many bones are found in caves, Will remarked, and she was once again delighted with his incessant search for the meaning behind the experience.

She borrowed a book from the library on funeral rites. They read it together and he was particularly fascinated by Mongolian lamas, who surround the corpse and make offerings of food to keep evil spirits away. When the time is right, they lift the body through a window to pass to the next world. And the Tibetans, where the dead body, merely a shell to their minds, is dismembered, providing sustenance for birds of prey. In Bali, Hindus line the path to the hut containing the body with lanterns until there are a sufficient number of corpses for a mass grave. Efficient and environmentally sensitive, Will commented, and he was also taken with the Vietnamese tradition of leaving wads of counterfeit money under gravesites, so the dead may purchase what they need in the afterlife.

Tibetan Buddhists believe the personality goes into a trance for four days. The individual does not know they're gone. In this First Bardo the monks recite chants only that person can hear. Until the dead one sees a bright light. They call it the clear light, and if the radiance isn't fearful they are welcomed to the higher place. But many are frightened by the light, so blinding they flee. They experience that moment when whole lives pass before their eyes. Like near-death experiences people describe in the same way.

They all talk about the bright light: the stairway to the empyrean. And from there, Anna believes, she might watch over, and await, her family. She has yet to see the light.

Will appreciated the Buddhist tradition of chanting to soothe the spirit in transition. The traditions of the bathers, the watchers. Civilized respect for the dead. No wailing, no dressing in black. He understood the meaning of celebrating life. This, she hopes, is what her friends and family will do. What her son will urge them to do. He will remember the rituals and he will remember the talks. He will explain to the others, to David and Karen, who will argue for a conventional memorial service, that his mother would want a Buddhist burial, and they will hopefully find common ground.

We must accept when we pass and we must be permitted to pass unencumbered. If she had ever experienced any doubt, the sanctity of death was confirmed by the patients she photographed in hospice care. Most of them had accepted their paths. So close to something those preoccupied with living never grasp: the splendor of the eternal soul. It was then she gathered her photographs together as living and dying, one and the same. A fitting epigraph.

All this time, Nell wondered where Anna was going the day of the accident. Where she was going then, or at any given time, is irrelevant, Anna might have countered. Where she is now and where we are all headed, that is the essence of destiny. That is what you want to know, Nell, and what you will never know, until your time.

She is still breathing. What if she is meant to resume this life? No, that is not what she has foreseen. It is her time. She has journeyed far. She must be patient. Her release will come at the right moment. As all things do.

Anna breathed on her own for six days. Her brain functions remained negligible; nonetheless, despite the prognostication, the anxieties, the legalities, she survived without interference. Her heart beat steadily, her breath shallow but even, exerting dominion over her body as if a rebuke to those who presumed otherwise. She never opened her eyes or spoke a word. Her skin tone remained pallid, nearly sepia, like an aged photograph, yet she survived long enough to defy the experts and infuse us all with a glimmer of the majesty of the human spirit.

No one will ever know for certain, of course, but Will and Beth concluded she remained alive in preparation for her passing, her spirit awaiting direction. I believe Anna sustained herself as a gift to me, to preclude any further family animosity, any lingering consideration of irresponsibility or murderous intent. Protecting me from whatever guilt remains in that place in our hearts where self-recrimination resides. Or, perhaps it is only as simple as this: she meant to give us a little more time to let go.

I visited every afternoon and on that last day, David was waiting for me in the hospital lobby when I arrived. I had only to see the look on his face to know she was gone. Disheveled, dressed in jeans and a sweatshirt, his eyes woeful and tired, he had been called to the hospital early morning, no recourse and no hope, a stark contrast to the determined young man in Anna's photographs. Twenty years later, his life built on a foundation that inexplicably crumbled overnight, with no blueprint for its restoration.

"I'm so sorry, David," I said, leaning in to him for an embrace, which he returned, and we held on just long enough to let the last of the animosity pass.

"So now it's done. She knew I would never let her go," David said, swiping the tears from his eyes and handing me a handkerchief to do the same.

"She was never yours to keep. She was just passing through."

"You believe that for certain now?"

"I am coming to believe," I answered.

"I still think it's ironic she chose you to be her executor."

"She was asking me to honor her life by living my own. I'm pretty sure of that now."

"Yes. I guess we will all have to do that."

I nodded, no further words to be said on this subject. Not now.

"We discussed the funeral in the lounge an hour or so ago," he said, his voice flat and level like a T-square. "Will has filled us in on the traditions. Karen wants a black and white motif. Maggie will prepare a feast, I'm sure. I will arrange for the choir at the church to chant and Will suggested readings from the Lotus Sutra. You know it?"

"Yes. Anna recited many sections to me in those early days, you know, those having most to do with the eternal path."

David nodded. "And Adrienne just stopped by, she is gathering nurses to bathe Anna for burial. A Jewish tradition."

I smiled. "An ancient tradition, I'm told."

"We're only arguing about the remains. Anna's will specifies cremation, but she was baptized, after all, and I think it best the kids have a place to visit their mother. I've got a lovely tranquil spot of land on a hilltop near town. I bought it some years ago. In the shade of a huge old maple tree."

I might have argued that Anna would have preferred her ashes scattered under such a tree, but David had the right to exert one last authority. And I too would visit her there in the years to come.

"Stay with us, please Nell. I never meant for you to be homeless."

"I'm not. I'm quite comfortable with Henry, and I have a feeling, not so much because of anything he has said or done, but I think we were meant to be together just now."

What I could not have known, but must have suspected, was that we would all gather together again in a matter of months to bid farewell to dear Henry.

After we parted, I made my way unannounced to Tim's house. He was putting the finishing touches to Anna's obit for the newspaper, which, he confessed, he had not been able to bring himself to write until it was certain to be an obituary and not the tale of a miracle. I asked him to help me do the one thing I have neglected to do: write Jason and Jeremy's official epitaph. Long after the fact, and never to be published, their obituary was a missing and necessary punctuation to the end of their story.

The writing took all night. A bottle of wine, a large pizza, and a pint of chocolate ice cream consumed. Lots of tears shed. And then it was done. I felt no relief, rather the expectation of relief over time, and that alone was a revelation.

On the day of Anna's funeral at the Congregational Church, a simple mahogany coffin rested on a pedestal at the alter, surrounded by tall vases filled with white lilies. Within, lay the body of Anna Miller, dressed by her sister in white silk with a black pashmina shawl, wearing an onyx necklace that belonged to her mother, and accompanied by thoughtfully selected photographs: the family at the beach last summer; Maggie, Adrienne and Anna together at an Eastover dinner; Anna's parents while still young; and one of Jason, Jeremy and me, all stolen from their frames by Beth, who sat with her mother through the night before the funeral, waiting for the first morning light to say good-bye.

The tenth anniversary of the World Trade Center attacks arrived soon after I helped Beth prepare and pack for college. That same week, Will returned to school, David to work, and their lives, which had taken a terrible turn months before, settled onto the paths ahead.

This anniversary was markedly different from the first. Anna was with me then. Many diverse commemorative events had been scheduled throughout the city. We attended the formal memorial at Ground Zero, having been favored with an invitation meant for families and coworkers of the victims by my neighbor, the policeman, who was there to honor the first responders. We stood respectfully to the rear of the legitimate mourners and sympathizers. Scofflaws, in effect. We listened to speeches and readings and wept. And, in the right moment, for the first time, I recited their names: Jason Herman, Jeremy Herman.

We fled immediately afterwards and made our way uptown through throngs of supporters waving miniature flags and wearing paper hats depicting the Statue of Liberty, as if a parade, to the Metropolitan Museum of Art, where curators had designated paintings and sculptures from the permanent collection to represent what they called humankind's indomitable spirit. Artworks meant to express the harmonic sentiments of despair and hope. We stood or sat before several of these, the museum's exquisite tranquility nullifying the anguish, for a time, before heading back to my apartment, where I collapsed on the couch and Anna sat on guard in Jason's chair through the evening and into the next day, until she felt I might be safely left alone.

Only now, looking back, I imagine how difficult it must have been for Anna to leave me every week, never knowing whether I might disappear between visits. I wonder if my trauma and my suffering all these years in part fueled her fascination with death, whatever her theories of acceptance and master plans. I will never know, and it is of no consequence now.

The tenth anniversary was an entirely different sort of day. None of the titanic global tremors of that first year. Most of the masses went about their daily activities with a glance at the news, a nod to remembrance, a posting on Facebook. Danny and I attended the morning ceremony at Ground Zero. The city was bathed in a nearly sapphire blue sky. We stood hand-in-hand before the commemorative pools marking the towers, marveling at their grandeur even as the elegant simplicity of that memorial reduced the once monumental scale of the towers to arms length. Rather than reaching for heaven, reflecting the heavens. And, once again, and always, I recited their names: Jason Herman, Jeremy Herman.

Afterwards, we walked the long walk home together in silence. Danny had moved in after Anna's death and I worried every time he left for work. Catastrophe hides on every corner for the fireman, in every building and basement, and each time I heard his key in the door, I was grateful for another day. I washed the ash from his skin. I scrubbed the soot from his hair. I listened to his tales and clung to his body through the night.

The day after the 9/11 commemoration, with few words, he gathered his belongings and moved out. Although Danny and I will always belong to each other, we no longer belonged together. Spokes on another wheel.

Increasingly uncomfortable with my shabby dwelling, I dumped the piles of old magazines and paperbacks and packed the last of Jeremy's things for donation. I reupholstered Jason's chair, ordered a new couch, and put the old couch on the sidewalk for salvage. While I could not bring myself to move away, I scrubbed every inch of the apartment, refinished the floors, and painted the walls a pearly white, the ceilings sky blue.

The fevered reclamation of my space was inspired in large part by Henry's housecleaning during the last weeks of summer. He enlisted me to help him box most of Margaret's collectibles to donate to the church bazaar, and regaled me with more stories of their lives. I miss Henry, I wish I had known him longer, and I confess I harbor envy at the thought that he and Anna might frolic somewhere together where I cannot be. Not yet.

Wednesdays with Anna are history. Now, frequent Saturday visits with Will anchor my calendar. We walk city streets, wander art galleries and stroll across the Brooklyn Bridge or saunter through Central Park examining trees. We frequently debate destiny over lunch. I have rediscovered the joy of a son, and Will, a mother. Much needed surrogacy for us both.

Every now and then, in the dead of night, or in the late hours of the day when dusk settles over the city and loneliness is most severe, I indulge the fantasy of going back in time. Only to the day before. Not to save them, I know better, rather to cherish a few waking hours together. Perhaps to warn someone that maniacs in jet planes would wreak havoc. To voice my concern to Anna she had grown misguided in her obsession with life and death. Foolishness, I know. We can never go back, only forward.

By my bedside, I keep a rock, round and mostly black, that Jeremy picked up long ago on a romp through the park. Remembrance seems embedded there, like childhood encrypted in one's psyche, and I have cherished that rock, all these years, gripping it in my palm when melancholy surfaces, examining striations as if never seen, and smoothing the hard finish with the tips of my fingers. A tactile meditative reimagining of the souls of loved ones.

No one should be expected to shutter grief, and that rock, the essence of memory, blends the earthly with the spiritual, where I reside most comfortably. That sweet sliver of space where the living and the dead embrace.

END

About the Author

Randy Kraft is a freelance journalist, blogger, book reviewer, and novelist. Raised in New York City, she currently resides in Southern California.

Her first novel COLORS OF THE WHEEL was published in January 2014 by Infinity Publishing. Through the lives of three generations – black, white and brown – the novel explores the challenges of blended families in contemporary America.

SIGNS OF LIFE explores the right to die and the nature of relationships in a culture that focuses on gains over losses.

OFF SEASON was produced in 2013 at the San Miguel Short Play Festival, in Mexico.

Randy earned a Masters in Writing at Manhattanville College, Purchase, NY.

Read Randy's book review blog at www.ocinsite.com, a culture and entertainment website serving Orange County, CA, and at randykraftwriter.blogspot.com Follow all things reading and writing at Twitter @ocbookblogger.

For book group information and to learn more about forthcoming fiction go to www.Maple57Press.com

Acknowledgements

Dedication
Dotty and Bernie, Rusty and David, never forgotten.
Dana and Julie, life support.
Paul, now and forever.

Readers
Carole, Chris, Deana, Deborah, Eliane, Elizabeth,
Hollie, Jane, Joan, Leslie, Liz, MK, Paul

Cheerleaders
Carol, Robyn, Laura, Ginger & Joe, Byron, CQ,
Carol F, Anne, Roberta, Edie, Amy

Advisors
Carole, Elizabeth, Joan, Wendy
Marianna, proofreader and believer
Sally Russell, Esq. Jack Prunier, MD. Sandy Groves, Ceramicist.
The novel started with a story written for MAW class at
Manhattanville College, NY

Hugs to Diane's Books of Greenwich and Laguna Beach Books

Cover by David Smith: www.designdsmith.com
Photography/Techmastery: Byron Cann

Inspiration
A Child's History of the World by V.M. Hillyer [1924 and 1951]
The Tibetan Book of Living and Dying by Sogyal Rinpoche
The Untethered Soul by Michael A. Singer
On Photography by Susan Sontag
River Flow by David Whyte
On Grief and Grieving, Elizabeth Kübler-Ross/David Kessler
Dr. Lyn Prashant: www.*degriefing*.com